FOREVER FAIRE BOX SET

BOOKS 1 - 5

HAZEL HUNTER

ALLURE PRESS

Hazel loves hearing from readers!
You can contact her at the links below.

Website: hazelhunter.com

Facebook: business.facebook.com/HazelHunterAuthor

Newsletter: HazelHunter.com/news

I send newsletters with details on new releases, special offers, and other bits of news related to my writing. You can sign up here!

HUNTED (BOOK 1)

CHAPTER 1

"There are worse places," Kayla Rowe said, as she stepped over a fallen tree trunk. Her foot sank into another fresh snowdrift. "I could be in the Sahara."

She slogged through to a more sheltered patch of ground and stopped, her heavy breaths billowing in the frosty air. With a grunt, she stomped off the clumps of icy powder that clung to her jeans.

"Not that I'd really mind the desert," she said. Talking to herself helped her ignore the fact that she couldn't feel her face or her hands anymore. "Camels aren't so bad, and my tan needs work. Mirages could be fun."

Kayla rubbed her ears and nose with her stiff gloves, hoping to restore some circulation, but didn't feel that either. Growing up in hot, sunny Florida left her ignorant of exactly what frostbite felt like. No doubt she'd find out soon enough. What she could feel was every gulp she took of the thin, sharp air. It burned her lungs before clawing its way out to form white clouds. Right now a bunch were drifting in front of her nose, like so much ghost tripe. The thought made her stomach sink.

"Add nausea to the frostbite," she muttered, and swatted at her floating breaths.

At sunset she'd abandoned her rental car to walk the rest of the way to town. She must have covered at least five miles by now, but the darkness made it hard to tell. Leaving the winding road to take a shortcut through the woods had seemed brilliant—until she found herself dodging trees, brush, and knee-high drifts. If not for the light filtering down from the full moon she'd probably be walking or falling face-first into them. Who knew Tennessee would have snow?

How Kayla missed Florida, and the little cottage she'd shared there with her sister. More than anything her heart still ached over giving up her job at the riding academy. The students and other trainers she'd worked with had been great, but leaving behind the horses she'd trained and cared for every day for the last three years had been like running out on family.

Cantankerous old Stan, who considered himself in charge of everything at the stables, had been particularly upset about her leaving.

You can't go, he pleaded. *We need you here. You're not like the others. You're one of us.*

I know. I'm sorry, she thought. She couldn't avoid the hurt in his big brown eyes. *But if I stay, and they found out where I work...what if they came here and hurt one of the kids, or you?*

Leaving her beloved job behind had been a smart if emotionally difficult choice. Hiking alone through the woods in winter, on the other hand, had been an exceptionally dumb idea. So had forgetting to charge her mobile. Kayla still couldn't believe she hadn't once glanced at the car's dashboard since leaving North Carolina. She'd never in her life run out of gas.

Until tonight.

The rental had begun sputtering as soon as she had gotten off the highway, and coasted to a long, slow stop just as she'd passed a sign that read ASHDALE 7 MILES.

Kayla couldn't blame her idiocy on the car, or anyone but herself. Though she'd been relieved to lose the thugs stalking her and her sister, Tara, the relief had made her careless. She'd been so busy congratulating herself on the success of her clever plan that she'd forgotten how often the universe liked to mess with that kind of thing. Now it seemed to be gloating.

You're not out of the woods yet, Rowe, and guess what? Now you might freeze to death in them.

Through the trees she could see the lights of the town as dozens of tiny jewels spangled the dark horizon. They promised warmth and shelter and her sister. But their distance meant she had at least another two or three miles to hike. If she got to Ashdale, she'd then have to find her way to the cheap motel where Tara was waiting.

"*When* I get there." Kayla pulled the edge of her wool scarf up over her mouth and nose. "No ifs. *When.*"

She trudged on, every step leeching more strength from her tired, overworked leg muscles. Once winter's teeth finished gnawing her limbs, she suspected it would start in on her chest and belly. If the cold got to her core, she might never make it out of the woods. Her younger sister would be left helpless and alone, with no one else in the world to look after her. Tara already coped with horrible bouts of depression, which had been especially frequent since their father had passed away. Losing her only living relative might finally push her to–

"Knock it off," Kayla yelled, though her lips were numbing.

She breathed in through her nose and out her mouth

until the shriveling knot in her chest loosened. She wasn't giving up, not this close to making it. She would get to town, and her sister, and then they would figure out where they could stay for the winter.

All she had to do was walk two more miles, and not die trying. Kayla thought about her sister, but the image of Tara's thin face soon faded. Instead she remembered the other reason she had to keep going—the reason they'd ended up in Tennessee—the stalkers.

CHAPTER 2

Kayla had first seen them over a month ago. Without warning the bikers had surrounded her and Tara on their way to the market. Kayla had gunned the engine and the pack of roaring machines had chased them through town. Though she had managed to lose them, she went straight to the police station to report the incident. But without license numbers the desk sergeant told her there wasn't anything they could do.

The next day Kayla came out of the market to find the bikers waiting in the parking lot, and called the police on her mobile. As soon as they heard the sirens the bikers took off. By the time the patrol car arrived they were gone. Over the next week the gang came after her and Tara three more times, yet as soon as Kayla called 911 they disappeared. There were never any witnesses or evidence to back up what she told the police. After the fifth call the cops stopped taking Kayla seriously, and the last time they even threatened to charge her with misuse of emergency services.

"Look, I don't care about me," Kayla told the cop. "I can

take care of myself. But these guys are huge and scary, and my sister is just a kid. If they grab her, she won't have a chance."

"Yeah, well, we've interviewed everyone and checked around town, lady," a ticked-off patrolman told her. "Nobody but you two has ever seen these bikers. So maybe you should talk about your problems with someone else. You know, like a therapist."

Kayla had stopped calling, but the bikers never stayed away for long. When one of the bastards had followed Tara into the fabric shop where she worked after school, she'd run out and disappeared. Kayla hadn't known about it until her sister's boss called several hours later, when a dazed and injured Tara had come back to the store and tried to start working again.

"I'm taking you to the ER," Kayla told her as she helped her to the car. "We'll get–"

"No," Tara said. She hunched her shoulders. "I'm okay."

"Okay?" Kayla caught Tara's hand and showed her the rapidly-darkening bruises on her knuckles. "This is not okay. And this?" She tugged on the torn, blood-stained sleeve of Tara's blouse. "How is this even remotely okay?"

"It's not my blood," her sister said, staring sullenly at the ground. "Would you just take me home, please?"

Tara had refused to offer any more details about the attack, but she was never the same after that day. When Kayla decided they should relocate, she didn't even argue. They'd quit their jobs, packed up and left town the next day, telling no one where they were going.

A week later the gang found them, just settling into their new apartment, and the nightmare started all over again. For nearly a month now they'd been on the run, never staying in any place for more than a few days. Yet no matter where they went, or how careful they were, the gang always caught up with them.

Kayla had no idea who the bikers were, but there was something very wrong with all of them. She'd assumed they were just another bunch of idiot thugs trying to look like badasses. But then she noticed the creepy similarities they shared. Gangs were big fans of uniformity, so it was no surprise they all wore sunglasses, black leather jackets, and trousers. Only theirs were identical. Each biker also had the same pale skin, quasi-military haircut, and bulging, bodybuilder frames. If not for the variations in the weird tribal tattoos they'd inked on their brows, the gang could have been twenty clones of the same jerk.

What was truly bizarre was how no one else seemed to see them. Everyone behaved as if they were invisible. Since none of the assholes wore helmets, or had license plates on their bikes, they should have at least caught the eye of the authorities. Yet Kayla had seen them go roaring past a state trooper at twenty miles over the posted speed limit, and the cop hadn't even blinked.

The last time the gang had attacked them had been during rush hour on a busy Georgia highway. One minute Kayla was looking for an exit sign. The next the passenger window exploded inward as a huge, dirty fist punched through it and clamped around Tara's neck. As Kayla screamed her sister broke free and grabbed the wheel, first swerving their car into the biker, and then across three lanes to an exit ramp.

"Are you out of your mind?" Kayla had shrieked at her sister as she wrenched her hand off the wheel. "What if you killed him?"

"I didn't."

Tara nodded at the rearview mirror.

Kayla saw the cars dodging the fallen biker. But as he

stood up, her eyes widened. He righted his bike with one hand and climbed back on.

"What the hell? No one could have survived that. What is he, Superman?"

"Whatever they are," Tara muttered, calmly brushing broken glass off her lap, "you'd better drive faster."

That day they hadn't stopped again until they'd reached the Carolinas, and by that time Kayla had come up with a plan.

"I don't know what they are or how they keep finding us," she'd told Tara, "but they have to be looking for two women traveling together, right? So we split up. I'll get rid of the car, rent something else and head south. You take the bus and go north."

Her sister started to shake her head, but when Kayla gently touched the bruises on her throat she stopped and finally nodded.

"Once I lose them I'll double back and meet up with you."

She picked up the complimentary travel map they'd taken from the lobby. A tiny motel symbol was stamped next to a dot in a sparsely-populated section of the Smoky Mountains. "Here, in Ashdale. There's a motel in town called..." She squinted at the minuscule type. "The Silver Birch Inn. Get a room there and wait for me."

Tara frowned. "Ashdale? Why does that sound familiar?"

"We used to live there when I was little," Kayla said, finger still on the map. "You were born there." Aware that they were both staring at it, Kayla quickly folded the map. "Dad said that if you or I ever got in trouble, we should go back to Ashdale." She handed the map to Tara. "He told me that we would always be safe there."

Her sister grimaced. "If it's so safe, then why did we move?"

"Dad hated it," Kayla said, moving to the window. She peered through the curtains at the nearly-empty parking lot. "He only took us to Florida because Mom left."

A few hundred yards later Kayla stopped again, resting her back propped against a nubby tree trunk.

"I'm fine," she gasped. "I could do this all night."

The lies enveloped her in more breath clouds that were thicker and whiter, as if the temperature had stopped dropping and had started plummeting.

"Okay, maybe not."

As her breath drifted off, a new light appeared, flickered and grew brighter.

Hello. Is that a cabin?

Kayla straightened and peered, and then grinned. The light was a lot closer than town, no more than a quarter mile ahead of her. She plodded forward as though it were a magnet.

The scent of wood smoke was in the air—and something else.

Cookies?

Her insides warmed as if she was already sitting beside a nice, hot fireplace.

Kayla hated asking strangers for help, but she had no choice. Once the people in the cabin saw how cold she was, surely they'd let her in to defrost by their fire for a few minutes. Or maybe they'd feel so sorry for her that they'd offer to drive her into town. She certainly wouldn't have to fake looking pathetic. Only when she got closer did Kayla see that the light wasn't coming from a cabin, but from a small campfire.

Who camps in the mountains in the middle of winter?

Kayla didn't really care. In addition to feeling numb she was also getting drowsy. Her legs quivered with each new step. The two miles to town might as well be two hundred. If she didn't stop and get warm she'd collapse.

Once Kayla got close enough to get a good look at the camp site, she stopped and hid behind a tree. Although she was a walking popsicle, the last month had taught her to spy first, listen second, and never trust the look of anyone —ever.

At first she could only see the flames, blazing but neatly contained by a ring of stacked stones. Smoke rose in an unsteady column to veil the moon. Firelight dimly illumi-nated two shapes near the hearth: a big one crouched beside it, head down and face hidden behind a long spill of dark hair; the other behind it even larger, with four powerful legs and a hide that gleamed like moonlight.

A man and his horse. Kayla already liked him.

All the guy wore was a denim jacket, white shirt and dark brown trousers, but what most reassured Kayla was his healthy tan and too-long, light brown mop. All of the hulking jackasses in the gang had had gray skin, tattooed foreheads, and short-cropped black hair.

He's not one of them.

For a second Kayla closed her eyes to wallow in the relief, but then her knees decided to buckle. She reached for the nearest tree branch to keep from falling on her face, and an icy twig caught under her hand, breaking with a loud, glassy snap.

The rider's brown hair fanned out as he spun toward the sound, revealing glittering dark eyes and the angle of a masculine jaw, but not much else. A silvery glint drew her gaze to the thin length of polished steel that appeared in his huge fist.

Okay, he's not an idiot, either.

Kayla could do the prudent thing and avoid him by going around his little campsite, and probably drop dead of hypothermia just on the outskirts of town. Or she could chat up a large, armed man alone in the dark woods and get warm. And possibly get herself killed.

Time to find out how stupid I am.

"I'm over here," she said. She stepped out and lifted an arm to wave. "Hi! Sorry. I didn't mean to startle you." She took a couple more steps until she emerged from the shadows. "My car broke down and I've been walking for miles." Keeping up the friendly, unconcerned tone was harder than she thought. "I'm, uh, really cold. Would you mind if I join you for a bit?"

The knife vanished, and the hair fell forward again as the rider ducked his head.

Kayla interpreted that as a nod. "Thank you so much."

She went directly to the fire, stripping off the gloves from her numb hands. She crouched beside the stones. The heat was so delicious on her stiff palms that she nearly moaned out loud.

"I thought I was hallucinating when I spotted you." She paused long enough for him to reply, and when he didn't she pressed on. "My sister is waiting on me in town, and I'm sure by now she's worried. Do you happen to have a phone with you that I can borrow to call her?"

"No," the rider said. He stirred the fire with a charred stick. Tiny embers swirled upward. "Phones don't work up here."

The deep, gentle voice wrapped around her, warm and soft. It was like one of her sister's handmade quilts. Even so, she was shivering.

"Okay, no problem," she said, her voice quaking a little. "I'm Kayla Rowe, by the way." She peered around him to get a better look at his ride. But somehow the big horse had shuffled back out of sight.

"Ryan," the rider finally said. He extinguished the glowing end of the stick by planting it in the ground. "Why did you leave your car on such a night?"

"Oh, you know. I didn't want to freeze to death in it." She heard the faint accent in his deep voice, but she couldn't place it. "You from around here, Ryan No-Last-Name?"

"No, but I stop by the place every winter." He lifted his head and for the first time looked at her directly. "Why are you here?"

"Same. Passing through."

Staring back was rude, but Kayla couldn't help herself. No one would call Ryan's blunt face handsome, not with that heavy jaw and broad-bridged nose. His mouth was more like a line than lips, and his thick eyebrows were a shade darker than his tan. But the rest of him was all man, and plenty of it. Beneath his denim jacket, heavy muscles padded his broad chest, wide shoulders and long arms. Because he was crouched in the shadows it was hard to tell how tall he was, but judging by the size of his hands, the long lines of his thighs and the gigantic boots he wore, he definitely wasn't a mini like her. No wonder he rode such a big horse. He'd squash anything smaller.

Being five foot nothing and barely a hundred pounds

had fated Kayla to be forever envious of substantial people, which was probably why she'd always been attracted to big men. Because she looked much younger and weaker than she was, the guys she liked never paid much attention to her. Ryan wasn't showing any particular interest, either. But Kayla's nerves remained on full alert, and she wasn't sure why. It might have been the odd scent blending with the smoke, which smelled stronger and sharper now—less like cookies and more like an exotic cocktail.

Vanilla brandy? Chocolate champagne?

Kayla rarely drank so she couldn't pin it down, but it was wonderful.

As for Ryan, apart from being super-sized, he seemed relatively harmless. But she was picking up a very strange vibe from him. As if there was something he didn't want her to see, or maybe that she'd missed altogether.

Or I've gotten so paranoid everyone looks to me like they're hiding something.

"Are you traveling with someone, Ryan?"

"Old friends," he said and tossed a handful of pine needles onto the fire. It billowed with a whoosh. "Do your parents know where you and your sister are?"

"Probably not. They're dead." The flaring flames erased the last of the shadows from his face, revealing long, narrow eyes that shouldn't have been such an ordinary brown. "I'm not a kid, either. I'm twenty-five."

"That's almost ancient," he said, sounding a little amused. "Now tell me the real reason you came here, Kayla Rowe."

CHAPTER 4

Christine Marszalek climbed down from the side stage, her spangled hair and skimpy costume glittering under the spot lights. The aroma of spilled beer, cigarette smoke, and sweat had lightened, which made her frown. The last of the Club Royale's regular clients had fled, leaving only the bikers, who weren't drinking, smoking or getting turned on. Oh, they watched, with their flat, muddy eyes, but not one of them had tipped her or any of the girls yet.

What the hell do they want?

The gang had roared in last night, taking all the empty rooms in the motel next door. They'd slept through the day, and then piled into the strip club at sunset. Old Fred, the owner and bartender, had gone back with one of them into his office, and had yet to come out. All the dancers acted as if nothing was wrong, but they were all scared.

Aisha, the dusky-skinned island girl who was taking her place, muttered, "Weasel's back."

Christine looked over to see the gang's leader, Dirk, getting a lap dance from Francine. But at the same time he was talking to a shorter, rodent-faced thug named Beck, who had been pestering all of them since the gang had come in. He handed the bigger man a paper, which he read and then crumpled in his fist.

"Keep dancing," Christine said under her breath.

"'Til when?" Aisha grumbled. "It's five a.m., girl. We were supposed to close at two."

Tiredly she climbed up to do her first whirl around the dull gold brass pole.

Christine went around the bar, which Old Fred was supposed to be manning, and made herself a club soda. As casually as she could, she moved to a spot just behind the two men.

"You're certain they were there?" Dirk demanded.

"Absolutely," Beck said, smirking at Francine. "The mortal at the hotel said they left yesterday."

They talked as strange as they looked, but it wasn't what they said that scared Christine. Since she'd started stripping she'd met every kind of jerk in existence, or thought she had. This biker gang was something else. They radiated strangeness, from their brow tats down to their shit-kicker boots. She'd never seen so many men look so much alike. Just meeting their eyes made her feel as if a million bugs had crept under her skin.

Without warning Dirk shoved Francine off him.

"Hey," Francine yelped as she fell on her ass. "You can't do shit like that."

"I can't?" Dirk said as he stood. "Bring the fat guy to me," he told Beck.

As Beck left, all of the dancers froze and looked over at Christine, who shook her head slightly. The music shut off, and Dirk scanned the room. Something slithered against Christine's skin as she watched the other girls' expressions blank. They slowly gathered around the biker.

"My men and I like this place. We're going to be staying for a time." He dropped a handful of white packets onto his table. "This is for you. You will not leave this place. You will keep the doors locked and let no one in but us. Do as you are told, and there will be more."

Christine swallowed hard as she watched her co-workers snatch up the coke, and then jumped as the gang leader glared back at her. Although she didn't do drugs, her silently screeching instincts made her go over and pick up one of the packets.

"Why are you so slow to take your pleasure?" Dirk demanded.

"Some of the girls have husbands, and kids," Christine told him tonelessly. "They need to go home, and take care of their families."

"And someday they will, but for now, this is their home." Dirk loomed over her.

It took all of Christine's nerve not to turn and run. "Their people will call the cops," she warned him. "They'll come here, and cause trouble for you. Let us work shifts, like our boss does."

"Your boss." He looked around until he spotted Beck dragging the rotund, perspiring Fred out of the back hall. "Ah, yes. Here he is now."

"Please," the man blubbered as soon as Beck pushed him toward Dirk. "I gave you what you wanted, didn't I? The place is yours. For free. Just lemme go."

Dirk tilted his head. "No, I'm not going to do that. Men in charge must provide an example for their underlings." He took him from Beck and stood him in front of Christine and the other dancers. "Tell your girls what will happen to them if they don't obey me."

The manager scanned the anxious faces in front of him.

"You ladies gotta do what the man says, no matter what. You do for him, he'll be good to you. I promise."

Dirk used one huge hand to affectionately rub Fred's bald scalp. "What happens if they don't do for me?"

"You'll, ah, punish them, I guess." The man cringed. "They're good girls, Mister Blackstone. Don't hurt them, please."

"I don't want to," Dirk said, producing a long, sharp-looking dagger. "But I think we need to show them an example, don't you think?"

CHAPTER 5

$\mathcal{C}$aught off guard, Kayla almost blurted out the truth. Then she saw how closely the big man across the fire was watching her.

"I don't know what you mean."

"The troubles that brought you here," he said. He propped his elbows on his knees. "It may help to talk about them. I'm a good listener."

"You're a stranger, too, and you know what they say about talking to them." Kayla saw him frown. "Look, I appreciate the chance to warm up, but it doesn't entitle you to my life story or anything. If that's what you're thinking."

The line of his mouth curled on one side. "So you can read minds, too."

"I wish."

Kayla squeezed the melting frost from her gloves. The painful tingling in her fingers meant her hands would be okay. If only her brain weren't so stiff and clumsy.

"But, seeing as I'm alone with you here in the deep dark

frozen woods," she said, "thank you in advance for having only good intentions."

"No need to be scared, girl," he said, watching her face. "You're safe with me."

She didn't know enough about him to believe that, but the gentleness in his voice sounded genuine. Incredibly sexy, too.

"I'm not a girl, but it's nice to hear I'm safe." She sighed a little as the knot between her shoulders unwound a little. "Because I'm really sick of being afraid."

He broke some twigs and tossed them on the crackling pine needles.

"Then you shouldn't be wandering around out here alone."

Definitely not an American, Kayla decided, *but trying very hard to sound like one.*

"I'm not wandering. My car really did run out of gas, you know, and I actually do have a sister waiting in town. How about you?"

"No car or sisters."

Ryan's head tipped to one side. Something flashed in his hair, as though something jeweled had caught the moonlight. Kayla blinked. But whatever it had been was gone.

"Anything else you want to know?" he said in that velvety voice.

There was plenty she wanted to know. How soft his hair was, what he smelled like up close, how it would feel to be in his arms–

She was staring again, and dropped her gaze. Her face flushed at where her thoughts had been headed. What was going on? She'd never been one for instant attractions, and she'd been around him for five minutes, tops. Except for his heroic build he wasn't even good-looking. She already had enough trouble in her life. The last thing she needed was a one-night stand in the woods with–

She glared at the fire. She'd done it again. Why was sex suddenly the only thing she could think of?

Hypothermia. He's big and warm, and I'm little and cold.

Kayla also hadn't had sex since dumping her last dead-end boyfriend a year ago, so maybe her hormones were finally waking up after their long sleep. She shook her head a little to try and clear it.

"What are you doing, riding out here in the dark?" she said, finally looking at him again but trying to concentrate on something else. "Most horses hate that, because they can't see as well at night. Every noise or movement spooks them."

"I like to ride, and I have excellent night vision." Ryan studied her face for a long moment. "Afraid I don't have a horse, though."

She peered over his shoulder again, and nearly fell over.

A motorcycle?

Her gaze darted one way, then the other. How could she have mistaken a motorcycle for a horse?

Oh, God, what have I done? The rest will ride up any minute and take me.

She shakily got to her feet, but the next thought froze her in place.

What if they already found Tara?

"Kayla?" Ryan's voice scattered her frantic thoughts in a million directions. "What's wrong?"

"Nothing."

She forced herself to let out the breath she was holding and take another. If she could keep him talking, there might be a way to escape.

"I feel so stupid," she said, telling the truth. "When I

walked up I could have sworn that your ride had a mane and four legs."

"Chrome and two wheels," Ryan said and smiled. "Moonlight plays tricks on the eyes out here."

It was certainly doing something. Up until that moment Kayla had thought Ryan had the most average eyes she'd ever seen, but his smile changed them into something not ordinary at all. The look he gave her shot across the fire like lightning, burning through her fear and enveloping her with wordless longings. Every inch of her skin prickled as she watched Ryan's mouth and felt her own throb.

He can't be one of them.

Her head spun as terror and desire played tug-o-war.

Every time I've been near them they make me sick. He does the exact opposite.

"Who are you, really?" she blurted out.

Ryan seemed surprised by the question. "I told you my name."

He rose to his feet and came around to her side of the fire.

Kayla looked up, astonished all over again by his size. The top of her head barely reached the lower vault of his chest. That put him close to seven feet tall. Up close his scent was so delicious that breathing it in made her feel drunk.

"I'm...I'm..."

Why couldn't she think of the right word?

"Yes?" he said, and lifted a hand to her cheek.

The touch of his cool palm barely grazed her skin. But the sensation plowed into her like a heavy fist wrapped in velvet. She swayed a little, and he took her shoulder.

"Look at me," he commanded.

Tiny white stars appeared in his hair, and she squinted up at them. "Did you know you have..." Her voice trailed off as she watched them flicker and grow brighter. "You have…uh, something." God, was she getting smashed on the smell of him? *She was.* "In your hair. Fireflies, maybe?"

"'Tis well," he murmured. "I want you to truly see me."

Kayla watched the glittering light pool gather, liquefy, and pour down his face to spread out over his chest and shoulders. Everywhere it touched him his body changed, emerging from beneath the light with new colors and dimensions.

"Holy cow," she muttered. "I don't think so."

Ryan's heavy, plain face had disappeared, altered into features that were much more refined and unearthly. His bronze skin had turned an unblemished porcelain white, and gave off a subtle glow from the deep cleft in his new jaw to the angular points of his ears. The light brown hair paled to a lustrous white-gold, and each strand caught the firelight and trapped it in long, thin rainbows. His brows formed light slashes over the same long, narrow eyes—only they had changed to a gorgeous sapphire blue with such long, thick white lashes they resembled jewels set in pearl filigree.

No man should be so beautiful. Some part of Kayla knew that, and she would tell him, just as soon as she remembered where her tongue was.

The final blow was the unsmiling, full-lipped mouth. Such luscious lips usually graced the faces of the hottest supermodels and were coveted by everyone else. One look suggested that spending your nights simply kissing such a mouth would be as good or better than sex.

"You have naught to fear, Kayla," he reminded her, his accent completely different now. "Have you come seeking our kind?"

As much as he unsettled her, his question made her heart jump into her throat. He'd turned into someone else, as if what she'd seen before had been an elaborate disguise. Nothing on this earth could let him do that, except–

The words Tara had muttered that awful day on the highway: *Not men.*

His hand tightened a fraction on her shoulder. "Tell me, Kayla."

She flinched. "I'm not sure I…"

Just now she realized his clothes had changed, too. He wore a sleek, dark violet tunic embroidered with strange symbols in silver. His tight trousers were made of black leather laced from knee to thigh with crisscrossing blue straps. From the straps hung dozens of small, curved blades that had to be knives, yet didn't look like any Kayla knew. His boots, which gleamed like black mirrors, were fitted with shin guards formed out of scrolled gold, and broad spiked clamps over the insteps. Somehow the exotic outfit reminded her of the strange clothes the bikers wore.

"You're far from home, aren't you?" he said.

Kayla jerked her head up. "Yes. I'm from Florida. And I have a…in town, waiting… Is my brain leaking out of my ears yet?"

"No, and it will not. You're doing very well." Ryan smiled again, breaking her heart and cradling it at the same time. His thumb edged along the bottom curve of her mouth as his voice dropped to a low, rough murmur. "The truth now, Kayla. Were you sent to us? Do you come with someone in need of our help? Protection, perhaps?"

"No. I told you, I saw your fire. Who's us?"

Her eyes stung, and when she lifted her hand to rub them she dislodged his, breaking the contact.

A heartbeat later he looked exactly as he had when she'd found him: a normal, brown-haired, brown-eyed giant guy in regular clothes. The strange hold he'd put over her likewise vanished, and she took a step back so she could bellow properly.

"What the hell is going on?"

"Nothing. It's all right. I made a mistake." He moved in and lifted his hand, resting it on her shoulder. The moment he did, the liquid light flowed over him again, shifting his form back into that of the pale, otherworldly warrior. "You are safe, Kayla, and nothing is amiss."

"Safe my ass." She wanted to shove him away, but the moment he touched her both arms quit working. "What are you doing to me?"

"Fighting a will of iron, it seems. For such a small thing, you're admirably resolute." Ryan moved his hand, curling it over the side of her throat. His eyes darkened as his fingers threaded through her hair. "So warm, so alive. I'd forgotten what it can be to touch a woman."

"Please don't tell me you're gay." Her anger faded as the strange, beguiling sensations streamed through her once more. "And while we're on that subject, what are you?"

"It doesn't matter." He bent down, and touched his forehead to hers. "You will have no memory of this."

"Why not?"

Kayla felt his hands encircle her throat. Was he going to strangle her?

"I cannot permit you to remember." He lifted his head and stared at her lips as his thumbs drew circles over her collarbones. "But I will have something of you that I may remember."

All Kayla had time to do was gulp before he pressed his mouth to hers.

Past experience convinced her to expect the usual, tentative first kiss. Even the grabbiest guy she'd dated in high school had initially given her a dry, gentle peck. It was as if it were some unspoken rule among boys interested in only one thing: *be nice, and maybe you'll get to second base.*

This exotic, beautiful man went at her as if he'd been starved for sex. His mouth was so wet, open, and carnal Kayla felt it down to her heels. The way he used his tongue and teeth sent a flood of pleasure through her so acute she heard the rush in her ears.

Ryan lifted his mouth only long enough to tip her head back before he was at her throat, his teeth catching her skin before the long, hot glide of his tongue stroked over the love bite, erasing the sting and sending new heat blazing down into her breasts and belly.

Slowly Ryan took his lips from her skin and set her at arm's length before he released her.

Still entangled in delight, Kayla staggered back a step and touched her lips. They were hot and almost painfully tender. One kiss, and it had been a thousand times better than all-night sex.

"Why did you do that?" she gasped.

"I could not resist you." He turned his face away. "I forgot myself. Forgive me."

Kayla barely heard him as heat spread out from her mouth and pulsed through her, burning past her fear. It reached deep inside, twisting with a frantic need, even as her mind raced. She couldn't leave him, not ever. It was all clear now. She was meant to be with this beautiful, breathtaking man. He'd care for her, and protect her, and she wouldn't have to deal with the bikers, or Tara, or the god-awful loneliness of her life anymore. With him, she'd never be alone again.

"Can you forget like that again?"

"Kayla," Ryan said and reached for her. But he turned his head as if he heard something and let his arm fall to his side. "Listen to me. A mortal– A man is coming who can help you. Go to the edge of the trees, wait there, and he will soon arrive. When he does, you will forget this. Forget everything that has happened here. Forget me."

"Sure," Kayla said, but then saw that he was serious. She shook her head and reached for him. "Please. Don't make me go."

Now he was the one stepping away. "You must leave me now."

She couldn't believe what he was saying. Didn't he feel it, too?

"I can't. I just found you. Since Dad died I've been so alone, so scared, and dealing with Tara and her..." Why was she telling him all this stuff? Despite knowing how crazy she sounded, she couldn't stop herself. "Ryan, I know you. I feel you, in here." She thumped her fist against her heart. "God, I think I've been waiting my whole life for you."

He looked down at her for a long time. "Kayla love, these feelings, they aren't real. As soon as we part, they will fade, and you will remember none of me. Now go." When she didn't move, he stepped back again. "You must obey, child."

Obey? Child?

The words echoed in her ears as her desperation faded. Part of her still wanted to throw herself at his feet, but now the rest of her wanted a good, sturdy branch to club him over the head.

Obey, my ass.

What had Ryan done to her? How could she have said those things? Bile crawled up Kayla's throat as she realized how close she had been to abandoning her sister. But since Ryan didn't seem to be aware of his effect on her, or that she had shaken most of it off–*thank you, God*–she could get away.

"Right," she said, keeping her expression bland. "Thanks again for, uh, sharing the warmth."

Kayla's stomach twisted itself into origami as she turned away and began to walk toward town. Although the wanting still burned inside her, she busied herself by putting her gloves back on and buttoning the flap of her hood. Behind her she heard the crackling hiss of water dousing the fire. The low purr of Ryan's motorcycle engine started and moved away. Eventually she slowed and finally stopped in her tracks.

It couldn't be coincidence. Ryan had a motorcycle, like the biker gang, but she could have sworn it'd been a horse. He'd been ordinary when she first saw him near the fire, and then he'd been gorgeous. She glanced over her shoulder. *Because he did something to make me see him as ordinary. Maybe the same way the bikers made themselves invisible to everyone but us.*

Kayla turned and ran back. Ryan and the motorcycle were gone, as expected, but undisturbed snow covered the ground where the fire had been. The only sign that anyone had been there were Kayla's own footprints, sunken into the drifts.

"No," she breathed. She spun around in a circle. "You can't be…damn it, where are you?"

In a falling shaft of moonlight, the faintest streak of tiny stars glimmered, like the lights she had seen in his hair. She hurried toward them, and found a barely-perceptible stream of sparkling light hanging in the cold air. It led out of the woods. Kayla ran as fast as she could, stumbling through brush and swatting branches out of her way as she followed Ryan's trail. She reached the edge of the woods and lurched onto the shoulder of the road. She searched in both direction. On her left the red taillight of a motorcycle shone about a quarter-mile away. But just before Ryan drove out of sight he turned right. Inexplicably he drove across the road, onto the shoulder, and headed directly for a barb-wire fence. Kayla put a hand to her chest and gasped. But at the last second Ryan pulled back on the handlebars and lifted the front wheel high in the air.

"Is he out of his mind?" she muttered.

But rather than crashing into the fence Ryan's motorcycle sailed over it, exploding in mid-air with a burst of gold and copper light. Kayla shrieked and ran toward him, but the light abruptly faded and Ryan landed on the other side of the fence. She stumbled to a stop and stared after him as he crossed the pasture. Instead of Ryan on a motorcycle, there was a giant, pale-haired warrior astride a huge white stallion with a wild golden mane. He galloped off into the pines and vanished from sight.

Kayla blinked a few times before she remembered to breathe.

"It was a horse. I knew it. But how did he–"

The glare of oncoming headlights made Kayla squint. She realized she'd moved onto the road. As she backed up onto the shoulder, a white and blue patrol car slowly rolled to a stop beside her. The passenger window lowered.

"Evening, Miss."

KAYLA TOOK a moment to compose herself. Not only had she just encountered the most gorgeous creature she'd ever seen, he'd vaulted over a barbwire fence on a motorcycle-turned-stallion. But if this police officer was like the others in Florida, he wouldn't have seen a thing. She glanced back at the pasture before she put on her best innocent-citizen face. True to Ryan's words, the promised help had arrived.

"Hi, there, Officer."

"Bit cold to be out walking tonight." He jerked his

thumb toward the back of his cruiser. "That your rental car five miles down the road?"

"Yes, yes, it is. I ran out of gas, and my phone is dead."

Kayla bent down so she could see his face and make sure he wasn't a dark-haired brute or a golden-haired demon. The cop was double-chinned, tired-eyed and completely bald. She relaxed a little.

"Could you possibly give me a lift to the nearest service station?" she said.

"No need for that. I called our tow guy for your car, and he carries gas for run-outs." He reached across to open the door. "Hop in and I'll drive you back."

The interior of the patrol car was comfortably warm, and once she belted herself in, Kayla took off her gloves to hold her hands in front of the vents.

"There's some coffee there," the cop said, nodding at the thermos cup in the console holder. "Black, but it's still hot."

"Terrific, thanks." Kayla removed the lid before taking a sip and sighing. "That's really good."

"My wife sends a thermos with me when I'm on patrol," he told her, "to keep me out of the donut shops."

Kayla cradled the cup between her palms and resisted the urge to glance back over her shoulder again.

"Does that work?"

"She thinks it does." The cop chuckled.

If she told him about her encounter with Ryan he'd take her to the nearest psych ward, so she'd have to be careful.

"While I was walking I thought I saw someone riding out in that pasture back there. Is it part of a ranch?"

"The fenced property across from the woods?" He shook his head. "That belongs to the old Moffett Ski Lodge. They shut down back in the eighties, but the Forever Faire uses it when they come to town."

"Forever Faire. Pretty name."

There was something about it that sounded familiar, too. Kayla tried to recall if her dad had mentioned it, but her memory came up empty. She took another sip of coffee.

"What is Forever Faire," she said, "like a county thing?"

"It's a traveling Renaissance fair," he said. "They spend every winter here in Ashdale. They set up their camp around the lodge, you know, like an old medieval village. They do archery and sword fights and jousts and such." He rolled his eyes. "I never got into all that Dark Ages stuff, but they're a good bunch. While they're here they always put on free shows for the townspeople."

"Must be fun." Kayla turned toward him and almost asked if they also liked to shape-shift while kissing lost women. "I thought I heard a motorcycle out there, too."

"All the Forever Faire guys ride them," he said. Kayla went still. "Saves them from having to haul those big caravans when they have to come to town for supplies, I expect. But up here at the lodge they use their horses. Looks more authentic. Easier to get around on horseback, too."

By the time they reached Kayla's rental car, she'd made a plan. Although she needed desperately to get to Tara, she'd never felt closer to figuring out the bikers. The motorcycles couldn't be a coincidence.

After a few minutes the tow truck arrived. Kayla paid the driver for adding some gas to her tank, and smiled with relief when the engine promptly started. After he left to go on another call she thanked the officer for his help.

"No problem," he said. "There's a couple of service stations in town where you can fill up." He climbed back into his cruiser. "Have a good trip, now, and watch that fuel gauge."

Kayla waved goodbye before she got back in the car

and drove to where she had seen Ryan jump the fence. But there was no way she could do the same in her car. She thumped the steering wheel with a gloved fist. But as she glared ahead at the patch of road illuminated by the headlights, she saw a break in the barbwire. As she nudged the car forward for a look, she wondered if she could climb over the fence. Except the last thing she wanted was to be in the cold again.

"A gate," she muttered, as she pulled off the road next to it.

Beyond was a small access road. Although she left the engine running, she checked for traffic in the rearview mirror, then up ahead, and hopped out of the car. The gate was closed by a drop latch, but it wasn't secured. She shoved it open and heard rusty hinges squeal, before she trotted back to the car.

"I'll just see where he went," she said, bargaining with her conscience as she turned off the headlights. "Then I'll drive to town, gas up, and find Tara. Then I'll have a breakdown, and get my head examined."

Despite the words, though, she was on to something. If she and Tara were going to stand a chance of not looking over their shoulders all their lives, she had to get to the bottom of this.

The gradual incline of the road led Kayla to the top of a rise where she slowed the car and then stopped. Moonlight sketched out a massive clearing encircled by towering pines and broad oaks. In the center stood a low, wide, stone-walled building that had to be the old ski lodge. Next to it was a barn with two wings of stables. Kayla shut off the engine and climbed out to get a better look. Scattered around the edges of the clearing were large trucks, horse trailers, campers and flatbeds.

The show people probably occupied the lodge. Most of

the windows were lit from within, and white wood smoke drifted from multiple chimneys on the roof. Someone had also built up a roaring blaze in a huge fire pit just in front of the lodge, around which several figures stood.

What Kayla didn't see was a single motorcycle–or snow–anywhere around the lodge.

She walked down, taking care not to stumble or make a sound like last time. As she drew closer she noted the big, rolled hay bales stacked in double rows beside the barn, as if they'd just been delivered. Judging by the size of the stables, the amount of hay, and the number of transport trailers, Kayla estimated Ryan and his friends had at least two dozen horses. If nothing else that indicated how prosperous they were. Maintaining a large, healthy stable was beyond expensive these days.

So he's rich as well as magical. But then, why bother performing? Maybe a Renfaire is the only place he can use his mojo without drawing attention.

Assuming Ryan hadn't changed his ride back into a motorcycle, he would have gone to the stable first to unsaddle the horse and bunk him down for the night. To take a look Kayla would have to circle behind or cross the camp, which would likely attract attention from the group around the bonfire.

"This better be worth it," she said as she started down the slope.

As she stepped out of the snow onto the lush, green grass, a strange shiver ran down her spine. She could feel the soil give slightly under her weight.

"A nice lawn?" she muttered, frowning. "In the dead of winter?"

She skirted the edge of the treeline and moved within earshot of those around the bonfire. All of them appeared to be large, normal men dressed in regular clothes. None had facial tats or short black hair. Every one of them looked as human as Ryan had, at least before he had changed on her.

Speak of the shape-shifting devil.

Kayla's gaze went to a larger man walking from the stable to the bonfire.

"You're late," a man said, his voice sharp.

"For what?"

That was Ryan, and he sounded just as annoyed.

"Trouble," the man told him. "Jannon caught two mortals stealing from us. He claims he disposed of them."

CHAPTER 6

*A*s he joined his men, Ryan Sheridan regarded his second-in-command. Like the rest of them, he still wore the glamor of his mortal guise. Fae nature made it impossible for Colm Longacre to utter an untruth among his own kind, and he wouldn't jest unless he was entertaining the mob.

"He did what now?" Ryan asked.

"Got rid of two vermin," someone else answered.

Jannon Ferguson elbowed his way to the front of the men as he took a drink from the oversize bottle of snowine he carried. In his true form, which was almost as large as Ryan's, he resembled a shining god.

"Caught our new groom and that needle-plying wench in the treasury, up to their elbows in our coin." He spat in the fire, which reacted with the Fae drink he'd been guzzling by sending up a bright blue flare. "Bloody thieving humans."

Ryan inspected the drunken warrior's garments for blood spatter, but saw only sparkling blue stains of drink on his tunic

"You did not report this to Colm until now?"

"All he does is coddle them. They needed learning, so I…" He raised one large, bulging arm and tried to snap his fingers, failed to connect them, and then batted the air with his huge hand. "I taught them."

In the past Ryan had seen Jannon use a single blow to cleave a boulder in two.

"By what manner did you give this instruction?"

"What the bloody hells do you care?" Jannon swayed and staggered a step sideways before he caught himself and drank again. "Weak, worthless scum, the both of them." He wiped his mouth with the back of his fist. "Got what they deserved, they did."

"Now I see," Colm said with an exaggerated nod. Then he sighed. "The fool wants you to think he did away with them, to goad you into thrashing him. I'll wager he did naught to harm a hair on either."

Ryan saw that truth echoed in Jannon's angry fists and guilty eyes, and considered thrashing him anyway.

"You wish to deceive me, brother? Why?"

"You know the reason. We all do." Colm regarded the drunken warrior. "You can wound yourself a thousand times over, Jan, and bleed on every mortal female in these mountains so they'll bed you and heal you. None of it will ever make you forget your clan."

"What would you know of women, Colm Longacre?" Jannon said, his upper lip curling as he fixed the other man with a sneer. "You've not pleasured one since you were gelded by that fucking witch." As the other men muttered uneasily, Jannon wobbled around to face Ryan. "Beg pardon, my liege. I meant to say Her Majesty the Queen, that fucking witch."

Colm folded his arms. "And now I'd say the great hulking idiot wants the both of us to beat him bloody."

"What did you call me?" Jannon said, his voice growing louder. He drew a dagger, squinted, and pointed it at the empty space beside Colm. "Come over here and say that to my face, you sodding Érien ponce."

Wallace Magee, the troop's blacksmith and spell tracker, silently moved up behind Jannon. At a nod from Ryan he seized Jannon's arm and plucked the weapon from his hand, all in one smooth motion.

Jannon spun around and smacked his face into Wallace's massive chest before he scowled up at him.

"What are you doing? Dint you hear? I've finally challenged that nosy cockless winge to battle. Give back me blade."

"Wouldn't be a fair fight, brother," Wallace said. The blacksmith tossed the knife through the fire to Colm, who caught it by the hilt. "Tomorrow you can gut him. I'll even hold him down for you. But for tonight, come." The blacksmith dropped his arm around the warrior's sagging shoulders. "Come and drink with me."

Ryan watched the pair retreat into the lodge before he scanned the faces of the other men.

"What set him off this time?"

"The wench he caught thieving, the new seamstress," one of the men told him. "Quite comely, that one." He used his hands to make a voluptuous female shape in the air, and then grimaced. "She also had very white skin, and long gilded hair."

Colm swore in the old language. "I told Lawrence to hire only dark wenches, rot his soul. I will crack his head on the morrow."

"Not so fast, brother," one of the men said. "If we're to perform we'll need replacements for them by week's end."

Ryan nodded his agreement. "Have new notices posted in town."

"Aye." Colm tucked Jannon's blade into a sheath on his belt before he glared at the rest of the men. "As long as he's drinking, Jannon stays here. Until he stops, bring no more women to camp. Seek your pleasures in the town. Do you hear me?"

As the other men made sounds of reluctant agreement, Ryan glanced over at the barb-wire fence separating their land from the roadway. He understood exactly how Jannon felt, for his own blood still ran hot. It would for the rest of the night, too, thanks to young Kayla, with her silken dark locks and topaz eyes. Oh, but she had been so luscious to touch and hold and kiss. He'd forgotten how good it felt, to take a woman in his arms for pleasure instead of a necessary healing. He never allowed himself such luxuries, but the sweet curve of her smile had intoxicated him. The kiss had brought him dangerously close to beseeching more from her, which her own desire would have compelled her to provide.

"I best adjust the wards to keep him penned tonight," Colm said in a low voice as the other men scattered to return to their cabins. "Walk the boundaries with me?"

Ryan followed his second to the trail surrounding the edge of the camp, where an unseen boundary of protective spells kept out the local wildlife, snow, and much of the cold. Beyond it he could see the roadway, on which a car now drove toward town. Someone had left the gate to the access road open—probably Jannon after he sent away the two thieves.

As Colm reworked the boundary spell to now include keeping Jannon in camp, Ryan absently checked the markers, which only he and the other warriors could see and touch. They remained bright and untested, disturbed only by his own passage through them upon his return to camp.

"Jannon likely mindfogged them before he sent them

back to town," Colm said. "'Tis the only spell he can manage when he's this pissed. I'll make sure of it in the morning."

"Aye, but spare Lawrence his skull and your spleen," Ryan admitted as he lowered his hand. "I am to blame. I paid no attention to the new hires. I should have noticed the woman had Fae coloring."

Colm grunted. "Mortal wenches all look alike to me."

Ryan might have agreed with him, but after tonight he suspected he would be looking for Kayla's golden eyes and exquisite face among every crowd of humans.

"Leave it to Lawrence," Ryan said, "after you remind him to hire no more pale-skinned blondes."

His second nodded. "Why were you so late returning from patrol? Did you find someone in need?"

"No Fae." Ryan saw the other man's expression. "Wallace may be wrong about what he sensed. He has been before now."

Light flared briefly between Colm's hands and the round, hovering ward he touched. "You don't want to find them."

"I've vowed to serve the lost and needful, just as the rest of you," Ryan reminded him. "I've no reason to abandon the course now."

Colm shook his head. "After what your clan did to you? You have every right to hold a grudge."

What his clan did to him? That made it sound so simple.

"There's more than enough pain and guilt to go around," Ryan said.

"The guilt is on them."

Ryan nodded, though he knew it wasn't true. His clan had disowned him because he'd broken the cardinal rule: never fall in love with a mortal. Though it was centuries ago, he recalled those days with bitter clarity. Maeve's pregnancy had gone badly in the last days. In desperation he'd taken her to his clan, but they had flatly refused to help. Ryan had watched his wife die along with their tiny infant son, and then the darkness overtook him.

The Sheridan clan, who knew that Ryan was a berserker, had come after him. He had cut his way through half of them before they had been able to imprison him. For months he had screamed and bled as he fought the bespelled chains holding him in the remote cave. By the time his self-control returned, the Fae king had judged him and issued his decree: death or exile. Some days Ryan still wondered why he had chosen the latter.

"Hardening my heart will not change what I did," Ryan said. "By royal decree we are all exiled to the mortal realm for eternity. We may help the lost Fae, and fight the dark, but we will never again know kinship with our own kind."

"The king enjoys twisting the knife as much as planting it," Colm said, and sighed. "But perhaps someday we can…" He stepped closer, sniffed, and frowned. "What is that smell?"

"Doubtless my horse," Ryan said quickly.

Colm was the closest thing to bloodkin that Ryan would ever have. If he told anyone about Kayla, it would be him—but not now, not with the taste of her still on his lips.

"As for these lost Fae," Ryan continued, "we will wait another night. Then Wallace can track them. They can't be left to wander about here."

"As you will," Colm said, but then frowned. "No, wait." He sniffed again. "It is not Titan. What is that?"

His second turned around slowly before he halted and breathed in deeply. Although Ryan tensed, he was careful to keep the concern from his face.

"There," Colm declared. "I have it. A spell trail, the

barest trace of one. You must have passed through it." He looked back at Ryan. "It's not our magick. Did you not feel it?"

Ryan released his glamour, emerging into his more powerful, natural form. As he opened his mind to the currents of energy all around them, his hair fanned out and his skin illuminated, drawing to it the particular heat of Fae magick. Within moments he found what Colm had sensed, a faint, subtle burn inside the air, marking the passage of something dark and strange.

"I have it." He tried to capture the magick with his own power, but it sifted through him and scattered itself across the winter darkness until every trace had disappeared. "It is old. Twenty years or more since 'twas cast."

Colm stared at him. "No enchantment could endure or linger that long."

"There is one sort that can," said a voice from behind. Wallace joined them, and glanced at Ryan. "Jannon sleeps. My fist may have helped him nod off."

"My thanks," Ryan said with half a smirk. He turned to examine the dark land around them, looking for any other sign of passing Fae. "I cannot tell if 'twas one or two. Can you, brother?"

"No," the blacksmith admitted. "But I can tell you the only enchantment that may linger so long in the mortal realm: a curse."

CHAPTER 7

Christine and everyone else in the strip club froze.

Dirk pressed the edge of his blade to their boss's throat.

"If they don't obey me, you'll be getting a new smile." He cut the man's neck just enough to stain the edge of his dagger. A bright bead of blood trickled down the front of his throat. "Right here."

Concealing a flinch, Christine let her eyes drift right and left. She quickly checked the surfaces around her. She'd never done her secret thing in front of anyone else, but if she was quick she might be able to get out before they realized she'd done it.

Dirk wiped his blade clean on the manager's shirt sleeve, and then clouted Fred, who collapsed in a motionless heap. Change spilled out of his pockets and rolled around the dancers' high-heeled shoes.

Christine's blood turned to ice, but none of the girls so much as blinked.

"My men have been on the road for a long time," Dirk

said, his voice taking on a weird resonance. "They need servicing, so you whores will attend to them. Now."

The women began to move like sleepwalkers toward the bikers, some stepping over Fred without even looking down. Christine ducked down to scoop up some quarters, dividing them between both hands as she straightened.

"Where is that mouthy one?" she heard Dirk ask.

Before anyone looked at her Christine whipped her hands out and released the coins. They ricocheted precisely off the tables, chairs and skulls she'd chosen. The quarters shot up at the spot lights like bullets. An instant later all of the bulbs shattered at the same time, plunging the club into darkness.

As the bikers shouted, Christine ran to the dancers' dressing room, grabbed her gym bag, and yanked up the only window. Once she'd climbed out, she kicked off her heels and ran barefoot through the snow to her little pickup. She kept the lights off as she started the engine, and floored it. In the rearview mirror she saw a spray of gravel shower a pair of bikers running out of the club.

"Oh, no, you don't," she muttered, pulling her seatbelt down and clipping it in place.

At the parking lot exit was a telephone pole. She wrenched the wheel, fishtailing the back end of her truck. With a loud crunch of metal, it slammed into the base of the pole. Wood exploded as she was jerked sideways against the seatbelts. As she righted herself, floored the gas, and steered away from the pole, it fell over and landed on the bikers.

"The bigger they are."

Tires squealing, she hurtled onto the road and accelerated, her heart hammering. As she drove through a labyrinth of streets and back roads away from the club, she kept an eye on the rearview mirror. No one appeared to be following her, and by the time she crossed the town border she felt reasonably safe. She drove up into the mountains, found an all-night truck stop, and parked behind the diner.

Taking her gym bag to the rest room, she changed out of her skimpy costume and put on a pink gingham blouse and a pair of jeans. Once she removed most of her makeup, and rubbed some baby powder under her arms, she stuffed her glitter-streaked hair under a long, strawberry blonde wig. She quickly braided the wig on either side of her face, and tied off the ends with some pink ribbon.

"Hi there," she said to her reflection, and then cleared her throat and tried again. "Hi there," she said in a softer, sweeter tone as she used her eyeliner to add some freckles on the bridge of her nose. "Could you help a girl out? Of course you could. Look at me. I'm practically your kid sister's twin. And if you touch me, I'll kick your balls up into your tonsils."

When she walked into the diner a few truckers gave her the eye, but when they saw she wasn't dressed like a working girl they turned their attention back to their plates. After inspecting the possibilities she walked over to the youngest, who was just finishing a burger. He looked up as she sat across from him, and quickly swiped some ketchup from his chin.

"Hi, there." She gave him her best, girl-next-door smile. "Could you help me out? I'm looking for a ride, and I can give you some gas money. Where are you headed?"

"Miami." He sounded a bit dazed. "But I'm not supposed to pick up any hitchers."

The thought of Florida tempted Christine, but she couldn't leave Aisha and the other girls at the mercy of the gang. Nor could she go to the cops, who would just barge in and get everyone killed. She hated cops anyway. No, what she needed was to hide, and think, but not too far away.

"I'm only looking for a lift to the next town." She tucked a twenty under his sweaty hand. "I won't tell anyone if you don't."

He glanced around them as he quickly tucked the money in his shirt pocket. "Sure, okay. Ashdale is about ten miles down the road. That all right?"

She glanced out the window at the dark, empty road. "That's perfect."

CHAPTER 8

Kayla drove through the tiny town of Ashdale, ignoring the way her heart still pounded as she searched both sides of the street. As soon as Ryan and one of the other men had started walking out of the camp in her direction she had panicked, and run back to the car. She'd been too far away to hear anything they said, but when she glanced back she saw Ryan change form again.

This time it had been even stranger, with his hair lifting and coiling as if it were alive, and his entire body lighting up with an intense, white-hot glow. The other man hadn't reacted at all to it, which meant he either didn't see it, or he could do the same thing. Like the drunken guy with the gold-streaked red hair who had tried to start a fight with Ryan and his friend at the bonfire—he hadn't pretended to look human at all. He'd looked like the drunk version of Conan the Barbarian.

They could be part of a gang, like the bikers.

But Kayla didn't want to believe that. Unfortunately,

given the motorcycles and the shape-shifting and the magic tricks, what else could it be?

The sign for the Silver Birch Inn appeared at the end of the main road, and Kayla gratefully turned into the lot. As the tires crunched to a stop on the gravel, she parked outside the front lobby. Under a flickering light, she simply sat. As she clasped her trembling hands in her lap, Kayla knew it wasn't the cold that made them shake. She could hardly believe what she'd just seen. After a few moments, she took a deep breath, got out of the car, and headed into the lobby.

A middle-aged woman who sat dozing behind the reception desk sat up as soon as Kayla's entry caused the bell over the door to ring. "Good evening," she said, her voice sleepy and soft. "May I help you?"

"Can you tell me which room Tara Rowe is staying in?" When the woman hesitated she added, "I'm her sister." The clerk still seemed unconvinced, so Kayla took out her wallet. "Here's my ID."

The woman glanced at the license Kayla held out, and then nodded. "When Miss Tara checked in she told me about you, but I've learned to be careful. We have her in room fourteen." She hesitated before she added, "I think she's been worried about you. Every night she comes up here to sit for hours and watch the road."

"I got delayed on the way here," Kayla said, forcing a smile.

As she closed her wallet, she glanced at the short stack of colorful flyers on the counter. A single word caught her eye: faire. She took one and skimmed it, noting the dates and events listed.

"Are you going to this Forever Faire show next week?"

The clerk smiled and nodded. "It's wonderful. They have archery contests, and all this amazing food, and all kinds of shows. Plus those men are so handsome in their shining armor. It's free, too, if you and your sister'll be here."

Kayla imagined Ryan in armor and felt her lips tingle. "Probably not, but thank you."

She went back out to retrieve her suitcase before she went to the room, the last one at the back of the motel. But before Kayla could even knock, her sister opened the door.

Tara had obviously jumped out of the shower. Her ash blonde hair hung dripping wet around her pale, narrow face, and all she wore was her old pink bathrobe. For an instant something shadowed her big gray eyes, and then she grabbed Kayla, dragged her inside and enveloped her in a tight hug.

"It's okay, I'm okay" Kayla murmured as she patted her sister's back.

New guilt ground a hole in her heart. How could Ryan have made her think about leaving Tara behind? Kayla was all she had in the world. As Tara's shoulders shuddered, Kayla found her own eyes burning and her throat tight.

"Don't cry," Kayla managed to say. "It gives you a clown nose, and a circus will steal you from me."

The old, lame joke from childhood worked its usual charm as Tara drew back and sniffed a few times.

"I wish one would. They'd never make me sit in a lousy motel for like forever."

"Forever is a bit longer than four days. The car broke down right before I got here, but a nice cop helped me." For the moment she would skip the real story. Kayla bolted the door. "Please tell me you have some food that didn't come out of a vending machine."

"Snack snob," Tara said, but gave her another quick hug. She gestured toward some take-out boxes stacked on the spindly table by the window. "I used the last of my cash to get some pizza. It's still warm."

"Good, I'm starving," Kayla said, and went to investigate. As soon as she saw the half-cheese, half-sardine and jalapeño, she glanced back at her sister. "You already knew I got here."

Tara had been able to sense Kayla almost since she was born.

"Like usual," she said, and shrugged. Tara wrinkled her nose. "Why do you stink like that?"

Kayla made a show of sniffing her sleeve, to which Ryan's delicious scent still clung.

"My desperate need to visit the nearest laundromat, I imagine."

She didn't want to think about him, or feel the ghost of his kiss on her lips. Instead she took a slice from the cheese half and bit off the point. Once she chewed and swallowed, she sighed.

"God, I love you," Kayla said. "Even if you do eat like a teenager."

"I am a teenager," Tara said, and handed her a can of soda. "So, what happened? Did you see them?"

"Not since the day we split up." She took a long drink before she dropped onto one of the double beds. "Go, finish your shower. I'll tell you everything once I've eaten and you're not so drippy, Fish Breath."

"Hey, I brushed."

Her sister tossed some napkins at her and retreated to the tiny bathroom. Only after she closed the door did Kayla set aside the food and drink, stand, strip out of her jacket and fling it across the room.

Son of a bitch. If she'd been alone, she would have shrieked it. *Why me? Why lie to me and change bodies and kiss me? Why couldn't you just stay on your side of the campfire? Why did you say I wouldn't remember if you knew I would?*

Kayla flopped back on the bed and pressed the heels of her hands against her eyes. She could hear Tara using the hair dryer in the bathroom, and knew she had only a minute or two to pull herself together. Tara knew her better than anyone on the planet. Lying to her sister had to be done by omission, or not at all.

The smartest thing Kayla could do was leave Ashdale first thing in the morning. Winter made heading north a bad idea, but there was still the southwest. They could even try driving all the way out west to some town along the Pacific coast. But traveling cost money, and theirs was almost gone.

No, what she'd given Tara was gone. *I used the last of my cash to get some pizza,* her sister had told her.

Kayla took out her wallet. She already knew her checking account balance had dwindled down to two digits, and she'd maxed out her credit card renting the car. A quick count of the bills she had left added up to seventy-four dollars in cash.

Not enough to get us to Kansas.

She pocketed her wallet and lay back to stare at the ceiling. She didn't want to go west or southwest or anywhere. What she wanted was to go back to the Forever Faire and to find out what sort of magicians Ryan and his men were—and how they were able to do what they did.

If we're to perform we'll need replacements for them by week-end.

Have new notices posted in town.

Kayla jumped off the bed and went to the window to check the parking lot. Her first job at the riding academy had been as a stable hand, while Tara had been making her own clothes for years. They could replace the ousted groom and the seamstress. The only problem was Ryan.

Unless...

Kayla went still.

He told me I wouldn't remember him, or anything. All I have to do is pretend I don't.

A finger tapped her shoulder, making her yelp and spin around to face her glowering sister.

"Quit sneaking up on me like that, will you? It's creepy."

"Next time I'll yell." Tara pushed a thin, folded towel into her hands. "Go take a shower. Use lots of soap. You really do stink."

If she was going to pull this off, Kayla thought, she needed her sister on board.

"No, sit down. I have to tell you what really happened to me tonight."

Tara scowled. "So you are keeping things from me. Again."

"The birds and the bees don't count. Just listen."

Kayla detailed everything that had happened to her that night, leaving out only the kiss Ryan had given her, and how it had made her feel. She then told her about how they might find out more about Ryan and his motorcycles by getting jobs at Forever Faire. Once she had finished Kayla waited for Tara to say something, but her sister seemed almost frozen.

"Come on. Tell me what you think."

Tara's thin brows drew together. "I think it scares me. I think we could get into a lot of trouble." She hesitated before she added, "And I think you're right. If Ryan and these other guys can help us with their magic, or whatever it is, it may be our only chance."

"So you don't think I'm crazy to believe in magic?" Kayla asked carefully.

Her sister's mouth twisted. "You're talking to the sister who can measure anything just by looking at it. Should I mention what you do with horses?"

A knot in her chest melted away. "We go tomorrow, apply for the jobs, and see what we can find out."

Tara nodded. "But we don't tell them anything about us. Not who we are, where we come from, or anything about what we can do. Not until we know we can trust them, okay?"

"Now you sound like the big sister." Kayla knew she was right, however, and grinned. "We're broke, and they suddenly need a groom and a seamstress. Pretty magical coincidence, huh?"

Her sister's thin face remained serious. "I don't believe in coincidences."

CHAPTER 9

Kayla woke up at dawn the next morning to dress in her least-feminine outfit. Stable managers preferred capable over pretty. The jeans were stretched out and baggy but—truth be told—she'd also lost some weight. The stress of the last month was taking its toll. She wore a roomy flannel shirt over a t-shirt she tucked into the jeans. With any luck, she could avoid attracting Ryan's attention and hopefully pass as a boy. That meant tightly pinning up her long, dark hair, and covering it with her father's old Tampa Bay Rays hat. He used to tell her that the sunburst over the big R also stood for the luck of the Rowes.

"Hope it works this time, Dad," she muttered as she walked out of the bathroom, and stopped as she saw Tara looking out of the window. "Anything wrong?"

"No." Her sister turned around, making the pale blue floral dress she wore float around her calves. "You look nice. Is this okay?"

"Who are you?" Kayla joked, "and what did you do with my sister?" To her horror she saw big tears spill down

Tara's thin cheeks. "Hey, it's great. We're going to be fine. I promise."

She went over and hugged her sister tightly.

Tara swallowed and swiped at her cheeks. "It's just seeing you with Dad's hat…I miss him."

"Me, too," Kayla said lowly, rubbing Tara's back. She stood back and held Tara at arm's length. "Donuts and coffee first. Then we go to the faire, apply for jobs, meet handsome, rich guys who shower us with money and take us off to live in mansions with servants and bathing-suit optional heated pools."

"Let's just get the jobs first," Tara said in an oddly resigned tone.

Kayla decided not to fuss, and drove her sister over to the local donut shop, where she bought their breakfast. More flyers for the Forever Faire were on the counter.

"Have you ever been?" Kayla asked the cashier.

"Nope," the girl said as she put the money in the register. "Not my thing." She handed Kayla back some change. "But it's not my brother's either, and he got hired."

Tara had taken her coffee to the cart with sugar and creamer. Out of the corner of her eye Kayla saw her listening.

"He got a job?" Kayla asked, pocketing the change.

"Oh, yeah," the girl said. "I don't think it's hard. He got hired onto the ground crew last week. No big deal. He went to the red booth, or some such thing."

On the way to the faire grounds Kayla went over their story with her sister.

"We're locals who have come back after working in Florida for a few years. We'll give him references if we have to, but don't volunteer anything. Look him in the eye and smile when you talk to him."

"I can't smile and talk at the same time," Tara grumbled.

"Then do that thing with your eyes you do when you want to get out of something," Kayla said, and glanced at her. More incredulous than flirty, Tara's eyelashes fluttered. Kayla nodded. "Like that."

They parked in a big, snow-patched dirt lot outside the gates to the faire grounds, and climbed out to inspect the entrance. Medieval flags and banners hung from the top of an old brick wall on either side of the gates, which stood open. Beyond them a straw-strewn dirt path led back to rows of tents and stalls. Behind those was the lodge, some kind of small stadium, and larger tents. She could see some men rigging something in the distance, but none of them looked like Ryan or his guys.

Kayla breathed in, and smelled honey, ginger and almonds warming the cold air. Bushes crowded around the red booth the counter girl had mentioned, which was more like a little house. Kayla looked up to see smoke pouring from its small chimney, and glanced at Tara, who gave her a tight nod. When they walked up and knocked on the door, a short, white-bearded man with a bald head and a big belly opened it and peered out at them.

"What do you want?" he asked, his voice gruff.

"To apply for jobs, sir," Kayla said, using the deepest tone she could manage. "I'm...Evan," she said, using her father's name, "and this is my sister, Tara. We heard you were looking for a groom and a seamstress."

The man squinted at both of them before opening the door wider and nodding his head toward the interior.

Inside, the booth was set up like an office, with a desk, several chairs and storage cabinets. Kayla noted the single rotary phone on the wall, which was the only device in the room. A dozen pair of boots were lined up next to the blazing fireplace, in the process of being cleaned.

"Sit down," the man said, wiping his hands on a rag

before trundling around the desk and dropping onto the stool. "I'm Lawrence, the crew handler." He gave them both another long look. "You've a horse that kicks whenever anyone goes near his rear. How do you break him of it?"

Kayla raised her eyebrows at the quick start.

"Start him bareback with a long rope in a pen," she said. "Train him to tolerate the touch of the rope on his hindquarters first, and then work up to rope and saddle. Once he's accepted that, you work him with your hands from front to back."

"So you're the groom." His gaze shifted to Tara. "You have to make up a lady's gown for the show. How much fabric will you need?"

"That depends on the lady and the style of the gown," her sister said. "For a slim fitted gown, height plus hem plus a foot. A fuller gown needs twice or three times that, depending on the draping, sleeves and any overlays."

He grunted and gestured toward her dress. "You made that?" When she nodded he sat back, and made a discreet motion with his hand, which sent twin flares of tiny red stars toward their faces. "Why do you want to work at the faire?"

"We need the jobs," Kayla told him, trying not to look at the swath of red stars floating in front of her nose.

Tara, thankfully, couldn't see them at all. "We also like the magic of the place," she put in, keeping a straight face.

"You two'll have precious little of that while you're mucking out stalls, and stitching up split trousers," Lawrence said as he took two forms from his desk. The red stars faded. "You'll fill these out, but if you can start today you're hired. You can live here while you work for us. We provide rooms at the lodge and meals with your pay."

Kayla exchanged a look with Tara. "We have a room at

the Silver Birch paid through next Thursday. We can move into the lodge on Friday."

Lawrence gave her another narrow look before he nodded. "See to the forms, and then I'll take you to your places."

CHAPTER 10

"You're trying to hide from me? Really?"

Titan shuffled out of the shadows of his stall to glare at Kayla. She suspected the big stallion considered her nothing but an annoying interloper, and given a chance would try to scare her off. He was the lead stallion, after all.

"I know what you're thinking, old man." Kayla stepped into the stall and hung the bridle on a peg. "You should know that you can't scare me off by pretending I'm invisible or giving me a well-placed nip. I'm here to stay, at least for the winter."

The massive stallion snorted and chuffed the straw with his hooves.

Since being hired by Forever Faire last week Kayla had kept her time with Ryan's big white stallion limited to strictly necessary care, mainly to avoid Ryan. With the first performance for the townspeople happening today, however, they'd have to come to an understanding.

"Come on, now. I'm not so bad." She unlatched the door

and stepped back. "And you've got, what, seventeen hundred pounds on me? You could squash me like a bug."

Titan's ears twitched as he bared his teeth and dipped his head.

"Yeah, you're a tough guy." Kayla stepped inside the stall and extended her hand, cookie on palm. "Riding across a field with that colossal tin-man on your back, another one coming at you with a lance in your face, you've got to be. I know I couldn't do it."

Titan chose to sniff rather than bite, and then lapped up the crescent-shaped cookie.

"Pretty good, right?" She leaned forward to whisper the rest. "Guess what? I've got more in my pocket for good boys."

Hinges gave a rusty squeal as someone entered the barn. "Groomsman." Heavy footsteps thudded across the packed dirt floor. "What's his name...Rowe? Where are you, boy?"

Showtime, Kayla thought as she patted Titan one last time before stepping out of the stall.

"Over here, sir."

As Colm Longacre approached, an elongated shadow cut through the lattice of sunlight that streamed through the barn's roof cracks. Like all the other Forever Faire performers he possessed ordinary features, but had a shorter, leaner frame. She'd heard everyone but his big buddies address him as sir, but when the other warriors didn't think anyone was listening they called him by his full name. The constant rounds he made of the camp while checking the work being done suggested he was some sort of manager—or busybody.

The head of every horse in the barn appeared as the herd assessed the situation. Kayla felt a waft of Titan's breath. The old rascal was probably enjoying this.

You want to see a real performance, pal, then now is the time to watch and learn.

Kayla couldn't keep up the ruse about being a boy forever—especially now that they'd moved to the lodge. She'd accidentally spoken in her normal voice a couple times already. For the first time since she'd been hired, she took off the baseball cap, which let her hair spill onto her shoulders.

"Damn and be done," Colm said and stopped. His sharp eyes caught a ray of light and turned to glittering copper. "You're the new groom?" Kayla let her smile answer him. "You're a woman!"

He made it sound as if she'd sprouted fangs and a forked tongue.

"Last time I checked," she told him. "Was there something you needed, sir?"

"We needed a bloody groom, not another damned female underfoot." Colm's expression darkened. "I've not seen you at the lodge. How did you get yourself hired?"

"I think I was the most experienced applicant. And I'm good with horses." That was true enough, in the same sense that the winter could be called somewhat cool, and the night a little dark. "We just moved to the lodge yesterday."

As Colm peered at her, Kayla openly returned the inspection. He looked like every other guy in the world, but she suspected underneath he was just as awesome as Ryan and the others. He kept up his disguise a little better, with his costume made meticulously from bronze shagreen and sage-colored linen. It fit him with glove-like perfection—possibly thanks to Tara.

Kayla noted the specks of soot on his hands and the manner in which he'd tied back his long black hair. That and the scent of wood smoke coming from his clothes suggested he'd come from building the fire in the gathering circle where the show's meals were cooked. He probably could have set it alight simply by standing beside it. She'd seen enough to guess that all of Ryan's men had some special talents.

"You're too little to manage, surely," he said. Though he frowned, he'd softened his tone.

It occurred to Kayla that he wasn't being insulting. He was worried for her. And in that moment she liked him, which made it harder to put on a properly meek and pitiable expression.

"I've done this all my life," she said. "We needed the jobs, sir."

She grimaced as soon as she realized her slip of the tongue.

Colm picked right up on it, too. "We?"

"Mr. Lawrence hired my sister, Tara, to work as your new seamstress," Kayla admitted.

"Did he now." Colm glanced down the rows of stalls. "What are you lot looking at?"

One of the horses whickered, and the others responded in kind. Tough hide grazed Kayla's cheek as Titan put his head over her shoulder, and she reached up to give him a pat and keep herself from smiling.

"Right." Colm nodded to himself, and reached for a bridle on the wall. "Doubtless you've heard that we're putting on a bout for the locals this afternoon. I'll need Sampson and Titan in full gear on the field in an hour."

At the sound of his name Titan jerked his head. The bridle fell off the hook into Colm's waiting hand. He hung it back in place as if nothing had happened.

"You've been shown how to properly outfit them?" he asked.

Kayla perched her cap back on her head. "Yes, sir. How did you know that was going to fall off?"

"I'm used to the oversized nag's tricks." He stripped off a glove and deftly tapped a finger against her cheek. "Forget that now, lass."

Kayla felt a tingle dance over her cheekbone, and assumed he was trying to make her forget the way Ryan had. With her best blank face she said, "Yes, sir."

Colm gave her one final, measuring look. "Right, then. Get on with it."

She went to work, but as soon as Colm left she slipped out the back door and hurried over to the big costume tent. Inside she found her sister eyeing a pattern, and cutting a length of wool into matching pieces.

"My cover's blown, and Colm knows you're my sister now. Brace yourself for an incoming interrogation."

"I don't have time for one," Tara muttered around the plastic-headed pins in her mouth. "One of the townies thought it was a good idea to wash their peasant tunic costume and toss it in the dryer last night."

Kayla saw the now-tiny tunic sitting on the table and winced. "Did they at least get you a sewing machine?"

"If you can call it that." Her sister nodded toward an ancient-looking contraption on the side of her work table. "It works off a foot pedal. That I have to actually pedal, like a bike."

Kayla made a sympathetic sound. "I've noticed the guys really hate technology. Maybe it messes with their magic."

"They don't have to use it. I do." Tara finished her cutting and set aside her shears before she faced her sister. "I hate this place. These people are creepy. The whole Renfaire thing is lame. How much longer do we have to do this?"

Her sister had been itching to leave from the day they'd

been hired, which perplexed Kayla. Since coming to the Forever Faire she'd never felt safer.

"Until I find out what kind of magic they're using to fool everyone," Kayla said. She reached out and touched her sister's stiff shoulder. "We need to so we can protect ourselves, remember?"

"Those bikers haven't shown up again," Tara said, and stabbed a pin into the wool. "Maybe this time we lost them for good."

"Or maybe they'll show up as soon as we try to leave." Kayla gestured around them. "At least here we're protected."

"From what? By what?" her sister demanded, throwing her arms up. "We still don't know anything about them."

"The show manager, Colm? He knew a bridle was going to fall before it did," Kayla said, pacing to the tent entrance. "Everyone is too ordinary, haven't you noticed that? Like they all don't want to be noticed. And Wallace, the guy who runs the smithy? I watched him while he was working alone, and he didn't see me. He waved his hand over a broken sword, and a bunch of little stars started floating over it."

Tara gave her a suspicious look. "Right. Like metal never reflected anything."

"After the stars disappeared, the sword wasn't broken anymore," Kayla said. "It looked brand new."

Her sister wrapped her arms around herself. "What about Ryan? What can he do?"

"Aside from change a motorcycle into a horse? I don't know yet. I've been kind of dodging him." She rubbed her temple. "He never practices in any of the duels they do. No swords, no staffs, nothing. The rest of them do, so that's a little weird."

"He's like the biggest guy here," Tara pointed out. "Maybe he doesn't want to hurt anyone else."

"I don't know. Maybe." Kayla sighed. "Look, kiddo, I have to go back and get the horses ready. Just, please be patient for a little longer. I'll find what we need, I promise."

"Sure." Her sister sighed and sat down behind the ancient foot-pedal contraption. "Just add a real sewing machine to that list, will you?"

"Hey, big guy." A brass-haired wench dressed in shabby garments perched her broad ass on the stool beside Dirk Blackstone. "Ain't see you around here before."

Over her shoulder Dirk saw his cousin Beck emerge from the shadowy corner his men occupied. Dirk shook his head slightly to send him back into the dark. Unlike the last tavern they had visited, this one was not full of mortal bikers eager to clash and draw blood. The Blackstone clan had left that one littered with their corpses, but not without cost. Dirk's wounds throbbed as he regarded the pushy mortal.

"I have never come here before today."

"Well, I have," she said. She leaned forward, pressing her arms against the sides of her large, drooping breasts. They bulged up from her too-tight, spangled top. "My name's Tina. Buy me a drink?"

He nodded to the bartender, who trotted over to give Tina a knowing smirk.

"A dirty martini, Jeff," Tina said as she shifted her thick

body closer to Dirk's. "So what brings you to Chattanooga, big guy? Got family in town?"

The smell of the sweat under her perfume filled Dirk's nose, bringing with it the acrid stink of chemicals. Dirk could see the cause in the faint needle marks in the bend of her arms, and the small open sore in the corner of her mouth. Yet atop her stench lay a far more inviting odor—that of his prey.

"Well?" Tina demanded.

Dirk imagined telling her that he and his clan had come on his father's orders to capture a cursed Fae woman who possessed enough power to level the city. Or maybe he would just tell her that her breath smelled of corpse rot.

"No. No family here."

She giggled. "Then why'd you come to Nooga, big guy?"

"I am looking for…" What was the word they used for their comrades? "Friends. Two sisters who travel together. One has light eyes, and the other is younger, and fair. Perhaps you have seen them."

"Waste my time checking out some other bitches?"

Tina made a flatulent sound with her thin lips as she accepted her drink from the bartender. From the glass she removed two small fruits skewered by an even tinier plastic sword.

"Not when there's a eye candy like you around," she said.

She watched him as she slowly sucked one of the fruits into her mouth.

Naught about the woman aroused Dirk, but her clumsy efforts at seduction brought back a vision of Tara Rowe. How pale her face had turned as he'd dragged her from the cloth shop. How viciously she had fought him. He'd held her close for a moment before she'd used her sharp little teeth on him, and wriggled free. The memory of how her slim, ripe body had felt against his could still made his cock stiffen. Someday she'd open her mouth for him. Someday very, very soon. And Dirk would wind his fist in that long, winter moon mane of hers, and make her pleasure him until her lips split.

"Come on, baby–" Tina placed her hand on his bicep, but snatched her hand back. She stood, staring at the dark wetness staining her fingers. "Shit, man. You're bleeding."

He seized her wrist before she could back away and shoved her back onto the stool.

"The women I seek. You have seen them."

"No, I told you," Tina whined. The wench whimpered as his grip on her tightened. "You're hurting."

"You are lying," he said through clenched teeth. Pain rose from her flesh and spread into his, seeping up his arm until it settled over the open wound. Dirk felt the edges closing and decided to attend to both his needs. "Come with me."

He hauled her behind him through the tavern and out the back entrance, where he found an empty alley. The wench was still whining and writhing when he turned and pushed her up against the brick wall, but once she looked into his eyes she fell under his power, quieted and went still.

Dirk grabbed a handful of her stiff curls and pulled until her eyes went wet. "Reveal."

"I'm a drunk and a drug addict," Tina said, the magick he cast rendering her voice flat and lifeless. "I short-change customers, and steal tips from the other waitresses. I shoplifted a bracelet to pawn it–"

"The sisters," Dirk said, twisting his fist in her hair until she released a high-pitched whine. "Are they here, in the city? I can smell them on you."

"There was a gal, last week." She stared past him as her

voice softened. "She had coffee and toast at City Cafe, the diner where I work. Pretty little girl. Prettier'n me. Strange, too. Like someone from a faraway place–"

He let go of her hair and grabbed her arms. He shook her hard enough to slam the back of her head into the wall.

"But you touched her. Why?"

Tina squinted at him. "She handed me a five and told me to keep the change. It felt so good when she touched me. Better than the meth."

So this one could still feel something other than her craving for oblivion. He released her arms and tore open her dress from collar to hem.

"Spread your legs."

Dirk unfastened his trousers and freed his shaft. He spat in his palm and dampened his club-like cockhead before stroking himself a few times. The wench stood unresisting as he kneed her legs apart and guided himself to her dry opening. Getting inside her meant fighting his own lack of desire as much as hers, and he could only shove half his length inside her before she began to mewl with pain.

"Please don't," Tina begged. "It hurts too much."

"Shut your mouth," he told her, gripping her throat and squeezing until she fell silent. Her funerary breath made him turn his head away and look down the alley as he forged deeper.

It would not be like this with Tara, Dirk thought as he mechanically pumped in and out of the wench. Tara already had the look of a wild thing about her. No, she would fight him, scratching and biting as she had before, until he beat her into submission.

Tina made a gurgling sound, distracting him from his fantasy, and he tightened his grip. "I told you," he muttered as he hammered into her. "Shut up."

He wouldn't fuck the little one on her feet, Dirk decided. He would strip her naked and tie her down. He'd fill her over and over until she cried out his name, and made herself his slave. He closed his eyes, imagining it was Tara sheathing him, and felt the hot surge tighten in his balls before he began to jet.

"Yes, you'll like it, little one," he murmured, driving himself into his root for the last, long spurt. "I'll make you love it."

A dark energy burned over Dirk's wounds, which the rough sex had been slowly healing. But Tina began to slide down the wall. He had to tilt his head to look into her bulging, dead eyes. Her protruding tongue made him jerk out of her in disgust, and she crumpled like a broken doll.

"You don't have to fucking kill them, Cousin," Beck said as he came out of the bar and nodded at the wench's corpse. "Or is it kill them fucking? I can never remember how 'tis said in this mortal prattle."

"Who fucking cares?" Dirk grumbled as he straightened his clothes. He lifted his hand, channeling his restored power at a broad swath of shadow. "One of them was here last week. Get the men. We're leaving."

Beck nodded. "And where are we to go now?"

Dirk reached down to grab Tina's hair and dragged her toward the writhing pool of darkness he'd created. "Some swill hall called City Cafe."

*R*yan knew that the old Moffett lodge had hosted many guests over its long history. A few illustrious politicians, country singers, and businessmen had even graced the wood-paneled halls where he now strode. But it had mostly served as a haven for renegades. Elias Moffett, the banker who had built the place before the market crash of '29, had hated the new-fangled electricity of his time, and outfitted the lodge to run on coal and gas. During the Great Depression Moffett had refused to sell the place, instead moving there to live with his wife. All their wealth gone, they had sometimes had to live on whatever wild game Elias could find in the woods, until their fortunes reversed again.

As Ryan exited the lodge and headed for the dressing tent, he still smiled a little when he remembered Elias. Like him, Elias had been exiled for marrying a mortal. The old Fae huntsman had welcomed the Forever Faire each winter, providing haven and kinship for Ryan and his men while they rested from their long year of traveling. Elias had also adored his lovely wife, Lily, despite the fact that she had never been able to give him children. She died smiling in his arms shortly after celebrating her ninetieth birthday. The next morning Elias had sent a courier with one last letter and the deed for the Moffett Lodge to Ryan, before choosing to follow his wife to the next place.

Once in the dressing tent, Ryan began to prepare for the bout by donning his armor. But his thoughts remained with Elias and his wife—and Ryan well knew why. He'd been in a melancholy mood since his encounter in the woods. Perhaps the joust would dispel his gloominess. If naught else it would give him something to do besides think of her.

The tent flap opened, and Colm stepped inside. "Our new groom's a female."

"What?" Ryan retrieved his chest protector and checked the straps before fitting it into place. "Why?"

"I asked Lawrence that, and the addlebrain swore— swore to me, Ryan—that he'd hired a lad. I went to the barn to tell the boy when to bring out the horses. And there she was." Colm brought over two lances and held them out. "The eight or the ten?"

"The ten, brother."

Ryan was set to ride against Gavan, who had been a champion of the tourneys since their invention.

"Is she a mannish woman?" Ryan asked. "What do they call it...transforming?"

"Transgender," his second said, but shook his head. "A wee thing, but definitely female. Could be Lawrence simply neglected to look down." Colm checked the length of the ten-foot lance for defects. "Titan's taken to cuddling her."

Ryan uttered a sour sound. "My horse doesn't cuddle."

"He does now. Hung his head on her shoulder and nuzzled her neck, as besotted as a boy. So sweet he was, it set my teeth to ache." Colm picked up his helmet and turned it over in his hands. "My gut says she's trouble."

He stopped cinching his straps. "How so?"

Colm made a frustrated sound. "I can't fault her work. She's managing it. The barn and the mounts are in good order. Our lads like her, too, rather a lot—even your Titan. She's a bit cheeky, but what female isn't these days?" He hesitated but then pressed on. "I just know there's more to this little wench than can be seen. I can't put name to the cause, but she unsettles me. The eyes, maybe. Like a cat's."

Ryan considered all that. "You're sure she's mortal, then?"

"Aye, as they come. I took a look from toe to head, and there's not a bit of Fae about her." Colm held up his right hand. "I saw a bridle about to fall and caught it. I mind-fogged it from her in a blink."

As his second Colm bore many burdens. He kept a keen and perpetual watch over their troop. His instincts, honed by battle and loss, always made the mark. If he thought the wench was trouble, then no doubt she was.

"Send her on her way after the bout," Ryan said.

"She'll need wages," Colm said, but he seemed relieved. "Enough to keep them until they find something else." He caught Ryan's glance. "Lawrence hired her sister as our new seamstress. You've seen her?"

"Aye." Ryan recalled the slim, ashen-haired female with the sulky eyes, fitting a vest on Gavan. He hadn't liked that she was fair, but her hair had none of the golden color so many Fae women possessed.

"They look naught alike."

Colm shrugged. "Sisters often don't, brother. Our groomswoman is the older, and to my eyes, more fetching."

Colm's concern for their temporary nuisance wasn't unusual. Although they treasured mortal females, the rigors of the show demanded the sort of stamina and strength rarely possessed by them. His second's interest stirred Ryan's curiosity.

"How long has it been since you've taken a lover?"

"Since I was cast out, as well you know," Colm told him. "Even if I had a mind to, which I do not, Kayla's too small. More than a peck at her would likely break–"

Ryan's gaze snapped to Colm's face. He quickly stepped to within an inch of the man.

"Kayla?" Ryan demanded. "Kayla Rowe is our new groom?"

"Aye." His second's brows rose as he glanced down at his shirt. The center of the garment was bunched in Ryan's fist. "You know her?"

"No," he said, almost shouting. He released his second and turned away. "I but let her warm herself at my fire on a cold night."

"Is that what they call it now?" Colm said. As Ryan spun around Colm held up his hands. "'Twas a jest, my liege. If you want her gone, she'll go."

Avoiding temptation by sending Kayla away was the only course that made sense. But as Ryan met his second's gaze, he remembered the delicious feel of Kayla's lips under his. Just the mention of her name buoyed his spirits. He'd let her go once, and it had taken every bit of willpower he possessed.

"Let her stay, for now."

If Colm had something to say about his decision, he kept it to himself.

Ryan draped his mail standard around his neck and picked up his jousting helmet. As he tucked it under his arm he picked up the ten-foot lance and stalked out of the tent.

Outside sunlight poured over the faire grounds, gilding

dozens of tents, shoppes, gaming stalls and performance stages. The sharp scents of ale and wine blended with that of roasted joints, sugared nuts and ginger cake. Mortals clustered and crowded everywhere. Despite the outlandish costumes that many wore, Ryan smiled. Somewhere out there, too, was Kayla Rowe.

"Good day to you, sir knight," said a willowy woman dressed in a neck ruff and low-cut scarlet gown. She dropped into a wobbly curtsy before him. Her long curls bobbled and her earrings glinted as she drew a small square of red silk from her sleeve and offered it to him. "Will you carry my favor?"

He eyed the over-large dagger she wore on her leather girdle, which was tied in the sheath with thin leather straps.

"Do you vow to keep your blade peace-bonded should I lose, milady?"

"But of course." She produced an ornate fan and peered at him over its edge. "You shall owe me a forfeit, however."

Colm stepped between them. "Alas, Sir Ryan of the Sheridans does not carry colors, but he is grateful for your favor just the same. If you would accompany me, I'll see to it that you have the best seat in the jousting arena. It is just the spot where all may admire your beauty, milady."

Wallace joined Ryan to watch Colm lead the simpering fan away.

"Should someone tell milady," Wallace said, "that back in those days, the only women who let their hair down, bared their ears, and wore red were trollops?"

"Best not to," Ryan replied, searching the crowd for Kayla's petite form. He handed the smith his helmet. "How is Gavan's mood?"

"His town wench threw him over for a mortal. You'll

need that ten," the smith said as they walked over to the entrance of the jousting arena.

KAYLA CHECKED over Sampson and Titan one last time before she took hold of their reins and led them out of the barn. The high pommels on the saddles looked odd, and she still couldn't understand why they needed to wear tail guards, but neither horse seemed to mind being laced into their armor. Someone took very good care of the mounts' gear, too. The riveted slats of the cruppers over their hindquarters had been lovingly polished to a mirror-brightness. Every bit of leather trim had been kept oiled and clean.

One of the performers halted in their path and stared.

"This is getting old," Kayla muttered under her breath as she stopped and looked up at yet another broad, ordinary face. "Hi. Kayla Rowe, new groom. Not a lad."

"I can see that," the man said, his tone as cold as his frosty amber eyes. "You're the sister, then."

This was Jannon, the drunk she had seen spoiling for a fight at the bonfire. "I am. You've met Tara?"

His jaw tightened. "Aye. She doesn't belong here anymore than you."

Kayla returned his evil glare. "You got a problem with us, pal, tell it to Colm. Or come find me and we'll chat. Leave my teenage sister out of it."

He stepped toward her, shook his head, and then pivoted and stalked away.

"So he's not a fan, obviously," she said to Titan.

Kayla felt suddenly cold, and looked down to see patches of frost on her jeans and jacket. Similar scrolls of ice appeared on both horses' armor.

"Looks like we've got an iceman to go with the horse-changer and the sword-mender." Titan nudged her shoulder and whickered. "Right, we have to go rumble with the other boys." She sighed. "Come on."

Once she reached the performer's passage into the jousting arena Kayla inspected the horses one final time. Satisfied, she led them out into the open-air makeshift stadium. A wood-post barrier divided the dirt field into parallel courses. Pennants and flags fluttered above the crowded stands. On either end of the field three men stood with a knight dressed in armor. The broad hilts of their lances matched the trims on their horses, so Kayla took Sampson down to Gavan. But as she returned to lead Titan to Ryan, she heard the bridle rattle as her hands shook. Sunlight glinted from Ryan's metal suit, almost blinding her. Even so, she couldn't help but stare. Heart pounding, she stopped and offered him the reins.

Her magical savior lifted his visor. "We meet again, Kayla Rowe."

He was as big and broad and breath-taking as she remembered, and she bowed to hide how much that flustered her. "At your service, Sir Ryan."

Thankfully he didn't answer. Instead he gripped Titan's pommel. He hoisted himself up into the saddle so effortlessly Kayla could only gape. Wallace handed Ryan his lance, and Colm checked his stirrups before straightening and nodding to him.

"Good luck," Kayla whispered as Titan trotted forward.

Ryan fit the end of his lance into the arret on his breastplate, sliding it back until the grapper on the hilt met the support. Then he looked back at her. For just a moment their eyes met. It was as though electricity crackled between them—and then he was off.

From the Queen's box the announcer introduced both

knights, who rode in a tight circle at the end of the barrier before taking their positions. The horses perked up as the men waved to the cheering crowd. After they both nodded to the announcer, the elegant old lady who played the queen stood, lifted a white handkerchief, and then dropped it.

The two horses took off. They galloped toward each other with tremendous speed. The impact of their hooves on the hard-packed dirt rolled like low thunder across the field. Kayla found herself holding her breath as Ryan and Gavan turned slightly in their saddles. They lowered their lances just before they met. The lances struck and exploded, sending Ryan to one side and nearly unhorsing Gavan.

As the horses circled back, the men serving as the ground crew rushed out to remove the broken lances from the field.

"We count no points for shattering both lances," Colm said as he joined her. "They have to make a shield or chest strike, or unsaddle the other. Or kill each other."

"Very funny," she muttered, her throat tight. She turned to see Ryan accepting a new lance from Wallace. "How long do they, uh, keep jousting?"

"Gavan's mooning over some town wench," Jannon said as he came up behind them.

"Not long," Colm told Kayla.

On the second pass Ryan struck Gavan's shield in the center, and took a hit on the arm, which the announcer called a point. Since both lances remained intact the men circled around and rode directly at each other again. Dust rose in a cloud, making it difficult to see what happened when they passed again, but shards of wood and a helmet soaring up into the air made Kayla press her hand against her mouth.

The ground crew hurried over to help up one fallen knight. Finally as the dust cleared Kayla saw it was Gavan.

"Does that mean he loses?" she asked. "Ryan is the winner?"

Colm regarded the limping figure. "'Tis a matter of opinion. But the joust is done. Go and fetch Titan, and I'll see to Sampson."

Kayla hurried toward Ryan, who had dismounted and removed his helmet. He stood near the stands, reins in hand, and bowed to the applauding crowd. But just before she reached him she felt something slither over the nape of her neck. She turned to see a tall, broad man dressed in black climbing down from the stands. He had his dark eyes fixed on Ryan, and when a breeze ruffled through his limp brown hair she somehow knew he was wearing a wig. She looked down and saw black gloves on his huge hands, and felt her skin crawl for a different reason. The man in black had one glove that looked shredded. As if he'd used it to punch through some glass to grab at a terrified girl in a car.

Rage that had simmered too long boiled up inside Kayla. She'd promised Tara they were safe. For once she'd even thought it was true. She'd had enough.

This time you're going to be roadkill, you bastard.

But before she could rush the man in black, Colm shouted something. Without warning Titan reared up, yanking the reins from Ryan's grip. The giant stallion roared before taking off toward the stands. A little boy in the very front row stood frozen as he watched the enormous creature barreling toward him.

There was no time to think. Kayla dashed in front of the horse.

"Titan, *no*," she screamed.

Just as the spooked stallion was nearly on top of her, Sampson darted in front of him. A gleaming gauntlet snatched Kayla off her feet. The two horses collided, with Titan whinnying furiously before dancing backward. She found herself cradled against Ryan's chest as Wallace caught Titan and dragged him back from the stands.

The faces in the crowd turned from horror to awe, and suddenly everyone was applauding and calling out to them. Kayla couldn't understand what they were saying, but Ryan smiled down at her.

"You're a brave one, my girl." He tugged off his gauntlet and used his thumb on her lower lip. "You've bitten yourself bloody."

She saw the crimson drop he took away and shook her head. "How did you do that? How did you move so fast?"

"Come on," a man shouted. "She saved the kid. Kiss her."

Ryan had pulled her up in front of him, nearly sitting her in his lap. She reached up and touched his cheek. Delicious heat and light poured over him and he changed again into the pale-haired, jewel-eyed warrior.

"You are real," she gasped. "I wasn't hallucinating."

Ryan's expression turned bleak. "Lass, what are you telling me?"

Anguish and relief made her tug his face down to hers.

This time the passion was hers, and she gave it all to him as their lips met. The raucous sounds of the crowd, the faire, and the rest of the world faded. He tasted hot and tart, as he cradled the back of her head. His tongue met hers and glided in deep.

Kayla's body shook as she struggled against his armor, longing to beat her fists against it, hating that steel separated their skins. She wanted to tear it away from him and run her hands over his brutal muscles, and drag him to the ground.

Ryan took his mouth from hers. "We cannot do this, lass. Not now."

"Then take me somewhere." She took a handful of his silken hair and laced her fingers through it, but it slipped free of her grasp. "I can't stand this. Please, Ryan."

But he did just the opposite and gently lowered her to the ground. With one final look, he rode off to the barn, leaving her staring after him. When she spun around to face the cheering crowd, she saw the dark man had also vanished.

Jannon loomed over her, his lips drawn into a sneer. "Nicely done, groomsman. Will you take up a lance next? Mayhap Ryan's, between your legs?"

Kayla's emotions boiled over into scorching fury. Without thinking, she walloped him. Reaching as high as she could, her fist connected with the bottom of his jaw.

As Jannon shook his head and scowled, she rubbed her throbbing knuckles and leaned closer. "Any other questions?"

"You've a spine, then." He rubbed his chin. "I like that."

"Obnoxious jackass," she spat.

She headed toward Sampson and Colm, the crowd still cheering behind her. Colm gave her a strange look.

"What, that?" she said. "He was being a jerk."

"I've no doubt," Colm replied lightly. But as he bent down to straighten the skewed flanchard on Sampson's right side, Kayla saw his shoulders shaking and nudged him aside.

"It isn't funny," she declared. But her own lips twitched as she secured the side armor. "Okay, it is, but don't laugh. I'm trying to be a groom here, not another damned female underfoot."

Colm patted her on the shoulder. "Today you've done that and then some, lass."

*O*nce the faire closed at sunset, Ryan watched from a nearby hill as Kayla left the barn and disappeared into the lodge. Inside it would be warm and bright, with all the mortal workers eating together and discussing the events of the day. No doubt the Rowe sisters would be made welcome by the others. Everyone was still talking about how Kayla had thrown herself in front of Titan. Part of him longed to join them, and sit beside the young sisters, and share in their merriment. If only that was what he truly craved.

Colm emerged from the pine grove. "You summoned me, my liege?"

He nodded, still looking down at the lodge. "Is she well?"

"I am happy to report that young Kayla is not begging for you," his second said. "Or pining. Or even looking. For that, brother, I think you must do more than kiss her."

"You know what I mean." Ryan leaned back against the shale outcropping behind him. "And as it happens, she's the one who kissed me."

Colm nodded. "I'll send her packing in the morning."

"That is not what I mean." He drove his head back against the rock, sending a small clump of shattered stone to the ground. "She has courage. She would have let Titan trample her to save that child."

"Aye, and when Jannon was rude to her after, she planted a facer on him." Colm smiled at his startled look. "Watching her do it 'twas the best moment of the day. Truth be said, the little wench tugs at my own heart. But she is mortal, Ryan, and trouble for you."

Everything his second said was true, yet Ryan couldn't bring himself to agree. Even now, when he was convinced she had seen his true form.

"I do have some good news," his second offered. "Seems we've a halfling among us."

Ryan pushed himself away from the rock. "Who?"

"Her name is Christine Marszalek, and she's working the children's archery range. Lawrence told me that he felt her Fae blood the moment he shook her hand." He sighed. "He also says she's unaware."

"Then she hasn't been awakened." Of all the Fae they tried to protect, the progeny of Fae trysts with humans were the most precious. "You'll get close to her, and discover what powers she may possess."

"As you wish." Colm dropped his glamor to stretch and shake out his garnet mane. "Lawrence claims she was a dancer before she came here. Perhaps she is of the Sylph-light clan to the north. Their leader has a peculiar penchant for mortal females."

"Watch her with the children," Ryan warned. "Sylph-lights use dance to mesmerize humans, and she could end up luring a horde of them off the grounds."

"No dancing," his second agreed. "What of the Rowes? Have you tired of tempting fate yet, or should I keep them on until you've had a proper taste of the little scrapper?"

"I tasted her today," Ryan said. His eyelids drooped as he remembered. "She's all firewine and honeybliss. You wouldn't think it to look at her, but she's fearsome when she's riled. I nearly yanked her to the ground to put her under me."

"You want her that much." Colm looked worried now.

"Aye, I want her." Ryan dragged a hand through his hair, and then found himself telling all. "I dream about her every other night. I can't forget the sweetness of her scent, or the softness of her skin. I want to wallow in her. All the while knowing that if I take another mortal to my bed, there is every chance I will plant my seed in her. No clan will take in one of our get. And if she dies–"

"She's not Maeve, Ryan. These modern girls, they protect their wombs like castles besieged." Colm clamped a hand on his broad shoulder. "And never forget that I've quiet footsteps, a stone cudgel, and a truckload of iron chains."

Ryan tried to muster a smile.

"One other thing needles me," Colm said. "I saw Kayla stare up in the crowd just before she flung herself in front of your Titan. Someone came today, and judging by her look, 'tis someone she has no love for."

Ryan considered that. "Mortal fear can look much like mortal anger."

"Aye, but fright wouldn't set her off on Jannon. She was still livid about something." Colm restored his human guise and yawned. "And I'm becoming the old woman who natters on about naught, so I'm to bed. I'll see to the Marszalek girl tomorrow. And you?"

"In your footsteps."

Ryan followed him down from the hill to the back of

the lodge, where he and his men kept their rooms. Once inside, Ryan bid Colm goodnight as they headed in opposite directions. In his large corner suite Ryan lit his oil lamp and closed the windows against the frigid night air. He'd kept Elias's sturdy furnishings, which the old huntsman had built to accommodate Fae bulk. But the big, empty bed held no appeal for him. He instead settled into the intricately-carved oak rocker by the fireplace, where Elias had spent so many nights with Lily on his lap. The love they had shared still lingered, permeating the wood, and comforting him as much as the heat from the flames.

His thoughts drifted back to the joust, and the sight of Kayla leading the horses into the arena. For a moment she had looked like a child between the two great beasts, and then she'd looked at him with those gilded eyes. He could almost believe her Fae, the way her skin had glowed, like a woman made of sunbeams and magick.

Ryan closed his eyes, and the arena in his memory emptied of mortals and Fae. Titan and Sampson left Kayla to shuffle off and graze, their armor falling from their brute bodies, their tails sifting in the breeze.

"Soon the battle is to begin," Kayla said as she came to him. She pressed her small hand against his bare chest. "Who do you think will prevail, my lord?"

He peered down at her, and staggered back as he saw the heart-shaped face of his lost bride.

"Maeve?"

"Aye, Ryan." She let her hand fall to her side as Kayla's jeans and blouse flowed into Maeve's favorite green gown. "Do not fear me, Husband."

He saw her fading and rushed to take her in his arms. "No, you cannot leave me again."

"My time has passed, and our son awaits." She touched

his face. "You have kept me in your heart so long, my darling, but you must release me now. It is her time."

"Her?" He looked over her head to see Kayla sitting in the empty stands. "She can never take your place, beloved."

"Not so, for I took hers." Maeve's smile turned sad. "And soon you will need her at your side. Death is coming again, Husband."

Ryan tried to hold onto Maeve, but her specter thinned into nothingness, leaving him facing Kayla.

She climbed down from the stands and left the arena. Ryan followed her through the empty faire, across the boundaries and into the snowy woods. The daylight faded to moonbeams, and dappled the drifts with silver pools.

"I'm here," she said lowly.

Kayla stood beside a campfire, her small form draped in bronze silk and amber lace. Everything about her tugged at him, but he could still see Maeve's sweet, sorrowful features.

"You are not my love," he said through clenched teeth. He went to her, gripped her by the arm, and dragged her against him. "You are my loneliness." He shook her. "My lust."

"If that's what you want," she said mildly.

She dropped to her knees and lifted her face as she unlaced the front of his trousers.

Ryan took in a sharp breath as he felt her long, cool fingers freeing him from his smalls. The sight of her clasping his shaft sent a surge of hot blood to his groin.

"You would put your mouth on me?"

Her eyes darkened as she locked gazes with him, and brought his engorged cockhead to her pretty lips for a feathery kiss.

"You thought of this the first time you saw me." She lashed her tongue over him. "And this."

He threaded his fingers through her hair, urging her mouth closer. As she engulfed him and suckled he let his head fall back and groaned.

Kayla's mouth glided on him, up and down, her head bobbing slowly as she relished his stiff rod. The soft, liquid sounds of her loving sank into him. The feel of her lips and tongue as she sucked him drew his balls up tight and hot. He wanted to pump his cream into her, and watch her swallow it, every pulse, every drop–

"Kayla," he moaned, and jerked awake.

Heart hammering and cock throbbing, he nearly fell as he staggered up from the chair. He stared back at it, and wiped the sweat from his hot face with a shaking hand. His eyes burned and blurred as he braced himself for the well of guilt and self-hatred that came with every thought of Maeve. But none came as his shaft pressed against his laces, as hard and swollen as if he'd just skewered Kayla's lips with it.

Ryan stomped out of his rooms and left the lodge, taking with him his seething temper as he stalked out to the forest. His boots left deep depressions in the frozen ground, and a trail of tiny, blazing stars hung in the air behind him. As he made his way through the evergreens, the rake of their needles set his arms to swinging. Showers of brittle green bits pelted the snow. Wood creaked and snapped as dozens of trees toppled in his wake.

Dirk left the drugged, bruised whore in his bed, and pulled on his trousers before he yanked open the motel room door. In the process it ripped off its hinges, and he flung it against the wall. The crash it made when it fell to the mottled carpet made the stripper open her bleary eyes before closing them tightly.

"Is the place burning down?" Dirk demanded of Beck.

"Worse," his cousin said, and gestured at the motel's frost-covered swimming pool. "Jarek awaits your report."

Dirk brushed the smaller man aside and strode over to the edge of the pool. They had removed all the lights from the exterior of the hotel, and the only thing illuminating the surface of the dirty water was an oval of shadow that glimmered around the edges.

Forcing himself down on one knee, Dirk bowed his head. "My liege. We have been awaiting your pleasure."

"So I am told. It seems that is all you have done since leaving the enclave." Jarek Blackstone's craggy face appeared in the center of the watery shadow. "You have found her again?"

"I have." Dirk rose to his feet and quickly related what he had learned. "When I discovered the sisters at Forever Faire, I would have captured them, but they are being protected by a large band of Fae outcasts disguised as mortals."

"You have forgotten how to fight, my son?" Jarek demanded.

"No, sire." He kept his expression bland. "Even now my hands itch for my blades. But your orders were to take the woman quietly. We cannot do that if we must first engage so many Fae warriors. They have also set up boundary spells to repel Dark Fae. I was only able to enter–"

"I care not what you have to do to get her," his father said flatly. "Kill the outcasts, take the changeling and her sister, and deliver them to me."

"Their leader is Ryan of the Sheridan," Dirk said. "You remember him, I think. He laid waste to near every Dark Fae clan in Ireland before he was cast out."

Jarek uttered a curse that caused the pool water to boil. Dirk fought the urge to back away.

"You are not a fool, my son, or a coward. Lure the women away if you must. Perhaps you may use Sheridan's weakness against him. Give it a good stir, and he may even help you do the work."

Remembering the tales of Sheridan gone mad, Dirk swallowed. "I will need more men."

"You have most of our clan with you," his father said, derision dripping from each syllable. "If the lot of you cannot outwit two females and a troop of exiles, what good are you to me?"

"I understand, Father." Dirk wasn't going to press the issue. He needed Jarek to believe he was still cowed by his will. "I will send word…"

Dirk watched the portal melt away into the filthy water.

Beck came to stand beside him. "He fears you, Cousin. He was the same with my sire when he ruled as clan leader. That is why Jarek murdered him. He cannot abide anyone who stands in the way of what he desires."

Neither could Dirk. "When I wrest control of the clan, I will give my father to you, as promised. Now, tell the men to assemble at midnight. I will need maps of the renegade encampment and the lands surrounding it."

As Beck bowed and hurried off, the sound of uneven footsteps made Dirk turn to see the stripper sneaking away from his room. He calmly strode over, freezing her in place. He seized her by the hair and dragged her back inside. As terrified screams pierced the night air, all of the shadows in the motel courtyard began slithering toward the open doorway.

CHAPTER 15

As usual, Kayla and Tara sat together in the canteen tent. Each morning Forever Faire's entire crew gathered there at the end of the concession lane to share the first meal, which the show provided as an employment perk. The choices offered were basic hot and cold breakfast foods, but since it was free and cooked well, no one complained.

A raven-haired girl with green eyes and tattooed arms parked her breakfast tray in front of Kayla's as she sat down across from her. "Howdy. I'm Christine," she said, a distinct Tennessee drawl in her voice. "I keep the kids from shooting each other with arrows."

Tara eyed the new girl's ink as well as her eyebrow, nose and lip piercings.

"I've lost my appetite," Tara said.

Before Kayla could chastise her, she got up and headed to the coffee urn. Kayla smiled sheepishly at Christine.

"Nice to meet you. I'm Kayla, the show's groom, and that rude little business is my sister, Tara, the seamstress." She offered her the Danish she hadn't touched.

"Thanks." Christine added the pastry to her heavily-laden plate. "How long have you and Goldilocks been with the faire?"

"About two weeks now." Kayla took a sip of her coffee and saw Colm weaving through the tables as he approached them. "Have you met the show manager yet? Because you're about to."

"Oh, yeah. He's my personal love puppy," the girl murmured before she looked up. "Morning, Colm. Sleep well without me?"

Kayla nearly choked, and stared at the new girl, who was still giving the manager a cheery grin.

"Aye, I always do. You're to work the hatchet-toss today, Miss Marszalek," Colm told her, his voice flinty. "No children permitted to play or to step past the roped lines. Three strikes inside the target for a prize. Any questions?"

Christine cocked her head. "Do you have a hairy chest?"

He blinked. "What?"

"I ask because that's kind of a deal-breaker for me. I prefer skin. Lots and lots of skin." She leaned forward to give him a better look at her perfect cleavage. "But you could shave." She smiled. "Or I could shave you."

Kayla watched Colm turn and stride off. "I don't think he's, uh…"

"Interested? Available? Hetero?" Christine laughed. "Some of the other girls say he's gay, but I'm thinking heartbroke. What's your take?"

"Not really my business." Kayla's eyes shifted to Tara, who was adding cream to her coffee, and then to Jannon, who stood behind her and looked as if he wanted to grab her and drag her off to his room. "Some of the faire guys are a little odd."

"A little? Honey." Christine watched Wallace pass their table. "They may not be much in the looks department, but they're all built like gladiators, talk like time travelers, and smell like dessert from a French bakery. That one is the hammer slammer, right?"

"The blacksmith," Kayla said. Christine's assessment might be colorful, but it was also right on the money. "Are you interested in anyone in particular?"

"I can never resist any big girl candy." She made a hungry sound. "Oh, now there's some serious sugar."

Kayla followed the new girl's gaze to the towering figure standing on the other side of the dining tent. Ryan had been avoiding her ever since the joust, but it wasn't working for either of them. Every time they saw each other the air between them seemed to buzz with unseen lightning. Kayla had also been losing herself in dark, erotic dreams about him each night. In her dream world they were always naked and touching and kissing, but before anything more could happen she would wake up sobbing with frustration.

Christine nudged her. "You hitting that, girlfriend?"

"She's not hitting anyone." Tara thumped her cup down, sloshing some coffee over the rim as she glared across the table. "And she's not your girlfriend, Pincushion."

"Hey," Kayla said, frowning at her sister's belligerence. "Manners."

"I heard you were a stripper," Tara said. She leaned forward, her stormy eyes intent on Christine's face. "What's it like, taking your clothes off and shaking your boobs and ass for money?"

Kayla slammed her hand on the table. "That's enough out of you."

"Easy, sweetie," Christine drawled, and smiled at Tara. "It's good money, kid, if you can smile, look sexy and dance for eight, ten hours straight, seven days a week. This would be on a tiny stage under a blasting a/c vent—

they don't like dancers to sweat too much—with lechers ogling all the time, and groping you the minute you step down. You have to treat them like princes, and pretend you're overjoyed by the dollar bill tips and the watered-down drinks they buy you. Once your shift is over, you hand a third of your take to the manager for the privilege of dancing in his place. Then you go home and try to scrub off the stink, fall unconscious, and don't move for eight hours. Then you get up, eat something that won't make you fat, and do it all over again. Piece of cake, really."

Tara, who had paled, sat back and folded her arms. "You could get another job."

"Oh, I tried, but I can barely read," Christine said, her smile tightening. "Dyslexia's a bitch. The foster home where I was raised kicked me out on the streets a week after I turned eighteen. Wal-Mart doesn't hire the homeless. Basically, it was starve or strip. But hey, if you want some lessons–"

"I'd rather starve." Tara shoved her chair back, rose and walked out of the tent, her ashen ponytail lashing her shoulder blades.

Kayla sighed. "I'm sorry. She's usually not so hostile." She saw the way Christine looked at her. "Okay, she is, but she's still a kid. Dad and I kind of spoiled her, too."

"She in trouble?" Christine asked. "'Cause that's the vibe I'm getting off her. Big time scared."

Kayla couldn't tell Christine about the biker gang, so she went with the next most plausible excuse.

"Our dad died a couple months back. Mom took off when we were little. I'm all she has now. It's been rough. Still, it's no excuse for her to be nasty to you."

"I was nasty back." Christine pushed her fork through her cold food before she dropped it. "I can't eat things that are congealed. You think that turkey leg vendor gal has anything cooked up yet at her stall? I love those things."

Kayla chuckled and accompanied Christine to the row of food vendors outside the dining tent, where she left her happily munching on a big smoked joint. There were no shows scheduled for the horses that day, so from there she headed to the barn and got to work on mucking out the stalls.

The unpleasant chore mostly kept Kayla from brooding over Ryan, although she couldn't help recalling the way he'd looked at her in the tent. Whatever this attraction they fought was, they were both losing. What would it be like, she wondered, to just give in.

Tara came after noon with a box lunch and a reluctant apology.

"I didn't mean to be like that," she said, and skirted around the barrow Kayla was filling with manure and urine-soaked hay. "I just didn't like the way she was sucking up to you."

Kayla and Tara's jealousy were old friends, but she couldn't let her off that easily.

"Christine doesn't know anyone at the show. She was simply being friendly."

"Everyone always likes you," Tara said, pouting a little. "Why aren't they like that with me?"

"Think about how you talked to Christine this morning. That might be a good place to start." She saw Tara's expression and set her pitchfork aside. "If you want people to like you, honey, give them something to like."

Her sister hunched her shoulders. "You want me to apologize to her, I will."

"That's for you to decide," Kayla said. She glanced down the row of stalls and saw all of the show's horses had stuck their heads out and were watching Tara. "Thanks for bringing me lunch."

"Don't be mad at me," her sister muttered before she trudged out.

Kayla took a few minutes to eat and rest before she finished cleaning the stalls. After she hung the pitchfork she went to tidy the tack room. Although the men took good care of the gear, they were lousy at organizing it. Kayla liked everything in its place. By the time she coiled up the last rope, the sun had set and the barn had gone dark.

"All right, boys," she said as she walked the stalls one more time to check each mount. "I'm calling it a night. See you tomorrow."

Titan whickered to her as she stepped out and closed the barn door, latching it in place. She took off her work cap and shook out her hair, rubbing the back of her neck as she turned to head to the lodge.

A burly figure stepped in her path, a cup half-filled with ale in his hand. He peered at her and then his mouth stretched, showing a gap-toothed grin.

"Well, now," he slurred. "You're awful purty."

Kayla nodded to him as she tried to go around him, only to halt as he blocked her.

"The show closes at sunset, sir. Do you need a ride?"

"You think I'm too drunk to drive? Maybe so." The redneck tossed his drink in the bushes and bent down to breathe ale fumes in her face. "How 'bout you gimme a ride, girlie?"

Kayla took a discreet step backward. "I can call a cab for you."

He reached down and massaged the front of his crotch. "Not talking about that kind, you little twat. Come 'ere."

Kayla did the exact opposite, spinning and breaking

into a flat run. Though she headed for the lodge, it'd never looked so far away. Behind her, she could hear the redneck's footfalls—gaining.

"Help!" she yelled.

She could hear his labored breathing just behind.

"Not so fast," he growled.

Although she managed a burst of speed, when she glanced back he was reaching for her.

"No!" she screamed, just as something clipped the back of her foot.

She went down hard, skidding along the grass. In the next second he was on top of her.

"Fucking tease," he breathed.

He grabbed her shoulder and forced her onto her back. As she turned, her fist sailed through the air. But he easily dodged it, backhanding her with a vicious slap. Pain radiated along her jaw and her ears rang. She tried to kick, but her legs were pinned to the ground.

"I'll show you–"

Suddenly the man's deadweight lifted. In one smooth movement, he was yanked to his feet and tossed against the broad trunk of an oak twenty feet away. He slid down, sagged over to vomit, and then fell into his own fluids.

Ryan picked her up and held her cradled in front of him.

"Did he injure you?" He looked all over her. "Are you hurt, love?"

"I'm okay." In fact she wasn't, but she could fake it. What she couldn't bear was Ryan calling her his love. "You can put me down."

His hair began to sparkle as he went still. "I cannot."

His big arms held her against his broad chest as he strode to the barn. Kayla clasped his neck as he opened Titan's stall and mounted the stallion without a saddle. He took her up with him as if she weighed nothing at all. He touched his heels to the big stallion's sides, and Titan carried them out into the night and away from the faire grounds. As soon as they approached the roadside fence Kayla cringed, but Titan made the leap and landed on the other side gracefully, still in horse form.

They rode deep into the woods, sending snow flying all around them as Titan navigated the white drifts. Several times Kayla felt pine branches drag at her hair, but felt no pain. When they finally stopped in front of a dark-windowed cabin, she felt as if she'd come home—although she had no idea where they were.

Ryan lowered her to the ground before he dismounted, and Titan retreated into an open-sided lean-to beside the cabin. Her magical savior stood staring down at her, and his sapphire eyes burned as if they were sinking into the molten heat of a furnace.

"You've come to me in my dreams," he said, his voice little more than a growl. "So often now I dare not sleep. You've offered yourself twice now, lass, and I cannot fight it anymore. Do you still want me?"

Kayla's throat tightened so much she could barely get the word out. "Yes."

He held out his hand. "Then come. Come inside."

RYAN TOOK Kayla into the unlocked cabin, and released her only long enough to light an oil lamp. As he turned up the wick, the glow illuminated the cabin's one-room interior, which held odd-looking, oversize furniture and strange tapestries. In one corner stood a bed so large it could sleep six comfortably.

Kayla gazed around her. "This place belongs to you, doesn't it?"

"Aye." He lit another lamp, and as he did she saw he wasn't using matches, but sparks from his fingertip. "'Twas left to me, along with the lodge."

The million questions she wanted to ask him fled from her mind. As unprepared as she was, at least she was on the pill. She walked over to the bed and sat on the edge of it. He watched her take off her jacket and boots, but when she began unbuttoning her work shirt he came and put a long pale hand over hers.

"Never do this out of gratitude," he told her.

"I'm not grateful." She pressed her cheek against the hard plane of his flat belly, and felt his big hand stroke the back of her head. "I'm tired, and angry, and confused. I know you're not going to tell me anything. When I leave here–"

"'Tis not meant to be, lass." He drew her to her feet, and caught her face between his palms. "We'll both suffer."

Kayla felt like hitting him. "You more than me. I've been working in the stalls all day, and I haven't taken a shower."

Ryan murmured something under his breath, and a cascade of light drenched her. When it disappeared it took with it all the dirt, sweat and stains on her clothes.

"That's a neat trick." Her skin also felt so clean she wondered if she were glowing now. "Can you turn straw into gold?"

He bent his head. "The horses can't eat coin," he said, the words caressing her lips.

Kayla breathed in deeply, relishing the heady scent of his skin. Tonight he smelled of dark wine and vanilla heat, and she wanted to taste that on her tongue. Wherever their bodies touched she could feel an effervescent tingle sinking into her.

"Okay," she managed to say, "just...um...forget that."

"I am busy anyway," he said, his smile grazing her jaw.

As his hair spilled around their faces, it threaded through and twined in hers.

"Is this even real?" Kayla whispered. "Or am I dreaming again?"

He said something in a language that tickled her ears, and suddenly their clothes vanished, and they were on the bed. He loomed over her, surveying her body as if he'd never seen a woman naked. Her fingers kneaded the heavy muscles of his chest. She took in the beauty of his tapered waist and long limbs, and let her gaze drift down to the plum head and thick shaft of his erect penis. It nested against the soft dark curls covering her sex, menacing and entrancing all at once. When he reached down she parted her thighs and lifted her hips for him.

As soon as he positioned himself his eyes glittered, and he rubbed against her, crowning himself with her slick fluids. Kayla's lashes fluttered as she felt him invading and stretching her. He felt so big she had a moment of panic, but as he forged in, the penetration set off a flood of sensations so exquisite she groaned with helpless delight.

"Oh, Ryan. Oh, finally."

As Ryan worked deeper, he watched her eyes as he began to stroke.

It wasn't a dream. She clutched at his flexing biceps, her body trembling as she accepted every deep thrust. Ryan was on her, and in her, his shaft so deliciously thick and hard it made her softness around him feel like silk and cream.

"I have you," he murmured, gazing into her eyes as he cradled her, and they floated above the bed. Nothing but air surrounded them as he glided in and out. "I can feel you in my heart now, Kayla love. Let me into yours."

Though she didn't know how, everything made perfect sense. The air warmed around them as she wrapped her legs around his waist, and felt his buttocks flexing under her heels. This was happening, over the bed instead of on it. When he took her breasts in his hands and bent to kiss each pink, pebbly nipple she felt his magic inside her. He was using it to take her, warming and thrilling her as he pumped in and out with his body.

"How can you…*ah.*"

He nipped one hard peak, and she arched against him, her desire mounting and rebelling and becoming some huge, impossible hunger that only he could feed.

"There," he breathed, watching her face as they both felt the force expanding inside her, around them, saturating their blood. "That belongs to me, love. Drench me with it, yes, you can. You know how much I need you."

Kayla cried out as he plowed into her, faster and harder, stroking her core until the enormous pleasure began to overtake them. He spoke again to her in that haunting tongue, words she almost understood. He put his mouth over hers, his breath filling her lungs and whispering his love in her heart. When she could take no more she let go, shattering and flinging the shards of herself into his light.

Ryan's voice dropped to a hoarse, heart-rending cry, and his big frame jerked against her as he poured into her, all heat and light and delirious bliss.

I can't bear it, Kayla thought, expecting to feel herself pour over him in one last wave of ecstasy. Instead darkness carried them away together, plunging them into the peaceful nothingness of the lovers' shared nowhere. Time had no more meaning for her as she held him, until she felt him slip away. She couldn't find a path to follow, and for the first time she knew real terror.

"Kayla." Her sister's voice dragged her into a different, piercing light. "Wake up."

Kayla tried to shade her eyes as Tara pulled her upright. She sat on the bed next to her and peered at Kayla's face. As Kayla came back to herself, she turned her head and saw that she lay on her bed in their room at the lodge. She remained fully dressed but for her boots, which sat on the floor by the closet.

Kayla frowned as the unlovely aroma of her body and garments filled her nose. When she tucked in her chin she saw all the stains and dirt she'd acquired while mucking out the stalls. Bits of straw and soil clung to her boots, too.

"Why am I dirty?"

"You didn't shower or change before you conked out." The mattress gave as Tara stood. "From the way you smell, you should have."

Feeling stunned, Kayla climbed off the bed, holding onto the side of it until her legs felt steady. Outside their window it was dark.

"You saw me come in tonight?"

"No. I was over at the hatchet toss, talking to Christine." Her sister grimaced. "I apologized. She was nice about it."

Kayla nodded absently as she walked into the bathroom they shared, and looked at herself in the small mirror over the sink. She looked exactly as she had when she'd left the barn, right before the drunk had jumped her.

Had that even happened?

Unable to decide, she ran her hand over her rumpled hair, felt something, and tugged it out of the tangled strands. Between her fingers hung a damp, broken pine needle.

Ryan looked up at the knocking on his door. It opened a moment later.

Colm entered but stopped as soon as he stepped inside. "'Tis naught important. We'll speak later."

"Stay," Ryan said, hefting the battle axe he'd been polishing since before dawn. He hung it up by the fireplace. "I'm not interested in taking your head. Yet."

"A cause for celebration, my liege." His second nudged the door shut and cautiously approached. "Is there another neck in danger, perhaps?"

"No." Ryan went to the window to stare out at the woods where he had taken Kayla. "I need you to fire the Rowe sisters, and take them away."

"The moment I leave you," Colm said quickly, and came over to join him. "We needn't hire replacements. Wallace is deft enough with the horses, and I've been known to ply a needle or two." Ryan didn't respond. "She'll be safer away, Ryan, and so will you."

He rested his brow against the cold glass and closed his tired eyes.

"Conjure some luck for them before you take them to town. I cannot… I should not see her again."

His second touched his shoulder before silently retreating.

Ryan moved from the window to Elias's old rocker, where he sat and beheld the mirror-bright gleam of his battle axe's blade. Taking Kayla to his remote cabin had been reckless. He'd been close to boiling over after dealing with her attacker. Making love to her he could not regret, much as he should. She had brought him back from the edge with her passion, and turned his rage into something so deep and pleasured and destroying he knew he would never forget it. It tore at him to know she would remember last night only as another dream, but after revealing himself to her he'd had no choice.

That he'd given not a single thought to his poor lost Maeve while loving Kayla didn't trouble Ryan as it should have. The lesson learned remained, however. He could not fall in love with another mortal. To do so was to court madness. He sat and stared into the flames, remembering every detail of the night. How long he sat there, he didn't know—or care. A sunbeam slowly drifted across the floor, reminding him of her eyes when she had found her pleasure.

Another knock intruded on his reverie, and he looked up to see Colm and Wallace enter.

"What is it now?"

"News." Colm gave the smith a troubled look. "I conjured the luck charm for the sisters, as you asked. The moment I cast it, it went null."

Ryan frowned. "What do you mean, null? The only thing that can do that is…" He regarded Wallace.

The big man nodded. "Colm asked me to perform a

trace and the spell track is unmistakable. The Rowe sisters are the source of the curse, my liege."

Ryan jolted to his feet in shock. "You mean to tell me that they are Fae? But we have all read them both as mortal."

"One of them was cursed to appear so," the smith said. "But the enchantment used is so powerful that it engulfs them both."

Ryan's eyebrows flew up. "The only reason to cloak them so powerfully as human is–"

"Because one of them is a changeling," Colm finished.

Ryan felt bile crawl up in his throat. A changeling was an unwanted Fae child left in the place of a stolen mortal infant. The practice had once been widespread among their kind, for mortal children had a strange, seductive power over Fae women. In the old days most babies often remained alone and unguarded while their peasant mothers worked in the fields, or their high-born parents left them to the dubious care of servants. Over time mortal couples grew to better cherish infants and safeguard their homes, which made it more difficult for the Fae to make the switch. He had been glad when the practice had dwindled away, for stealing mortal babies was just as horrific as abandoning a Fae child to live as a changeling.

"But a changeling could be enchanted to pass as the human child they replaced," Ryan said. "Why curse her?"

Wallace's expression grew uneasy. "A simple enchantment would not be enough to mask a changeling with a dangerous power, or the capacity for great evil. Such things are almost always done for the very worst reasons."

"It smells to me of Dark Fae," his second added. "You know how they favor such scheming."

Ryan knew their enemies to be power hungry and ruthless, but to use babies as pawns? The Dark Fae must have been desperate. He looked from Colm to Wallace. They had already come to the same conclusion.

"What is the course you advise?"

"We must discover which sister is the changeling," Colm said. "And then try to fathom why she was hidden among mortals."

Ryan eyed him. "Kayla is brave and good and true. She is the mortal, I am sure of it."

"Or the enchantment makes her seem so," Wallace countered. "My liege, such is the curse that she herself would not be aware."

Ryan looked out at the forest, and felt his roiling emotions settle into a bleak despair. If the Dark Fae were involved, their scheme would likely threaten both the Fae and the mortal world.

"How do we learn which one is the changeling?"

"We can begin by separating them, and questioning them," his second suggested gently.

"The curse is stronger when they're together," Wallace said. "The true mortal sister may know something about her sibling that would reveal her dark nature."

It couldn't be Kayla. Everything in Ryan said so. But he had a duty. Ryan faced his men.

"Keep watch over the seamstress, Wallace. Colm and I will take Kayla to town and question her."

"I'M A LITTLE CONFUSED," Kayla said as she followed Colm out to the cluster of pickup trucks they used for supply runs into town. "First, you said we were fired. Then you made us go over to the smithy to watch Wallace stare back at us. Now you need me to help you with a feed order." She stopped when she saw Ryan standing by the pickup. "Oh, no. I don't think so."

"You still have a job, and today it's to load grain on the truck. Come on, then." Colm took her by the arm and urged her forward. "You'll drive, and he'll not bite."

"It's me who will bite," Kayla said, but she climbed into the cab and behind the steering wheel.

When Ryan took the middle seat, the air between them seemed to heat. Kayla's hands tightened on the steering wheel, but she kept her gaze straight out the windshield.

"Let's go," Colm said, pulling the door closed behind him.

She took the access road she'd seen the first night, stopping long enough for Colm to jump out and open the gate.

"I know I didn't dream last night," she said to Ryan as she stared stonily out the windshield. "So don't even go there."

"I wasn't planning to," Ryan said.

"You can also stop pretending to look like Mr. Average whenever we're alone. I remember all about the sun god hair, sparkling eyes, ivory skin, the incredible sex, and you trying to hide it all from me, which if you hadn't noticed, isn't working very well. Does Colm change, too, or is that just your deal?"

"Kayla," Ryan said gently, "Be quiet now."

As soon as Colm climbed back inside she drove through the open gate and onto the road.

"The boss wants me to shut up," she told the show manager. "So you do the talking."

"It's a lovely day, isn't it?" Colm said. He looked at both of them before he settled back against the bench seat. "I think we should visit the market while we're in town. And perhaps dine out for luncheon."

Out of the corner of her eye Kayla caught something dark in the side mirror. She looked to see seven motorcycles emerge from the woods behind them. Fear dropped in the pit of her stomach like a stone. Nausea spread through her, but there was no time to process it. A dozen more bikers appeared on the road ahead of them.

"Ryan…" Colm began.

When Kayla checked the mirror again, the men behind them were close enough for her to see their forehead tats. She floored the gas pedal, aiming at the center of the pack up ahead.

"That's not going to–" Ryan said.

Although the pack parted, tire irons appeared in their hands. Every window was pummeled as they passed. The windshield shattered, spewing shards of glass all over the cab. As Kayla struggled to control the steering, Ryan's giant hand cranked the wheel hard. The tires screeched as the truck did a 180.

"Take us back to the faire grounds," he bellowed, his foot on top of hers as the engine roared.

"We'll not make it, Ryan," she heard Colm say.

The biker pack had reformed and was almost on them. Kayla jerked the wheel and sent the truck off into a field. The vehicle bucked and swayed, but kept moving forward —but not fast enough. Bikers passed them on both sides. Without warning, Ryan stomped on the brake.

"Colm," he yelled. "Get her clear."

Kayla was thrown forward as they came to a sudden stop on the edge of the field. In her peripheral vision, both men burst with light. A very different-looking Colm appeared at her door, yanked it open, and dragged her out. Ryan was right behind her, saying something. But she couldn't hear over the din of the motorcycles. Together he and Colm lifted her off her feet and sprinted toward the center of the field. As the bikers pursued them Ryan stopped, gestured to Colm, and shoved Kayla behind him.

The gang stopped and climbed off their bikes, letting

them fall over. But without hurry, they spread out to form a circle. The one who had tried to drag Tara out of Kayla's car approached them. He took off his shades to squint at Ryan and Colm.

"No need to fight, exiles," he said. His gravelly voice drove invisible splinters into Kayla's spine. "Give us the woman and her sister, and we will let you live."

Ryan lowered his head as white light encircled the three of them. "Leave now, Dirk Blackstone, and I will not gut you in front of your mewlings."

The rest of the bikers chuckled as if he'd made a joke.

"I can compromise," Dirk said. He smiled faintly as he focused on Kayla, stepping closer. "This one, then, in return for safe passage back to your little faire."

Although Kayla waited for Ryan's rejoinder, there wasn't one.

"Ryan, no," Colm muttered.

A wave of heat rolled off Ryan as the light around them darkened to scarlet. The sunlight dimmed and, to her shock, his eyes blazed even hotter than they had last night. Then several things happened at once.

Dirk reached out to grab her, Colm lunged at Ryan, and Ryan's eyes turned solid black. Kayla watched in horror as Ryan batted Colm away as if he were nothing more than an insect. Then he went for Dirk, and the other bikers rushed at her.

Colm pushed her into the center of the circle of light. "Don't you move!" he yelled.

His long garnet hair whipped across her face as he looked over at Ryan. He had Dirk on the ground and was using a strange, bloody dark club to beat him in the head. Kayla saw the body of another biker on the ground, and nearly screamed when she saw his left arm was missing.

Two of the biggest bikers flung themselves at Ryan's

back, stabbing at him with knives. He stopped bludgeoning Dirk long enough to shake them off. Quicker than a man his size should have been able to move, Ryan spun, caught both by the neck, and hurled them to the ground. Before either could even raise their heads, Ryan kicked one, then the other. Kayla thought she heard breaking bones.

His face bloody, battered and bleeding, Dirk crawled backward and drew his own dagger.

"Look out!" she screamed.

Dirk flung the blade at Ryan, striking him in the side of the neck.

"Ryan!" she shrieked, as Colm grabbed her arm and kept her in place.

Ryan dropped to his knees, his expression puzzled as he gripped the hilt of the weapon. The rest of the gang grabbed Dirk and the other wounded men, hauling them toward the trees.

"You should know this, Sheridan," Dirk said, struggling to his feet and staggering backward. "The changeling you protect is evil. As black a soul as my own. She merits no sanctuary among you and yours."

He nearly fell over before gripping one of his men's shoulders and limping into the woods.

Kayla watched as the bikers vanished into the shadows, and jumped as their motorcycles started on their own and followed, riderless, after them. The circle of light faded away, and she rushed over to Ryan, Colm right behind. The only evidence of the battle was the knife Ryan had pulled out of his neck, and the bloody, dismembered arm, which melted into the ground a moment later, leaving only an oily black stain on the snow.

She knelt in front of him. "How badly are you hurt? We have to take you to a hospital!"

"No need." Ryan smiled faintly as he touched the

shallow cut on his neck. It slowly closed beneath his fingers. "Colm will take you back to the faire. I'll stand sentinel while he does."

"Are you crazy?" She stood up. "We're not leaving you here. What if they come back? You'll be alone, and—"

"I'll go berserk again, and kill anything that moves," Ryan finished for her. "Including you and Colm, love."

"His affliction is very rare," Colm told Kayla, weighing his words.

He'd left his liege as ordered, and he and the girl were nearly at the faire grounds. She'd had to run to keep up with his long strides.

"Naught but a handful of true berserkers have ever been born among our clans," he continued. "Most of them die the first time they lose control, or must be beheaded to be stopped. Not our Ryan."

She gave him a wide-eyed look. "He's done that before?" she said between breaths.

The woman had seen so much now he might as well tell her. "Six times that I know. Most when he served our clan leaders. He fought in many wars. Well, perhaps not so many. Two or three that I recall."

"I know you're not human, Colm," she said as they moved through the boundary spell protecting the Forever Faire. "So you're going to tell me all of it. What you are, what you're doing here, why the Blackstones want me and my sister, what a changeling is, the magic, everything." She waved at Wallace, who came trotting toward them. "Just go get Ryan now, and bring him home."

"Go to your room, and wait for me there," Colm said. For a moment she wavered and looked like she might try to go with them. "You've seen what happens when you leave the faire. I'll not ask twice."

Colm didn't wait for an answer as he took Wallace to the nearest vehicle, a van. Gavan and several others joined them. He checked over his shoulder to see Kayla retreating into the lodge.

"Ryan's been hurt," he told the men. "The Blackstone clan attacked us on the road. They wanted the woman, so he made me bring her back first."

"Then drive," the smith said, and piled into the van with the others.

Colm sped back to the scene of the battle. But at first he saw no sign of Ryan. Wallace pointed to a dark blue heap, and he stopped the van to climb out and hurry over with the men to their injured leader.

Ryan had dropped the glamour he had used to convince Kayla he was unharmed, and opened his eyes as Wallace touched the broad, ugly gash in his neck.

"You took your time," he said weakly. He coughed, and blood welled from the side of his mouth.

"Is this how you mean to forfeit the next bout?" Gavan asked as he tore off some of his tunic and pressed it over the wound. "Not a very clever ruse, my liege."

Wallace picked up the dagger that Dirk had planted in Ryan's neck. He immediately shoved the blade in the soil. He looked at Colm.

"The blade was enchanted, brother. A Fae-slayer. The wound will keep growing wider and deeper, until it decapitates him."

Colm cursed the cowardly Dark Fae as he and the men carried Ryan back to the van.

"Wrap that cloth around his throat," he told Gavan. To Wallace, who'd started the van, he said, "Drop me at the lodge, and then take him down below. I've a cure for this."

The smith's expression turned grim. "Then you'd better bring it soon."

Though the trip back was quick, Ryan lost consciousness. Even before the van had stopped in front of the lodge, the door was open and Colm jumped out.

"Get him below," he said over his shoulder as he ran for the lodge.

Kayla must have heard him coming. She had her door open before he could knock. She stepped out into the hall to look both ways.

"Where is he?"

"We've taken him downstairs," Colm said. "Come with me."

She peppered him with more questions as he led her down into the basement, where the oil lamps had already been lit. As soon as she stepped off the stairs she saw the crates that had been moved to reveal the giant hole in the back wall.

"What is this?"

"I hope you'll forgive me," he said.

"None of this was your fault," she said. "I'm the one who screwed up with my lousy defensive driving." Kayla peered into the tunnel. "I don't see Ryan."

"You will," Colm said, and clouted the back of her head with his fist. He caught her as she fell and carried her limp body into the entrance.

Kayla felt heat and light and pain, and opened her eyes to slits. The dazzling things around her slowly sharpened from big blurry dots to prismatic crystals, thousands of them. They covered the ceiling over her head and wrapped around her sides and feet—which were bare.

"This is bad," she murmured.

Her voice spread out in soft whispers that agreed with her.

She raised her pounding head as much as she dared, and saw she had been stripped naked.

"What the..."

She lifted her oddly-heavy hand, and the links attached to the wide cuff around her wrist clinked. The other hand had been shackled, too, and the chains disappeared over the end of the soft mattress beneath her back. She turned her head the other way and saw Ryan, his big body white and bare, and his face shrouded by a long swath of scarlet-stained white-gold. For a moment her heart stopped. Then his diaphragm moved up and down. She exhaled, but again she went still. Although she didn't hear anything, she was almost positive someone else was close.

"Hello?" she said.

Kayla waited for the echoes to die away before she called out again in a louder voice.

"Hello? Please, is someone there? We need help. This man—Ryan Sheridan—is hurt."

No one responded, and now the silence seemed to press against her ears.

Slowly she propped herself on her elbow, making the chains rattle, and winced as a spot at the base of her skull throbbed sharply. Her fingers shook a little as she took the cloth from Ryan's face. He was so pale!

"Do not die on me," she told him.

Around his neck was a darkly-stained, makeshift bandage. Gingerly, she lifted it to see the gash in his neck that she had watched disappear. It now looked twice as long, gaped horribly, and steadily seeped blood. Something compelled her to cover it with her hand, and she felt his blood warm her fingers. A soft blue glow shimmered under her palm, making her gasp. When she snatched her hand away the bleeding had stopped.

Ryan stirred, and opened his eyes. "Kayla," he whispered, his voice thready. His brows drew together as he regarded her. "How?"

"Pretty sure it was Colm, whose ass I'm going to kick all over the faire once I get out of here." She held up her hand enough for him to see the shackles and chain. "I'm naked and chained in a cave. You're in a lot worse shape." She gazed down at his face. "How do we get out of this without making you go black-eyed?"

"He wants you to heal me." Ryan closed his eyes. "Better if you don't."

"Better?" she said, ignoring the echo. "Better for who?

The Blackstones?" She stopped herself. "How exactly do I heal you?"

"Sex." His mouth hitched. "When a mortal makes love to an injured Fae, it heals our wounds."

He was Fae? As in the fairy fantasy folk type Fae? A couple hundred things about him suddenly wanted to make sense, but she didn't have time to deal with that now.

"That's why you stopped bleeding when I touched your neck?" She moved over him. "Maybe I should just do more of that. Ryan? Ryan?" She patted his cheek until he opened his eyes a little. "We're alone and I'm in chains. Please, do not faint on me now."

"If you wish me to live, make love to me," he whispered. "If not, then move away. It won't be long."

Make love to him. She'd wanted that more than anything only last night. But like this? She gazed down at the chains. For a healing? How could that work? But as Ryan's eyes closed, Kayla knew time was running out. Quickly.

She started wiping the blood from his mouth, and then swore as she bent over to kiss him anyway. He murmured something in that strange language of his before their lips met. He stirred slightly as her mouth gently kneaded his. But when there was no further reaction, she straddled him, bracing one hand on his shoulder. With the other she reached down for his shaft. She flinched when she felt it instantly swell and go rigid.

"That helps," she said, hoping he heard.

As scared as she was, she expected to be dry, but the moment she tucked him between her legs she felt herself go wet. Then it was just a matter of fitting him to the right spot and bearing down. She should have felt awkward and awful, but the moment his thick cockhead lodged inside her, shivery delight shimmered through her limbs and drew a low moan from her lips.

This time they didn't float over the bed, explode with light or any other repeat of their first surreal coupling. Instead, Kayla worked herself slowly up and down, taking him in and rising up to let him almost slide free. As she did she watched the wound in his neck, which began to shrink and close again. Something told her to put her hand over it, and the blue glow reappeared.

Ryan opened his eyes, which shone with the same gentle light. "Kayla."

"I'm healing you," she said, panting the words a bit as her own need welled up inside her. "Can you feel that? It's so strange." It took her another moment to figure out what it was. "Our hearts are beating together."

It was as though the blood in her veins spoke to his. His arms moved, and he clasped her hips with his hands.

"You're pouring your life into me. Your heart to mine."

She rode him a little faster, a little harder.

The edges of the neck wound sealed together, and the scar they made began to flatten.

"Oh, that feels good," he said, his voice stronger. "You feel good on me, Kayla love. Why did you choose to save me?"

"You know why." She rolled her hips to take him deeper. "You knew it the night I walked up to your camp-fire. When we looked at each other, and all the nonsense dropped and I could see you. Could you see me?"

He nodded slowly, and then pulled her down to him. He took the chains that bound her and pulled them until they snapped. His hips surged under hers as he clasped her bottom and began driving into her, his big body tensing along with hers.

She kissed his chin and let him take over, her body

shaking with the force of his thrusts. Nothing felt as good as his shaft stroking her, and his big hands squeezing her. Her hips moved in time with his, meeting each penetration. She took him deeply, his heated flesh parting her, then pushing into her core. A groan escaped her lips as a sweet familiar tension unwound in her belly. In moments, the ecstasy blossomed, and Kayla came with a low, keening cry that seemed to echo forever.

Ryan wrapped his arms around her as he followed her, his shaft jerking with every thick jet he pumped into her. When she collapsed on his chest he rubbed his cheek against the top of her head, and murmured to her until she almost fell asleep. But as he drew out of her, and gently rolled her to his side, she reluctantly opened her eyes. There wasn't a mark left on his neck.

"Sorry, Kayla love," he said, smiling. "I would tarry here forever, and never let you go. But we cannot stay."

Slowly she sat up, rubbing the tender place on the back of her head. Ryan frowned as he sat up too.

"Colm will answer for what he did to you," he said.

"He'll answer," she agreed. "But to me. You get a little over-excited, and arms start tearing off bodies."

Ryan rose from the padded platform and retrieved a neatly-folded pile of clothes, which turned out to be hers. She took them and began to get dressed. He found his own, blood-stained clothes and started pulling them on.

"But he knew bringing me down here would save your life," she said. "Right?"

Something flickered across Ryan's face. "Yes, he did."

Once they'd dressed, he stood in front of her and took her hands.

"The Blackstones are Dark Fae," he said. "They do not care about mortals, or this world, or anything but themselves. In every sense they are our enemy. They will not leave until they have what they want."

Her chest tightened. "Me and my sister."

He grimaced but nodded. "Come," he said, tucking her in by his side.

Ryan guided her out of the cave and through a long, dark tunnel to a narrow staircase made entirely of carved crystal. Kayla shivered a little when they climbed it and emerged into the lodge's basement.

Wallace stood waiting with a lantern. "My liege." He bowed to Ryan before turning to Kayla. "My lady."

"Next time, just ask me to do the sexual healing, okay?" Kayla said. "I would have said yes."

The smith nodded. "Miss Rowe, I waited so that I might tell you. We went to, ah, warn your sister about the Blackstones, but she was gone. We cannot find her now."

"What?"

Kayla pushed past him and ran up the stairs. Blood pounding in her ears, she dashed to their room. It was empty but Tara's clothes were still in the closet. Kayla spun and sprinted back into the hallway. Tara might be at the costume tent. But no sooner had she emerged from the room than Ryan intercepted her.

"She is likely out walking the grounds. She would not leave without telling someone."

Kayla glared up at him. "Of course she would leave. She's probably out looking for me, or hiding from your men, who like to knock women unconscious and use them like big Band-Aids." She saw Colm walking toward them, and felt her stomach knot. "What did you do with Tara?"

"Naught—nothing." He turned to Ryan, his gaze shifting to his neck. "It seems you were right, my liege."

Kayla's hands became fists, and her heart rate doubled. She pushed herself between the giant men.

"Right about what?" she demanded.

"Come with me, and I will explain." Ryan held out his hand.

"I'm not going anywhere. Right about what?" When he didn't reply, she turned on Colm. "Then you tell me, right now."

"Tara is the one that the Blackstones want, Miss Rowe. Not you. She is the evil one."

Before Kayla even knew what she was doing, she slapped him as hard as she could. He didn't so much as flinch.

"Only a true mortal could have healed Ryan," he continued. "That you did proves you are not the changeling."

"You mean…" She looked from him to Ryan and back again. "You risked his life to find out?" Then she recalled how she'd sensed another presence in the cave. "You were watching, weren't you? To see if I'd heal him." She hugged herself. "You cold-blooded bastard."

Colm met her gaze. "It had to be done."

She had to get away from them—and find Tara. But this time she didn't run. Instead, she simply walked away. Without a word she turned her back on them. With tears filling her eyes she made her way down the hallway, and then outside. Inside the empty costume tent she stopped. She wiped furiously at her eyes, trying to think. Where would Tara run this time? Where could she possibly go? In the cold and the–

The tent flaps opened and Ryan came in.

"Kayla love," he said, in the same kind tone he used with kids. "Tara is not your sister. She is a changeling. She is a Fae made to seem as though she were human. Colm told me what Dirk Blackstone said before he ran. We know she is dangerous, and evil. You must stay away from her now."

He wore his mortal guise, and still he was the most

stunning man she'd ever met. She could still taste his kisses on her lips, and feel the aching softness he'd filled between her thighs. She was fairly sure she'd never get the delicious smell of him out of her head. From the moment they'd met, she'd been so sure that he was the love of her life.

But she'd been wrong.

The love of her life wouldn't tell her to abandon her sister.

"You don't know anything about Tara or me," she said in a quaking voice. "But I know who I have to stay away from, Ryan." Kayla took in a shaky breath. "You. I quit."

"You are leaving us," a deep voice said.

Kayla closed the last suitcase and looked over at Jannon, who stood in the doorway of her room.

"And you're a genius. Get lost."

"You are going to look for Tara." He stepped inside and closed the door. "I can help you track her."

She picked up the suitcases and tried to squeeze past him. "Do you want me to punch you in the head again?"

"All living things leave traces of their life forces where they have passed. They do not last long, but they can be followed for a time." He moved his hand, and two bands of color appeared in the air between them. He pointed to the vivid golden trail. "This is from you." He tapped the much fainter, dark violet trail. "This is from Tara."

Kayla's jaw dropped. "You can track her with that stuff?" When he nodded she dropped the cases. "Let's go."

"I have already traced her last movements from here." He pointed at the window overlooking the oak groves.

"She went into the woods. We will need horses to follow her trail in there."

Fifteen minutes later Kayla rode across the faire grounds beside Jannon to enter the forest bordering the east side of the lodge. She didn't know how he could see her sister's trail, but he seemed to have no difficulty following it. The trees and snow drifts slowed their mounts to a walk. They were taking too long.

"If we don't find her soon," she said, "she could freeze to death out here."

"Tara was on foot," Jannon said. "She could not have walked more than a few miles." He glanced at her. "I do not believe your sister is evil."

"Good. That makes two of us." A thought occurred to her. "You and she aren't…involved, are you?"

"We are not. Yet. I have hopes."

"She's only nineteen," Kayla said, about to warn him off, but they were wasting time. "Never mind. Let's just find her."

They rode for another fifteen minutes before Jannon halted and motioned for her to dismount. After they tethered their horses, he guided her through a snowy thicket on the edge of a mountain lake. Kayla heard her sister's voice and surged forward, only to be yanked down by Jannon.

"Dark Fae," he muttered, moving his hand. He showed her a muddy trail crisscrossing Tara's. "They must have lured her to this place. I will rescue her. You will stay here."

Without waiting for her to answer, he took off. Kayla waited exactly two seconds before she hurried after him. But they both came to a stop at what they saw. A few yards in front of them, just beyond the trees, stood Tara. But she was wiping away the dried blood from Dirk Blackstone's battered face.

"I have to go back for my sister," Tara was telling him. "I can't leave Kayla with those assholes."

Jannon's head reared back at the words.

"We can get that bitch later," Dirk said. He snaked an arm around her waist, and pulled her against him. "Do you know how long I have thought about this?"

Tara didn't struggle as the Dark Fae kissed her, and Kayla cringed as she watched her sister's hands creep up around the biker's thick neck.

Jannon turned on his heel and walked back the way they'd come, as a blast of icy air slapped her in the face. She started to go after him, but she couldn't leave Tara just to soothe Jannon's hurt feelings. No, what she had to do was get her crazy sister away from the even crazier gang leader. Then she and her sister would get the hell out of here.

Kayla crept up behind the trees, and felt her stomach turn as she saw Dirk tearing at Tara's clothes. When her sister struggled against him, he shoved her to her knees. Tara pushed at the front of his trousers.

Then it dawned on Kayla what was going to happen. In a moment of calm, she saw it clearly.

Dirk doesn't know who the changeling is. But if he has sex with Tara, so that he can be healed, it won't work. Then he'll know the changeling is Tara.

"Please," Tara begged him, turning her face away. "Not like this."

"It's time for you to grow up, little sister," Dirk said. He tugged out his penis, which was as dark and ugly as a club. "Now open your mouth, damn you. You're going to give me a nice, long cocksucking before I fuck you."

Kayla straightened up. It was now or never.

"Hey, Blackstone," Kayla called as she stepped out where he could see her. "I'm the one you want. I'm the changeling. Let her go, and I'm yours."

• • • • •

The End of *Hunted*

• • • • •

Kayla's story continues in *Outcast (Forever Faire Book Two)*.

For a sneak peek, turn the page.

COPYRIGHT

OUTCAST (BOOK 2)

CHAPTER 1

S ILENCE STRETCHED ACROSS a remote lake in the Tennessee mountains, the water mostly petrified by winter. Only thin, rick-rack ribbons of determined currents interrupted the ice. Framed by steep banks of leafless trees silvered by frost, and evergreens blanketed by constant snowfall, the blue-gray water huddled under its crystalline mantle, waiting for spring—or perhaps dreading what was about to happen on its banks. There terrible possibilities formed a menacing triangle between a hulking, battered brute, a weeping teenager on her knees, and the small, fierce-eyed woman confronting them both.

Squinting against the sun, Kayla Rowe kept her eyes on Dirk Blackstone's bloodied face. He and his biker gang had been stalking her and her sister, Tara, for months. They'd forced them to run from their home in Florida to the small town of Ashdale. They'd taken jobs at Forever Faire, a traveling Renfaire run by unearthly, powerful Fae warriors who used magick to disguise themselves as humans. Kayla had hoped the Fae would help them, but now things had come to a disastrous turn. She had never imagined offering herself in trade for her younger sister, but she'd rather die than allow Tara to be raped by the Dark Fae biker gang leader.

"I mean it, Blackstone," Kayla said as she took another step closer to the massive thug. "Let her go, and you can have me. I'm the one you wanted, not her."

His bruised features twisted with a sneer as he shoved the swollen club of his penis back into his trousers. "Little sister is mine." He jerked Tara off her knees, and slowly licked a tear from her cheek while watching Kayla. "Now so are you." His voice took on a spine-clawing resonance as he added, "Come here, you tiresome bitch."

His cold, dark magick wrapped around Kayla like a frozen, invisible fist, jerking her a step closer. A shockwave of raw panic flashed through her, and something buzzed in her ears. The sound grew louder until a trio of motorcycles roared out of the woods on her left. Just as she saw the furious faces of Colm Longacre, Jannon Ferguson and Ryan Sheridan, the huge bikes bucked and exploded with a burst of copper-gold light.

The power gripping Kayla vanished as the light transformed the three motorcycles into massive horses. As soon as they spotted Dirk they reared in unison. Only their rider's powerful grips and horsemanship kept them seated. But in a split second, Ryan dismounted and hit the ground running. Colm and Jannon did the same, all of their bodies shifting into their unearthly Fae forms.

Kayla had no intention of wasting the massive distraction. She darted in front of Dirk, grabbed Tara, and dragged her back. The Dark Fae warrior only had a moment to glance after them before he turned and fled for the trees. The Forever Faire men nearly reached him before he jumped into a pool of shadow. He sank into it as if he were melting, finally disappearing from sight.

Jannon halted beside the women as Ryan and Colm went after their mounts. He looked at Tara for a long moment before he turned to Kayla. "Did he harm you?"

"We're good," Kayla said, though she didn't particularly believe it. She put her arm around her sister as she looked up at Jannon's godlike face and his bristling mane of gold-streaked copper hair. "Thanks for coming back with the cavalry."

He grunted and sheathed his long dagger before heading toward the other men.

Kayla faced her sister. "Hi. Nice to see you again. Mind telling me why you were kissing that asshole?"

"I don't know," Tara said, tucking her chin in. Her long, ash-blonde hair veiled her face. "I couldn't help myself."

After personally experiencing the force of Dirk's dark magick, Kayla should have believed that. But she didn't. At the same time she knew her sister had nearly been raped, and that was enough trauma for a teenager to handle—for now, anyway.

"We're going to talk about this later. Right now we need to get out of here, pronto."

"If you leave Forever Faire, he'll take you," a deep voice said.

Kayla spun around to face Ryan Sheridan, the master of Forever Faire. At nearly seven feet tall, he loomed over her, his big, tough body a sculpture of heroic muscle and other-worldly beauty. The breeze stirred his long, white-gold mane, which perfectly framed his gorgeous features and stern, jewel-blue gaze. He might look like a prince straight out of a fantasy movie, but he'd been lying to Kayla from the moment they'd met. Oh, she'd fallen hard for him—no woman with a pulse wouldn't have—until he'd tried to convince her that Tara was not her sister. According to him Tara was some evil changeling the Blackstones wanted. That was when Kayla had slammed the door to her heart in Ryan's face.

"Go to hell," she told him flatly, and guided Tara away from him. "Come on, honey. Road trip time."

"He's right, lass." Colm stepped into her path, his glittering garnet-colored hair darkening to black as he shifted back into his average, normal mortal disguise. "You'll not get more than a mile away. The Blackstone clan use shadows like doorways to any place they wish to travel. But Dark Fae can't pass our boundaries, so they and their filthy magick can never breach the faire grounds."

"Really?" Kayla said hotly. "So the last place on earth I want to go is the only place that's safe. How convenient." At least now she understood why the biker gang had kept finding them while seemingly appearing out of nowhere. "You also made it clear that Tara isn't welcome at the faire anymore. What do you expect me to do? Dump her outside the gates? How long will it take for that rapist asshole to snatch her and force himself on her again? Five minutes?"

Colm glanced over at Ryan before he said to her sister, "Jannon told us he saw you kissing Blackstone."

"He made me do it," Tara shrieked, and then buried her face against Kayla's shoulder as she sobbed.

Rubbing her sister's narrow back, Kayla closed her eyes for a moment to force back her own tears before she glared at the men.

"I know you guys are magical fantasy warriors who battle dark forces, slay dragons, and save princesses, or whatever. Well, we're not, okay? I'm a groom. Tara is a seamstress. She's not evil. She doesn't have super powers. She's never hurt anyone in her life."

At that Tara wailed even louder, and Jannon muttered something under his breath and turned away. Colm looked as if Kayla had kicked him in the groin. Kayla eyed the man she'd lost her heart to, but his expression remained unmoved.

"For God's sake, Ryan," she spat at him. "What's the matter with you? She's just a kid."

"So she is." The grim line of Ryan's mouth softened for a moment as he looked into Kayla's eyes. "Very well. You may both stay at Forever Faire."

Kayla couldn't believe he had to think about it. "Maybe we'd better take our chances on the road. I wouldn't want to put anyone out."

When he took a quick step toward them, she handed Tara off to Colm, and went toe-to-toe with him. Despite her seething fury, her fists quickly unclenched. It was like that first night she'd met him. He smelled hot and delicious, like dessert and wine and sex under a pale moon, and she wanted to throw herself into his arms and beg him to take her away. Which was another problem she had with Ryan—the minute they got within a foot of each other the only thing she wanted was him, naked and on top of her. It had to be another of his magick tricks.

"Stop doing that," she said through her teeth.

He stared down at her lips. "I will if you stay."

Was he lying to her again? Would she fall asleep tonight and end up floating in his arms while he once more used that beautiful mouth on her body? Or would he have her chained naked beside him in a crystal cave for another emergency that only sex could solve? Her cheeks flushed hot at the memory. To be truthful, she wanted that badly. But it had to be her choice, not magick.

Yet what choice did she have? Forever Faire was the only place where the Blackstones couldn't get at them.

"I don't trust you," she finally said. She jerked her chin at Colm and Jannon. "Or them. But the Blackstones are worse, and I can't keep Tara safe by myself. Those are the only reasons we're staying, is that clear?"

Ryan's jaw tightened. "We are sworn to protect those who come to us."

"Good, then do your damn job." She went over to Tara, who had managed to stop crying and now simply looked shattered. "I'm sorry, but we have to stay here." Her sister gave her a blank look, as if she didn't comprehend what she was saying. "Only until I figure out something else," Kayla tacked on.

Tara took a deep breath and turned to Jannon, reaching out to him with her thin hand.

"Thank you for saving me," she said, her voice shaking. But rather than take her hand, Jannon recoiled from it. "I know what I did…it was…"

Colm uttered a sharp sound and darted forward. Kayla didn't understand why until Tara fell like a swan shot out of the sky. Colm caught her thin body before it touched the ground.

"I've got her," he said, cradling her to his broad chest. "I'll take her back to the lodge." He waited for a nod from Kayla, and then stalked off in the direction of the faire grounds.

Ryan dragged a hand through his hair, which changed along with the rest of him into his only-average-looking mortal guise. He followed Colm without a word.

Jannon watched them leave before turning to Kayla.

"Blackstone cast no spell over her," he said. "I would have felt the burn of it."

"Well, it happened," Kayla snapped, but suddenly she felt very old and utterly exhausted. "She's nineteen years old. She's never had a boyfriend, or gone on a date. In fact, I'm pretty sure that was her first kiss."

"Aye." Jannon's expression darkened. "And 'twill be his last."

*P*RETENDING TO PASS out had been lame, but Tara remained limp and motionless on her bed. She could feel Colm Longacre staring down at her, and wondered if he knew she was faking. But Tara didn't think so. Kayla had told her that the show manager's weird power was to see things a few seconds before they happened. Like her phony faint.

"Rest now, lass," was all he said before switching off the lamp by her bed and leaving.

Tara opened her eyes to stare at the dark ceiling. She couldn't see the thin, mildewed crack in the plaster that ran from one corner to the other, but she knew it was still there. Just as Dirk Blackstone had always been there, lurking in the shadows ever since he'd found her and Kayla in Florida.

Tara dampened her dry lips, and tasted blood on them —his blood. It had flavored that awful kiss, along with his lust. She'd always thought a man's mouth would taste warm and wonderful, not cold and coppery. And still, some part of her had wanted it. That part had let him stick his tongue in her mouth, and made her clutch at his neck, and it had been horrible and terrifying and something else, something she would never, ever think about again.

Pushing herself up, Tara listened, but heard no sounds from outside in the hall. No doubt Kayla was beyond pissed with her now, but she'd never show it. She'd just shift into her mommy mode, like always. Tara didn't want to sit through another kind, gentle, stupid-ass lecture. She'd already endured thousands of them. She was all grown up now anyway, wasn't she? She could deal with her own problems.

Tara changed out of her dress, which still smelled of Dirk's icy sweat. She wanted to shower, but knew Kayla would be back soon. After dressing in a dark blue sweater and black jeans, she stuffed her hair under a black knit cap and pulled on her heavy gray down coat, which made her look fifty pounds heavier.

Climbing out the window felt silly and awkward, but Tara was glad she had when she dropped to the ground and heard her sister's voice calling her name from their room. She hurried around the back of the lodge, keeping her head down whenever she passed someone. She saw Colm and Ryan having an argument by the barn, and did an abrupt turn toward the smithy on the other side of the faire grounds. There she saw Wallace Magee dressed in a leather apron and hammering on something, and stopped to watch the blacksmith for a while.

Like the other guys he used a nothing-special illusion that made him look ordinary and human, at least in the face. He wasn't wearing a shirt under the apron, and his roof-beam shoulders and car hood of a chest flexed with so much muscle he should have toppled over from the weight. One of his arms had to be bigger around than her whole body. Her gaze shifted as another big man joined him, and her heart clenched.

Jannon.

Since the day she and Kayla had started working at Forever Faire the guy had been watching her. She'd thought it was creepy in the beginning, and braced herself for another attack, but Jannon had kept his distance. She did the same, but gradually she realized he wasn't doing it because he disliked her. When she looked in his chilly golden eyes she'd sometimes catch a glimpse of something soft and almost wistful, right before he turned away. It was like he was crushing on her, but couldn't work up the nerve to say anything.

Jannon hated her now, Tara reminded herself, but couldn't resist creeping closer to the smithy so she could listen to their conversation.

"'Tis a bad business," Wallace was telling him, and tucked his enormous hammer in his belt before using tongs to shove the blade he was hammering into a barrel of water that sputtered and hissed. "Mark my words, whoever cursed that girl intended it for more than passing a changeling as mortal."

"She's a wisp of a thing. What could she do?" Jannon swatted at the huge cloud of steam that rose from the barrel. "Snip off our ear points? Stick pins in our arses? Stitch our smalls to our balls?"

Good suggestions, Tara thought, smiling a little.

"You do fancy her." The smith set aside his tongs to smack Jannon in the back of the head. "You bloody idiot. Do you not remember what Blackstone said about this changeling? Did you not see her kissing that piece of filth this very day? She's meant for evil purposes, not you."

"'Tis a choice to go over to the dark," Jannon said,

snarling the words. "She's not made it." He stalked away from the smithy.

"Yet," Wallace called after him, and then turned his head to scowl in Tara's direction.

She shrank back behind the tree trunk, holding her breath until she heard Wallace begin hammering again. She fled, using the straw-stuffed targets at the archery range to cover her movements. Only when she was out of the blacksmith's sight did she slow to a walk as she thought about everything she'd heard. Three words kept screeching silently in her mind.

Cursed. Filth. Evil.

Tara went to the costume tent, where she sat in the dark among the performer's gowns and tunics. She picked out a hooded cape she'd made out of an amber velvet to match Kayla's eyes. Her sister was probably looking for her right now. Tara hugged the cape to her chest. But instead of recalling Kayla's voice, she remembered Jannon's. He'd said it was a choice to go over to the dark.

"Jannon," she muttered, sitting on the ground. She pulled the hood over her head and wrapped her arms around her knees, tightening into a miserable huddle. "Stupid name."

But Jannon didn't believe she was evil—even after seeing her with Dirk. It made Tara wish she'd kissed him first.

Brooding turned to shivering as the temperature dropped, until Tara reluctantly got up. Taking the cape with her, she left the tent to return to the lodge. On the way there she passed men gathered at the nightly bonfire and pretended not to notice their hard gazes. When she saw Jannon, however, she gave him a small nod and smile. He reacted by turning his back on her and took a drink from the glittering blue bottle in his fist.

Tears stung Tara's eyes, and her throat tightened up. But she wouldn't cry. It was time to behave like what she really was: an adult.

The thought of going back to the room she shared with Kayla made her stomach knot, so she changed directions and walked into the wing reserved for the Forever Faire men. It felt odd and was too quiet, as if a thousand eyes watched her from mouthless faces. Tara shrugged off the feeling and went down the row of doors. Near the end of the wide hall, the doors were open. As she peeked in the first, she realized why: they were unused, and therefore perfect. She immediately went over to shut the open windows. After turning on the heat and warming her hands in front of the big vent, she found matches on the bedside table and lit the oil lamp. Though there were no bedclothes on the large mattress, she stretched out on it.

Cursed. Filth. Evil.

Pulling her velvet cape around her like a blanket, Tara closed her eyes. The men would spend a couple of hours talking and drinking by the bonfire. As for her, she'd rest a few seconds, and then she was leaving.

JANNON FERGUSON WANTED nothing more than to drown himself in drink, but no amount of snowine would wipe the memories of watching sweet, innocent Tara Rowe kissing that foul, stinking, son of a poxed whore, Dirk Blackstone. It had been branded on his brain, likely forever, and so he would endure it. As he endured all the rest of the utter fucking plagues upon his heart.

Colm Longacre came to stand beside him. "In town there are wenches more than willing to help a man forget his worries."

Jannon gave him a sour look. "How would you know?"

"Ah, you remind me." Colm nodded. "I'm not a man, but a nosy, gelded, sodding ponce of a winge. Still, you're not, so I wager you'd manage."

Dimly Jannon recalled hurling those insults at Colm during his last wallowing, and felt regret grind salt in his wounds. "'Twas the snowine speaking."

"Aye." Firelight burnished Colm's copper eyes to a dark gold. "This lass. She's lovely, and helpless, and everything that stirs a man's heart. Changelings are made to be so, Jan. Beneath all that pretty hair, behind those haunted eyes, there's darkness waiting. It will bide its time, but when it's ready…"

"…it will eat her soul alive," Jannon finished for him. He wanted to pummel Colm, but all the man did was offer the truth. "My clan once took in a changeling. He'd been left in the hills to die by a mortal family too frightened to keep him. Tristan, they called him. He was only a wee lad when we brought him into the clan."

"Changelings are spelled to be beguiling," Colm said carefully. "But your family must have known he would turn."

"Aye, and when my father and I caught him tormenting one of our hounds with his fire magick, he smiled so sweetly at us. As if he were only playing. He was almost too small for the chains." He rubbed his eyes. "My father wanted him done, but my mother loved him, and slipped into the cave that night to release him. All she found were his charred clothes, filled with his ashes."

"Tara Rowe is likely worse," Colm said. "She's wanted by the Blackstones, brother, and all they covet is power."

"Aye, so it seems." Jannon saw how he was looking at him. "Only know that I am not my mother."

Colm nodded, clapped him on the shoulder and retreated to talk to some of the other men. Jannon left the fire and walked to the lodge, where he planned to spend the rest of the night drinking himself unconscious. Once inside he passed the hall leading to the Rowe sisters' room, he paused, and then forced himself to keep moving.

Jannon wondered if there was enough snowine in the world to keep him from thinking about Tara. With every step he felt her presence more keenly. When he stopped at his door he could swear that he even smelled the delicate fragrance of her pale skin and moonlit hair. Suspicion made him glance up and down the hall. Light spilled from an open door at the end —an unused room. He stepped silently to stand in its opening. There seemed to be a bundle of velvet on the bed. But it turned, revealing a narrow face and a tendril of pale hair.

Despair and elation dueled in his chest. Had she come looking for him? Hadn't she reached for him at the lake, and smiled at him by the bonfire?

He should wake her and send her back to her sister. He knew he should. And yet when had logic ever ruled his heart? Tara was so close. Quietly he stripped off his shirt and pulled off his boots, but left his trousers on as he approached the bed. She stirred as he drew near, her pretty lips parting on a sigh as he stretched out next to her. He thought she might wake as her silvery lashes fluttered for a moment, but she only sidled up against him. Jannon moved his arm around her, and the sound she made as her cheek nestled on his shoulder made him close his own eyes. For all the trouble Tara Rowe might be, a changeling poised on the path between the light and the dark, she felt as weightless and warm as a sunbeam.

During the few hours that followed Jannon did not sleep. He listened to her breathe, and thought of home and all that he had lost after being cast out. He had deserved nothing less for what he had done to his wife and her lover.

Bryn had been his greatest love, and his cruelest mistake. The daughter of a neighboring clan leader, she'd tantalized him from the moment they'd met. So ensnared by her was Jannon that he refused to believe the whispers about her. When his parents had tried to withhold their blessing, he'd even threaten to end himself. Bringing her into the clan as his bride had been the happiest day of his life.

Jannon's clan wondered why he had been so blinded by Bryn's wiles. Surely with all her flirtations, secretive glances, and disappearances he should have suspected something. But no, he had thought her a good and faithful wife. When he'd gone off to battle a rival clan, however, he'd been spell-wounded early, and sent home to recover. Jannon had found Bryn in their bed, slumbering naked in the arms of one of her many lovers. A moment later his power escaped him in one great, seething burst of rage, killing Bryn and her lover. It had left Jannon close to death for days.

Such a crime called for Jannon's life in return, but on the day slated for his execution Bryn's clan had come forward to reveal her power over men. The seductive enchantment she had used to control Jannon had been absolute until the battle, when the enemy had torn his body shields from him. That had also damaged Bryn's secret enthrallment spell. Once confronted with her true nature, the enchantment had backlashed on Jannon, resulting in his lethal reaction. For that his life was spared, but he was cast out of his clan and forbidden to ever join another.

With his shattered heart Jannon had not cared about his fate after that. He no longer needed kin, or believed in love. He would likely be dead now if Ryan Sheridan had not found him drinking and fighting his way across Ireland. The master of Forever Faire had challenged Jannon to a contest of skills for an enchanted purse of gold against a hundred years of service. Knowing any manner of violence would bestir Sheridan to go berserk, Jannon had agreed, even allowing his opponent to choose the weapons and the field of play.

The game of chess that followed had been mercifully short. Ryan had trounced him in ten moves.

Once he had served his century of service, Jannon might have gone back to his pursuit of death by pub brawling. By then Ryan and the other men of Forever Faire had made themselves his brothers, so he stayed. There had been mortal females—too many, for he had always been reckless—but none of them had once touched his heart.

Yet somehow this slender thread of a lass had, the moment he'd looked into her ghost-gray eyes.

Jannon watched her sleep, and made himself remember Tristan, and the sly look he sometimes glimpsed in the boy's bright eyes. Yet until the day they had taken him away in chains, he had been the best of brothers. Jannon might have saved him, if he'd known Tristan had been struggling against the dark path. The same could be said of Bryn, and her sad inability to honestly win the heart of any man.

And now Tara. Was she to walk Tristan's path? Had she enchanted him, like Bryn? Or was she worse than either of them?

Finally Jannon rose, got dressed, and lifted Tara into his arms. She murmured something but remained asleep as he carried her out of his rooms and through the lodge. Kayla opened the door at his soft knock, looking as if she had searched the grounds, which she likely had. When she began to speak Jannon shook his head and carried Tara over to her bed, where he put her down and covered her with an old, soft quilt.

Kayla followed him out into the hall, and closed the door.

"Has she been with you all this time?" she demanded.

"She has." He saw the fury blaze in her eyes, and added,

"I found her in the men's quarters. I let her sleep there, and that is all. She needs rest, and care, and kindness now."

Kayla strode away from him, turned around and came back.

"Look, I appreciate you being nice to my sister, especially when everyone else around here is treating her like a disease. But Tara really is just a teenager. You need to leave her alone."

"I do." Jannon glanced at the door. "Yet I fear I cannot." He looked down at the little mortal's irate face. "Keep her close, Rowe. Keep her away from me."

IN THE MORNING, Kayla wanted to shake Tara awake so she could demand answers about her behavior. But the bruise-dark crescents under her sister's eyes made her leave the room instead. Jannon was right. She did need rest. Nor was Kayla in the mood to hang with the crew at their communal breakfast. None of them had any idea of exactly who was running the faire. On her way out she stopped long enough to grab some apples from the dining room before she headed to the barn.

The head of almost every horse under the roof appeared over the stall doors as Kayla came in and latched the door.

"Yes, I know I'm late," she told them as she hung up her jacket and tucked the extra apples in the pockets before she took a bite of one. Once she swallowed, she said, "My sister is driving me crazy. The guy I just fell for turns out to be a complete jerk. Then there's the magical asshole biker gang." She shook the bitten apple at the horses. "Don't even get me started on them."

She didn't see Titan's big, noble head at his stall, and went over to peer inside. The enormous white stallion stood with his nose in a corner and his hindquarters facing her, his long golden tail drooping.

"So it's talk to the butt day? I don't think so."

Kayla took down a coil of rope and unlatched the door. Standing just inside, she slapped the bundle of rope against her leg. Titan swung his head around to glare at her.

"I can make the kissy sound if you want," she told him, measuring out a two-foot length between her hands. "Or we can go straight to an ass tap. Your choice, pal."

The big stallion made a rude sound, but grudgingly turned to face her, his big eyes meeting hers.

She knew exactly what he was thinking. "Yeah, yeah. I'm being a whiny bitch, and Ryan's still your guy. Peace offering." She held out the rest of her apple, which Titan delicately retrieved from her hand. "If only a nice snack would solve all *my* problems."

"Hey, Rowe," a woman called out. "You in here?"

Kayla stepped out of the stall and latched the door before walking over to the raven-haired girl who had come into the barn. Christine Marszalek hadn't yet changed into the peasant girl costume that she wore while running the faire's hatchet-throw game. Instead she wore snug black jeans and an ivory sweater that loved her curves. She'd rolled up the sleeves to show off her colorfully tattooed arms, and while Kayla never much cared for body ink, Christine's looked gorgeous.

"Hey," Kayla said. She had liked the former stripper from the moment they'd met. "What's up?"

"Serious shit, girlfriend." Christine shut the barn door behind her. She had the kind of green eyes that invoked oceans and emeralds, and not even her liberal use of black eyeliner and smoky shadow could dim their beauty. "I heard Colm talking to one of the other guys. He said something about you and your sister having a tussle with someone named Blackstone." Her soft Tennessee drawl turned chilly as she asked, "This guy, is he big and ugly, and running around with a biker gang?"

"Yes." Even talking about them made Kayla's chest tighten. "They've been hassling me and Tara for a while now."

"Okay." Christine seemed almost relieved. "So they probably don't know about me working here."

Kayla didn't bother to hide her surprise. "You know them?"

"Not personally, girl. They took over the strip club where I was working before I hired on here." Christine's hands fisted at her sides as she told Kayla about the Blackstones' invasion. "I got away, but Fred and all the other dancers are still trapped there. The bikers might know about my thing, too."

Kayla frowned. "What thing?"

"It's better if I show you." Christine glanced around before she reached down and picked up a pebble. "Just trust me, and don't move an inch for the next ten seconds, okay?" When Kayla nodded she took a deep breath, and hurled the stone at her face.

Kayla felt a little puff of air against her cheek as the rock whizzed by and hit something metallic behind her. A pitchfork in front of her suddenly fell from its hook. The tool's handle hit Kayla's jacket on the way down, knocking one of the apples out of the pocket. The apple bounced between her and Christine, who bent to catch it in her hand.

"Ta-da." She straightened and held out the fruit. "What do you think?"

"Very neat trick." Kayla stared at the apple. "So can you

put it back, too?" She watched Christine eye her jacket, and then gasped as the woman tossed the apple, which sank neatly into the pocket. "All right, how did you do that?"

"I don't know, but I've been able to do it since I was a kid. Maybe my folks were circus people or something." She saw Kayla's expression and grimaced. "I don't know who they are. I grew up in foster care."

Kayla suspected the other woman's gift of precision had something to do with the Fae, but if she told her that Christine would probably think she'd lost her mind. "Did the Blackstones see you do your…thing?"

"Maybe. I used it to get away from them." Christine went over and perched on a work stool. "These guys, they've got some kind of weird powers that let them take over people's minds. I'm the only one it didn't work on. The big, nasty one that runs the gang, he's also got the other girls on drugs, and he's using them like whores for his boys. I can't go to the cops—these guys'll just take them over, too, but I've gotta do something."

"For now, you need to stay here at the faire. The Black-stones can't, ah, get past our guys." Kayla hung up her rope as she tried to think of what to tell her friend. "You should talk to Colm, too. Tell him all about it. You can trust him."

"Yeah, I know he's a good guy." She stretched and sighed. "I only wish I knew what he looked like naked."

Kayla smothered a chuckle. "I don't think he's really…available."

Christine grinned wanly. "I got that message, too. He's nice and all, but the minute I flirt with him all those big old 'No Trespassing' signs go up. I don't know what his last gal did to him, but it sure put him in a cast-iron chastity belt."

Telling her friend that Colm's last gal had been the Fae Queen also wasn't an option. "Maybe he'll bust out of it one day."

Christine laughed. "Yeah, that would be something. Maybe I'll talk to Louisa and see if she'll come out here. She reads the tarot, and she's always been right about everything she's told me."

Kayla swallowed a chuckle. "I'd never guess you were one for fortune-tellers."

"Me, either, until one of the dancers at the club took me with her when she went for a reading, and had her do one for me. That woman turned over three cards, and saw things about me that I'd never told a soul. Last time I went she said I'd be leaving my job in a hurry, which turned out to be true." Christine's expression grew thoughtful. "I could ask her to do a spread for you and Tara. She's way good."

Before coming to Forever Faire Kayla would have scoffed at such a suggestion, but now that she knew about the Fae she couldn't dismiss anything even the least bit paranormal. "Sure. I'll take all the help I can get."

After Christine left, Kayla saw Titan and all the other horses were eyeing her. "Don't look at me like that. I didn't spill any beans."

Sampson whinnied, setting off the other horses, while Titan shook his head, making his golden mane shimmy.

"Be nice to me," she told them as she walked back to the big bins that stored the feed. "I may not be able to make a pebble defy the law of physics, but I am in charge of your breakfast."

CHAPTER 5

"WE'VE HAD SOME requests for the feast," Lawrence Sharpe said, stroking his white beard. "It seems the mortals would like more modern fare for the visitors."

In Lawrence's little red cottage, Ryan Sheridan sorted through the menus and sketches in his hands without really seeing them. Disguising his clan of outcast Fae warriors as performers in a traveling Renaissance Faire required him to stage regular events for their mortal visitors, such as Forever Faire's Winter Feast. With all the tourists coming to town for the holidays they could expect a large crowd, which usually cheered him. This year, however, he had a changeling on the faire grounds, the Dark Fae lurking just outside the gates, and a lovely, stubborn mortal woman fully capable of driving him mad in the center of it all.

Kayla Rowe.

"The food stall vendors also ask that we not choose foods that must be fried," the older man added, peering at the list in his big, work-worn hands. "It seems there are issues with the power needed for the deep fryers."

Even now Kayla was somewhere on the faire grounds, working with the horses, smiling at other mortals, safe under his protection from the Blackstone clan. He had been fool enough to make her his lover, and he felt sure she still silently seethed with all that bright, hot emotion they had shared along with their bodies.

Ryan heard a tearing sound, and looked down to see he had ripped the papers in half.

"My liege, perhaps you could look upon the plans for the feast another time," Lawrence said, his tone a bit strained. The short, bald old half-Fae gave his snowy beard several unconscious, nervous tugs as he added, "I'd be happy to discuss the matters tomorrow."

"Calm yourself, before you pluck your chin to match your pate." Ryan tossed the ruined papers on the desk between them. "Forgive me, but I am much preoccupied at the moment. Colm has told you of the Blackstones, and the changeling?"

"Yes—aye," the old man corrected himself. "Forgive me, my liege. When one has only mortals to speak to day in and out, one begins to sound like them. If I may ask, why do you keep the Rowe girl here, when you know she is a cursed changeling? I thought such creatures always turn to the dark."

Ryan suspected the rest of his men shared Lawrence's concerns, but none of them had spoken a word. He felt a grudging admiration for the halfling's mortal directness.

"Her human sister, Kayla, is an innocent. She believes Tara to be the same, and will not be parted from her. Until the changeling proves differently, I must allow her to remain, to protect Kayla."

The bald head bobbed. "As you say, so shall it be."

Another of Lawrence's finer qualities was that he never argued, Ryan thought, and rose from the chair. "I will have much on my mind until the matter is resolved, so I will leave the preparations for the feast in your capable hands, brother."

The old man gave the pile of boots by the fire a wistful glance before forcing a hearty smile. "I will not disappoint, my liege."

Leaving the cottage, Ryan made his way through the encampment to the lodge, where the mortal crew had gathered in the dining hall for the morning meal. Once he saw that both Rowe sisters were absent Ryan helped himself to a mug of dark, strong brew and sat down with Gavan, who was working through a plate with enough food to feed a dozen humans.

His jousting partner's glamour made him appear like any other gray-headed, burly, middle-aged mortal among their crew. The dull disguise hid the dazzling looks Gavan had inherited from his clan, the Watersons, who had cast him out for reasons never explained. Ryan had always suspected it had been something invented, for the clan leader of the Watersons was a vain, foolish Fae matriarch who expected all the men under her rule to cater to her.

"Any sign during the night?" Ryan asked.

Gavan, who had supervised the new patrol of their boundaries, shook his shaggy head. "If the Blackstones hover, they do so at a cowardly distance." He lowered his voice to a level no mortal could hear. "The changeling spent time with Jannon. Dyrak saw him carry her back to the sister in the wee hours."

Ryan noticed how the other man was avoiding his gaze. "You think me a fool to permit them to stay."

"We, all of us, know how dangerous changelings are. I've not gone against the Blackstone clan myself, but I've heard enough monstrous tales from those who have. Even among the Dark Fae they are feared and reviled." Now Gavan looked at Ryan. "If you say we are to fight them to save an innocent, my sword is ready."

"And if I command you to fight them to protect the changeling?" Ryan had to ask.

"My gut will disagree, and I may want a rematch in the arena after." Gavan's mouth stretched into a grim smile. "But you are my liege, and I am your man. Dark Fae are scum. My sword is ready."

Ryan had no stomach for food, and left Gavan to find Colm and assure all was in readiness for the day's performances. Yet as he walked out of the lodge, he found himself on the path to the barn. When he passed the empty costume tent, where Tara should have been working, he paused and stepped inside.

The work of creating and repairing garments for the faire's performers required some skill, and every season Lawrence struggled to hire a seamstress able to keep up with the demands. Three racks of new, handsomely made costumes now stood finished to one side of the work table, attesting to Tara Rowe's talents. He saw another stack of older garments that had been sent over for mending, and when he examined them he saw how flawlessly she had rejoined the burst seams and patched the worn spots. Like all Fae he appreciated the beauty of any handwork, and from what Tara had sewn her mastery equaled that of any Fae maker.

Dark Fae had no desire or patience for such labors. How could one of their changelings be capable of such artful, meticulous work?

"She's not here," a cool voice said. "We're letting her sleep in this morning."

Ryan turned to see Kayla standing behind him. She

smelled of sunshine and woman instead of perfume, and as he breathed her in he saw the palest shade of pink roses bloom on her cheeks. He could see she had been working, for stains mottled her boots and jeans, and bits of straw clung to her jacket like odd confetti. Seeing the damp tendrils of her dark, silky hair that had escaped her cap made him remember how it had felt brushing against his flesh.

"She must be weary after her night with Jannon."

Kayla's eyes narrowed. "Nothing happened, and picking a fight with me right now is a bad idea."

"Angering me is *always* a bad idea," he countered.

"True." She pursed her pretty lips. "Sorry."

In that moment Ryan wanted Kayla in his arms, Titan, and a clear path to the forest beyond the lodge.

"Come with me to my cabin. Alone there, we can speak freely."

The pulse beating in the hollow of her throat fluttered frantically. "The last time we went you didn't want to talk much."

His own heart hammered in his chest. "Then we'll find other things to do."

"You promised to stop doing those things if I stayed," Kayla said, her voice soft and almost regretful, until she cleared her throat. "Look, the only reason I'm here is because Christine told me something this morning that you need to know."

Ryan listened as Kayla repeated the dancer's claims of what the Blackstones had done. He felt no surprise at learning that Dirk was using drugs and magick to control the women, for Dark Fae regularly abused mortals in such ways. The details of Christine's demonstration of her power for Kayla also confirmed Lawrence's suspicion that the dancer was part Fae, particularly when she related that Christine had been abandoned.

"I hope you're not going to tell me that Christine's a changeling, too," she said once she had finished the tale.

"She's likely a halfling—a child borne by a Fae's mortal female lover," he admitted. That brought an image of Maeve, her belly swollen with his baby. Yet for once the bleak despair such remembrances always brought did not come with it. "We are forbidden to marry mortals, but that does not stop us from dalliances."

"Is that what you were doing with me?" she demanded. "Dallying?"

"You know better." He came around the work table, stopping only when she took a step back. "Kayla."

She held up one hand, which she dropped as soon as she saw it was trembling. "We're not talking about us, Ryan. What happens to Christine?"

"We search for halflings as we travel with the faire. If they are grown, and we can unveil their Fae bloodline, we take them to their father's clan." He could taste her desire for him warming the air between them. "They are bound by blood to watch over them. A few are even brought into the clan, although that is rare."

Kayla considered what he'd told her for a moment. "Okay, but what if it was her mother who was Fae?"

"A Fae woman could never bring a half-mortal child back to her clan. It is undeniable proof she has broken our laws. She and the child would be cast out." He hesitated before he added, "The woman would also fear retribution from her Fae husband. I have heard of a few who took revenge by murdering the halfling child."

"Kill the kid instead of the cheating wife. Right. How charming." She shook her head. "Back to Christine. However she got here, the girl needs to know who and what she is. Since I'm just a lowly mortal, I can't answer the million questions she's going to have. Have Colm explain it to her."

Ryan folded his arms. "You think I am not up to the task, my lovely one?"

"Oh, no. She just likes him. I think you're driving me crazy." She strode out.

CHAPTER 6

ON HER MIDDAY break Christine used the ancient landline in Lawrence's office to call Louisa Hayes. When she didn't answer, Christine left a message asking her to come to the faire to perform a reading for the Rowe sisters. As she hung up she grinned at the surly old man, who sat laboring over a stack of lists.

"Want to find out your future, Larry?" she teased. "Louisa will give you a peek for twenty-five bucks."

He glowered up at her. "My name is Lawrence, and no, thank you. I have no future. I have nothing but these bloody menus to sort out. Roast turkey legs. Black peasant bread. Shepherd's pie. Bah. The little ones will want none of it, and then they will cry, and I will be blamed. Again."

"So add on some burgers and hot dogs," Christine advised him. "Or pizza and chicken nuggets. Those are the only four food groups for anyone under twelve." She leaned over to kiss his gleaming scalp. "Say thank you, Larry."

"Thank you, saucy wench." Lawrence's lips twitched. "Now go on with you."

Christine didn't mind that the old guy watched her butt as she left. He was a man, and she had a particularly fine ass. Most of the Forever Faire guys gave her appreciative looks when they thought she couldn't see. Since she did the same to them, she figured it was fair. She never got a glance from Ryan, the big dude who ran the whole show, but he was too busy watching Kayla to notice her.

And then there was Colm, who mostly gave her the stink eye.

Christine saw the object of her affections standing in front of the cleared patch of ground where they'd set up the hatchet-toss game. He hadn't taken down the CLOSED clock sign, she noted, but he was studying the targets like there'd be a pop quiz later.

"Got a special going today," she said as she joined him. "Six throws for a dollar, or a nice, slow kiss."

"We don't charge for the games, and I don't kiss the help." For once he didn't glare at her. "We need to have a word, Miss Marszalek."

"One day you're gonna call me Christine," she warned. "And I'm going to rip your clothes off."

His face turned to stone. "Please come with me now."

As she followed him to one of the tents where they stowed the show equipment, Christine wondered if she was still going to be employed in ten minutes. Something was up, judging by how polite he was being.

Colm held the tent flap up for her to enter, and let it drop once he was inside. "I hope you've enjoyed working at the faire."

"Sure, I've loved everything. The job, the kids, looking at you, the food, the cool costumes, smelling you, the nice folks, your weird friends, wondering what you look like naked, and..." She stopped and thought for a moment.

"Nope, that's about it. Do I get my last paycheck before you boot me out the gate, or do you mail it to me? Because I don't really have an address per se, and oh have mercy *Colm*."

The burst of dark light had lasted only as long as her cry of horror. A cascade of softer, golden stars erased the Colm that Christine knew, and replaced him with a lean, gorgeous upgrade. Her gaze bounced from his long mane of garnet hair to the silver filigree on his gleaming black boots and up again to meet his polished copper eyes.

"'Tis easier to show what we are than it is to explain," he said, his voice so warm and melodic each word caressed her skin. "I and the other men of Forever Faire are not mortal— not human—but Fae. Like me, they use the illusion of glamour to appear unremarkable."

"Uh-huh." Christine felt woozy now. "So, you're not going to eat my face off now, are you?"

"We don't eat mortal faces, or any other parts they possess." His smile flooded her with gentle warmth. "We are your people, because you are only half-mortal. Your other half is Fae, like us." He stepped quickly toward her, and supported her by the elbows a heartbeat before her knees buckled. "You have nothing to fear, Christine."

"Says the mighty, morphing, power stranger. Don't let me pass out," she told him as he led her over to a stack of crates, and sat her on top of them. "At the very least, I want to take a selfie with you."

"'Tis is a shock, but 'twill pass." He urged her to bend forward until her forehead nearly touched her knees, and kept his arm around her shoulders. "Did you never wonder why you were so different from the other children around you?"

"Too busy trying not to get my ass kicked by the older kids. Group homes suck." His hands left her, and as Christine straightened she had to grab the edge of the crates to stay upright. "So my mom or dad was like you?"

Colm nodded. "'Twas likely your father. Mortal women are very hard to resist, especially when we are hurt."

Christine listened with increasing awe as he told her about the Fae, and how they lived in secluded clans hidden from the rest of the world. While they looked mostly human, they were bigger, stronger, and more intelligent. They possessed superhuman abilities from birth that were related to their bloodlines and their own personal powers. They used magick, too, not only to disguise themselves but to protect their property and their people from their enemies, known as Dark Fae.

As soon as she heard that Christine muttered, "The Blackstones."

"Aye. They're among the worst of our darkest kin." Colm sat down beside her. "I'm told you escaped them by using your power."

"That, and a lot of luck." She touched a lock of his dark red hair, which curled around her fingers as if it were alive before slipping free. "What the hell am I gonna do with all this, Colm? I'm just a dancer with a good eye for angles. I never finished school– God, I can barely read. Maybe all that wonderful Fae stuff skipped me, or I took after my human mama."

"Without weapons or aid you outwitted and escaped a horde of Dark Fae," he reminded her. "There are battle-hardened warriors I know who would quail at the same prospect. Your clan would be very proud."

"Since I'm a half-human love child, maybe not." She bumped her shoulder against his. "You still like me, though, right? Maybe you could introduce me to your folks someday."

A muscle on his jaw ticked. "I have no clan. I am an

outcast, as are all the other Fae here."

"They kicked you out?" She felt indignant. "I thought they were supposed to be smart people."

That startled a chuckle out of him. "You flatter me."

"Not really." Christine wanted to do a lot more than that. "So why did these dumbasses do it?"

His amusement abruptly faded. "For our misdeeds, each of us was sentenced to dwell forever in the mortal realm as eternal exiles. We have tried to make Forever Faire our clan, but it can never truly be the same. We are shunned by our kind. No Fae woman would leave her clan to be wife to an exile, or bear his children. The men take what comfort they can with mortal females, yet we must still conceal what we are. We do not age as they do, and their lives by comparison are so brief, it seems a cruelty to expect more than a brief dalliance."

The way he said that made her eyes sting. "Is that why you never…"

"I am not like the others." He gave her hand a gentle pat. "Your attentions are gratifying, my lady, but they are wasted on me. Since I was cast out I have been incapable with women."

"Okay." Christine blinked. "I mean, not okay. Not okay at all. Colm, have you even tried?"

Before Colm could answer, someone shouted for him outside the tent.

"We will talk again later." He stood up and moved away from her, disappearing for a moment in another shower of tiny stars before he changed back into a regular guy.

"Hey." Christine climbed off the crates. "You gonna tell me what you did to get kicked out of the Fae club?"

"I fell in love with the Fae Queen, and gave her my heart." Before he stepped out of the tent, he glanced back at her. "She still has it."

"I'M TIRED," TARA complained as she finally came out of the bathroom. "Do I have to do this?"

"Why, no," Kayla said in her nicest voice. "You can go back to your bed and sleep for another ten hours. Or you could go ask Jannon if he minds babysitting you for another night in a shared bed. Or you can walk out the gates and go look for that Blackstone jackass, and see if he'll let you crash at his place. You know, after he rapes you."

"Fine, I'll let the witch read my palm. God." Tara stalked past her.

"She's not a witch, and she reads tarot cards." Kayla slammed the door to their room shut, and followed her sister down the hall. "She's also a friend of Christine's, so you're going to be polite to her."

Tara heaved a theatrical sigh. "Yessah, boss."

"Wait a minute." Kayla caught her sister's arm and pulled her around to face her. "Have I yelled at you? Demanded an explanation for your little disappearing act last night? I haven't even mentioned how I felt when I found you *kissing our stalker.*" As Tara opened her mouth Kayla gave her a shake. "Don't lie to me, kiddo. He didn't make you do it."

"He said some stuff. No guy ever talked to me like that." Tara's face reddened, and she ducked her head. "I thought that was why he was chasing us. For me. I thought he cared about me."

Kayla felt her exasperation drop a notch. "All right. We'll forget about the kissing. We need a plan, and Christine thinks this lady can help us see what's coming. Let's give it a shot, okay? That's all I'm asking."

Her sister nodded quickly, and meekly accompanied her the rest of the way to Christine's room, where they were greeted by the dancer and introduced to Louisa Hayes.

"Nice to meet you," Kayla said, taking in the stout woman's bright eyes, apple-cheeked face, and frizzy ginger perm. Instead of dressing like a gypsy she wore a pale green wool twin set, complete with a pearl necklace. Although she had to be at least fifty, she had skin as tight and smooth as a teen. Something about her made Kayla take a harder, longer look. "Thanks for coming out here today."

"My pleasure, my dear." Louisa gestured at two folding chairs on the other side of the card table. "Please, sit down. Before I read your cards I will need you to shuffle the deck, so they can know your energy."

"Sure." Kayla watched her remove a stack of big cards from a burgundy velvet bag embroidered with golden symbols, and felt a sudden, strong urge to call off the whole thing. Maybe it was the possibility that Louisa really could see the future. "How long have you been at this?"

"Reading the tarot? Since I was a girl. My Gran taught

me." The older woman placed the overlarge deck in the center of the table. "Who would like to be first?"

Tara, who had barely mumbled a word to Louisa, scooped up the deck and awkwardly shuffled the cards before handing them to the older woman. "If I get a full house, do I win?"

Kayla gave her sister a glare, but Louisa ignored the jibe and calmly laid out a spread of three cards, faces down, before setting aside the deck.

"We will begin with your past," Louisa said, and turned over a card. It had one long blade crossed by four others. "Here we have the five of swords. You waited to hear, and be heard, but a powerful force imprisoned you in silence. That is why there were so many dark days for you, my dear."

Tara swallowed hard. "What does that mean?"

"Your past has been difficult for you," Louisa advised gently, and turned over a second card. "Now, the present." On the card eight more blades formed a cage around a blindfolded woman. "The eight of swords."

Christine leaned close to Kayla to murmur, "That's an awful lot of blades."

"You feel trapped," the older woman said, and paused, staring at the card before she added, "Someone close to you wishes to keep you from your destiny. You are blind to this, not by choice, but by the will of the other. This is why you struggle now, Tara. You have traded one prison for another."

"Maybe she should reshuffle the deck," Kayla suggested and reached for the deck. "Or you could do my reading now."

"No," Tara said, grabbing her hand. To Louisa she said, "Finish it."

The older woman's bright eyes shifted to Kayla before

she reluctantly flipped the third card. She paled as she stared at the tall building being struck by lightning, and then looked into Tara's eyes.

"The future is The Tower. You are in great danger, and that which surrounds you will come to…" She stopped and shook her head. "I can't see, exactly, because it is hidden, like much in your life. I think you should be very careful in whom you place your trust. Like those who seem good and kind. They wear masks made only to deceive you." She quickly collected the cards and put them in Kayla's hands. "Now for your sister."

The cards felt oddly cold as Kayla shuffled them and handed them back.

Louisa silently dealt another three card spread, and turned over the first, on which a radiant-looking woman wearing a crown sat before an enormous forest.

"Your past is The Empress. A great and benevolent presence in your life protected you, my dear. I'm sensing that it was your mother. She meant for you to arrive at this day to do the same for another."

"My mother abandoned us when we were little," Kayla said flatly. "We haven't heard a word from her in eighteen years."

"Perhaps by leaving, she protected you from some evil in her life." Louisa's hair bobbed around her red cheeks as she turned over the second card, which showed a man with the number eight floating sideways over his head. "The Magician occupies your present. He represents a powerful, clever force that means to undo the Empress's work. This could be a man you've met, who you believe has feelings for you. He makes you believe this so that you won't resist his will, but I think he underestimates your love for your sister."

"That seems a little confusing," Kayla said, frowning as

she thought of Dirk Blackstone. He didn't fit Louisa's description, but Ryan certainly did. Was this all some kind of game he was playing, so he could use her for his own purposes? "Are you sure about this guy?"

"I can only read the cards that are dealt," Louisa admitted. "The Magician is often a favorable card, but not in this position. For you, he means upheaval and pain." She turned over the third card.

They all stared silently at the skeleton riding a horse.

"The future," Louisa said, her voice shaking. She swallowed several times. "I'm sorry, but I'm not feeling well." Quickly she picked up the cards and put them back into her velvet bag before she stood. "Christine, there's no charge for the readings."

Kayla quickly got up and blocked her path to the door. "What does it mean? Do you think I'm going to die? Tell me."

The older woman looked as if she might shove her out of the way. "The Death card is about what is coming for you, brought about by the Magician. I feel it is very close now, and will come by night when shadows are at their darkest. This omen also reflects back on the past and the Empress. I think your mother was destroyed by hatred disguised as love, my dear. Now the same may happen to you and your sister. I sense a great threat, but not only for you. You see, I must pair the readings, as you are sisters. It means…" She leaned close to whisper the rest. "If you don't leave here before the full moon, Tara will die."

· · · · ·

THE MAN DRIVING the black taxicab stopped a few yards outside the gates of Forever Faire, and watched as a slender, black-haired beauty embraced his older, plumper fare.

"I have to go out of town for a few weeks," the old lady told the younger. "I'll call you when I get back to see how your friends make out."

The driver hid a smirk, but then, he knew that the Rowe sisters' luck had almost run out.

Once the old lady climbed into the back of the cab, the driver adjusted his rearview mirror and performed a somewhat clumsy three-point turn. He watched his passenger look out the back window and wave at the girl. As she disappeared around the curve behind them, the old woman turned around to scowl at him.

Beck Blackstone shifted from the illusion of the mortal cabbie to his true form. "How did your readings go? Make any money?"

"I planted the seeds," she said. Her lips stretched until tiny splits appeared. "They will water them with their fears. By the full moon they'll grow so large that nothing will keep them under Sheridan's wing."

Beck watched as murky light enveloped his passenger. "And the new cloaking spell? She did not see through it?"

"This time she saw nothing of me." Bright eyes turned the color of mud as they met Beck's gaze. "Christine Marszalek has befriended the sisters. Perhaps when they leave, they will bring her with them. I should like that very much."

Beck nodded. "When the time comes, I will have her set aside for you."

"She's half-Fae. That is how she was able to escape the club." Plump fingers probed the halo of crimped ginger hair. They reemerged stained a wet, dark red. "Fucking cunt. Drive to the cottage, and hurry. I am already coming undone."

Beck nodded, and turned off on a side road and followed it to a rustic little cottage surrounded by firs and pines. Clothing ripped in the back seat as Beck parked the cab in front of Louisa Hayes's home. He rolled down his window to breathe in the smoke drifting from the brick chimney, which even now still smelled of burnt mortal bone. The scent that reminded him of the old days, when his clan could slay as many humans as they wished, and no one dared challenge them. This modern world had too many eyes and ears.

The cab's back door flung open, and Beck watched with amusement as his fare staggered out naked. Pendulous breasts swayed as bloated hands began to tear at the placid features. Eyes, nose, and mouth sagged, then slid down from Dirk Blackstone's blood-covered face.

As Beck watched his cousin wrestle with his hideous garment, he nodded to himself. It had been his idea to question each of the dancers at the club about the one who had escaped. One of the girls had mentioned how often the little bitch went to have her cards read, which led them to the old woman. Even under the kind of duress that drove mortals insane, Louisa Hayes had repeatedly denied knowing where Christine had gone. Then the girl herself had called the old witch, and left a message on her telephone machine, asking her to come to the faire and do a reading for the Rowe sisters.

Beck's eyelids drooped as he remembered snapping the bones in Louisa's fingers. It had taken seven before she told Dirk which cards to use.

"Do I amuse you?" Dirk demanded, as he worked one arm out of the lifeless mortal flesh. "Perhaps for my next foray I will don your hide."

"Ah, but you cannot filet a faithful cousin, or any other immortal you would make your masque." Beck climbed out of the cab and walked over to him. "Sard my ass, but even with the fat and the wrinkles that mewling witch must have been a tight fit."

Dirk said nothing as he peeled away Louisa's skin until he could step out of it naked. He kicked the boneless flesh at Beck before he strode into the cottage.

"Time to go to your reward, my lady," Beck said.

He dragged the flaccid remains over the threshold, inside, and across the living room. With a heave, he cast the flesh into the enormous fireplace, then wiped his hands clean on the old witch's lace curtains.

"I would offer some manner of mortal prayer," he said. "But you were a pagan. Perhaps you will be reborn as a cow in some land where fools worship them. Not that there would be much difference." Air shifted around Beck, and for a moment he smelled the thick, warm perfume of blooming flowers. "You think to haunt me?" The light from the window dimmed as his anger swelled. "Begone, old woman. You have served your purpose."

The flames in the fireplace roared up, while outside snow began to pelt the windows. The smoke from the burning flesh wafted in his eyes, forcing him back, and then the fire vanished. Beck went still as he saw a burst of warm pink light. But when it faded, all that remained of the old witch had crumbled to gray ash.

"So you possessed a few drops of Fae blood," he murmured, nodding in agreement with himself. "They are burnt away now, along with the rest of you."

The storm outside cleared as Beck sat in the old woman's overstuffed chair and waited. The little house smelled of blood and death, but so did everyplace they went, eventually. Having a cousin who could wear human flesh like clothing could be a messy business, but this time it had allowed Dirk to pass through Forever Faire's bespelled boundaries.

"It would be useful if we could all masque ourselves with mortal hides," Beck called out, and heard Dirk snarl something in response from the bath. He went into the kitchen where they had first questioned and then butchered the witch, which now resembled a small slaughtering pen. He picked up the mound of clothing Dirk had shed before slipping into the old woman's skin. "Then the rest of the clan could cross the faire's boundaries, and get our changeling."

His cousin emerged a short time later, now dripping wet from the shower as he snatched his clothing from Beck.

"She is mine, Cousin. Mine alone. Forget that, and I'll have your head as my footstool."

Beck offered him a mocking bow, and found himself slammed against the nearest wall.

"You know all I want is a quiet corner, Jarek in chains, and a sharp blade," Beck managed to croak. Despite the massive fist around his neck he grinned at Dirk. "'Tis a shame you cannot wear him. Not that there will be much left when I am done."

"So you say."

His cousin released him. Beck staggered back and massaged his throat, as Dirk roughly pulled on his clothes and boots.

"Set fire to this hovel," he said. "I want no trace of our work left for that mad cock Sheridan to find."

Without waiting for an acknowledgement, his cousin stalked out, leaving Beck to start the blaze.

A deck of the old woman's tarot cards still lay on the kitchen table. He grinned as he picked them up and took them to the fireplace. One by one, he lit them and dropped them around the cottage. By the time he'd lit the final card the place was burning merrily around him. Beck placed the last flaming card on the old woman's chair, and frowned as he saw the picture of a grinning skeleton on a horse staring up at him. Suddenly he remembered that Louisa had done something strange when she'd showed Dirk the Death card. She had stopped weeping, and closed her eyes a moment before his cousin had snapped her neck.

"You knew you were going to die," Beck muttered as he watched the card curl up and blacken. Fear constricted his throat. "What more did you know? What did you see in those bloody cards?"

Flames engulfed the chair, but when their smoke reached his nose, Beck smelled the flowers of an eternal spring. He spun around, and saw the fireplace filling not with flames but blooms made of soft, pink light.

"Fuck you and your witchery, you old hag."

He turned on his heel and walked out to the cab where his cousin waited. Someday there would be no limit to the mortals he would kill. Someday he would kill enough to build a house from their bones. Someday…

"Why are you grinning like that?" his cousin demanded.

"I think I know how to get all of us into Forever Faire," Beck said, his tone placid. "We will need more bikers. Many more bikers."

"My father refuses to send more men," Dirk reminded him.

"Not our clansmen." He started the engine. "Mortal bikers."

"HAVE YOU SEEN Tara?" Kayla asked Christine as she delivered the last platter of burgers to the dining hall buffet table.

"Last I heard, she went to run up a few more tablecloths for the feast tables." Christine scattered a handful of cherry tomatoes over a large salad, each landing in precise, evenly-spaced spots on the mixed greens. She glanced up and frowned. "You've already checked the costume tent, huh?"

"She probably went back to the lodge to take a shower." Kayla felt something stir the hairs on the back of her neck, and gritted her teeth. She didn't have to look to know who was causing it. "So what are you wearing tomorrow night?"

"Only the latest fashion for serving wenches." Christine whipped off her apron to reveal the white linen blouse, black leather bustier, and full red skirt she wore. She turned from side to side. "What do you think? Doesn't it shriek 'Tug on my laces, Hot Stuff?'"

Kayla's gaze shifted to Colm, who stood talking with one of the cooks. "I don't think he's a tugger, honey."

"I see someone who is," her friend said, and nodded past her. "If mine doesn't work out, can I have him?"

"Sure," Kayla said. For a moment she wondered if throwing Christine at Ryan would actually get him off her back, until a startling surge of jealousy raced through her. "I've got to get the horses bedded down for the night. See you later."

Pulling down the cap that went with the squire costume Tara had made for her, Kayla walked quickly out of the back of the tent. She made it halfway to the barn before Ryan stepped in front of her.

"You cannot outrun me. My legs are twice the length of yours," he said, eyeing her hose-clad thighs. "Hiding will not work, either. You leave a trail of your scent as well as your life energy wherever you go. I have played this game of princess and monster for sevenday now. I will not permit you to win it again."

So he knew she'd been avoiding him. "We call it hide and seek now. What do you want, other than everything you're not going to get?"

As a group of vendors passed them Ryan took her hand and led her to a more secluded spot between two tents. "I know you wish Tara to be safe, but as long as she is here, the Blackstones will not leave. Neither of you can go beyond the faire grounds while they are here, or you will be taken."

"Haven't we been over this?" She realized she was still holding his hand, and pulled it away. "We won't step foot outside the gates."

His lovely, sexy mouth tightened. "This is a stalemate, Kayla, but it will not remain so. The Dark Fae are not only powerful, they are resourceful. Eventually they will ferret out a way to breach our boundaries."

She silently agreed with everything he said, and hated

herself for it. "So what do you suggest we do? Call in the National Guard? They can't see them."

"Wallace believes the Blackstones are tracking you by the curse that cloaks Tara." He stepped closer, and before she could back away, he caressed her cheek. "It is too powerful and well-cast to be removed, but we can make it weaker."

Although his touch made her want to fling herself into his arms, Kayla forced herself to focus on his words. "By separating us."

Ryan nodded. "There is a Fae clan whose leader is indebted to me. I can arrange for him and his kin to take Tara, and move her somewhere far from Forever Faire."

That he'd even consider such a thing made her blood boil. "No."

"They are kind, good people, and will safeguard her against the Dark Fae," he assured her, "until such time as we can defeat the Blackstones. Once she is away, you and I will–"

"Shut up." She shoved him as hard as she could, which was the same as trying to push over a brick wall. "You think I don't know what you really want? You and me, alone here in our little medieval love nest, without Tara to spoil things. Well, it's not happening, Ryan. You're not sending my sister anywhere. But I'll tell you what: first thing tomorrow morning, we'll leave, together. As for you and I, we're done now. Stay away from me."

So angry she could barely see straight, Kayla left him and ran to the barn. Once inside she slammed the door behind her, falling back against it and beating her fists against the old wood until she saw every horse in the barn staring at her.

"Sorry, I'm– Sorry, guys."

She rubbed a hand over her hot face and retreated to

check that she had all the gear she would need for tomorrow night's show. As she passed each horse, they stretched out their necks, trying to nose her. Surrounded by saddles, blankets and bridles in the tack room, Kayla felt calmer. She switched on the light, and surveyed the wire racks of show accessories. She might as well start pulling and organizing things now.

"Send Tara away, my ass." She jerked down a handful of blankets and sorted through them, picking out the colors that would complement the Winter Feast's theme of white and blue. "Why don't we just kill her? No more changeling, no more issues. Isn't that the perfect solution?"

The door to the tack room suddenly opened with a squeal of hinges, and a shower of tiny white stars cascaded down to bounce around the floorboards. Ryan stepped inside and kicked the door shut before he finished transforming.

"We are not done," he told her, his eyes glowing so brightly his gaze seemed to burn into her head.

Kayla set aside the blankets and folded her arms. "You touch me, or use your magick to make me want it, and I swear to God I will find a way to hurt you. Even if it takes me the rest of my dumbass mortal life."

"I don't have to touch you." He swept up his hand, and bridles began to fall off their brackets. "Nor does my magick."

Kayla felt something curl around her ankle, and glanced down to see two coils of rope encircling her boots. Regret finally seeped through her fury, for despite his thick skull and utter unconcern for her feelings, this was Ryan. Ryan, whose passion had taken her apart and rebuilt her. Ryan, who had made her feel hope…and this sick, twisted love that wanted her to go along with his horrible plan.

"Please, don't do this." She hated how pitiful her voice sounded. "I can't take anymore, Ryan."

"'Tis the same for me, my lovely one." He flicked his fingers, and the buttons on her jacket fell off and rolled away. He bent down, not touching her at all as he breathed in. "I see you and it seizes me inside, with the gilt talons of your eyes. The dark satin of your hair peace-bonds my heart. I am bound to you by every blink of your lashes, by every crystal ring of your laughter."

He had her bound by the wrists and ankles, and when the leather and rope tugged her back against the shelves of curry combs, Kayla didn't fight them. Some perverse part of her wanted to see just how far he would take this.

"I dream of us now, every night." Ryan unbuttoned his own tunic, stripping it off to reveal his broad, beautifully muscled chest. "In the cabin, in the snow, high atop some icy waterfall. We are naked and the world dwindles as we reach to each other. You whisper my name just before my hand covers your naked breast, and then I awake, alone and cold and hard. So hard."

Kayla's jacket simply evaporated, leaving her in her tunic and hose. She kept her gaze locked with his as he stripped off his boots and trousers. His pale white skin took on a subtle glow as he straightened, naked and fully erect. Only then did she feel the rest of her costume peel away from her skin, leaving her in her underwear. She could feel her panties clinging to her sex, which had grown damp and throbbed urgently now.

Ryan moved close enough for his body heat to sink into her skin, and put his mouth beside her ear. "I never have to touch you for you to make me like iron, my lovely one. Then all I must do is what is necessary to find peace."

The whisper of his breath against her ear and cheek made her swallow a moan. "What do you do?"

He stepped back, watching her face as he reached down and wrapped his hand around his engorged shaft. "This." Slowly he began stroking the length of his cock, his arm flexing and his chest heaving as he dragged in more air. "I remember how it was in the cabin, that night we first had each other. Touching you. Putting my mouth on you. Fucking you."

Kayla turned her face away, but listening to his hand pumping made her clit pulse, and her nipples pucker into tight beads. "Is this why you tied me up? To torture me?"

"No." He murmured something else, and light filled the room.

When Kayla's dazzled eyes cleared, she saw Ryan bound by rope and rein to the shelves, and she was standing where he had been. Her panties and bra were gone, too. She should have run for the door, but her feet took her to him. "I think that spell backfired, my man."

"This is how you have me." He looked down at the full, straining bulb of his erection. "And I can find no relief from it. Not even when I use my hand and pretend it is you." He lifted his head and smiled wanly at her. "Why should tonight be any different?"

Kayla imagined walking out of the tack room and leaving him there to stew, but her heart brought her closer still, until she could rest her cheek against his smooth skin. She felt the hammering of his heart increase as she brushed her lips over one small, flat brown nipple, and smiled against it before she caressed it with her tongue.

"Whatever is said, whatever is done," Ryan told her, his voice going so deep it growled against her ears, "I am yours, my lady, to do with as you please."

Kayla kissed her way across his chest to his other nipple, giving it some attention as she curved her hands over his tight, bulging shoulders. That this huge, brawny man was telling her that he was her toy made all kinds of ideas fill her head. "I like how you taste."

"Then have me." His eyes searched hers. "Feast on me."

Putting her mouth and tongue on his body gave Kayla a heady sense of power. She reveled in it as she ran her hands over him, mapping every long stretch of skin and the delicious strength knotting beneath it. She toyed with him, pinching his nipples until he groaned. She caressed them with her fingertips as she used her tongue on his belly. The columns of his thighs turned to steel as she knelt and shook her hair back, wanting him to see as well as feel the moment she kissed the slick, satiny bulb. It throbbed so strongly now it tapped her chin.

"Hmmmm." She kissed him, and let her lips linger. A pearl of bitter sweetness seeped from the velvety eye of his cock, and she lapped it up before she opened to engulf him.

"Ah." Ryan shook, making the shelves rattle behind him. "Now you make me dream again, oh, my lady. More, yes, take more of me. Take all of me."

Kayla slowly worked her lips down, sucking firmly as he glided in and out. She didn't know if his hips were thrusting or her head was bobbing. They were one instead of two now. He possessed her, his cock pushing in her mouth, and she devoured him, her lips caressing as she took every inch. He felt so large and hard she wondered if he could last much longer, and prayed that he would. Nothing felt as good as this. Rubbing her palms against his thighs, she reassured him, and then goaded him by cradling the tight bulge of his balls with her curious fingers.

Rope tore, and leather shredded, and when Ryan pulled her up into his arms Kayla wrapped hers around his neck.

"Again I break my promises." He walked her back until he braced her on the work table, and stepped between her thighs. "You make a liar out of me and I do not care. I must be inside you. Will you let me give it to you now, love?"

Kayla leaned back, using her legs to draw him closer as she tasted him on her lips, and smiled. "Yes, Ryan. Unless you want me to throw you to the floor and–"

He pushed his hands under her bottom as he thrust inside her, his hips jerking frantically as he worked into her clenching opening. "Kayla, help me. Look at me, show me your eyes. I cannot stop, I cannot wait, I cannot think."

He had filled her so completely that she could no longer tell where she ended and he began. "Then stop trying," she whispered. "Nothing matters but this." She tightened around him until he began to move.

Ryan draped her over his arm, urging her back so he could get at her breasts. At the same time he worked between her thighs, plowing in and out with deep, hard thrusts until the table under her began to pound just as rapidly against the wall. Kayla gripped his strong arms and rolled her hips up and down, fucking him back as she heard herself make a soft keening sound. He was going to split her in half soon, and she didn't care. It meant nothing as the tides of hunger swelled and rose within her. When he came into her in the next moment she jutted her breasts against his mouth and cried out as lights burst behind her closed eyelids. The rest of her exploded in fast and furious surges of pure, hot ecstasy.

Ryan said something as if from a distance, and then released a guttural sound as his big body shuddered over her. Deep inside, his shaft swelled even larger and then pulsed with every thrust as he pumped his creamy seed into her again and again.

They held onto each other until the last of the delight faded, and Kayla shivered and huddled close to him. Ryan held her against his chest, murmuring to her as he rubbed his cheek on the top of her head.

"We do not have to dream in solitude," he told her as he drew out of her and lifted her from the table to her feet. "We can have what we desire. If you will only hear me, and trust in me, there is nothing that can come between us, love."

Kayla looked down as her clothes settled over her naked body, and turned away from him. She took in a breath and smelled the scent of their bodies and sex, blended now like some secret, erotic perfume. This moment should have been glorious and satisfying, but he'd reminded her of what did stand between them. Tara. Nineteen years old, frightened and helpless, and with no one in the world but Kayla. God forgive her, but Kayla found herself wanting to agree with him.

All right. Send Tara away with your friends.

But the words never left her tongue. They soured there as she faced her own selfishness. She wanted him more than her sister. She was tired of taking care of her. Everything about Tara was dark and depressed and a dead end. Tara gave nothing back. She was like a vampire, always demanding more and more because no matter what Kayla did, it was never enough. It never defeated the nightmares, the depressions, the despair. Since they were kids it had always been about Tara. Every time her sister looked at her Kayla could almost hear it: *Help me, save me, love me and only me.*

If Kayla could have hated Ryan as much as she hated herself in this moment, none of this would have happened. She felt him reach out to her.

"Don't," she said, without turning. "You should sleep well enough tonight. I know I won't."

What began as a walk quickly broke into a run. Kayla

had to get away from him. Her temper was barely leashed. As she passed the stalls, every horse made furious sounds. They reared, kicked, and pounded their stalls. It sounded as if the barn was about to shake itself to pieces.

But as Kayla flew through the door, she didn't care. Instead all she could hear was Tara trying to explain what she had done. *He said some stuff. No guy ever talked to me like that. I thought he cared about me. He made me do it.*

Now, at least, Kayla understood. Her sister had been telling the truth after all.

CHAPTER 9

JANNON FINISHED HAMMERING the last peg into the wooden stand, and gave it a firm shake to assure its sturdiness. Since the Winter Feast joust always proved to be the most well-attended of their shows, the additional seating would be welcome. Jannon only welcomed the opportunity to pound something other than his skull against a wall.

Still, he'd managed to keep away from Tara Rowe for another day.

Tomorrow he would rise before dawn and take a nag and the old logging cart into the woods. Perhaps he'd build a hovel for himself there. Ryan often retreated to his, and if Jannon locked himself inside, in time he might rid himself of this damnable awareness of her. Even now he swore he could feel the willow-o-wisp warmth of her body, and smell the tantalizing scent of her skin.

"I didn't know you were a carpenter," a low voice said behind him.

Jannon kept his back to her as he plied his hammer against nothing that needed it.

Tara came around him and stepped under the stand, bracing her back against a strut. "You can talk to me, you know. My sister won't tear your head off if you do."

"Think again." He shoved his sledge into his work belt. Perhaps rudeness would send her away. "Why do you plague me now?"

"Sorry. I wish I wasn't a disease." She looked away from him. Regret instantly lanced through his chest. "But I can't stop being a changeling, right? Can't hand in my evil little sister card. Can't escape whatever is coming."

Jannon tugged her out from under the stand and studied her delicate face. "You are not evil. I could not abide evil in my bed. The slime, the flesh-piercing spines—none of which you have." He forced himself to let her go, but tapped the tip of her nose. "There. Give back that card."

Tara didn't laugh as he'd expected. "Not quite yet. My sister had this woman come to read the tarot for us. My cards were full of swords and prisons and darkness. It was like the worst tarot reading ever."

Jannon wondered if he should tear off Kayla's head. "Tell me you did not pay coin for this foolishness."

"No, it was free." Her chin wobbled. "I think that makes it worse."

Tucking her against his chest felt as natural to Jannon as stroking a soothing hand along the delicate arch of her spine. "Prisons can be escaped, and darkness may be defeated by no more than a single candle. As for the swords, I am very good with blades, so you may give them to me." When she didn't reply, he asked, "Have you spoken to your sister about this?"

She shook her head against his chest. "She's mad at me. Sick of me, too. She wants to be with Ryan, and I'm always in the way. Well, not for much longer."

Alarmed now, Jannon drew back, holding her at arm's

length. "What are you saying, Tara? You know you cannot leave the camp. Never tell me you are thinking of going to Dirk Blackstone."

"It's okay. I'm staying. I have to." She looked down at his boots, and then jerked her head up, a strange urgency in her eyes. "Will you dance with me at the Winter Feast?"

Jannon grimaced. "I am not much for dancing. Brawling, now, I am your man." As soon as the words left him he silently cursed himself. "What I mean to say is, there will be others more capable as partners."

"But no one else likes me but you." Her smoky eyes filled with shadows. "Just one dance, please?"

The little wench had his battered heart in her grip, Jannon thought, and he was never going to pry it free. "Wear stout slippers tomorrow night."

"You'd never hurt me." A sad smile touched her lips before she turned and walked toward the tents.

As Jannon watched her go, he wondered why she left him feeling that her words had meant more. He swatted at something crawling over the back of his neck, and then felt the uneasiness leave him.

"So I am to dance." Jannon bent to retrieve the sack of joining pegs. "'Twill be easier than brawling, surely."

"WE MISSED YOU at the evening meal, my liege." Wallace carried a tray of food into Ryan's rooms, but set it down as soon as he saw his face. "What now?"

"The Rowe sisters." Ryan gestured for the spell tracker to sit in the chair opposite his. "I need you to take a closer look at them. Do you have your crystal with you?"

"I have been carrying it of late." Wallace removed a black cloth from his vest pocket and unwrapped it to reveal a small, opaque shard. "What do you wish to see?"

"Their past," Ryan told him. "Take me to their childhood."

The blacksmith spread the white cloth over his hand, and placed the shard in the center of it. As he murmured in the ancient tongue, the crystal came alive with shimmering light. The shard rose from the cloth to hover over it, slowly turning and sprouting new angles. When he had finished the spell, the shard had expanded into a whirling, glittering sphere.

"Open," Wallace said, deftly moving his hand through

the silver light. The crystal elongated and flattened. When it formed a two-sided oval mirror, he touched his fingers to the crystal surface. "Kayla and Tara Rowe, as children."

Ryan watched as a young girl appeared. She held a blanket-wrapped infant, and watched an older man packing suitcases in the back of an old car.

"Aren't we going to wait for Mama?" the girl asked the man. When he didn't reply, she tightened her arms around the infant. "Daddy, what if she comes back, and we're not here?"

"She's not coming back, sweetheart." The man took the infant from her, which made the baby cry. He ignored her screams as he strapped her into a safety seat. "Now get in the car. Go on, Kayla. I want to be in Georgia by tonight."

"There," Wallace murmured, and pointed to a barely perceptible, dark glow surrounding the car seat as well as the young girl. "Spell trace from the curse placed on them. To be so visible it must have been cast just before this event."

"Can you see earlier?" Ryan asked, but when Wallace passed his hand over the surface it filled with a thick, dark seething smoke.

"More enchantment," the blacksmith said, drawing back his hand. "The spell not only cloaks the children, it forms a barricade around the time of the casting. Whoever cursed these children made sure no one would ever discover who did it, or why."

Wallace didn't have to tell Ryan that such safeguards were almost always invoked to protect a changeling.

"Take me to their home in Florida, and show me the rest of it."

The dark mass cleared, and more images appeared on the mirror. This time it showed young Kayla giving bottles to the baby Tara, and changing her diapers, and bathing her. Ryan noticed the man always hovered somewhere in the background, not helping the girl but never taking his eyes off her.

"Would you take her, Daddy?" Kayla asked as she finished feeding the infant. "I need to do my homework."

The father's mouth thinned. "Then put her in the playpen. She'll only scream if I hold her."

Kayla's eyes swam with tears, but she carried the baby to a high chair, and put some cereal on the tray before she started reading a text book and making notes on a sheet of paper.

The baby, Ryan noted, didn't touch the cereal, but watched her sister as closely as the father had.

Wallace summoned more images that showed the father, drinking himself unconscious, the baby teething, and young Kayla falling asleep in class. He watched the times the children had gone hungry as their father spent his wages on drink instead of food. Somehow Kayla always managed to find something to feed Tara, even if it meant asking a neighbor for a cup of milk, or stealing some fruit from a grove on her way home from school.

Many times he saw Kayla crying in her bed, but always sobbing into her pillow so that the baby in the crib beside it would not wake. He also watched her sneaking money out of her father's wallet while he sat unconscious in his chair, a half-empty bottle still clutched in his hand. Even when she went to the grocer to buy food, Kayla was never alone. Tara nattered happily to her sister from the store cart's baby seat.

"They were inseparable," Wallace said as he regarded the mirror.

"Aye." If the father had still been living, Ryan would have found him and throttled him. "I wonder how she speaks so fondly of that man."

Wallace passed his hand over the crystal. "Answer."

The next image showed an older Kayla struggling to take Tara from a grim-faced police officer.

"You don't understand," the girl had to yell the words to be heard over her screaming sister. "My dad will be home from work soon. I'm babysitting her for him."

The patrolman handed the writhing, squalling child over to a tired-looking older woman. "Honey, your dad is in trouble. He drank too much and crashed his car. Where's your Mama?"

Kayla stared at the floor. "She's dead."

"I'm real sorry about that," the officer said. "You got any other family?" When she shook her head, he sighed. "Well, then, until your Dad gets everything worked out, you girls have to stay at the children's shelter. You'll be safe there, and the ladies who run the place can look after the little one."

Kayla hardened her eyes, and her expression grew calm when she looked up at the man.

"Tara doesn't like strangers. I'm the only one who can take care of her."

Ryan's stomach clenched. "Oh, love."

Wallace brought up another image, this of the two girls arriving home with their father, who had a bandage on his head and looked defeated.

"No, Daddy," Kayla said as her father went to the refrigerator. "You heard what the judge said. No more drinking, or they'll take us away from you for good."

The father knelt before her. "I don't know if I can do that, sweetheart. I can't stop thinking about your Mama. I miss her so much."

Tara, who was in Kayla's arms, leaned out and clasped her tiny hands around the father's neck. "We miss you, Daddy."

Over her head the man's eyes filled with tears, and he embraced both girls.

Ryan and Wallace watched the rest of the images, which showed the girls' childhood gradually improving. The father never lost his gaunt, haunted look, but from that point he stopped drinking and devoted himself to his daughters. The images made it plain, however, that it had been Kayla who had held the family together.

"I understand now the bond between these girls," Wallace said as the last image faded from the crystal. "Kayla had to be both mother and sister to Tara. But why did you wish to see the whole of their childhood?"

It took a moment for Ryan to realize what Wallace had asked. "I think this curse on them protects more than the changeling," he told the smith, and described how the horses had behaved when Kayla had left the barn.

"The nags are very fond of her," Wallace reminded him as he collapsed the crystal, and pocketed it. "Still, she has an uncanny way with them. You think her gifted, too?"

"I think I have never seen every horse in a barn try to break out of their stalls when there was no fire." Ryan rubbed his eyes. "And when I went to Titan to try to calm him, he bit me, hard enough to draw blood." He showed the blacksmith the fading crescents of his horse's teeth embedded on both sides of his right hand. "I have had Titan for five hundred years, since he was gifted to me by my father's stable master. In all that time, he has never so much as nipped me once."

"You already know the truth of it, my liege," Wallace said, and sighed. "No mortal can control a Fae horse, much less an entire herd of them."

"Could a curse account for such a talent?"

Wallace's brow furrowed, but he shook his head. "Not to my knowing. Mask them, yes. Hide their true nature, yes. A curse would likely ensure they produce no children, cloaking their true life energy. But bestow a gift? No."

Ryan saw how Wallace was looking at him. "She is no changeling."

The blacksmith grimaced. "I should hope not. One in camp is enough."

CHAPTER 11

"CAN YOU SET my wife up as the target?" a skinny redneck asked Christine, and grinned at the chunky, scowling brunette beside him. "Come on, baby. It'll be fun, and you know my aim is for shit."

"Well, if I do that, sir," Christine said, "it's only fair to let her have a turn at you. Ladies go first at my game." She regarded the embarrassed woman. "How's your aim, hon?"

That made the skinny husband go still, while the wife grinned and said, "Mighty good, and he forgets I'm part Shawnee."

As the couple tossed their hatchets together, but not at each other, Christine spotted Colm walking with Ryan out of the lane of medieval craft shoppes. It hurt a little now to see other women walk by him, unaware of the amazing face he hid under his boring mortal mask.

Glamour, Christine corrected herself as she turned to award a stuffed dragon prize to the redneck's wife. *I wish I could do that. I'd make myself so beautiful he'd never think of that heart-stealing bitch of a Fae Queen again.*

A sweet sensation raced up her right arm, and Christine

looked over to see Kayla leading a pair of horses in jousting gear toward the arena. She measured the distance between her friend and Ryan, in the process catching Colm's eye. She tilted her head toward the armored horses before she clipped up the CLOSED sign and trotted over to Kayla.

"Hi there, my favorite lunch pal," she said quickly, keeping one eye on Ryan as Colm stopped and gestured in a different direction. "I didn't think there'd be a bout today."

"Gavan and his crew want to practice some new razzle-dazzle for the sunset joust," Kayla told her. "Listen, about lunch."

"You're not hungry, I know, but you can sit there and have some coffee while I stuff my face," Christine told her firmly. "I have the best gossip in camp. Like how I saw turkey leg gal doing the walk of conquest at the lodge this morning. You'll never guess whose room she sashayed out of, either."

Kayla handed the horses off to a member of the arena ground crew before she turned to Christine. "Jannon's?"

Odd how she never suspected Ryan, Christine thought. "It will cost you lunch to find out."

A few minutes later she and Kayla sat in a corner of the dining hall. Christine gossiped and ate two chicken sand-wiches while watching her friend mope over the coffee she'd let grow cold.

"So Gavan is definitely in a better mood today," she told Kayla, and offered her a slice of her apple. "Maybe you should go to his room tonight, and attack him. Turkey leg gal has nothing on you, girlfriend."

"Uh-huh." Kayla absently nibbled on the fruit while watching the nearest window.

"Or I could come with you to visit your favorite

jouster," Christine offered. "I think Big Guy likes me—when he notices me, which is only when you're not around. Maybe I could give him a lap dance while you cry over him. Bet he'd noticed that."

Kayla picked up her cup, took a sip, grimaced and went back to window watching.

"Tell you what. We'll let him pick who he'd like to kiss all over until dawn. The other one has to watch." When that didn't get a rise out of her, Christine added, "Kayla, look, it's Ryan, right behind you, and he's naked."

The other woman whipped her head around before scowling. "Very funny. Excuse me, I have some real shit to shovel." She got up and stalked out.

"So that went well." Christine got up and disposed of her lunch remains.

Colm stood waiting outside the lodge, and came over to Christine as soon as he saw her. "He's at the arena."

"She's at the barn." She checked her watch as she fell into step beside him. "I can keep an eye on her until tonight, but then what'll we do?"

"I'll keep her dancing while you talk to Ryan about the Fae." Colm sounded as harassed as she felt. "Take him away from the feast. Perhaps to your room. Ask as many questions as you can. Pretend you don't understand his answers."

She scowled a little. "He knows I'm not that stupid," she snipped, "and I wanted to dance with you at the feast." She gave a quick wave of her hand. "Never mind."

She turned to walk back to the hatchet toss, caught her foot on a root and fell. Colm grabbed her, but not before her knee hit the ground. A sharp pain erupted at the front of it.

"Damn it all," she muttered.

Colm helped her up and eyed her leg. "You're bleeding."

Before she knew what was happening, he swung her up into his arms and carried her back toward the lodge.

Although Christine tried to see what had happened to her leg, and where he was taking her, in moments he was shouldering his way through a door and some curtains. He set her down on a soft, pillowy surface, where he left her and moved away. As he flicked on the lights Christine turned her head around, and stared in astonishment at the splendor that surrounded them.

The room had been furnished like some fantasy movie, with moss-colored drapes and velvet-upholstered furnishings in every shade of brown. Antique lamps with stained-glass shades glowed in bronze, green and gold panels shaped like leaves. She didn't recognize the dried flowers and herbs hanging from the ceiling, but they must have been what scented the air like a forest. She got hungry again as she counted the huge brass bowls of fruit and nuts, and smiled at the bird feathers arranged in fanciful displays on the walls.

Colm knelt by the settee. "Be still." He gingerly lifted the torn and bloody skirt of her costume, and raised the hem to her thigh. A piece of broken glass protruding from from the skin. "It is not so bad."

"You sound disappointed." She watched him leave her again to retrieve a large red bottle and a small wooden box from a shelf. "This is your room, isn't it?"

"Aye." His black hair took on a reddish glow as he opened the box and took out more herbs. "You expected a pallet and some books?"

"No." She'd never expected to be invited in, not that she'd spoil things by mentioning that. "I just never thought you'd be so…artistic."

"We spend many months here every winter, and I like my comforts." He came back to her, and put his hand just above her knee. "I will remove the glass now. It will hurt, but be still."

She nodded, and winced as he slowly eased the dagger-like glass out of her flesh. Blood streaked down the side of her leg, which he mopped up with a piece of white linen.

He uncorked the red bottle and eyed her. "This will hurt more."

"I'm not a baby," she assured him, and then howled as he poured the dark liquid over her wound. "All right, I am."

"'Tis firewine," Colm told her, his face and body shifting into his Fae form. "It will keep it from festering." He folded the cloth into a long bandage and tied it around her knee before offering her the bottle. "It tastes better than it feels."

Christine snatched the bottle from him, sniffed the opening, and took a healthy swallow. "Mercy," she gasped when she could breathe again, and pushed the firewine back in his hand. "You didn't buy that at the liquor store in town."

"We saved the son of a clan leader, who to this day keeps our cellars stocked." He took a swallow, and sighed. "I should have seen your tumble before it happened. Forgive me, Christine."

"Is your mojo on the fritz?" she teased.

"I was distracted." He checked the bandage and stood, holding out his hand. "Come, show me if you can bear any weight on it."

She placed her fingers over his palm, and gingerly got up, wobbling a little as a flicker of pain danced up her thigh. Her hand moved to his arm as she shifted her weight, and his hand went to her waist to help support her.

"It's not so bad." She looked up as he bent his head to peer at her knee, and their noses bumped. "Sorry."

"I should not have asked you to help me keep Kayla and

Ryan apart," he admitted, and kissed her forehead. "'Twas my responsibility."

"I'm usually not such a ninny." She leaned against him, and the feel of their bodies pressed together made her sigh with pleasure. "But you can play doctor with me any time."

"Brazen wench." His hand crept up her back, splaying over her spine before he tucked her head under his chin. "Even when I know it can come to naught, you tempt me."

She could do with a bit more of that, Christine thought, and turned her face to nuzzle his throat. "I love how you smell. You're Christmas morning, and the first night of carnival, and hot caramel on chocolate ice cream with a great big old cherry on top."

Colm tipped her chin up to look into her eyes. "I am not for you, my lady."

Christine kissed him anyway, and the world upended.

Somehow Colm got her down on the settee again, and covered her with his long, strong body as he kissed her back. His mouth was so hungry that at first all Christine could do was hang on for the ride. Then her own, much-ignored desires woke up and started issuing demands for the hostages of her breasts.

Colm must have heard them, because he freed them from her blouse and cradled them in his clever hands, squeezing them as he wrenched his mouth from hers and attacked. He engulfed one throbbing peak and then the other, rubbing his face over and over against the firm curves.

Between her thighs Christine felt the delicious nudge of his erection, and wanted to shriek with joy. Incapable? Her ass. He was big and hard and ready for her, and her starved little pussy practically gushed with anticipation. Christine covered his face with soft, eager kisses as she reached down between them to give his confined cock a nice, long, slow stroke of her fingers.

Someone hammered on the door before opening it. "Colm, I need–"

Ryan stopped short as he stared at them.

"I need him more," Christine said. "Come back later. Like tomorrow. Or next Tuesday, okay?"

Slowly the weight of Colm lifted, and he covered her damp, heaving breasts with what was left of her blouse. "Forgive me, my liege. How may I serve?"

"Hey." Christine sat up. "I was here first."

Ryan looked from Colm to her and back again. "I will speak to you when you are… I will speak to you another time." He left.

Colm stood with his back to Christine. "This should not have happened." He shifted into his mortal form. "Can you walk?"

"After that? I'm not sure," she snapped. "Get back here and make sure I can't."

He finally looked at her. "You are a lovely woman, and any man in this camp would be proud to have you as his. I cannot take you. No, that is not the truth. I do not want to take you, Christine. I have never cared about you as anything but a woman who shares kinship with me. I never wanted this, but it is more than that. I cannot have you."

She went rigid. "You're a liar."

"I should have told you." His mouth flattened. "We're both Fae. We can't lie to each other."

"That's good, because I hate–" the last word stuck in Christine's throat, and she stared at him in horror.

"Not even when we should," he said sadly.

"Well, then, I apologize for my confusion. Must have been that rod you were trying to rub through my clothes."

She would not cry in front of him. Instead she struggled to her feet and hobbled out of the room. Kayla was right. It was time to leave this place in the dust.

Christine only had one bag to pack, so in ten minutes she was changed and headed out to her truck. She promised herself that this time she wouldn't stop until she reached Miami, where the winters were warm, the clubs were plentiful, and the men supposedly tipped with tens and twenties.

She drove through the gates, stopping at the nearest gas station to fill up her tank for the long haul. She didn't realize tears were streaming down her face until they started plopping on the handle of the gas pump hose.

"I love him." Christine wanted to spit, but it seemed she couldn't even lie to herself. "I love him, and I'm going back, and I'm making him into a liar."

Digging her wallet out of her bag, she wiped her face with her sleeve and went in to pay the attendant, who gave her a ridiculous grin and too much change.

"I gave you a twenty, not a fifty," Christine said as she offered him the extra bills. A big hand clamped on her wrist as the attendant shifted into the weasel-faced biker from the club.

"Why don't we take it out in trade?" Beck Blackstone asked.

HUNDREDS OF COPPER torches blazed against the twilight blue of the sky, and marched along the crowded path leading to Forever Faire's Winter Feast celebration. Three additional dining tents had been erected for the banquet, and special blue-white banners and flags adorned the rest of the encampment. In the jousting arena Gavan pitted himself against targets rather than an opponent, showing off his mastery of the lance as the spectators cheered and applauded. The mortal crew worked every stall, shoppe and performance stage to entertain the visitors, while the Fae presented sparkling white silk roses to every girl child and blue pinwheels to the boys.

Kayla manned the horse pen, leading the gentlest of the Fae's horses over to the fence to be admired and petted by small hands. She also kept an eye on Tara, who stood outside the costume tent handing out soft garlands of flowers and ribbons for the smallest infant girls to wear.

"Let me look after them," Wallace said as he came into

the pen. "Go and have something to eat. If you tell me you are not hungry, I will send Ryan to fetch you."

Kayla took off her squire's hat and perched it on his much bigger head. "I am hungry, thank you. Have you seen Christine?" When he shook his head, she sighed. "She must really be pissed at me."

Wallace grunted. "Then she will have to stand in line."

Kayla went to grab Tara so they could take their break together, but when she reached the costume tent she found another woman manning the garland racks. "Did my sister just leave?"

"She went dancing with one of the guys," the woman said, nodding toward the couples waltzing around the bonfire, where a band was playing ancient tunes on medieval instruments.

Kayla couldn't see her sister, but imagined Jannon was likely the one whirling her around under the stars. She tried not to feel resentful as she went into a banquet tent, as she was honestly glad Tara was enjoying herself for once. Jannon might be an immortal exiled Fae warrior, and way too old for her sister, but even he was a huge improvement on Dirk Blackstone.

After loading up a tray at the buffet, Kayla went to sit at a table of guests dressed up like peasants. She managed to eat and laugh at the same time as the guests, who were experienced Renfaire visitors, told ribald jokes and sang drinking songs. One younger guy kept asking her questions about the joust while sneaking admiring looks at her, which made her feel less like a wallflower. Everyone at the table looked up when a tall shadow fell over Kayla, and she turned to see Ryan in his knightly finery.

"May I have this dance, my lady?" he asked, holding out his arm.

Although the seething fury that had filled her at their

last meeting had dwindled, the relentless tug on her heart hadn't. Even in his human guise, he was irresistible in costume.

"Is this part of the show?" asked one of the guests behind her.

"It would not do to disappoint, my lady," Ryan said, smiling. "Do I ask so much?"

He knew damn well he did. But as Kayla glanced around, every gaze in the vicinity was on them. Kayla stood and tucked her arm through his, and every woman at the nearby tables sighed. He walked her out of the tent and over to the bonfire.

"I'm supposed to be a groom," she said. "I'm pretty sure that back in medieval times magnificent knights didn't ask lowly grooms to dance."

"I remember a few knights who spent much time with their grooms in their arms. They simply indulged in a different form of dance." As they reached the edge of the dancing couples Ryan turned to her. "Take down your hair, and everyone will know I dance with a proper female."

"Who said I was proper?" Kayla clasped one hand in his, and rested the other arm atop his, and laughed as he whirled her directly into the mass of spinning skirts and thumping boots.

"Waltzing is not medieval, you know," Kayla told him after they'd made one circuit of the fire. "It came out in the eighteenth century."

"There were dances like this long before that." Ryan lifted her off her feet and whirled her around three times. "Like this one. I danced it as a boy at a clan wedding."

Kayla almost stumbled trying to keep up with his intricate steps. "You're being awfully nice. What do you want?"

"Only to hold my groom in my arms." The music ended, and as everyone around them stopped and applauded Ryan looked down at her. "I would like to show you something. You may need to make use of it."

She resisted the urge to glance down at his pants. "And what would that be?"

"Another entrance to the caves," Ryan said, his smile evaporating. "I have given our last conversation some thought. Should the Blackstones find a way to enter the camp and attack us, you will be safe there."

Kayla accompanied him from the bonfire into the woods at the south end of the camp. Ryan stopped in front of an enormous black oak, its long, twisted limbs making shadow play against the moonlit sky. She glanced around it but saw nothing but heaps of dead leaves.

"I'm not seeing the way in. Do we need a rake?"

"Only this."

Ryan took her hand, and placed it in a small hollow on the tree's massive trunk. Light flared briefly under Kayla's palm. The great slabs of bark dissolved, revealing an arched opening and crystal steps leading down into the darkness.

"Now that is a very neat trick." Kayla leaned in to see the steps ending several feet below in a stone tunnel illuminated by a pair of flickering lights. "Is someone down there now?"

Ryan drew her back as the lights floated up toward them, glittering blue and white, before drifting back down and disappearing into the tunnel.

"Likely not, but wait here."

"I'm much better at going with than waiting," Kayla said, following him inside the arch and down the steps. The tree trunk portal closed behind them, but as soon as it did two stakes in the walls flanking the tunnel entrance burst into flame. "Motion sensor torches. I'm impressed."

"'Twas none of my doing. The spells down here were

cast by Elias Moffett, the Fae hunter who built the lodge." Ryan peered into the tunnel, and took a step back as the two lights reappeared, swirled in front of him, and zipped off again. "Beckoning lights. They're left behind as guides for those who enter."

"Guides to what?" Kayla asked.

"The caves are extensive, some parts unexplored." He held out his hand. "Stay close to me."

They walked down the tunnel and emerged into a larger chamber with three more passages. The two lights hovered over them before flying into a craggy stone wall and disappearing.

"You're going to need a pickaxe," Kayla said as she went over and touched the stone, which dissolved under her fingers to reveal a fourth passageway. "Or not."

The lights swirled around her, and something tugged at Kayla now. She entered the passage and walked down another short set of hewn crystal steps into a cave filled with mist. The lights grew brighter, and their power reflected off the sparkling walls to illuminate a small spring. Kayla moved to the edge, and felt the steam rising, caressing her face like a lover's sigh. Logically the small space should have smelled dank and mildewed, but instead a spicy-sweet fragrance scented the air, as if the stone were made of fresh-baked gingerbread, and the pool was filled with hot apple cider.

"It's a spring." She bent down to hold her hand over the surface of the water, which felt deliciously warm. She glanced back at Ryan. "How can it be hot at this time of year?"

Before he could answer the lights flew around her head, swirling around her until she swiped at them. The moment her fingers touched the light it stretched into a filament and wrapped around her wrist, and dragged her over the edge into the water.

Kayla splashed furiously before she went under, and more light enveloped her. Her eyes widened as she saw the walls of the pool glowing with thousands of small, polished crystal domes, which began to release colorful bubbles into the water. Ryan jumped in, and put his arm around her as he hauled her up to the surface.

"Wow," she managed to get out before coughing. She pushed soaked hair out of her eyes and looked at the surface of the glowing pool, which bubbled merrily now. "Is this going to boil us alive?"

"If it had been meant to, we would already be stewed." Ryan pulled her over to a recess in one side of the pool that formed a little bench. "I think Elias fashioned this for his wife, Lily. She was mortal, and suffered from joint pain when she was older."

Kayla felt something caress her bottom and glanced down to see bubbles swirling around her hips—her naked hips. "This doesn't feel like a therapy pool, especially with the pretty lights and disappearing clothes feature. It feels more, ah, romantic."

Ryan grinned at her. "Elias did enjoy surprising Lily with gifts of magick. This trysting pool must have been one of them."

"He sounds like he was a loving husband." Kayla wondered what it must have been like for Lily to spend a lifetime with a man who never aged, had superhuman powers and looked like a God. "He gave up his people for her, right? The Fae exiled him for marrying a human woman?"

"Aye."

Stars glimmered in Ryan's hair as he dropped his glamour, and the lights of the pool intensified. Looking into his sapphire eyes made something in Kayla's chest tighten.

"So the magick was meant for Lily," she said.

He swam closer, and water streamed from his shoulders as he braced his hands on either side of her. "But what happens now is you and me, my lovely one."

Kayla curled her hand around his neck, pulling him down until his mouth touched hers. He tasted sweet and spicy from the pool, but when she took the kiss deeper he was all hot, dark hunger. Water splashed as he turned with her, taking her place on the crystal ledge and holding her on his lap. His hands moved under the surface to grip her waist, and he lifted his head to look into her half-closed eyes.

"I will build you a waterfall by my cabin," he murmured, using his lips to caress her jaw and cheek. "But it will pour sunlight over you instead of water, so that you never feel cold again."

Desire had that task in hand. Kayla could feel her softness fluttering and heating even now for him. Watching his face she straddled him, and moved until she could rub her folds over the thick bulb of his cockhead.

"Ryan." She stroked the pad of her thumb over his full lower lip, and shifted until she lodged him where she needed his heavy girth. "This is all the magick I want."

He groaned as she sank down on him, his big hands coming up to cradle her bottom. "Oh, Kayla. 'Tis all the magick we need."

The walls of the cave grew as bright as the pool, painting Kayla and Ryan with their sparkling glints. She held onto his shoulders as she took him in, catching her breath as he stretched and filled her. Rising again, she pulled back her shoulders, offering him her tight-peaked breasts. When he put his mouth on her she thought she might explode, and shook with aching need as he tugged on one nipple and then the other.

The pool grew cooler, or their bodies burned hotter. Kayla couldn't tell which. All she knew was this dance now, her wet, clenching tightness stroking over his hard, swollen length. The pool lapped at her waist, sending rivulets of the water up to caress her mounds and Ryan's cheeks, and when he drew back the enchanted spring took them under and into the crystalline light.

She should be drowning, Kayla thought, not whirling and clutching and taking Ryan as he pumped in and out of her. Then nothing mattered but the building pleasure they created, their slick bodies sliding like silk together. When her climax came she put her mouth to his so he could taste her cry of joy, and drank down his moan as he filled her like the rigid shaft pulsing deep inside her body.

Somehow they ended up on the side of the pool, a cushion of warm sweet water shimmering under them as they held each other.

"I'm sorry I was so hateful to you." She smoothed a wet strand of his pale hair back from his brow. "Christine had a friend come and do a tarot card reading for us. Everything she saw, or said, was pretty bleak. I got a book from one of the vendors, though, and looked up the cards she read for us. Some of what she said was wrong, particularly in regard to you."

"I have been wrong about you as well," he said, and stroked her cheek. "I have never seen Fae horses take to a mortal so completely. When you left after we were together, in the barn, they almost tore it to pieces trying to follow you."

He wasn't asking her to explain, but Kayla knew it was time to tell him. "There's something you need to know about me, but we have to go to the barn so I can show you how it works."

Though the last thing she wanted to do was leave the trysting pool, she couldn't keep this from him any longer. The look on her face must have told him it was serious. Ryan used his magick to dry them off, and as soon as he did their clothes reappeared on their bodies. From the cave they returned to the surface, and walked across the camp hand in hand.

Inside the barn Wallace was putting Sampson in his stall, and smiled at both of them before he left without a word.

"Your blacksmith is a mind-reader," Kayla said as she latched the barn door and went to Titan's stall. "Which brings me to me." She opened the door, and led Titan out into the center of the straw-covered floor. "Horses and I have a strange connection. There's no other way to put it than just telling you: I can talk to them in my head."

Titan looked at her before he heaved a very human-sounding sigh.

Don't give me any attitude tonight, pal, Kayla thought to him.

She left him there and walked up to Ryan. She whispered to him what she was going to do, making him frown, and then she began telling Titan.

Sidestep, and then show him some break dancing.

The big stallion glared at her back before he began stepping sideways. As Ryan stiffened, the big horse abruptly dropped, rolled onto his back, and pawed at the air before righting himself, shaking off the dust, and coming over to Kayla to nuzzle her hands.

"You used no signals," Ryan said, his eyes narrowing. "You wish me to believe that you can command them by thought alone?"

"I can if I have to, but I'd rather ask," she murmured back. "I also know what they're thinking. I can sense when they're in trouble, and sometimes, I can call them to me as far as a couple of miles away." From the doubt still in his eyes Kayla knew she'd have to do better. "Ask Titan a question, something only he would know, and I'll tell you the answer."

Ryan scowled and cocked his head back, but just for a moment. Something must have occurred to him.

"During the Battle of the White Cliffs, someone stopped me in my rage by clouting me, and dragged me from the field to the sea," Ryan said, and reached up to stroke his horse's neck. "I never knew who it was. Does Titan?"

Kayla met the stallion's gaze. *Well?*

I did it. We were losing the battle, and I could not permit him to be butchered by the enemy, or to cut me down in his madness.

The horse shared his memories of the chaotic scene, during which he turned and kicked Ryan in the head, and then used his teeth to drag him by the arm down to the water's edge.

Kayla repeated everything Titan told her, and added, "Your left arm probably had some strange-looking bruises where he grabbed hold of you. Assuming the Fae bruise."

"I wore protectors over my arms, but I remember the dents I later found in them. I thought them made by an enemy's heel, not my mount's teeth." He touched his forehead to the horse's. "Thank you, my friend. On that day, you saved my life."

Is he going to kiss me now? Titan thought to Kayla. *Because I can kick him in the head again, if need be.*

Kayla laughed, which made Ryan turn to her.

"Titan prefers not to be kissed," she said, "but I'm happy

to stand in for him. So what do you think my horse telepathy means?"

"You may have some Fae blood," he told her, looking a lot happier now. "It would explain a great deal that has happened between us. Such as why we are so deeply drawn to each other." He took her hands, and rubbed his thumbs across her knuckles. "Kayla, I have no right to ask you to come to me—to be with me. I know there are matters left unsettled. But when we were in Elias's trysting pool, nothing else mattered. I should like to have that again. As many times as I may before we are parted."

"I think that can be arranged. By the way, Titan would like to take a ride around camp and see all the kids, not that he'll admit it." Kayla went to retrieve Ryan's saddle. "He also likes to take rides at night for any reason," she said as she saddled the stallion. "It ticks him off when you leave him behind and walk."

Ryan swung up into the saddle before bending sideways to haul her to sit in front of him. "You will ride with us," he said, and kissed the side of her neck.

Kayla leaned back against him, feeling completely content. "I can swing that, too."

OLM STOOD SENTINEL with Lawrence by the gates as the last of the visitors left the grounds.

"The children's buffet was a great success," Colm said. "Ryan will be very pleased."

"It was—'twas Christine who suggested the pizza and such," the old man admitted. "She will make a fine mother someday."

Being reminded of the dancer should have twisted like a knife in Colm's gut, but he could still feel her kisses on his face. "So she shall." He walked out to help Lawrence close the gate, and heard soft, muffled sobbing.

"What is that?"

"I will fetch a torch," Lawrence said, and disappeared into his cottage, returning with a rag-wrapped branch, which he set ablaze with a lighter. "Forgive me, but I did not inherit the gift of sparking from my Fae side."

"Stay here," Colm said, and took the torch from him.

He followed the sound to the very border of the faire's boundaries. As he held up the torch, he looked from side to side. Emerging from the gloom was the pale, nude body of a woman in the ditch. Someone had left her there, gagged and bound.

"Lawrence," he shouted over his shoulder. "Go and get some men."

It was a trick, of course. Dark Fae took pleasure in using wounded humans as bait. Colm moved to just inside the outer boundary as he peered, looking for Blackstones hiding in the brush. The light of the torch flickered over the woman's arms, revealing her tattoos.

"Christine."

Without thinking Colm dropped the torch as he emerged from the boundary and ran to her. Something came whizzing at him, and a blade sank into his upper chest, flanked by another that gashed the top of his shoulder before flipping away. Dark Fae rushed out of the shadows, and Colm flung himself on top of Christine to shield her with his body. More blades rammed into his back and legs as the Blackstones crowded around him, jeering and laughing as they stabbed him over and over.

Blood pooled in Colm's mouth as he lifted his head, and saw Ryan and Kayla on Titan. The mortal woman jumped off before Ryan sailed over the boundary, his mount transforming into a motorcycle. More of the Forever Faire warriors did the same, and plowed into the Dark Fae, knocking them aside as Ryan reached Colm and jumped off.

"You would take on the whole clan yourself," his friend muttered as he flung Colm over his shoulder, and scooped up Christine with his other arm. "Selfish of you, brother."

Colm wanted to laugh, but coughed up some blood before he could. Ryan kicked a Blackstone out of his way and mounted the bike while holding both of them tightly.

"Now, Titan," Kayla shouted.

The motorcycle roared back toward the boundary,

clearing it with a high jump before landing as the stallion on the other side. Ryan's men followed as the Blackstones evaporated into the night.

Kayla took Christine down and covered her with her jacket, while Ryan carried Colm into the red cottage. Lawrence spread a blanket before the fire, where Ryan gently lay him, and Colm smiled a little as he heard Gavan cursing outside.

"He hates ambushes," Colm told Ryan, and shifted his gaze as Kayla and Christine came inside. The dancer fell down beside him, her bruised face streaked with tears. "Do not cry, my lady. We prevailed this night."

"You are a crazy man," she told him flatly before she looked at Ryan. "Am I mortal enough to heal him?"

"I cannot say," Ryan told her softly.

"Then get out and I'll try." Christine handed Kayla's jacket back to her, and began unbuckling Colm's belt.

With great effort he found her hands with one of his. "No, my little dancer. I love you for it, but I cannot have you." The room was dimming. He couldn't hold on to her hands. "I love you, Christine."

Though more words were in his mind, his lungs refused to move.

"Colm," she cried, almost too dim to hear. "Colm."

He strained to hear her, but found there was no sound at all. The great, long arc of his life played in front of his eyes. Centuries slipped past, no more than a string of moments, like glittering jewels on a delicate chain. Love and loss, love and loss, and finally love again. As the images faded, peace settled on him.

Until Christine's soft lips brushed his.

Colm had imagined many ways to die. But her mouth on his, catching the last of his life, turned out to be the finest of all.

RYAN LEFT KAYLA with a sobbing Christine, and went out to tell the men that the Blackstones had taken their brother from them.

"Fucking cowards," Gavan shouted.

He mounted Sampson, and drew his blade as he wheeled the big horse around to jump the boundary. Seething, Ryan stepped in front of him.

"This is what they intended, to draw us out in a furious quest for vengeance. I will not give them what they want."

"Then I will," Jannon said. He swung up on his mount. "You can remain here and nursemaid the mortals." The sound of approaching motorcycles made him give Ryan an ugly grin. "It seems they are stupid fucking cowards."

Ryan turned to see a horde of bikers coming at high speed toward the boundary, but as they drew closer his blood froze in his veins.

"Gavan, Jannon, stay where you are. Where is Tara?"

"I was out looking for her when we heard the commotion," Jannon said. "She left the dance suddenly and went off toward the lodge, but I did not find her there."

Gavan stood up in his stirrups. "Ryan, those riders are not the Blackstones. They are– Blind me, they are mortals."

As the first biker reached the outer perimeter of the boundary, he deliberately laid down his bike, tumbling off it to roll in a crumpled heap just outside the protective barrier. More bikers inexplicably did the exact same thing, falling atop the first man. Ryan counted thirty bodies and smashed bikes before he realized what they were doing.

"They're making a bridge of bodies."

Dozens of bikers crashed into the heaps of bodies and machines, growing the pile higher. When the last of the mortals had sacrificed themselves, the shadows beyond them began to seethe.

"Sound the alarm," Ryan shouted as he drew his blade, and looked over at Kayla and Christine. "Get the crew to the lodge. Take them down into the caves."

"You do it," Christine said to Kayla, and pulled on her jacket. She started picking up stones. "I'm staying."

Kayla hesitated.

"Go," he bellowed.

Ryan felt the dark, furious surge of his power well up inside him as he faced the bridge made of dead flesh and twisted metal. If he went berserk, he knew he would build another, out of any living being that crossed his path. As Kayla took off at a run, he glanced over at the red cottage.

"Forgive me, my friend."

More motorcycles came screaming up the road to the gates. But when they reached the piles of bodies and bikes, they used them to launch high into the air, over the reach of the spelled barrier. Blackstones jumped off their bikes and landed on the ground, ringing Ryan and his men. But their motorcycles did not join them. Instead they trans- formed. In the air overhead, dozens of dragons swirled in furious flight. Scaled, orange-eyed, and immense, they swooped down, blasting swaths of fire.

· · · · ·

The End of *Outcast*

· · · · ·

Kayla's story continues in *Hidden (Forever Faire Book Three)*.

For a sneak peek, turn the page.

COPYRIGHT

HIDDEN (BOOK 3)

CHAPTER 1

CELEBRATING THE WINTER with a night of shows and feasting at a traveling Renaissance faire had worn out the residents of Ashdale, Tennessee. As they returned to their homes in the small, remote mountain town, most had to carry their sleeping children inside. Gently removing pinwheels and flower wands still clutched by small hands, they tucked in their little ones, and kissed their dreamy faces. The magick of Forever Faire would have their young sons staging mock sword battles and jousts for days, while their little sisters dressed up as fairy princesses and begged to have ribbons woven into their hair.

Yet as the tired parents sought their own beds, some saw from their windows bursts of light illuminating the sky over the faire grounds. It puzzled some, for Forever Faire was closed now, and the performers had never put on fireworks shows.

"Nothing to worry about, hon," one husband told his wife as he put his arm around her, guiding her back to their bedroom. "They're probably having a little after-party of their own."

Up on the mountain, Kayla Rowe sent the last of the show's ground crew into the basement of the old Moffett Ski Lodge. At least there they could take refuge in the system of tunnels and caverns running beneath the faire grounds.

"Keep everyone down there until I get back," she called.

She rushed upstairs to give the same instructions to the men evacuating the rest of the staff from their rooms. Window panes shook beneath the buffeting wind of the snowstorm surging down the ridge. It howled over the distant clamor of men shouting and steel clashing. But nothing could drown out the unearthly roars that echoed over the roof, or the acrid stench of sulfurous fire.

Running out into the rising storm, Kayla raced to the big barn and flung open both doors. Inside she hurried down the row of horse stalls, unlatching each door as she went. Her hands shook so violently it sometimes took her two or three tries to release the latches. When the horses stepped out they herded around her like concerned friends.

Kayla rarely used her ability to communicate and control horses with her thoughts. When she did she only linked with the mind of one horse. It would take too long to do that now, so she dragged in a deep breath and reached out to the entire herd.

The Blackstones have broken through our boundaries and are attacking Ryan and his men. Their motorcycles have shifted into flying, fire-breathing dragons. We have to get them to safety.

Such violent thoughts would have spooked ordinary horses, sending them skittering back into their stalls. But these massive animals were battle-hardened Fae warhorses and, like their masters, they never ran from a fight.

Grania, a gentle, cream-colored mare who often gave rides to visiting children, knelt down before Kayla so she could mount. Once she was astride, the big mare whickered to the other horses. The herd fell in behind her as she trotted out of the barn. Kayla wound her hands in Grania's bronze-streaked mane and gripped the mare's sides with her legs.

"Go."

The mare took off, and the rest of the herd spread out to flank her, assembling into a charging formation. Kayla kept her head down and held on tightly as they left a hail of dirt clots in their wake. The storm and the battle flung blasts of snow and glowing ash at her. The icy crystals and fiery embers pummeled her face with a thousand tiny, stinging blows. She hardly felt it as they drew closer to the faire's entrance, scanning the melee of brawling warriors to find Ryan Sheridan.

Sparks exploded from a group of seven Dark Fae bikers, all of whom belonged to the Blackstone clan. They surrounded one towering, golden-haired Fae warrior who was snarling and holding them off with swords in both hands. His gilded mane flew as he turned toward Kayla, revealing the darkness that filled his eyes. Blood painted a terrifying mask over his handsome face. Though he could see her, Kayla knew her lover didn't recognize her. Violence turned Ryan into a brutal berserker who would attack and try to kill anyone who came near him. To see him like this nearly tore the heart from her, but until he was seriously wounded or the battle ended, he would remain in this savage state.

Ryan is over there, by the gates, Kayla thought to her mount and the rest of the herd. *Stay away from him.*

She looked around for Tara but saw no sign of her. Her teenage sister had disappeared from the dance after the feast. Since the Blackstones had only attacked the camp to grab her sister, Kayla felt reasonably sure Tara wasn't with them.

Had her sister known the Dark Fae were coming for her? Is that why she'd run off?

If she knew and didn't tell anyone, Kayla thought, *then maybe I should let Ryan send her away.*

A blast of fire came from overhead and smashed into the ground in front of Grania, who reared and launched herself and Kayla over it. The impact of landing on the other side nearly jolted Kayla off the mare. When she righted herself a massive, black-scaled dragon dropped down to snap at her with fanged jaws.

Kayla ducked and locked her hands and ankles around the mare's strong neck. When the dragon tried again to seize her she swung around out of reach under the horse's head. Grania skidded to a stop just beyond Ryan, and Kayla dropped to her feet. Since she sensed the Blackstones were controlling the dragons, who were out of reach in the sky anyway, she directed the herd toward the Dark Fae.

Get to our guys, and help them take down the bikers. As many as you can.

"Hey, Rowe." Breathless, smeared with soot and wearing only a long jacket over her battered body, Christine Marszalek joined her. "Not a good time to be unarmed." The half-Fae former stripper handed her a dagger and hauled her behind a charred tree. "Everyone in the caves?"

"Headed that way. Have you seen Tara?"

Christine shook her head.

Kayla peered around the scorched trunk, and jerked back as a Blackstone snatched at her. The Dark Fae bared his teeth, and then yelped as Grania grabbed him by the collar and dragged him away.

"Son of a bitch," Kayla muttered. She turned to her friend and saw the blood spatter on her face and neck. "You all right?"

"No, girlfriend." Christine's mouth flattened as she glanced at the little red cottage by the gates. "I'm definitely not."

Kayla felt like kicking herself. Inside the cottage lay the body of Colm Longacre, the Fae warrior Christine had fallen for. The blood on her friend belonged to him, and had been spilled when he'd used his own body to shield the half-Fae dancer from the Blackstones. Once Ryan had brought them both back into camp, Colm had refused to let Christine try to heal him. He'd died in her arms.

"I'm sorry," Kayla said, touching her friend's shoulder.

"Sorry will come later." Christine dug in her pocket, taking out three small rocks. "Right now we get some payback."

With a broad swing of her arm she hurled the stones at the battling men. A heartbeat later three Dark Fae bikers dropped to their knees, their hands clapped over their wounded eyes.

Kayla swiped at the sludge of ash and snow dripping down her face, still awed by Christine's Fae ability to precisely target anything.

"You have to teach me how to do that," Kayla said. A waft of air made her look up to see a dragon hovering over the burned tree shielding them. "We've got to find better cover."

"No time."

The other woman broke off a thin, blackened branch and hurled it at the creature just as it opened its jaws. The makeshift spear lodged in the dragon's mouth, and a fireball engulfed its head as it crashed to the ground.

"Down!" Christine yelled, and gave Kayla a hard shove.

Kayla plowed into the ground as fire streamed over her. When the scorching heat passed, she pushed herself up. Christine staggered away, her body engulfed in flames.

"Christine, no!" Kayla screamed.

The other woman lunged at one of the Blackstones. She tackled him and set him on fire as they both collapsed.

Time slowed, and the lashing wind died. The thick snow fall drifted in languid diagonal patterns. The men trying to hack each other to pieces went still, staring at the ghastly tableau of a dead dragon and two bodies burning to death on the ground. Ryan stood over the last of his tormentors, his eyes clearing as he slowly turned his head toward Christine. Except it wasn't Christine. It was a charred husk shaped like a woman, her hands still locked around the thick neck of a dead Dark Fae.

Nausea roiled in Kayla's stomach, and bile rose in her throat, as time snapped back into place.

Christine!

Her friend had sacrificed herself to save Kayla's life.

She wanted to scream, but clutched her chest instead. The air that filled her lungs folded in on itself, becoming impossible to breathe. All of the sounds around her went away, as if they were being plucked one by one from her ears. Something more terrible than the dragons and the Blackstones had come—something she couldn't hear. But she felt it in her bones. Sunlight and wordless whispers filled her head, blending and rising into a song so beautiful and powerful that she thought her heart would shatter.

No blood stains love's blade.

No valiant heart shall be ended.

That which was made is unmade.

That which was broken is mended.

A bomb went off in the center of the battlefield, exploding in all directions.

The blast knocked Kayla back against the tree, where she remained pinned and helpless. Her eyes widened as she saw every Blackstone swept off their feet and hurled over the boundary, along with their dragons. Trees flattened in their wake as they sailed into the air. Where they landed, somewhere miles away from Forever Faire, the horizon exploded with ice and snow. Kayla slid down the tree, blinded by snow and tears.

"Kayla love," Ryan said.

He appeared from nowhere, his sapphire eyes searching hers as he snatched her up from the ground. He wrapped his cloak around her and held her against his chest. He whirled to his men.

"To the lodge," he shouted. "Now!"

Kayla huddled against Ryan as he ran. She wiped her eyes clear but winced as she gulped in some icy air. Her lungs felt bruised, and her head pounded so hard she thought her throbbing skull might explode. But even through the pain, a new smell intruded. It was smoke, but of a different kind. Peering past Ryan's cloak, she saw it: the roof of the old lodge was on fire.

Flames leapt up into the darkened sky as horror gripped her throat.

Where is Tara?

The wind buffeted Ryan, nearly knocking him over, but he managed to keep running. But luckily the same frigid gale hurled sheets of snow at the lodge. In moments the flames snuffed out, and Kayla could have cheered. But no sooner had the fire died than a low groan rolled out from the building. Stressed timbers screeched, then snapped. The center of the lodge collapsed.

CHAPTER 2

THOUGH RYAN TRIED to hang on to her, Kayla squirmed furiously. He barely had time to release her before he dropped her.

"Tara!" she yelled, landing on her feet. "Tara!"

She surged toward the collapsed lodge but Ryan gripped her arm.

"No," he said. "That will do no good."

"She might be in there!"

"If she is, I will find her." He saw Wallace in the distance. "Wallace! Get to the west wing. We'll send the injured there. Make litters to carry them down to the caves."

The blacksmith nodded and hurried off.

"Kayla," Ryan said, though she was struggling to free herself. "Kayla! Concentrate." He shook her a little, and her wild eyes focused on his face. "Call the horses. We'll need them to transport the wounded."

For the first time since the dragons had appeared, Kayla's face calmed. Her thoughts would go directly to their sturdy mounts. If she was in a panic, they would panic too. She visibly calmed herself and closed her eyes.

Jannon Ferguson caught Ryan's other arm, and gestured to show he was going in the back of the lodge. Ryan nodded and motioned for his other men to spread out and do the same.

Kayla opened her eyes.

"I'll search for survivors and get them out," Ryan told her, still gripping her arm. "When I do, I'll send them to Wallace. Go inside and help him."

Kayla shook her head, her hair tossing in the icy wind. "Not when my sister might be in there."

The sound of galloping filled the air, as the show's horses arrived with saddle blankets, coils of rope and other objects clamped in their teeth. But Kayla didn't so much as glance at them. Instead, she stared hard into his eyes.

He would have argued the point, but people were trapped. And the storm was growing worse. He also knew that, because she was much smaller, she might be able to fit into spaces he could not.

"You stay by me," he said over the howling wind, and finally released her.

He trotted toward the lodge, Kayla right behind, and ducked through the skewed front door.

The storm had blown out the gas torches that illuminated the interior of the lodge. In near darkness, Ryan made his way to the back kitchen. He grabbed the strobing emergency flashlight from the wall—triggered by the electricity shutoff—and handed it to Kayla. Quickly he found the main gas valve and shut it off. From there he led Kayla toward the crew's quarters, which were located directly below the collapsed roof. As soon as he encountered the first pile of debris he expanded his senses to reveal any trace of mortal presence. When no life energy or smell of blood hung in the air, he began clearing a path through the rubble.

Kayla aimed the flashlight in different directions, and called out at regular intervals.

"Tara! Shout if you can hear me."

"Is anyone there?" Ryan yelled.

No reply came.

Adrenalin still coursing through his veins, he began shoving aside the biggest sections of debris first. He grabbed anything within reach, picked it up, and heaved it left or right. Though dust rose, a partially intact passage came into view.

"Help!" came a dim voice.

Three mortals were pinned under what appeared to be flooring, a woman and two men.

"Oh thank god," said one of the men, before he started coughing.

Cautiously, Ryan lifted one corner of the thick slab, tilting it upward. When it seemed stable, he pushed it higher.

"Go," he said.

Kayla darted forward and dragged out the woman. The two men managed to get to their feet, then leaned on one another to hobble clear. Ryan pushed the slab to one side, where it landed with a crashing thud.

Kayla knelt next to the woman, who was conscious but grimacing in pain.

"She has a broken foot," Kayla told the two men. Though bruised and cut, they appeared to have escaped major injuries. "Take her outside to the horses. They'll take you to safety. Just go with them."

Carefully, Ryan bent low, scooped up the woman, and slowly set her on her one good foot. He motioned to the two men, who each put a shoulder under arm. When the three limped away Ryan turned back to the debris. He tossed aside a broken door and looked back at Kayla.

"When we find Tara, do I thank your sister for saving us all?"

She blinked. "I don't understand..." But then understanding dawned on her face. "You mean that atomic bomb thing that nearly blew out my ear drums and broke my back?" She started to shake her head, but stopped. "Do changelings have that kind of power?"

"Not to my knowing," Ryan admitted. "Yet we do not know what she can do. If the Blackstones want her so badly that they'd willingly force me to go berserker, then I think yes."

"Well, if my sister saved us, it proves one thing," Kayla said. "She's not evil. You did notice that not one of our guys or horses were hurt when the Dark Fae were defeated."

Ryan didn't trust Tara Rowe, or any changeling for that matter. The teenager's perpetual brooding sullenness had always troubled him, particularly when she used it to manipulate Kayla. He also did not believe that Tara was responsible for driving off the Blackstones. If she had been capable of such power, why had she not used it against Dirk when he'd tried to rape her?

But voicing his doubts would only infuriate Kayla, who saw her teenage sister through the eyes of love. She'd also been the only one to care for and protect the girl since their mother had abandoned them. Their father had only concerned himself with drowning his sorrows with drink.

Kayla and Ryan must have heard it at the same time, since both of them looked past the debris and down the hall. Though he was ahead of her, he moved her directly behind him—with only a second to spare. The wall exploded just beyond the door that Ryan had tossed aside.

Although he braced for another collapse, he needn't have. Jannon shouldered his way through the gap, carrying someone wrapped in a dirty blanket. Plaster dust whitened his coppery mane, and he had bleeding gashes on his arms and hands.

"There are no others," he told Ryan as he carried the body out of the rubble. "The rest got to the tunnels before the roof caved in. But someone saw Tara run into the lodge."

"Tara?" Kayla said, pushing past him.

Jannon knelt and gently laid his small bundle down. He brushed Tara's ash-blonde hair away from her still, pale face.

"Oh my god," Kayla whispered. "*Tara.*"

"She's alive, but only just," Jannon said, his voice strained. "I found her buried so deeply she could not breathe."

"She is a changeling, not mortal," Ryan said, touching Kayla's rigid shoulder. "There is only one way to heal her."

"No one is having healing sex with my sister," she said flatly. She looked up at Jannon. "We have to take her to the hospital."

"This is what he means, Rowe."

Jannon took out a blade and sliced his palm open, and before Kayla could stop him, he held the wound to Tara's lips. Ryan held Kayla back as they both watched Tara's mouth slowly close over Jannon's wound and the color slowly return to her face. When Kayla went still, he released her.

"Dark Fae can be healed by pain and blood as well as mortal life-sharing," he said.

"Perhaps you might then explain my healing," a very familiar voice said.

Ryan spun around, not believing his ears. Was it some trick of the Dark Fae?

"Colm?" he said, not trusting his eyes.

Colm Longacre strode from the shadows.

"What?" Ryan muttered. He had watched his comrade die not an hour before, his lifeblood seeping into the floor of the cottage.

"What evil is this?" Jannon said, as he got up and drew a long dagger. "He may be a Blackstone, my liege, wrapped in glamour. Let me have him."

"No, Ferguson," Colm said. "I am the same cockless, sodding, ponce of a winge you so admire." He cocked a heavy eyebrow. "But if proof is needed, I can recount the events of a night when you went to a certain bawdy house in Paris. You remember, the one where you quickly discovered all the pretty girls under the roof were in fact pretty boys–"

"'Tis Longacre," Jannon told Ryan. "Not even Wallace knows about that."

Ryan closed his eyes briefly as relief flooded through him. But when he opened them to look at his second's calm face, the image of him lying cold on the floor came to him.

"What brought you back from death, brother?"

"I cannot say. I remember much pain, and Christine giving me a kiss before I went into the dark. Then I heard something, and opened my eyes, and find I am well again. More than well." Colm lifted the blood-soaked tatters of his tunic to show his muscular torso, which looked smooth and unmarked. "Dare I say there is not a scratch on me." He dropped the tunic. "But when I came out of Lawrence's cottage, I found the other miracle of my life."

Kayla made a strange sound as she stared past him. "No. It's not possible."

"You're telling me, girlfriend."

A slender woman came to stand beside Colm, who took her hand in his.

"Christine," Kayla whispered.

Ryan peered at her. She had wrapped herself in a cloak, but that didn't disguise the changes in her appearance. Her tattoos had vanished. Her hair, which had been raven-black, now flowed over her shoulders in brown waves streaked with gold. Like Colm, there wasn't a mark on her.

"But I saw you…" Kayla breathed.

"Burn to death? Yeah. I did. Took one of those Blackstone killers with me." The half-Fae woman rested her head against Colm's shoulder. "I don't believe in miracles, but I'm fine with this one."

AYLA KEPT PACE with Jannon as he carried Tara down into the tunnels beneath the lodge. Behind them the howling of the storm finally faded. They emerged into a wide crystal cavern where the show stored their supplies and equipment. All around them was the Forever Faire crew, helped there by the Fae. Most of the mortals had arranged blankets and pallets into beds, and shared food brought down from the lodge. All of the Fae used their glamour, so the humans saw them in their usual mundane appearances.

Kayla walked alongside Jannon and noticed no one seemed to be upset over discovering there were dragons in the world.

"Did someone drop a spell on the crew to keep them from freaking out?" she asked.

"The memories have been mindfogged from them." He ducked down under a low opening in the cave wall. "All they know is the storm and the fire in the lodge." He glanced down at the bundle he was carrying. "'Tis enough."

Kayla followed him inside to find Wallace wrapping a

clean bandage around the shin of the vendor who sold roasted turkey legs. The woman lay on a pair of crates covered with a tarp. Next to her was a large first-aid kit, and Gavan standing by.

"'Twill be sore, lass," Wallace said, "but if you'll rest it, by morning it should be walkable."

Wallace helped her down and handed her off to Gavan, who swung the smiling woman up into his arms and carried her out.

Jannon carefully lowered Tara onto the makeshift exam table.

"I found her buried by the collapse," Jannon said quietly. "I revived her by blood-sharing, and see no wounds, but within there may be something amiss. She does not wake."

Wallace met Kayla's gaze. "Have I your permission to use spell on her, to reveal her injuries?"

When she nodded, he took out a shard of crystal, and placed it in the air above Tara's body. The crystal began to glow as it expanded and flattened into a mirror, in which a Tara made of mist appeared. The blacksmith murmured something under his breath, and tiny lights began to appear in the mist-form.

"She has no internal wounds," Wallace told them, and gestured to the dimmest of the lights, which shimmered in her neck. "It seems she took a hard blow to the base of her skull. That is most likely what keeps her from waking now."

"So she probably has a concussion?" Kayla asked, and when Wallace nodded she placed her hand on her sister's dirty brow. "I should take her to the hospital."

"If she were mortal, I would agree," the smith told her. "But we both know she is not. Some or all of the Black-stones may have survived the night. If so, they will track her to the hospital, and cut their way through the mortals there to get to her."

"God, I hate this," Kayla murmured as she took her sister's thin, limp hand between hers.

"We'll keep her here," Wallace said. "There are plenty of blankets."

With Jannon's help Kayla made a bed for her sister against one wall of the cave. But as she laid down the final blanket, she remembered the horses who'd brought them. Instantly her mind reached out to them. Thankfully, like the sensible creatures they were, they'd sheltered together in the barn. She had just enough time to send them a brief thanks, before Jannon laid Tara down.

Though Jannon stood, Kayla sat next to Tara, but both stared at the teenager's drawn face. As Kayla took her sister's hand again, she remembered Jannon giving his blood to Tara. Her heart sank a little at the thought. Was that proof that Tara was Dark Fae?

"I've heard it said you were too damn stubborn to kill," Wallace said.

Kayla looked up to see Colm and Christine. Wallace grinned as he slapped Colm's shoulder, though his expression changed as he inspected Christine.

"Miss Marszalek, 'tis you, is it not? But I saw you burn, child."

"Yes, I did. Not a way you want to go, either," she told him, and extended her arms. "You remember my tats, right? Every one of them is gone, including the really cool rose on my right butt cheek."

"You'll have to take her word for that," Colm put in. "Or I'll tear off your head."

"Baby, relax. Almost every man in this county has seen my ass. Also, this?" Christine pointed to her head. "Is my natural color. Which I haven't seen since I decided Goth black was more badass back in the ninth grade. Explain that and I'll give you a cookie."

Wallace examined both of them with his crystal mirror, which showed their mist-bodies glowing with so many tiny amber stars they appeared to be made of golden light. Kayla noticed how quiet the smith became as he studied the crystal mirror. He exchanged a strange look with Jannon. Something was wrong. Of that Kayla was sure. But somehow it wasn't scaring them. They were confused. Wallace closed the mirror back into a crystal and pocketed it.

Ryan came in and, though he glanced at her briefly, joined his men and spoke to them in their ancient Fae language. Though Christine raised her eyebrows at Kayla, all she could do was shrug. Jannon shook his head, and Colm raised his hands and dropped them. In the silence, Kayla realized she was squeezing Tara's small hand, and let it go.

"What is it?" Kayla finally asked.

"We cannot say as yet," Wallace said. He turned to Christine. "Will you tell us what you remember before you came back as you are now?"

The dancer nodded. "Kayla and I were attacked by one of the dragons. I tried to put a cork in him, but he blasted us. I pushed her away before the fire hit me. The heat and the pain… It was like being dropped into Hell. I knew I was done for, so I jumped on a Blackstone to take him with me. We fell, and I could feel the fire spreading to him, and burning inside me…" She paused and swallowed hard. "I wasn't afraid to die. I knew it would take the pain away, and I'd be with Colm."

"Aye," he said. He put his arms around her waist and kissed the top of her head. "I was waiting for you. It seemed like eternity."

"Now you know how it feels," she said, her voice unsteady. She sniffed and swiped at her cheek. "Anyway, I let go and went into the dark. It felt good to be there—safe, you know? Then it started lighting up, and I saw this beautiful woman. She reached out to me, and I felt something twine around me like a vine. It might have been, too, because it smelled like flowers. I never felt anything so soft and gentle. I thought the woman was speaking to me, but then I realized she was singing to me, and it was her voice wrapped around me. I went to sleep, and when I opened my eyes Colm was there, wrapping me up. You know the rest."

"Can you tell us what the woman looked like?" Wallace asked.

"I couldn't see her too well," Christine admitted. "I remember she had long golden hair, and wore a gown that sparkled like sunlight on water. When she started singing her hair moved around her face, like it was dancing. Was she Fae?" She looked at all the men. "Why are you giving each other the stink eye?"

"What you may have heard," Ryan said slowly, "was a resurrection song, sung by a spell singer. It is a very rare Fae power that, among other things, can bring the dead back to life."

"How rare?" Kayla asked.

All turned to her, and then to Tara.

"None but royalty possess it," Colm said. "It manifests only once in ten thousand years. But the last princess to possess the gift of spellsong was murdered by Dark Fae."

"Another may have been born since," Ryan said. "As outcasts we cannot know."

"Well, you can rule me out," Kayla said. "I'm human, and I'm also tone-deaf." She glanced down at her sister. "But Tara has a beautiful singing voice."

Just then her younger sister stirred. But when she opened her eyes she looked up at Kayla as if she didn't recognize her.

"Hey," Kayla said, smiling down at the teenager. "Welcome back to the land of the living."

Tara cringed away from her.

"Don't you touch me." She glanced around the room. "Jannon?" He quickly stepped forward. "Jannon, please, help me."

Kayla gaped at her, not quite believing what was happening. But as the Fae warrior rushed to her side, she had no choice but to get up and back away.

"I am here, my lady," Jannon told Tara, holding her hands in his. "You are safe now. Do you not know your sister? This is Kayla, who loves you dearly."

Tara looked over his shoulder, her eyes narrowing as she met Kayla's gaze.

"She doesn't care about me. I heard her say it in the barn. She wishes I was dead."

WHETHER COLM WAS trying to avoid the family drama or not, Christine didn't know. But she saw him silently leave and slipped out to follow him. Tara's accusations had to be absolute bullshit. She knew Kayla would sacrifice herself before hurting a hair on her sister's head. Christine would have stayed behind to point that out, but she wasn't sure how much longer she could resist slapping some sense into the whiny little blonde.

Out in the main cavern, the Fae had doused most of the lights, no doubt to allow the exhausted crew to get some sleep. After making her way carefully across the darkened cave, but seeing no sign of Colm, Christine took the tunnel back to the basement of the lodge.

"Colm?" she called out, but only the faint echo of her voice answered her.

Slowly, she climbed the stairs. The smell of burnt wood lingered, making her wrap her ink-free arms over her churning belly. She'd kept most of the details of what it was like to burn to death from her friends, but that didn't mean she'd forgotten it. Being stung by all the yellow jackets in creation all at once wouldn't have hurt that much. Even though the lodge was as cold as the storm outside, Christine still felt the ghost of searing flames haunting her skin.

"Colm?" She waited and listened. "Come on, is this any way to treat a girl who cheated death with you?"

The wind rattled some windows, but there was no other sound.

Christine wandered in the halls that remained intact, eventually finding herself standing in front of Colm's room. He was probably still down in the tunnels helping the crew. Or maybe he'd made his way back to Ryan to help him deal with the Tara drama, though that made her feel like screaming. They'd been brought back to life, hadn't they? Beaten death, gotten healed, the works. If anyone should be falling to pieces, it was Christine. She'd kissed Colm for only the second time since falling head over heels for the man, and he'd died in her arms. Then she'd been barbecued by a dragon, for crying out loud. Hadn't she earned a little attention?

But as soon as the thought occurred to her, a knot tightened in her chest. She was only half-Fae—and definitely no match for Fae royalty. She shrunk back from the door. Maybe she wasn't enough for Colm. Maybe he was still in love with that bitch Fae queen. That thought got her blood boiling.

"Over my dead body," Christine muttered.

She tried the door and found it open. Inside she didn't bother with the lights, but dropped onto his velvet settee and slid over onto her side, pulling a pillow against her chest. She wanted to cry, but she had no reason. Her body wasn't dead anymore. She had been given a second chance. All the traces of her past had been scoured away. She wasn't black-haired, tatted-up Christine anymore. She'd risen from those ashes and been made new.

"I am not calling myself Phoenix," she told the pillow. "That's just too obvious."

"I am rather fond of Christine, myself," Colm said softly, and came out of the shadows.

She sat up and nearly threw the pillow at his head. "Didn't you hear me yelling for you?"

He struck a match to light one of the oil lamps. "I did." He placed the glass chimney over the flame and turned up the wick until the light illuminated his long garnet hair and copper eyes. "I also knew if I waited you would come to me."

"Happy to know I'm so predictable." Suddenly tired of his oh-so-noble bullshit, Christine surged to her feet. "You told me you loved me. You remember, right before you died on me. Before that, you told me we were just pals and you couldn't offer anything more. So which is it, Colm? Should I find you a daisy so you can pull off petals until it tells you, or what?"

"Before I was cast out, the Queen came to bid me farewell. It was then she bespelled me so that I would always love her and only her."

Christine scowled a moment, processing what he'd said. Then her eyes went wide.

Colm nodded at her expression.

"I never told anyone of it, but 'twas well-known the sort of man I am. I'd never used women for pleasure. I had to share my heart as well as my body. The Queen believed she should be the last lover I ever knew, and saw to it that she would be. By keeping my heart bound to hers, she condemned me to eternal celibacy."

"Never let me anywhere near this selfish harpy," Christine said through clenched teeth. But then a thought occurred to her. "Wait a minute. When we were kissing, right here, before your big just-friends speech, you wanted me. I felt it."

Colm nodded. "I can feel physical desire as any man does. My body responds to it by growing hard and ready. But when I have tried to be with a woman—and I have, Christine, several times—my lack of feeling for her puts a quick end to it."

"All right," she said, relaxing a little. That explained most of her frustrations with him, but not everything. "You told me that Fae can't lie to each other. If you can't love me, then why did you say you did before you died?"

Colm shrugged and slowly shook his head. "I cannot say for certain." He stepped forward and drew her down on the settee beside him. "I've heard it said that as we begin to die, our powers leave us. But so do any spells cast over us. They turn to memories that flash in front of us. In that moment, just before you kissed me, I felt as though I'd been freed of the Queen's enchantment." He took her hand. "Somehow my heart returned to me, and I wanted the last moment of my life spent giving it to you."

Christine smiled slowly. "But you're not dead anymore."

"No." He raised her hand to his lips. "I am come back for you, Christine Marszalek. I am your man now. But if you have no more feelings for me–"

She tackled him and knocked them both to the floor, but Christine didn't care. As he rolled to his back, she flung herself on top of him. Her mouth covered his, devouring him as though she were starving. She tilted her head one way, then the other, straddling his hips.

Colm's big hands pressed against her back. His lips worked furiously as he took every lick, nip and moan and gave them back—with interest. He kissed her deeply, his tongue dueling with hers, as he pressed inward, melding their lips. Breathing no longer seemed important, but feeling Colm's hard chest against her aching nipples did. She groped for the buttons of the shirt he'd borrowed from Lawrence.

Colm took his mouth from hers to roll her onto her back. He grabbed the edges of the shirt and ripped it open, baring his amazing chest and abs. In moments he tore it from his sculpted body and tossed the fabric aside, as she quickly unbuttoned her blouse.

"Tell me if I am too rough."

She arched her back as he cupped her breasts and put his mouth to her throbbing peaks. His tongue worked over her breasts like a hungry cat with two bowls of cream. She sucked in a ragged breath.

"Yes," she hissed, as she wrapped her legs around him and rolled her hips.

Her confined sex rubbed against his bulging erection, which made him groan into her cleavage.

"Next time we'll go slow and be romantic and stuff," she panted, as she unfastened his trousers and curled her fingers around his engorged shaft. "This time I want it right now."

He smiled and muttered something, and their clothes suddenly vanished, leaving them both naked on the floor.

"As my lady commands," he said between breaths.

Christine guided him to her, and drew her knees up so she could take him deep. But the first touch of his dome startled her. He was feverishly hot. As he worked the broad head into her, the heat sank into her softness, and spread through her lower belly. She moaned as the red-hot pressure mounted inside.

Colm's face was that of a tortured man being freed from decades in a dungeon.

"All the silken, rain-washed delight that you are inside,"

he groaned. "Oh, my love. You make me your bed slave now."

She bit his jaw. "Then chain us up together, because I'm most definitely yours."

His thick erection stretched her hungry pussy while he sank into her, inch by slow inch. Using the strength she'd gained from dancing, she massaged him from within. His eyes squeezed shut as her walls tugged on him, luring him ever deeper. With a final push of his hips, his full length was packed inside her—and nearly too much. But Christine knew she had to set him free, and rip off the leash he'd worn so long.

"I know it's been a long time for you," she gasped, and cupped his lean, tight buttocks with her hands. "But if you don't fuck my brains out right this minute, Colm, I'm going to ride you like a stallion that needs breaking."

"Aye," he groaned, his eyes fluttering open. A dark pleasure flickered over his face, as he hoisted her legs up to thrust even deeper. "I want to fuck you. I've spent night after night imagining it. You, under me, crying out my name as I plowed into you. Is this how you want it then, love? Does this stoke your fires as hot and high as mine?"

"Oh, yeah." Christine pressed her heels against his strong back, and writhed as his cock pumped in and out of her. His hips were picking up speed. "Yes, Colm, oh, that's so good. Give it to me, come on, we both need it like that."

She met his powerful thrusts with her own, their bodies growing slick and hot from the duel of their sexes. Lost in the primeval rhythm, Christine found herself suddenly being scooped up in his arms. He reclined beneath her, gripping her hips and urged her down on him.

"Now you may ride until you break me," he said, his voice dropping to a hungry growl.

"I don't ride," Christine breathed. She dragged his hands up to her breasts. "I dance."

She planted her knees, and began moving on him, sliding up his pole and then back down as she worked her hips. As his fingers stroked her nipples she thrust out her breasts, teasing his palms and making them jiggle under his grip. She would have gone on teasing him, too, but something was happening inside her now. The hot girth of his cock stroking her pussy stirred some long-dormant beast inside her. It came awake and took over, bringing her up on her knees so she could fuck herself on his beautiful, thick shaft. Dimly she heard sounds spilling between them as she fucked him harder and faster. Her whimpers harmonized with his deep grunts as a savage clenching began deep inside. He thrust his shaft upward in time, until the climax took her.

Like a wrecking ball of heat and delight and love, it smashed into her and then through her. Colm shouted something and jerked under her as his cock emptied the jets of his come deep inside. Her entire body shuddered, absorbing wave after wave of ecstasy. But as Colm's hips finally stilled, she swayed over his glistening body. Colm eased her down on top of him and stroked her sweat-soaked hair away from her cheeks and brow.

"I hope I came back immortal," she whispered into his skin. "Because that kind of fucking might be lethal." Instantly ashamed for being so crude, she propped her chin up. "Sorry. I'll have to work on my romantic pillow talk. I want to be your lady in every way."

"You are now." He traced the outline of her lips. "Never regret what you say to me. I love that you are bold, and earthy, and speak the truth. I have never known a woman to be so forthright and honest. I never thought I would find you, but I knew it when I first set eyes on you. I felt it.

That is why I behaved like an indifferent ass. And to think I first wasted my heart on a woman who would rather geld me than permit me to love again…" He stopped and shook his head.

"But you did find me, and I'm here, and Colm?" She pressed her lips over the low throb of his heart. "I love you."

"I thought I knew what that meant," he whispered. A tear rolled down his angular cheek. "You teach me, my lady. You teach me."

*W*ITH A SUDDEN jerk, Dirk Blackstone roused from the black ashes of defeat. Though the wind still howled, freezing sleet was coming down. The blinding storm was abating, which meant his cousin was dead or unconscious. He felt stiff scales abrading his face, and pushed himself away from the belly of the wounded dragon beside him. More lay scattered in the drifts around him, along with his unconscious men. Huge stretches of black stain on the white snow indicated that as many as half their mounts had died.

Of one thing Dirk was certain: Ryan Sheridan could not have done this.

He staggered to his feet, and kicked snow in the slack faces of his kinsman until they began to wake. His cousin crawled out from beneath the broken tail of a keening dragon and struggled upright.

"Bloody fucking outcasts," Beck said, pressing his hand to the gash across his tattooed brow. "What was that infernal spell they used against us?"

"That was no spell." Dirk made an abrupt gesture, and

the surviving dragons groaned before they evaporated into muddy gray light and shifted back into motorcycles. "Share the remaining mounts between you. We will need the whores to heal us. Back to the club."

On the ride back to their temporary lair Dirk recalled every detail he could of the battle—one they should have won. In fact they would have except for being driven out by that unknown force. A Fae spell could not have defeated them with such ease. He, his men, and their mounts were used to combat magick. But to wipe a battlefield clean of only Dark Fae required the spell be channeled specifically at them, all at once. Not even his father had that much power.

But she did.

As Dirk parked his bike outside the strip club, he glanced back in the direction of Sheridan's ridiculous faire. If the changeling had awakened, her power might have done this thing. It made his task more complicated, but all the more rewarding. If she was a woman unaware of her potential, he could use that. He squinted at the horizon. He would use that power and her love to bait a trap.

With all that strength under his control, Dirk would rule both Fae kingdoms.

He went into the club to find the dancers sleeping off their latest dose of drugs. He grabbed a serving tray and slammed it against the bar repeatedly until they roused.

"Take off your clothes," he ordered.

He scowled as he counted heads. It seemed three more sluts had slipped away in his absence. He would have to do something about that after the men were healed.

The rest of his kin arrived a few minutes later. They shoved the tables and chairs away, toppling some, as they created enough space for an orgy. Dirk watched them strip and drag the naked dancers to the sticky carpet, where they pinned them under their battered bodies. Beck shared a young brunette with two other men, his brow knitting a little more with every thrust of his cock in the mortal's rump. By the time he jerked his seed onto her back his wounds had mended. He slapped her ass before pulling up his trousers and striding over to the bar.

"So it seems my uncle did not exaggerate," Beck said to Dirk as he poured them both a large measure of bourbon. "This changeling does command powers great enough to level a city. You need healing, Cousin. Shall I bring a pair to your room?"

"Later." Dirk drained his glass. "Did Fallon survive the battle?"

"He did." Beck nodded toward the back of the club. "He cannot shift back to machine form yet, so I told him to hide himself in the trees. We wouldn't want the locals to think their dismal little village overrun by monsters."

Dirk went out the back door and stood in the moonlight to cast the summoning spell. From the forest came a low, deep groan, and trees began falling into the snow as the dragon trudged out onto the back lot.

The largest and strongest of his herd, Fallon towered over Dirk. His black-scaled body bore numerous deep wounds, and half of his talons had been shorn off. Still, his large, vertically-slit green eyes appeared clear and focused, and he stopped the proper distance from Dirk to lower his head in subservience. His smoke-scented breaths puffed through his large nostrils, streaming up like chimney belches in the icy air.

"How is it that so many of your herd died tonight?" Dirk demanded.

Like most of his father's creations, the creature could communicate by thought with his Dark Fae masters.

'Twas a spellsong, my lord. The like of it we have not known

since the clan wars of old. Nothing may stand before it unscathed. Those lost were killed because they were too close to the source. It enveloped them whole.

Blackstones cared nothing for the old legends, particular those of the Fae. Yet even Dirk had heard tales of spellsong being used long ago against the Dark Fae clans.

"How did it kill them?"

They were unmade. 'Tis what happens when an enchanted creature is engulfed by spellsong. Fallon extended a foreleg and spread his stubby digits. *It took from me my talons.*

The blunt ends looked as smooth and unmarked as if they had always been so. Dirk grunted.

"Did you see the singer? Was it the changeling I was sent to capture?"

I cannot tell you, my lord. None of the herd or I caught sight before the blast.

"What fucking use are you, then?" He flung a hand at the trees. "Go back and hide yourself. As soon as you can shift, return."

As you command, my lord. The dragon slowly turned around and limped back toward the forest, hesitated, and then turned around to face Dirk again. *There is more I must say.*

"I am in no mood to chat with you, behemoth." Though that was true, Dirk had never known one of their dragons to volunteer information. "What is it?"

Ten millennia pass before a Fae of royal blood is born with spellsong. Your father hunted the last singer but could never capture her. She died while fleeing him.

Dirk snorted. "That was no ghost that flung us like toys from the camp."

No, my lord. Fallon ducked his head and lumbered off.

As Dirk walked to the courtyard between the club and

seedy motel, Fallon's words began to sink home. Could the changeling possibly be a spell singer?

He stopped in the center of the stained concrete deck. A small, filthy swimming pool had frozen over with a thick layer of leaf-clotted ice. Looking down at his own vague reflection, he pulled off his jacket to reveal the wounds on his arms and chest. With a motion of his hand, he dragged a nearby shadow to the edge of the pool. As he flung it on the ice, he invoked the portal spell. An oval of yellow light appeared and melted into the frozen surface. With a hiss of steam, dark water appeared in its place. Though it churned for a few moments, it quickly stilled. The broad, brutish face of Jarek Blackstone appeared.

"My liege." Dirk went down on one knee before his father. "We carried out a direct attack on the Fae encampment tonight, but we were repelled. I and all of my men were injured, and half our mounts slain."

His father's upper lip curled with contempt. "How like you to kneel before me with news of yet another failure. What was it this time? Did you not drive Sheridan berserk?"

"We did." He looked into his father's small, glittering eyes. For now he would keep silent on the matter of the spell singer. "I believe we might have prevailed, had you sent the additional men I requested."

"How dare you put the blame on me?" his father roared.

Dirk's cheek twitched. "'Tis true and you know it." He slowly rose to his feet. "Now I must have them, or return to you empty-handed. It is your choice, Father. You know how the men talk with their kin. Once the other clan leaders learn of my failure, I wonder what they will make of your obsession with this changeling."

Though Jarek sneered, his gaze shifted sideways. He

was silent for a few moments. Dirk felt sweat roll down his back.

"I will send reinforcements," Jarek finally said, his mouth so tight his lips barely moved. "But beware, my son. This time I do not provide more fodder for Sheridan's sword. I send you death incarnate. If they cannot gorge on fallen Fae, they will feast on more familiar meat."

Dirk watched his father's furious visage melt away. Though some tension released in his shoulders, he didn't leave the pool.

"You must stop eavesdropping, Cousin," Dirk said over his shoulder. "'Twill be the death of you."

"But your sire has such good ideas," Beck said as he guided two dancers over to the pool. "Imagine, suspending him in his creation chamber. Lowering him slowly, inch by inch, to meet his death incarnate. At my leisure it might take days, even weeks."

Dirk enjoyed torture as much as any Blackstone, but sometimes even he found his cousin's incessant musings repulsive.

"Get that storm going again," Dirk ordered. "It might pick off a straggler or two." He took hold of the women and marched them to his room.

JANNON BROUGHT ANOTHER blanket to the pallet he had made for Tara, and carefully draped it over her thin, tense form.

"You did not eat tonight," he said. "Shall I fetch you something? I think there are sandwiches and those bubbling drinks that make me sneeze."

"No, thank you." She turned over to face the crystal-covered wall. "You don't have to babysit me, either."

"Indeed. I was all a-hope I might earn some extra coin." He smiled as she rolled back over to glare at him. "There you are. You think you are angry with me, but you are not. You only wish to arm-wrestle me. I can tell." He stretched out beside the pallet and offered her his hand. "Come. I am not very good at it. You will likely prevail."

"Right. Your bicep is as big around as my waist." She made as if to push his hand away, and then gripped it. "What happens if you break my arm?"

"I say I win, and I am very sorry?" As she giggled he grinned. "That is better. Now I will teach you the trick to arm-wrestling. It is all in how you begin."

Jannon showed her how to pull his hand toward her and move her palm up to steal his leverage. When she pinned his arm to the stone her eyes lit up for a moment—before she scowled and snatched her hand away.

"You let me win," she accused.

"Of course I let you win. If I had won, you would have a broken arm. Now let me show you one pitiless variation I learnt from a tiny girl at the feast. But I warn you, 'tis not for the faint of heart." He held up his smallest finger. "Pinky wrestling."

"Children's games?" said a voice from behind him. Jannon glanced over his shoulder. "How charming," Gavan said, crossing his arms. He stood just inside the small cave, his stern face set in stone. "Have you questioned her?"

Jannon jumped to his feet. "For what purpose? To learn how it feels to be buried alive? Or to be hunted and mauled by Dark Fae scum?" He glanced down at Tara, who looked stricken. But once ignited, his temper grew unruly. He glared at the other Fae. "Come, Gavan. Have you met the cave walls? Permit me to introduce your pretty face to them."

"Someone told the Blackstones that Christine had left the grounds," Gavan said, looking pointedly at Tara. "'Tis well-known this girl had harsh words for our new sister." Gavan took a step toward Tara. "I think 'twas you who told them of her. Do you even know what Blackstones do to helpless women?"

"Yeah. I do."

Tara got up more quickly than Jannon would have guessed she could. She also grabbed his arm to keep him from swinging it at Gavan's head.

"It's no secret I don't like Christine much," she said. "But how do you think I got in touch with the Blackstones? Do you think I have them on speed dial? Oh, that's right, the only phone in this place is in Lawrence's cottage. Which he keeps locked when he's not inside."

"There are other ways," Gavan insisted. "And we know Dark Fae to be loyal only unto their kin."

"I didn't know that," she said, still clutching Jannon's arm with both hands. "Does that apply to changelings too, or is it just a Blackstone thing?" Tara turned to Jannon. "I have got to get a Dark Fae how-to guide. Do you think that lady with the book shoppe sells them?"

Her flippancy pushed back Jannon's outrage a notch. He fixed his gaze on Gavan.

"Tara is not the traitor you seek, brother. I watched her all day, and danced with her at the feast. She did nothing untoward. Look for your traitor elsewhere."

Gavan grunted something in their Fae language and stalked out. Wallace immediately ducked his head in, surveyed them both, and then followed Gavan.

"You shouldn't have lied to him." Tara sat down on the pallet and propped her chin on her knees. "I didn't do it."

"Fae cannot lie to each other." He dropped down to sit beside her. "I did watch you all day. I watch you most every day." He tapped the end of her nose. "I liked the way you put Gavan in his place. It reminded me of your sister."

"Sure. Wonderful, amazing Kayla who doesn't deserve to be treated so nastily by her evil changeling little sister." She extended her arm. "Go ahead, break it. It'll be more fun."

Jannon heard the pain under her snideness and stroked his hand over her narrow back. "Whatever you heard Kayla say in the barn was not in earnest. She was but angry with Ryan. Your sister adores you."

"Maybe she used to, but now she wants me gone. Without me she can have a life, and him." She sagged a little. "I'm so tired, Jan."

"Then permit me to be your pillow." He tugged her down to lie beside him, and wrapped his arms around her. "Close your eyes, my sweet. I will not let anyone harm you."

With a sigh she curled up against him. "I wish."

"WHAT DO YOU mean, she doesn't want to see me?" Kayla demanded.

Though she'd slept like the dead, the news that Tara didn't want to see her had her nerves instantly frazzled.

"Just that," Wallace said. He led her away from the cave where Tara had spent the night with Jannon. "She took a hard blow to the head," he continued, once they were out of earshot. "'Tis not uncommon for such injuries to give one's emotions a stir."

Kayla pressed the heel of her hand to her temple, where her frustration was hammering away.

"She thinks I want her dead, Wallace. I'd like to clear that up, so the kid doesn't run away screaming every time she sees me."

"And you will," he said, "when she is more ready to brace the subject." He gave her shoulder an awkward pat. "Later."

Kayla glanced past him at the cave. She knew Jannon was in there with her sister, but there was nothing she could do about that. At least she knew he would watch her like a stalker. She blew out a breath.

"All right. But tell her I love her, and I hope she's feeling better." Wallace turned to go, but she caught his arm. "Also, remind Jannon that she's nineteen, and innocent." Wallace tried to leave again, but she held him fast and looked him in the eye. "And she'd better stay that way."

Wallace looked confused. "You mean, she has never… But she is a changeling."

Now it was Kayla's turn to look confused. She let go of him.

"Dark Fae consider innocence repugnant," he said. "They become, ah, physically active at a very young age. As much to heal wounds as to know…well, more of the flesh."

"Not Tara," Kayla declared, shaking her head. "She makes driven snow look trampy. Hey, maybe you're all wrong about her, and she's not Dark Fae." Now she patted his shoulder. "Lot to think about, huh?"

Kayla left the confused blacksmith and made a circuit of the cavern, but most of the crew still slept in their makeshift beds. Lawrence was supervising the cooks who were up preparing a hot breakfast over some camp stoves. It looked like they had the meal well in hand. Colm and Christine were off somewhere probably having some much-deserved private time. Since she couldn't talk to Tara that left her with the prospect of heading up to the barn to check on the horses, which she really didn't want to do by herself. A rush of loneliness chilled her, and she looked around for Ryan, who had also disappeared.

Gavan sat by a tunnel entrance whittling a long stick, and she stopped to admire the wise old face he was carving into the wood. "That's pretty neat. I didn't know you were into wood."

"I'm not," he assured her. "It is this or pace, which is annoying the mortals who wish to sleep."

"I understand completely." She sighed. "Have you seen Ryan?"

Gavan pointed his face-stick at the tunnel across from them. "He went to the barn to look after the horses, and bring down more food from the lodge for the mortals."

"Oh, so he's doing my job now." What the Fae warrior had said made her assess their situation again. "We can't keep everyone down here forever. We'll have to get the local people out to their families, and send the others to hotels or something."

"When it is safe to move them, we will," he told her. "They can't keep up the storm forever."

"The Blackstones are doing this?" she asked, astonished.

"It would be quite the coincidence if they were not."

"Right," she said quietly, gaining a newfound appreciation for Fae power.

Kayla thanked him and went up to the basement in time to meet Ryan carrying down a large stack of boxes, covered in snow.

"How are my boys and girls?"

"They're weathering the storm well. I gave them all an extra measure of grain." He set down the boxes and pulled her into his arms. "Good morning."

The kiss he gave her made Kayla's whole body wake up. Where their lips touched, tingling erupted, as though an electric current connected them. His mouth smothered hers as his giant arms folded around her. Her hands found the hard planes of muscle on his back, and held on tight. As he leaned forward, her body curved to his. She pressed close as his delicious heat and scent poured into her. His lips were tender, insistent, and soon moved under her chin, and down the front of her throat.

"I remember this," she whispered, trying to get her breath. He bent her back and nipped at the dip between her collar bones. "And that." Her heartbeat jumped up a few notches.

"You taste of honey and cinnamon," he murmured against her skin. His warm, moist breath washed down her. "The sweet and the spice."

But as though he'd reminded himself of something, he slowly kissed his way back to her mouth. With one last nibble, he finally drew back. He glanced at the boxes.

"Were it not for the delivery," he said, "I would eat you from head to toe."

Kayla gulped, her heart pounding against her rib cage. "I'll remember that too." She let him go, backed up a pace, and took a deep breath. "Good morning."

He smiled a dazzling smile. "Come and help me deliver this."

She picked up one of the boxes, which seemed to weigh more than her.

"What are you feeding our people? Bricks?"

"Canned goods," he said with a chuckle. "Most of the fresh food was frozen by the cold."

He took the box from her and picked up the rest.

The extra food made the cooks happy, and the smell of breakfast soon roused the crew. Kayla and Ryan helped serve the hot meal before joining the other Fae to eat. Jannon came out of the adjoining cave only long enough to retrieve two trays before he returned to Tara.

"Let it be for now," Ryan said, following Kayla's gaze. "A day of rest might sweeten her tongue."

Kayla forced a smile, and made herself finish her food. She'd spent her whole life worrying about Tara. If Jannon was watching over her, maybe she would take a day off and do something else—not that she had much choice.

As it turned out there was a great deal to do. Ryan announced the unhappy news that the show was closing for the rest of the winter, and as soon as safe transportation could be arranged the crew would be sent home. He and the other Fae then took turns escorting small groups of the crew up to the lodge to retrieve clean clothes and other necessities, and brought down some mattresses salvaged from the few rooms left intact. Kayla helped the rest of their people do what they could to make their temporary shelter more comfortable, including setting up portable lavatories and camp showers. Just before the evening meal Lawrence also went around handing out cash in pay envelopes. Kayla saw how thick they were and guessed that Ryan had paid everyone through the end of the season.

After dinner had been served Kayla dressed in several layers and went up to the barn. The driving snow had turned to pellets of ice. But like Wallace had said, the gale was lessening. Even so, she found herself awed once again at the enormity of Fae power, even if it was Dark Fae. As she entered the dimly lit stable, her thoughts turned to Tara, but she forced her sister from her mind. Tara didn't want to see her.

As she passed the stalls, Titan, Sampson, and Grania seemed to sense her unease, their noses snuffling gently under her outstretched hand.

"I miss you too," she said to them.

After she'd bedded everyone down for the night, she made her way back into the lodge. As she shook off the ice from her jacket and boots, she decided to see someone else she missed. She stopped by Colm's room to check on Christine. Her friend answered the door, yawning and wearing a sheet.

"We're fine. Just taking a long nap." As Colm called her

name, Christine glanced over her shoulder before she whispered, "You would not believe this guy in the sack, girlfriend. Holy shit. Best. Sex. Ever."

Kayla was still chuckling when she went back down to the caves. Ryan came to meet her.

"All four-legged Fae are good for the night," she told him. "I think we might want to turn them out for a few hours tomorrow, though. They're getting grouchy and thinking things like 'Why shouldn't I kick out the side of the barn? There's nothing better to do.'"

"Aye, they dislike being separated from us." He plucked a piece of straw from her hair. "If you're not too tired, I'd like to show you something."

CHAPTER 8

KAYLA FOLLOWED RYAN from the big cavern into the first of several tunnels lit by Elias Moffett's magick torches. They flamed to life as they entered at one end, and went dark as soon as they left through the other. The further they went, the more heavily encrusted with multicolored crystals the walls became. It was as if they were walking inside a giant prism. She tentatively reached out her hand. The faceted surfaces of the stones were cool to the touch, but then seemed to absorb some of her body heat as they took on a brighter glow.

"This isn't Tennessee anymore," she said. "Is it?"

"We left the mortal realm behind when we entered the tunnels," Ryan said, and stopped at what appeared to be a dead end. "Now you enter Fae territory."

He removed the crystal he carried in his pocket, and pressed it against the wall. Light danced along the surface, which disappeared to reveal a carved archway.

Kayla took Ryan's hand as they walked through the arch and into a very large, dark void where there seemed to be nothing but the sound of rushing water. With a single step forward Ryan seemed to activate another illumination spell. It raced away from them to light up a long, wide crystal path. It gracefully spiraled around a pretty little cottage made of polished stone walls and a wood beam roof.

"How beautiful," Kayla said. "Did you...build... Oh my god."

The light continued past the cottage and illuminated another, larger house, and another, and then a dozen more. Gardens of moss and crystal appeared around a waterfall that drove an enormous wooden wheel. Sculptures of pale stone stood guard around a shimmering pool. Above the buildings a large orb in the high stone roof glowed into life. Its gentle light revealed a marketplace and—in the distance—an amphitheater and archery range. By the time the entire cavern lit up Kayla could only stare helplessly at the small city.

"This is Tarman," Ryan told her. "One of the first clans to seek haven in America built it, about the same time your pilgrims landed in Plymouth."

Even with her dazzled eyes Kayla could see the city was empty. "Why did they leave?"

"Over time the clan grew, and needed more space to thrive. They went west with the mortal pioneers, and founded another, larger stronghold in New Mexico." He tugged on her hand. "Come. There is nothing to fear."

As she walked along the path through the fairytale scene, Kayla realized why the Fae chose to hide themselves. Countless precious gems framed the windows and doors. Their knobs and hinges looked like solid silver and gold.

"Our presence activates all the amenities," Ryan said, "just as for the original settlers."

A fountain that they passed spouted gaily. Through open doors, Kayla noticed cozy furnishings, delicate linens, and intricate tapestries. Some were so finely worked they belonged in a museum. She wished her sister was here to see them.

"Tara would love this," Kayla said as she admired a wall hanging depicting fairies dancing in the center of an oak grove. She paused for a moment. "Do you think she's going to hate me forever, or just until she needs me again?"

"Perhaps your sister wishes to divert attention from herself," Ryan said, and put his arm around her shoulders to give her a side-hug. "Making these accusations against you may be her ploy to distract us from something she fears we will discover."

"I don't know what to think," Kayla said with a sigh. She looked up at him. "If she's in trouble, or she's made a mistake, I'm not walking away. She *is* my sister."

Ryan kissed her brow. "I know, love."

As they resumed their stroll, she tucked herself against his side.

"Why show me this?" she asked. "I mean, it's beautiful and all, but we can't stay."

His sapphire eyes gazed down at her. "This is not unlike the place where I grew up. I wanted to share it, so you would know more of me."

It struck her then. The glittering surroundings and the glorious Fae warriors—they were of a piece. In the world up above, without his mundane disguise, Ryan stood out like a sun god. Here—she glanced around—he fit.

As they made their way to the waterfall Kayla slowly became aware of something tugging at the back of her mind: a very real and nagging sense of déjà vu. Often she knew what something was before Ryan identified it for her. When he reached out and touched a floating crystal globe, she was half-expecting the sparkling stream of water that cascaded over his palm. She also saw patterns in the carvings and sculptures that made her smile fondly, as if they were old favorites. Yet she had never seen anything like them in her life.

"Will the clan ever come back here?" she asked as she looked inside a white stone entrance to a dwelling built alongside the water fall. The structure, which had been hewn directly from the cavern stone, looked almost painfully plain next to the other homes and buildings in the city.

"Unless they are in need of temporary sanctuary, no." Ryan looked around them. "Elias Moffett laid claim to Tarman when he was cast out and created the lodge above. He gave both to me before he died. No clan would live in an exile's territory. It would be beneath them."

"Like it's not good enough anymore because it's yours?" She frowned. "That's ridiculous."

"That is Fae snobbery," he corrected, and tilted his head. "What is amiss with you? You are like a cat skirting hot coals."

Kayla touched the smooth white stone. "This place… I know this is crazy, but I swear I've seen it, or a place like it, before now." She let her hand fall away. "We used to live in Ashdale when I was a little girl, but I don't remember ever going to a cave, or anything like that." On impulse she walked through the entrance.

"You could not access Tarman, or any Fae stronghold, without a key crystal. It is how we protect our realm from discovery by mortals." Ryan ducked his head as he followed her into the structure. "This was a storage barn, used for grain. There will be naught to see here."

"Maybe, maybe not."

She turned around slowly, letting herself take in the empty chamber. Though the floor was paved in a geometric pattern of blue, green and violet tiles, she noticed some of the tiles in one corner where shaped a little different. She walked over to them. As soon as she gingerly stepped onto them the back wall of the barn dissolved. Beyond was a wide, shadow-filled recess that stretched out of sight.

"Is this more of Elias's secret Lily stuff," Kayla asked, peering in. "Like the trysting pool?"

"No, he never came to Tarman itself. It brought back too many unhappy memories for him." Ryan breathed in deeply, and then chuckled. "You have uncovered a snuggery."

Kayla had never heard the word, but felt her face grow hot. "Is that what I think it is?"

"Likely yes." He took her hand and led her over the threshold, turning to watch the illusion of the barn's wall restore itself. "As you may have noticed, we Fae are a passionate people. That can sometimes be inconvenient when living among a large clan. Often a couple will create a private retreat like this for their more private interludes."

As they walked down the passage torches flickered to life. The walls were adorned with colorful frescos of lovely, ethereal women and strapping, handsome men. When Kayla saw that all the figures were nude, and engaged in very erotic activities, she grinned.

"So a snuggery is a cozy little place where you, ah, snuggle up with your honey?"

"'Tis something like that," Ryan said as they stopped at another dead end.

He pressed his palm against it. The wall vanished, revealing a secret room.

If the Fae city had dazzled Kayla, the sheer size and beauty of the snuggery dumbfounded her. White marble formed an oval floor the size of a football field. Silk-covered lounges, chairs, armoires and tables of inlaid gold dotted the expanse. Above their heads a colossal chandelier made of cascading prisms twinkled as it shed soft light in all the colors of the rainbow. Part of the waterfall had been diverted to shower like rain over a steaming sunken bath. Urns fashioned from dusky jasper and striated agate were filled with fruit, berries and nuts. Two goblets by the largest of the divans were filled with something that looked like champagne. The air trembled with the sound of delicate strings being plucked, and became suffused with the heady scents of a lush garden.

"This isn't little or cozy," Kayla said, awe in her voice. She walked to the center of the snuggery and turned around slowly to take it all in. "Ryan, this is a freaking palace."

"To a human, I suppose it is." He plucked an apple from one of the urns. "Fae palaces are somewhat larger. A small one might fit in the outer cavern." He took a bite of the gleaming fruit and thought for a moment. "If the gardens were kept modest."

"Modest. Right." She wandered over to an elegant cabinet and opened the doors. Shelves of strange objects and racks of skimpy garments filled it. When she picked up a short transparent wand, it curled around her finger. "Magic toys?"

"Of a sort." He nodded at her hand. "That is used by a male to ensure his stamina."

Kayla watched the wand settle around the base of her finger, where it contracted, as it might have on a man's–

"Oh my god."

Ryan laughed. "Implements of pleasure are not solely used by mortals. We enjoy them as well."

"Good for you." She gingerly removed the wand, which straightened as she placed it back on a shelf. She closed the armoire and went over to check out the goblets, which smelled like honeyed champagne. "What is this stuff?"

"Heartwine. You can drink it. Mortals find it pleasant, although it has no effect on them." He joined her, and picked up the other goblet. "But for my kind, it unlocks hidden desires."

"You said I might have a little Fae blood." With a grin she took a swallow, and felt a shimmering warmth spread from her throat to her belly. "Okay, very nice. Now what happens?"

"We discover just what you are, Kayla love." Ryan kept his gaze locked with hers as he drank from his goblet. "And what we two have been hiding in our hearts."

Though she waited, Kayla didn't feel anything beyond the shimmering warmth. Though she was disappointed, she approached one of the lounges that had an odd shape. The cushions rose to a peak in the center, and both ends of the lounge were armless. She walked around it, trying to imagine how two lovers would use it, and felt something tickle the small of her back.

"Do they sit on either side, away from each other?" she murmured as she sat down on one of the lower ends, and rubbed her back against the center peak. "No, that's not it. Come and help me figure this out."

Ryan came to stand at the end, and pulled off his tunic as he watched her. "What does your body tell you?"

"My body is feeling a little smothered." She unbuttoned the front of her shirt, and fanned the dampness between her breasts. "Especially looking at that gorgeous chest of yours." She turned on the lounge so she could lean back against the center bulge and admire her lover's magnificent torso. "You should never wear a shirt. Or pants. That should be like a Fae law or something: Ryan Sheridan must walk around naked forever. What do you think?"

He braced an arm on the back of the lounge as he bent down. His mouth hovered an inch from her lips.

"I think you are feeling the heartwine now, love."

Kayla teased him with the tip of her tongue along his lower lip. "So I'm a little Fae after all."

KISSING RYAN SHERIDAN on a lumpy couch in a secret Fae pleasure palace had to be the most excellent moment of Kayla's life. He had the best mouth for kissing, too: beautiful lips and a clever tongue and oh, the way he tasted. A banquet of bliss. She also couldn't keep her hands off him, but that was his fault for having so many smooth, hard muscles. He was a treasure map of a man, and she wanted to explore all the lovely booty he was keeping from her.

Ryan ended the kiss on a sigh. "More of that, and I will show you how to use this lounge."

"Then kiss me again," she said, rolling over and pulling aside her hair to expose the back of her neck. "Right here. I love feeling your breath on my nape, right before you do– Yeah, like that." As he fastened his mouth on the spot his body pressed her against the rise of the cushions. He lifted her shirt so he could work his way down her spine. As soon as he reached the small of her back she shivered. She reached down to unbutton her jeans.

"Permit me," he murmured. In the next instant they

were both naked. His big hands smoothed over her bottom. "Now this part of you I could happily kiss for a year or more."

Kayla wriggled her hips to rub back against his caressing palms. "It's not as nice as Christine's, but I think it's okay. Oh." He slid his fingers between her buttocks and stroked her rosebud. The warmth in her belly turned to a wild, excited heat. "You are a wicked man, Sheridan."

"Kayla love, you have only begun to know me." He rubbed his thumb against the tight pucker as he kissed the curves around it, and then nuzzled her with his lips. When she tensed, he stopped. "There is nothing to fear. I want only what you are willing to give."

"I know that," she said, and pressed her hot face against the cushions. "I've just never...done anything quite *this* wicked."

He turned her over onto her back, and looked down at her with a decidedly hungry smile. "Would you wish to?"

Now she understood the purpose of the lounge. The prospect of trying it out should have given her pause. This was the only virginity she had left—the last, untouched part of her that she could offer him. Her own curiosity burned inside her, too, wanting him and only him to satisfy it.

"I believe I do," Kayla said at last, and glanced down at the thick swell of his erection. With anyone else she might have been afraid, but this was Ryan, and he'd tie himself up rather than hurt her. "I'll need some help on how to manage it, though."

"My brave lady." He ran his hands from her shoulders to her hips. "Only be open to me, and I will show you the rest."

Kayla wrapped her arms around his neck, holding him tightly for a moment, and then released him. Slowly she turned over, stretching herself out for him. Ryan clasped her hips, lifting and draping her over the rise of the cushions.

The lounge moved under Kayla, puffing up under her cheek to support her head and extending two rests for her arms. As soon as she moved her hands to the latter they filled her palms and stroked her wrists, as if reassuring her. Then Ryan knelt behind her, and pressed his mouth to her sex, his tongue gliding from her slick folds up to the tight opening. Kayla groaned as he lavished slow, wet kisses there, and woke all the slumbering nerves to a throbbing awareness.

The erotic torment soon swept away the last of Kayla's tension, and replaced it with a shivering, wild anticipation. Ryan moved over her, tracing the taut muscles of her back with his lips as he slipped a hand under her to caress her aching breasts.

"Now we begin," he told her, his voice as rough as his touch was gentle. "You have only to be a flower now, and open your sweetness to me."

Kayla nodded, too wound up to speak, and felt his hot, satiny dome poised between her buttocks. She gripped the soft supports under her hands as he fit himself to her little bud, and pressed in. The stretching of her tight opening to accommodate the heavy bulb of him made her take in a quick breath, but the heat of the heartwine spread through her hips to encircle him.

"Oh, Ryan." The sensations of his penetration and her body's response fluttered through her, stroking her insides and teasing her nipples. "More, please. I need more of you, all of you."

"Easy, love. We have time enough to play all night." He worked gently inside her, sinking his hard shaft into her by exquisite degrees. The deeper he pushed, the more his muscles coiled against her. "If only you could feel this, how you glove me. You wrap me in chains of the sweetest softness, Kayla."

She groaned as he filled her to his root, and her whole body shook under him as the pleasurable shock of his possession racked her. "This is…not what I thought. Ryan, you need to, ah, do something."

"Something like this?" He remained planted in her as he filled his hands with her breasts. He tugged on her nipples until she shuddered.

Kayla would have laughed if she wasn't burning up for him. "Think lower."

His slow withdrawal made her bite her lip, and then he plowed back inside, steady and tender all at once. Her bottom tightened as his thrust created a dark, delicious friction. It fed a bite of bliss to her now-ravenous need.

"Again, like that." She lifted her hips, and when he stroked out and in again she gripped him with the strong muscles of her channel, making it his turn to groan. "Oh, yes, like that."

Ryan kissed her shoulder. "You make me forget this is your first time, love." He nipped her ear lobe. "I wish to be gentle."

"That's nice." She squeezed him tighter. "I don't want nice. I want more."

The next thrust he gave her bordered on powerful, and when she released a gasp of relief Ryan uttered a low, guttural laugh.

"You want more, more of me, all of me, then take it." He pumped in and out of her, his shaft gliding against the tight ring of her pucker as he plumbed her channel. "There, my lady, you have me now."

He seized her hips, and her breasts began to bounce with every plunging thrust he made into her bottom. The heartwine seemed to blaze out from her belly to her head and heels and fingertips in continuous flaming ripples. It made her pant through the waves as something huge gathered around Ryan's swelling shaft.

"You are mine now, all of you, every secret, every desire," she heard him say, and felt him put his mouth to her nape again. This time he bit her like a stallion covering a mare, and she shrieked his name as he worked impossibly deep in her and began to jet.

The feel of him pumping her full of his seed rolled through her, setting off her own release—unlike any she'd ever felt. Their bodies seemed to melt together as the earthy, blissful tremors stormed through them, and Kayla lost herself in an endless rain of lightning-bright sensation.

Sometime later Ryan eased his slick shaft from her throbbing rosebud and lifted her from the lounge to carry her over to the sunken bath. He walked down the curving steps into the water, which felt cool and crisp against her overheated skin.

Kayla hid her face against his chest until he murmured her name with a note of concern. "I'm okay. Well, no, I'm not, but since this is better than okay, I'd rather not be." She peeked up at him. "Think we can steal a bottle of that heartwine?"

"Gavan has a case hidden somewhere in the lodge." He gave her a slow grin. "And he still owes me a forfeit for losing the last joust."

Her joke suddenly made her realize something. "We don't really need it." She pressed her hand against his cheek. "You're my heartwine. I get drunk on you every time you touch me." What she wanted to say next almost hurt coming out of her. "We also now know I'm not a hundred percent mortal. Does that change anything?"

"For me, no. For you, it means that you have another

family somewhere. We could try to trace your Fae blood-line, and bring you to your clan." He looked all over her face. "Or you could stay with me."

"Go find my snobby immortal family, who may or may not want to know I exist, or be with the guy I'm crazy about and his cool friends and a herd of adorable magick horses. Hmmm." She tapped her chin. "Not really a tough one. You. I pick you."

Ryan touched his mouth to hers, and they slowly sank under the water.

ITH THE STORM ended, Forever Faire officially closed for the season. Ryan's patrols saw no sign of the Blackstones, so he had Lawrence charter several buses. They transported the crew to their homes or other renfaires where they had secured jobs for the remainder of the winter. Most of the mortals went off gladly, for living in the caves hadn't been very comfortable, but there were a few tearful farewells. Gavan accepted fervent kisses from his latest lover, and then stoically mindfogged the memories of their affair from her. She left smiling and chatting happily about her new job selling roasted turkey legs at a large outdoor fantasy convention in Georgia.

Once the humans had been taken to safety, Ryan summoned his men to the lodge's dining hall to discuss their next move. He first invited the others to put forth their opinions, and was not surprised to learn that nearly all the Fae wished to hunt down the Blackstones.

"If we account for the deathsign we saw by the gates, then they have lost at least ten men," Gavan pointed out.

"Our number is made greater than theirs. We should strike now, before they send for more scum to aid them."

"Aye." Jannon slammed his fist against the table. "We find them, and wipe them clean from this realm, my liege."

The other Fae roared their agreement, until Colm stood and held up his hands.

"No man here wants Dirk Blackstone decorating his blade more than I," he said, his expression calm as he scanned the room. "For what he did to my lady, I would send him in small pieces back to the shadow hell that spawned him. Yet as much as I thirst for vengeance, there will always be Dark Fae, and battles, and time enough to fight them, brothers. We must first protect our women."

Mutters echoed around the room, and as if on cue Kayla joined Ryan.

"I've got the kitchen up and running," she told him, and glanced at the scowling Fae. "Lunch will be canned beef stew, I'm afraid, but I added some stuff to perk it up. Why does everyone look pissed?"

"We decide what next to do," Ryan said, but he saw an opportunity. As he rested his hand on her shoulder, he looked at his men. "I share Colm's view. We vowed to stand guardian to Fae lost in the mortal realm." His gaze shifted to Christine, who sat beside his second. "Our halfling sister has already sacrificed herself once for us. Kayla has also proven her worth."

"Damn straight I have," she murmured.

"And what of the changeling?" Gavan countered, glaring at Jannon. "Do you ask us to risk our lives to stand guardian over her, after she kisses Dirk Blackstone and betrays our sister?"

"Hang on," Christine interjected. Before anyone could speak, she got to her feet. "I was caught because I had a fight with Colm, and left the faire. Blackstone had men all over town, watching for anyone they could use. And they already knew I was half-Fae because they saw me do my thing at the club. So quit blaming the kid. She had nothing to do with it."

Ryan saw Kayla give her friend a grateful look. Since coming up from the caves Tara still refused to speak to her sister, and had taken the room next to Jannon's for her own.

"If that is what you believe happened, sister, then I accept your account." Gavan folded his arms. "But what of her affections for that murdering bastard? Is she to be pardoned for those without question?"

"She kissed him, once," Christine corrected him. "Which was a mistake. I've made plenty of those myself. Are you perfect?" She glared at another man. "Are you?" When the men averted their gazes she planted her hands on her hips. "Your clans kicked you out for screwing up, so you know how it feels to have everyone bail on you. Can't you at least extend the kid a little compassion, instead of judging her unworthy, too?"

"The last woman who sought my favor had me cast out for refusing her," Gavan said. He pushed up out of his chair. "Forgive me for repeating *my* greatest mistake."

Ryan watched his jousting partner stalk out of the lodge.

"I am with Colm," Ryan said, "and this is my decision. On the morrow we will move Forever Faire to Totten Lake. Prepare what you need for the journey."

Kayla turned to him as the men began discussing his decision, some in grumbling tones. "Totten Lake? In Florida?"

Ryan took her hand and led her back into the kitchen. "Aye. It should not be far from where you spent your childhood."

"Tara and I lived about ten miles away from it, in Starling Park." Her expression turned bleak as she crossed to the stove. "The Blackstones know that, too. It's where they started stalking us. When we leave, they'll just follow us back there."

"Not this time, love." He took out his crystal and held it up. "This is our transport. Every Fae stronghold contains a portal that we can open. It is done by joining the power of our crystals. We pass through them as easily as the Blackstones do shadows."

"So there's a city like Tarman where I use to live?" When he nodded she grew thoughtful. "They'll probably think we would never go back to our hometown, so maybe we'll be done with them." She glanced up at him. "Or can they follow us through this portal?"

"No Dark Fae would dare try. Our enchantments would kill them." He pocketed his shard. "When we have all passed through, I will also close the portal so they cannot see where we have travelled."

Kayla went over to stir a pot of stew bubbling on the stove. "I never thought I'd go back home. Is that why you chose Totten Lake? Because of me and Tara?"

He didn't want to upset her, but hiding his other aim would only cause strife between them later.

"There is a very powerful Fae clan some miles north of the place. They are called the Cloudstar, and over time I have had favorable dealings with them. I think they could be your natal clan." When she began to protest he held up his hand. "I know you made your choice last night in the snuggery. I do not mean to persuade you differently. You should meet your kin, however, and they may provide us with some knowledge of your bloodline. I also think the curse placed on Tara would have prevented them from sensing you. It does make you seem entirely mortal."

"I don't know. This whole thing seems like some Pandora's box we shouldn't open." She turned off the burner and slipped into his arms. "What if it's bad, like my great-grandfather was exiled for being a bad guy, or my…never mind."

"Before you stands a berserker, who married a mortal," Ryan said. "After she died with my son, I lost my mind, and tried to slay my entire clan. They had to keep me chained like a wild animal until I emerged from the madness. I have not changed overmuch since that terrible time. Defending you, I tore the arm off one Dark Fae, and tried to beat another to death with it."

"That isn't you," she insisted, her expression turning stubborn.

"But it is part of me, my lovely one." He bent his head to press his brow to hers. "You have faced the nightmare I carry within me. Whatever your Fae kin did to cause you to be raised in the mortal realm, it cannot be worse."

AT MIDNIGHT COLM rose from his bed to dress, taking care to be silent so he didn't wake Christine. She mumbled something and pulled his pillow against her naked breasts, her lips curving as she drifted off again. Standing over her in the dark made his heart swell, for while she stole his blankets and spread out like a little star fish, she also welcomed him with kisses each night, and would not rest until they found their pleasure in each other.

"I know how much you like to watch me sleep," her husky voice said suddenly. "But if you don't get a move on, you'll be late to the secret meeting I'm not supposed to know about."

He knelt down as she turned to face him, and kissed her soft lips. "I should have insisted you be part of it."

"So invite me to the next one. I can take notes in a short skirt, and flash you when the others aren't looking." She swallowed a yawn. "I would mention to Ryan that Gavan and Jannon are about ready to rumble. You need to deal with that as well as Tara, or we're going to lose one of them." She hugged him. "Now go."

Colm made his way from the lodge to the barn, where Ryan, Wallace and Gavan stood waiting. He glanced down at the horse stalls and saw into the empty tack room. "What of Jannon?"

"He can no longer be trusted," Gavan said, all his anger gone, and only the shimmer of regret in his eyes. "Ryan bid me play the thorn in his side, so that we might test his loyalty. He no longer stands with us. The changeling has him fast in her grip."

"I cannot agree," Colm said, looking at Ryan. "We all know Jan has feelings for Tara. You know his heart to be unwavering. Perhaps you have mistook love for possession."

"She uses him like a shield against the rest of us," Wallace said. "I read him while we were in the caves. There is spell trace of the curse on him now. It spreads, brother. I think her capable of infecting anyone she wishes to do her bidding."

"We have not yet fathomed the nature of this curse," Colm said. "It is likely dark magick, but we have not proven that." He studied the other men's grim expressions. "Never tell me you mean to do this girl harm."

"If she is Dark Fae, going through the portal will kill her," Ryan said, as he dragged a hand over the back of his neck. "Since we believe her to be, I cannot permit her to attempt the journey with us."

"I must disagree now, my liege," Wallace put in. "The enchantment that protects her is absolute. It will cloak her when she passes through the portal, which will respond to her as we have. It will read her as mortal."

"There is a solution that will spare all of us grief," Gavan said. "We keep her to the last, and send her for something left behind that is needed. When she goes to fetch it, the rest of us step through and close the portal before she returns."

"Indeed. And how do you propose to prevent my lady from returning through the portal to retrieve her sister?" When Gavan shrugged Ryan turned away, and went to Titan's stall to rub his stallion's questing nose. "We will take the changeling with us to Totten Lake, and there we will find the means to break this curse."

"The Cloudstar have some very powerful mages among their kin," Wallace said. "They have devoted themselves to spell practice since the days of the clan wars. But they are not particularly fond of outsiders."

"Devalan—one of their own—fought beside me at the White Cliffs," Ryan said. "He yet owes me a life-debt. Gavan, you will attend to Jannon. Assure that the changeling only holds him under her sway, and does no more with him. Colm, I will need you to scour the records available in Starling Park, where the girls were raised. I want to know what happened to their mother, and anything more that seems suspicious."

Wallace frowned and looked over at the tack room. "Did you hear something?"

Colm strode back to see one of the shutters outside the window moving and creaking as the wind buffeted it. He glanced down at the floor, and thought he saw a bug creeping under the straw. He stomped on it before he rejoined his brothers.

"Not a word to Kayla," Ryan said before they made their way back to the lodge. "I think she is no longer under her sister's control, but until we are certain of that, we must keep this from her."

THE BITTER COLD of the night should have numbed Tara, but all she could do was burn inside as she watched Ryan and the other men leave the barn for the lodge. Her sister might adore the master of Forever Faire, but Tara could see now what he was under his handsome mask. He pretended that he cared for Kayla while he lied to her and used her for sex. Now he was deceiving his own men with his schemes and all this talk about her corrupting Jannon. He didn't want her to have any friends, or lovers. He wanted to hurt her, maybe even kill her, and he'd make everyone believe he was trying to help her when he did.

"But now I know what you're going to do," Tara muttered as she trudged around the back of the lodge, where she could slip inside unnoticed. "If you can't get me into the portal, then you can't take me anywhere to break my curse, or my neck, or whatever you really want to do."

She followed the back hall to the room she'd moved into, but stopped short when she saw Jannon sitting outside it. His patient expression tugged at her heart. It didn't matter to him if she stayed away all night. He'd be sitting in the same spot come morning. Ryan was wrong about him, too. She hadn't done anything to make him her slave or whatever. Jannon actually cared about her.

Tara walked up to the Fae warrior, who slowly rose to his feet. "What are you doing?"

"Waiting for you." He lifted his hand to her face, and frowned when she flinched away. "What is amiss? Why is there snow in your hair?"

Of course that was the first thing he'd notice. "God, why don't you just for once leave me alone?" she snapped, and then went still as Jannon's eyes blanked. He turned around, disappearing into his room.

Tara put a hand to her mouth. Jannon had done exactly what she said. As she stared at the closed door, she nervously twined a lock of her hair around her finger. Since coming out of the caves he'd brought her meals and clean clothes and sat with her when she was lonely… But that was only because he loved her.

Wasn't it?

Tara went into her room, shut the door, and flopped on the bed. She pressed her hands over her face. Her eyes burned and exhaustion dragged at her bones, but there was nothing she could do about it. Since that day by the lake she hadn't been able to sleep more than a few minutes without the nightmares coming for her.

The one she dreamt most often was the first that had come to her in childhood, the one about the battered, beautiful lady in chains. She'd had long, white-blond hair, and eyes the color of the sea. She was imprisoned some-where awful, and lay huddled in a corner of a filthy cell. Her pretty white dress was ripped and stained. The only time the lady left was when a huge thug tore off her manacles and dragged her out. He always tossed her back in and chained her again before leaving.

The lady wept all the time at first, holding herself and rocking back and forth, but eventually she stopped and lay unmoving on the stone floor. She grew thinner and dirtier, and then something changed. She puked into her toilet bucket for days. The guard brought her more food, and she stopped vomiting. No one dragged her out anymore as her belly began to swell.

One night the lady managed to lift a blade from one of the thugs. She passed her hand over it, making it glow. The shape of the blade changed, and she used it to pick the locks on her manacles. But rather than remove them, she left them around her wrists and ankles so it would look like she remained shackled. The next time the thug delivered her meal, she stabbed him and ran.

The nightmare always ended the same way, too. They brought the lady back to the cell with so many terrible wounds Tara knew she couldn't survive them. Then a big, dark man came in with the blade she'd bespelled, and used it to cut open her belly.

The woman had opened her swollen eyes to look at the baby girl he wrenched out of her womb. She died smiling at her wailing child, and Tara woke up covered in sweat, her own scream locked in her throat.

Something nudged her foot, and she sat up quickly. There was no one in the room, only the oil lamp she'd left lit. She glanced down and saw a black, bottomless pit beside the bed, and scrambled backward as Dirk Blackstone looked out of it at her.

"I've been waiting for you, little sister," he said, and held out his hand. "Come to me now. You and I must talk."

Tara jumped over the pit and fled the room, running

down to the basement, where she stood on the threshold of the tunnel to the caves.

"I can't follow you there," Dirk told her, standing in a shadowy corner. "But I can come into your dreams again. You liked it when I did, back in your little house." Part of the darkness around him stretched across the floor toward her. "All those nights you went to bed early, hoping I would come. I'm here now, little sister. Do you want kisses, or caresses, or something more satisfying?"

The air around her turned to icy ink, and she shoved herself out of the darkness and into the light.

The single bulb overhead flickered as she stumbled up the stairs and opened her mouth to call to Jannon, but something tightened around her throat like a fist. She clawed the writhing shadow from her neck and flung it from her as she ran for her old room, only to find a small mountain of broken wood and plaster blocking the hall.

"Tara?" Jannon called from the back of the lodge. "Where are you?"

Pale light filtered through a broken window, and the tiny shadows cast by the rubble began to skitter around her feet like cockroaches.

"No," she whispered.

She rushed into the kitchen, where all of the lights had been turned off. Where there was no light, there were no shadows. She would be safe here for now, and have time to think of what to do next.

Jannon walked through the dining room and out of the lodge, still shouting her name, his voice growing more distant. Soon he would be too far away to hear her answer him.

Tara groped her way to a chair and sat down. She trembled so violently that the table legs vibrated on the wood floor. She hadn't done anything really bad so far. There was still time to take it back. She could tell Kayla the truth about her and Dirk, and how he'd convinced her that he only wanted to help them. It would be harder to admit what had actually happened down by the lake, but that wasn't her fault, either. She couldn't help how she'd been born, or the way the clan had planned to use her. She'd only been a tiny baby.

Kayla loved her. Kayla would save her. She always did.

Tara smelled icy sweat, and knocked the kitchen chair over scrambling out of it. She tried to find the back door to the kitchen, but something slithered across her back and around her waist. It dragged her down to the floor and back through the door into an inky pool.

Shadows engulfed her, filling her mouth, nose and eyes. They seeped into her ears and enveloped her body, encasing her in the black. She couldn't move or breathe, and only when she thought her lungs would burst did the darkness release her. It expanded around her, becoming the universe.

"We meet again, little sister."

Tara spun around to find Dirk standing just behind her. "What are you doing here?"

"Welcoming you back into my arms." He reached for her, his eyes glittering as he watched her cower away. "What is the matter? Don't you love me anymore?"

She had loved him, from the first time he'd come to her in her dreams. He'd held her and stroked her hair, and promised to make her his someday. She could still remember the icy touch of his lips on her brow. Then there were the other dreams, the dark and sexy ones, where they'd done more than hold each other and kiss.

Dirk Blackstone had been her first love, up until the moment by the lake, when he'd released her, and whispered the ugly truth to her.

"I don't love you anymore," she shouted. "You're sick. You tried to rape me."

"You needed me to force you," Dirk said, and circled around her slowly. "'Twas the only way to awaken you, little sister. Now you will explain to me why you have not provided me with the means to defeat Sheridan and his men."

She hugged herself. "I can't do anything about them, I told you. And stop calling me that."

"But my sister is who you are, Tara Blackstone." Dirk reached out to caress her cheek. "I awakened our blood bond in you, that day by the lake. You became disgusted only when I told you we share the same sire. Still, you agreed to help me overthrow our father so we may take control of the clan."

Tara swallowed a mouthful of bile. "I can't break the curse. I tried everything you said. Kayla still believes she's a mortal. She even thinks I was the one who blasted you during the battle. They all do."

His enormous hand wrapped around her throat. "Did you confess your sins to her? Is that what awakened her power?"

"No. I swear–" She clawed at his hand as he cut off her air. When he allowed her to gulp down a breath, she wheezed, "I don't know what made her do that. Neither does she."

Dirk backhanded her. "Then you are useless to me, except as my whore." He began dragging her deeper into the shadows.

"Wait. I'm not strong enough to break the curse, but you are." Tara met his gaze, and told him the rest. "That's what you really want, isn't it? To get her away from the Fae before they find out what she is."

His muddy eyes glinted with interest. "So, you are a

Blackstone after all. I know this offer comes at a price. What do you want?"

"My freedom. You never touch me again." She used the back of her hand to wipe away the blood trickling from the corner of her mouth. "If I do this for you, I want Jannon Ferguson as my slave, to make sure you don't break your promise."

Dirk dragged her up against him, and licked the blood from her hand. "You fancy yourself in love with that drunken fool? 'Tis the enchantment we placed on you. You are a changeling, made to enslave the Fae to you. When you are brought back into the clan, the spell will end, and your Jannon will return to his senses."

The bottom fell out of the world, and Tara saw herself clearly for the first time. "When he does, you can chain him in my mother's cell."

CHAPTER 13

IN THE MORNING Kayla rode with Ryan on Titan up to his cabin, where he collected some clothes and books to take on the journey. While he packed she wandered around the cabin, feeling sorry for the first time that she would be leaving Ashdale.

"Do you ever wish you lived in a place like Tarman, instead of having to travel all the time?" she asked him.

"No, but I have grown accustomed to life on the road." Ryan took a heavy cloak from a hook on the wall and folded it. "Our winters here were as close to a home as we should ever have."

She put down a snow globe she was shaking and eyed him. "Were? You're coming back next winter."

"With the lodge in ruins, and the Dark Fae made aware of our annual presence, 'tis no longer safe." He sat on the edge of his big bed and held out his hand to her. "There are other places, Kayla. Other homes we might build."

She went to him, threading her fingers through his shining blonde hair. "You're going to miss this place even more than I will."

"But thanks to you, my last season here I shall remember quite fondly." He hooked his fingers in the front of her jeans, and tugged her between his thighs. "And this morning, if you are willing."

"I'm willing to go into the scary crystal portal that we hope will magically transport me to Florida without spreading my atoms across another dimension," she reminded him. "So anything you might want to do to put that off for another hour is fine with me."

"I do wish to try something." He brought her hands up to kiss her fingertips, and then placed them against his chest. "Close your eyes. Imagine the tunic I wear now removed from me."

She smiled. "Why don't I just take it off?"

"Humor me, love." He put his hands on either side of her head. "You want my tunic gone from me. See it in your mind, and feel it in your fingers. Ah."

Kayla felt his chest under her hands and opened her eyes. His tunic lay in shreds around his waist. "Uh-oh. What did you do?"

"'Twas not me." He surveyed the tatters with a rueful grin. "You are most definitely of Fae blood, but your control needs work."

"Stand up and let me give it another shot."

She repeated the exercise, placing her hands on his hips. This time instead of imagining herself tearing his clothes off she thought of his faded jeans unfastening and sliding down his legs. As soon as she felt the heavy denim moved from under her palms she looked to see his jeans in a puddle around his feet—a real puddle of fabric turned to a denim-colored liquid.

"You might want to unpack some of your clothes," she said. She bent down to touch the liquid, which turned back into his jeans. She snatched her hand back. "What was that?"

Ryan stepped out of the jeans and picked them up from the floor. "You unmade them, and remade them." His brows drew together. "By touch."

What he said brought back some of the words Kayla had heard, just before the blast that had ended the battle with the Blackstones. *That which was made is unmade. That which was broken is mended.*

"Is this a way every Fae can undress?" she asked.

"Yes, with proper focus. It is a wordless thought-spell." He glanced down at her clothes, which abruptly vanished, and pointed to them where they sat in a neatly-folded pile on the table. "With practice you can do it faster."

She nodded. "But my clothes didn't melt or shred, and I'm guessing that never happens when you do it."

Ryan drew her onto the bed, and stretched out beside her. "When Fae and mortals have children, they are born with abilities and powers different from ours. Some, like Lawrence, come into the world with but one gift. I thought you like him, but you prove me wrong again. When we reach Florida, we must learn what more you can do—and how you may control it."

"So I might be a halfling, like Christine." Kayla rolled onto her back. "I've hated my mother for so long I can't stand to say this, but now I wish I knew more about her." She turned her head toward him. "She took off when Tara was just a baby, and I was in kindergarten. Dad never took pictures, and I can't even remember what she looked like."

"If your mother was Fae, and cast out for marrying your father, the Cloudstar may know of her." He shifted over her, propping himself on his elbows as he studied her face. "We should dress and go back. There is much to do."

She made a vague sound of agreement as she twined

her legs around his. "I still need to get some stuff from the barn for the horses."

His features grew taut when he felt her hand move down between their bodies. "Colm is likely wondering what we do here so long."

"Christine isn't." She smiled up at him as she took hold of his straining shaft. "She'll tell him." Then she stroked her fist up and down as Ryan sucked in a breath. "By the way, Titan knows exactly what we're doing."

"Tell my damned horse to keep his thoughts out of our bed."

Kayla guided the full, throbbing bulb of his cockhead to the center of her folds.

"So wet and hot," he murmured. Then his eyes narrowed. "You were thinking of this before I said anything about clothes."

"I have a couple fond memories myself."

His sapphire eyes glittered. "Then let us make one more," he said, and forged into her.

As his girth spread her and the sweet pressure filled her, her eyelids fluttered. Impossibly, each time was better than the last. Ryan lowered his head to hers, kissed her mouth, and began to stroke in and out.

Kayla held him, returning his kisses as she rode the long, languorous thrusts. It was sweet and a little sad to know this would be the last time they would make love in this bed. She wished she could pack up the entire cabin, and push it through the portal so they could hide it away in some oak grove. The pleasure palace in Tarman had been thrilling, but the cabin was more like home.

Ryan moved onto his side, and draped her thigh over his as he pumped harder and deeper into her softness. "Look at me, love." He slid his hand down to caress the hard nub of her clit. "This is my home, inside you. I'm going to fill it with pleasure and lust and love, and me. As much of me as you will have."

The sudden earnestness in his voice tightened her throat. "As much as you can give me," she said, and he plunged deep.

Her back arched at the sudden penetration. As his shaft pistoned, his fingers rubbed her swollen clit. As much as she wanted the moment to last, her pussy clenched frantically around him. Kayla came with a cry, shuddering against him as he kept pumping into the core of her delight. As she felt a second, softer climax rising in her, Ryan clutched her against him. He shook as he spurt one silken stream after another into her.

Kissing Ryan through the tremors afterward kept Kayla occupied until she heard Titan's grumbling thoughts. "Your damned horse says it's almost noon. We'd better get back before Colm sends a search party."

"When we arrive at Totten Lake," Ryan said, drawing a heart shape around her nipple, "I want a week in bed with you."

"Only a week?" she teased. "I was thinking more like a lifetime."

His expression sobered. "That might be longer than you think."

"Oh, I hope so." Kayla pressed his hand over her breast. "See, I've been waiting for you all my life. I'm ready to start a new one—and if it lasts forever, that may be just long enough."

THAT NIGHT KAYLA carried the last of her grooming gear from the barn down to the caves, where Colm and Wallace had the horses penned. She was relieved to see Tara near the far edge of the portal, which was already open. Colm and Christine stood at the entrance.

Ryan and his men had used their crystals in unison. A near-blinding beam of light had burst from them, opening what had seemed to be a wall. But as the energy faded, a towering arch was revealed, inscribed with Fae language. Between the inscriptions thousands of triangular blue diamonds twinkled.

Kayla stowed the gear out of the way.

"Those pretties are journey stones," Colm was telling Christine. "The rarest of all Fae gems, and unknown in the mortal realm. After the territories were settled, all of the clans agreed to use their stockpiles to create the portals. They permit us to move entire cities without being detected by anyone above ground."

As interesting as the explanation was, this was the first

time Kayla had seen Tara since she'd woken up after her concussion. Ryan had sent Jannon and Gavan through the portal first, so maybe now was a good time to talk to her—when she couldn't hide behind Jannon.

But just as Kayla passed Colm and Christine, Gavan emerged from the portal in a burst of blue light.

"'Tis a bit musty," he said, as though he'd just stepped off a bus, "but I set Jan to opening the ventilation shafts. Once we work some comfort spells, it shall be most habitable." The Fae warrior handed Christine and Kayla some large, fragrant white flowers. "The magnolia are in bloom." He held onto the third cluster of blooms as he looked around the cave. He spotted Tara and approached her, holding them out.

"These are for you, Miss Rowe." He offered her the magnolias, and bowed. "I hope you will forgive me for my ill-temper. It was unkind to hurl such accusations at you."

Though Tara glanced left and right as though she might bolt, she finally took the flowers.

Tension released in Kayla's chest, and she and Christine exchanged a little smile. Maybe it was a new beginning after all, not just in Totten Lake, but for all of them.

Tara held the flowers to her nose, and nearly dropped them as she groaned. "Oh, I can't believe it—I left my sewing box upstairs. It's the one my Dad gave me." She shook the bouquet a little. "With white flowers on the lid." Her shoulders slumped. "I guess it's too late to go and get it."

"No, it's not," Kayla said. She glanced at Gavan, who nodded. "Come on. I'll go with you."

Having this time alone with her sister made Kayla determined not to waste a second of it. "You don't feel nervous being alone with me?" she said, as they climbed the stairs in the basement. "I am the sister who wants you dead, after all."

"Jannon told me you were mad at Ryan that day, and what you said was sarcastic." Tara ducked her head. "I'm sorry about the way I acted. I don't know why I thought you were serious."

"You took a hard blow on the head during the lodge collapse," Kayla told her. She followed her into the hall-ways and then the room next to Jannon's. "Anyway, I'm glad you're feeling better, especially toward me."

"Honestly, I don't feel much of anything."

Tara lit an oil lamp and put it beside the bed, and sat down to look through the night stand drawers.

Kayla cocked her head at her. Why did she sound like she was going to her own funeral?

"Maybe we should have Wallace take another look at you."

"I don't mean physically," Tara said and smiled. "I'm pretty good at faking emotions, but I haven't felt any for a while now. Not since that day with Dirk. That was a big reality check."

"Honey, I know he traumatized you, but you have to let it go." Kayla went over to sit beside her sister, and took her hand. "We're going home, where we'll be safe from the Blackstones. We're going to get help with this curse, too. Everything will be okay if we stick together, and love each other."

"That's just it, Kayla," Tara said, squeezing her hand. "Everything is not okay. You don't love me. You only think you do. They made me lovable as part of my guise, so you and Dad would take care of me and protect me until I was old enough to serve my clan."

Kayla blinked. "Excuse me? What clan?"

"The Blackstones, of course. Dirk and I have the same

father." She released Kayla's hand and stood. "After he kissed me, he whispered it in my ear. That's why he calls me little sister. Because I'm his, not yours."

"No!" Kayla felt her stomach churn. "I don't believe this. Dirk lied to you, Tara. I have known you your entire life, and you have never been a Blackstone."

"I didn't believe him at first, either." Tara lifted her hand to her brow, smoothing her fingers over it as a heavy tattoo appeared. "Then this showed up on my face, after he tried to rape me. It's the first thing the clan does after you're born. They mark you as theirs, right where everyone can see it. Mine stays hidden because of the guise. So you'd think I was normal."

"It's a trick," Kayla insisted, and started to rise. "They cast some kind of illusion spell, to make you think you're tattooed. It sounds like something that sick bastard would do, to turn you against me. If we go to Ryan—"

"Sit down," Tara said, and shoved her back. Kayla's eyes filled with tears. "You really don't get it. I tell you the truth after all these years, and you don't believe me. You think I was actually depressed all that time? I hated you and Dad. I faked it so you'd leave me alone. So I could stop being lovable for a couple of hours."

A sob escaped Kayla. "But you sat with Dad at the hospital. You held his hand. You loved him."

"I don't feel love, Kayla." Tara went to the wall mirror, and stared at herself. "My brother thinks he's in love with me, or whatever love is for Dark Fae. He definitely wants me to be his slut." She glanced back over her shoulder. "By the way, I'm only technically a virgin. He's been fucking me in my dreams since I was thirteen."

"God, no, Tara." Kayla reached out to her. "Please, don't let him do this to you anymore. Let me help you put an end to this abuse."

"I appreciate that," she said, and moved back to the bed. "It's why I brought you here." Tara sat down next to her. "I don't want to be his incestuous whore, so I had to make a bargain." Tara put her arm around Kayla's shoulders. "My freedom for you."

Kayla didn't understand until she looked down. A shadow on the floor slithered over in front of her.

"You wouldn't do this to me," she gasped. "Tara, we're sisters!"

"No, we're not. I'm a Blackstone, and you're my enemy."

Her sister kissed her cheek, and gave her a hard shove.

Kayla fell headlong into a bottomless pit.

• • • • •

The End of *Hidden*

• • • • •

Kayla's story continues in *Denied (Forever Faire Book Four)*.

For a sneak peek, turn the page.

DENIED (BOOK 4)

CHAPTER 1

A N ENDLESS ABYSS of utter darkness swallowed Kayla Rowe alive. She couldn't see or move or breathe. But as she fell deeper into the bottomless void, she let go of her terrified panic and took refuge in her memories.

There she found Ryan Sheridan, the Fae warrior with whom she'd fallen in love. He towered over everything else like a beacon of hope. She saw his glittering white-blonde hair, and the tenderness in his jewel-blue eyes. Since she'd come to work as a groom at Forever Faire, Ryan's traveling Renaissance Faire, he had shown her secret magick, hidden marvels, and passionate, life-changing pleasures. Being with him these last weeks had changed her from a frightened stalking victim to a confident, strong woman. If she died happy, it was only because of him.

This is my home, inside you, he told her in his rich, deep voice. *I'm going to fill it with pleasure and lust and love, and me. As much of me as you will have.*

Yet as the blackness wrapped around her, Ryan's image

dissolved into a thin, gray-eyed teenager watching her from the shadows. The fragile spill of moonlight hair on her narrow shoulders made Kayla reach out, but the girl turned and ran away.

Her baby sister, Tara. She was so afraid.

You don't love me. You only think you do.

Kayla didn't understand the words, or the cold voice that had uttered them. She couldn't remember what had happened before she'd dropped into the abyss. Had they been separated again? Was it her fault? She felt almost sure that it was. But how could she have left her sister behind?

She'd looked after Tara since childhood, when their mother had abandoned them. Her baby sister had been so small and helpless, and Kayla's father had crawled into a whiskey bottle. Some would say she'd had no choice, but Kayla had chosen to be sister, mother and father to that innocent infant.

Kayla hadn't minded. She'd never tired of holding that chubby hand and listening to her birdlike chattering on the way to and from school. Teaching Tara how to dress and tie her sneakers by herself had been little victories for them both. If their father hadn't given up the bottle, Kayla would have gone on being everything to Tara anyway.

Tara had been Kayla's entire world. She could never abandon her.

Even when her sister had begun suffering from terrible depressions, Kayla hadn't stopped loving her. She'd checked out self-help books from the library, and when those hadn't worked she'd nagged her father until he'd taken Tara to a therapist.

You think I was actually depressed all that time? I faked it so you'd leave me alone.

No, that had to be wrong. All of this was wrong. When

her father had died, Kayla had promised Tara she would never leave her alone—and she'd kept that promise. She'd never once turned her back on her little sister. Tara would never hurt her, either. She loved her just as much.

I don't feel love, Kayla.

I hated you and Dad.

Kayla's head began to spin as she clutched at what she thought she knew. Tara was the only family she had left. She loved her. Her sister would never–

I'm a Blackstone, and you're my enemy.

A body dropped on top of Kayla, and knocked them both out of the darkness into some kind of empty dressing room. As soon as she could breathe she wrapped her arms around her sister and held onto her tightly.

"You came after me," she said, sobbing out the words. "Oh, sweetie, I had no idea, I'm so sorry–"

"I'm not," Christine said. She sat up and looked all around them. Her soft Tennessee drawl went flinty. "So. This is really fucking bad."

Kayla swallowed against the lump in her throat. Why had she thought Christine was Tara? It made no sense. But instead of her sister, her friend had come after her. The final gap in her memory filled in as she remembered the last moments before she had fallen into darkness. Tara had traded Kayla for her own freedom by betraying her to the Blackstones—by sending her to them.

Tara had shoved her into the abyss.

The dancer said in a low voice, "We're at the strip club where I used to dance. Where all the Blackstones are, remember?" She listened for a long moment. One of the overhead lights made her green eyes flash, as hard and cold as jade. "I don't think they know we're here yet. That's good. We might just make it out of here alive."

The lump in Kayla's throat swelled until she thought she might strangle. "Tara–"

"I know, I was there. I heard all that shit she said. We'll talk about it later." Christine helped Kayla to her feet and went to a curtain to peek through it. She came back and started undressing. "Strip."

The order made Kayla wonder if Christine had gone crazy, too. "I'm sorry?"

"Take off your clothes," the dancer repeated with thin patience, "or we're going to die."

Like a robot Kayla jerked off her shirt and jeans, and then her underwear as Christine raided a nearby rack of what looked like skimpy, sparkling bikinis. She handed Kayla a bra and thong made of lime green satin with hot pink sequins. When she put the costume on it barely covered her breasts and mons, and almost completely exposed her bottom.

"Good girl," Christine said. The dancer retrieved two wigs made of tinsel from a drawer and fitted one over Kayla's dark hair. She used the other to cover her golden-brown waves. "Show how you would look if you were completely stoned."

Kayla blinked. "What?"

"Never mind, just look like that. Don't talk, don't smile, and don't move or blink too fast." Christine grabbed some hairpins and went to check the curtain again. "There's a back door behind the stage outside. That's our way out. Come on, we can do this."

Kayla grabbed her hand and followed her through the curtain. They emerged in the back of a dark, smelly bar. She kept her head down and focused on the heels of Christine's stilettos, flinching as a big, heavyset man with an unconvincing comb-over staggered out of a men's room.

"Hey. Nobody told me there were twins dancing

tonight." He swayed and leered at Christine's breasts. "You two like to tag-team, or what?"

What he said made Kayla frown. She and Christine didn't look anything alike. Yet when she glanced at the mirrored wall, she had to stare. In the costumes and wigs they were almost doubles of each other.

"We like anything you like, sugar," Christine said, her voice a coy purr. She sidled closer, and rubbed up against the drunk as if he were the sexiest man on the planet. "Come outside and we'll give you a private preview."

Kayla didn't understand why Christine wanted the man to go with them, until she saw how his big frame blocked them from view. Dark Fae were scattered around the club. She nearly froze when she spotted Dirk Blackstone. He was grunting and jerking behind a naked woman who he had propped against the bar.

The most horrifying thing Tara had told her burned in her ears: *He's been fucking me in my dreams since I was thirteen.*

Dirk Blackstone wouldn't touch her sister again, Kayla thought, a strange calm settling over her. She'd cut off his hands with a hacksaw, if need be. His penis, too. Maybe she should take care of that right now, just to be on the safe side.

Christine's hand clamped on Kayla's shoulder. "No," she said flatly. "You're not doing this now. We're outnumbered, and he won't kill us. Not right away. Do you understand?"

Feeling as if she might vomit, Kayla nodded, and followed Christine and the drunk outside.

Christine closed the door gently and turned to the fat man, who gave her a big smile.

"So what do you two do?" His expression froze as he looked down at the fist gripping his genitals.

"We say good-night," Christine said. She took away her hand and rammed her knee into the same spot.

The drunk went down like a sinking ship, toppling over to whimper and clutch at his crotch.

Christine started searching the man's jacket pockets, but Kayla saw something move in the trees. A motorcycle without a rider slowly rolled out of the shadows and stopped to idle in front of her. She knew it only looked like a motorcycle. In its true form it was an enormous, fire-breathing black dragon, created to serve the Blackstones. But something made her reach out to it.

"Hell, Kayla." The dancer grabbed at her. "Get away from that thing,"

"It's all right," Kayla said, though she didn't know how she knew. But when she touched the bike she felt a powerful surge of determination and fear, not evil intent. "It isn't here to hurt us."

Christine uttered a sound of disbelief. "Are you kidding? One of these things burned me to death. You remember, right before I came back to life with boring brown hair, and all my tattoos gone?"

You must leave this place now, lady, the dragon whispered inside Kayla's head, his deep voice rumbling inside her bones. *Only take me with you, and I vow I will guard you both with my life.*

Kayla's telepathic ability allowed her to communicate by thought with horses–and now, it seemed, shape-shifting dragons, too.

"Why should we trust you? You helped the Blackstones attack our camp."

We were given no choice.

Hundreds of horrific images poured into Kayla's thoughts, but as gruesome as they were, she felt completely disconnected from what she was seeing.

I'm in shock.

It felt bizarre to realize that she really didn't care about anything but hurting Dirk Blackstone for what he'd done to her sister. But Tara wasn't her sister. She was Dirk's.

"Stop the slideshow, please." Kayla climbed on the motorcycle, and said to Christine, "Get on."

The dancer shook her head. "I'd rather walk back to Forever Faire."

As the back door of the club started to open, Christine divided the hair pins she carried between her two hands. A heartbeat later she staggered backward as the bike shot forward. It was all Kayla could do to hang on to the handlebars.

Hold tight.

Kayla's legs gripped the beast as though it were a horse. A second later, its front tire rammed into the door, slamming it closed. With a screeching squeal of tires and the smell of burning rubber, the engine revved as the motorcycle turned in place. The entire machine shuddered as a blast of white-hot fire shot from its tailpipes, welding the edges of the door to the frame.

Someone inside the club shouted, and a heavy weight rammed into the door from the other side.

The motorcycle lurched forward and stopped next to Christine. Her astonished expression matched Kayla's shock. There was more shouting from behind the door.

"I hate walking," Christine said, and climbed on behind Kayla.

Once her friend settled into position, the bike made it's way through the parking lot. Though Kayla looked like she was steering, she only gripped the handlebars to stay mounted. She looked over her shoulder just as the Blackstones emerged to stare at the fallen drunk.

"Here they come."

The motorcycle's engine revved.

"Got it," Christine said. She whipped out her arms, flinging the hairpins at the Dark Fae trotting toward them. Three of the men at the front of the group shrieked and fell, covering their eyes with their palms.

CHAPTER 2

"WE SHOULD RETURN to the faire grounds and search for them there, my liege," Colm Longacre said as he coasted to a stop beside Ryan Sheridan's big, white motorcycle. "I cannot believe the Blackstones would try to take them into town. We have too many friends here."

The master of Forever Faire scanned the nearly empty streets around them. Though they'd been plowed clear of the snow from the enormous storm, few residents were venturing out. Ryan clenched his jaw. Perhaps his second was right. When he'd realized that the sisters were no longer at the portal, he'd gone directly to Tara's room.

"Tara must have lied about what she saw," Ryan said. "I do not believe her claim that she fainted, either. You saw how she kept rubbing the back of her head."

"Aye, as if she'd been clouted."

They would have to start at the beginning and use spelltrace. It would be slow but–

"Fuck me," Colm muttered.

Ryan followed the direction of his gaze and went still.

Two nearly naked women were driving toward them on a Blackstone bike. Both had on wigs made of thin metallic strips, and tiny costumes covered with spangles. The driver yanked off her wig, revealing long, dark silken hair.

"Kayla."

The Blackstone bike stopped on the other side of the intersection. Ryan sped through it, screeched to a stop, and jumped off his own bike. In moments he snatched Kayla into his arms.

"Where have you been?" He looked down at her skimpy garment and tore off his jacket to drape it over her. "Why are you dressed like this?"

"I'll explain when we get back," she said, and looked back down the road. "The Blackstones are coming after us."

"Yeah," Christine said as she leaned over to kiss Colm, who wrapped her in his long coat. "And they're pissed, and we stole one of their dragon bikes. So let's move, boys."

They all quickly remounted. Ryan and Colm flanked the women, and the odd trio of bikes sped back to the faire grounds. Once inside the boundary, Kayla's bike stopped and parked, and she headed for the lodge. Ryan knew exactly where she was headed. But before he could step in front of her, Christine did.

"We need to get rid of the dragon first," she said.

Ryan eyed the Blackstone's motorcycle, which disappeared in a shimmer of silvery light. In its place a huge, black-scaled dragon appeared, smoke pouring from its nostrils as it arched its long, leathery wings.

"Take cover," Colm shouted as he drew his daggers.

"He's not going to hurt anyone," Kayla yelled. She darted between him and the huge creature, and said to the dragon. "Down, Fallon." She turned back to Colm. "That's his name."

"I don't care what the bloody thing calls itself," Colm said as he shoved Christine behind him. "Get out of the way, Rowe."

The long wings folded as the creature dropped down on his belly, making the earth shake beneath their feet. Tucking his muzzle in so that his smoky breath wafted away from them, he went still and watched Kayla's face.

Ryan regarded her in disbelief. "You control this monster?"

"I haven't had to yet." Kayla reached out and placed her hand on the dragon's brow. "But I can hear his thoughts, just like the horses. It's okay, Colm." She stroked the reptile's head. "He and the other dragons were created to serve as slaves for the Dark Fae. I think they're a lot like your Fae horses, except the clan has been seriously abusing them for centuries."

Titan shifted out of motorcycle form and trotted over to Ryan. The big stallion eyed the dragon and gave Kayla what could only be called a look of disgust.

She lifted her hands in a gesture of surrender. "Okay, horses are better than dragons. The point is, he got us away from the Blackstones." She hesitated, frowning at Fallon. "And he's asking for sanctuary."

Colm uttered a short laugh. "The evil fucking thing wants us to protect him? After he attacked us, and burned Christine alive?"

"He wasn't the one who hurt Christine. Some guy named Beck forced another of the herd to burn her." Kayla glanced at Christine. "If they don't obey the clan, they're tortured."

The dancer sniffed. "He could be lying, too."

"He can't. Neither can the horses. I'd know the second they did." Kayla looked into the dragon's eyes, and the creature shifted back into a motorcycle. "Fallon is the herd leader, and he wants to save the dragons who survived the battle. He also knows everything about the Blackstones, including a lot of things that we don't."

Ryan had never seen a Dark Fae creature behave as docilely as a rabbit. But seeing was not believing. He crossed his arms, eyeing the bike.

"I've seen his memories," Kayla said. "I know it's a risk, but he wants to help."

"So it says," Colm retorted.

"He just saved Christine and me," Kayla said. "We wouldn't be here if not for him."

Though that was likely true, it wasn't what persuaded Ryan—it was Kayla. Her way with creatures was beyond question.

Ryan nodded. "Take it down to the portal–"

"My liege–"

Ryan raised his voice. "And have it crated in its motor-cycle form, and spell-shielded for the jaunt." When his second hesitated, he added, "Wrap the crate in spellbound iron chains before you send it through, and that should prevent it from shifting again."

"Aye," Colm finally said.

"Can I borrow one of those daggers?" Christine asked her lover. With raised eyebrows, Colm handed her one. She faced Ryan. "Did Tara tell you that she shoved Kayla into a shadow portal to send her to the Blackstones? No? I saw her do it, and then I knocked that bitch out and jumped in after Kayla. We landed in the strip club where I used to work. Dirk and his boys are using it as a flop house."

"But they weren't waiting for us," Kayla tacked on quickly. "Dirk may have forced her to turn me over to the clan, but she didn't tell them I was coming."

"The Dark Fae wanted you, not her?" Colm's expression grew thoughtful. "I wonder why."

Ryan rested his hand on his lover's shoulder. "Tara lied to us after you disappeared, and claimed you had been taken. She has been deceiving everyone since you came to Forever Faire. You cannot deny what she is any longer, my love."

"Yeah, and that's not all," the dancer said flatly. "Tell him exactly who Tara is."

Kayla swallowed hard. "Tara said she's a Blackstone, and Dirk is her half-brother."

"Right," Christine said. "Now, are we all convinced that the little bitch is an evil Dark Fae changeling?" When no one said anything Christine nodded. "Terrific, it's unanimous. Let me go take care of her ass, and then we can get out of here."

"You can't kill her." Kayla turned to Ryan. "Tara told me that Dirk has been molesting her in her dreams for years. She only found out he was her brother that day down by the lake. Sending me to him was the only way she thought she could put an end to the abuse."

Ryan thought of the teenager's haunted gray eyes. "I am sorry for her suffering, but that does not justify her actions. Dirk would have done that and worse to you."

"I know." Pain darkened his lover's topaz eyes. "But we still have to take her with us."

CHAPTER 3

IN THE CAVES deep below the faire grounds, Kayla stepped up to the faceted stone arch of the crystal portal. The Fae's triangular blue journey stones formed a glowing halo as Ryan used his crystal to activate the enormous device. The circle of mist in the center shimmered, shaping itself into a hazy view of a lake. Moonlight revealed a dozen rustic cottages scattered among the twisted-limbed black oaks and towering pines. The Fae warriors who had already gone through were working to set up their new camp.

Nothing looked scary, but after her experience in the shadow portal, Kayla felt her stomach clench.

"Making the jaunt will not hurt you," Ryan said, taking her hand in his. "You will see light, and you may feel warm, but that is all."

"Okay," she said, not really sure that was true. But she looked up at his handsome face, and drew a little strength from the love she saw in his brilliant blue eyes. "Just don't let go of my hand."

Ryan nodded, and stepped with her through the arch.

Time stopped for Kayla, who glanced down to see her petite body turn into thousands of tiny amber and blue stars. They kept her shape as she flew through a tunnel made of prismatic crystals—all of which reflected her and Ryan's faces. The promised warmth suffused her like being wrapped in the softest, lightest of blankets. Another step, and the damp, sultry air of a Florida night enveloped her.

"Whoa." She staggered a little, as Ryan caught her and held her steady. When she glanced down at herself she saw a few remaining stars trickle down her legs to disappear into the grass. "That was…interesting."

"My liege."

Wallace Magee, Ryan's spell tracker, joined them. The big blacksmith had shifted into his ordinary mortal guise, but carried several large chunks of crystals from the caves in his arms.

"The rental agency just delivered the vehicles we ordered. I am set to cast the spell boundary to safeguard the camp. How shall I fashion it?"

"Keep us unseen and unheard by the local mortals," Ryan told him. "Have the men sweep the entire property for squatters. I want no humans in the camp."

Wallace nodded, before turning to Kayla. "It is good to see you unharmed, my lady." He bowed his head before he strode off.

The unhappy reminder of her ordeal made her finally ask the one question she hadn't.

"Where have you stashed my sis– Tara?"

"Gavan brought her through and has her secured in one of the cottages." Ryan studied her face for a moment. "Do you wish to see her? She is chained with spellbound iron, so she cannot use her magick or harm you."

The thought of the frail teenager in chains made Kayla

feel sick. But it was the only thing to keep Tara from hurting someone.

"I don't even know what I'd say to her." She sighed. "What about Jannon? Has Wallace been able to break whatever spell Tara cast over him?"

"Aye. Her enchantment works by proximity," Ryan said. "As long as he keeps his distance, she should not be able to steal his loyalty again."

"But you put a guard on Tara, just in case he doesn't," Kayla guessed.

"Aye." His beautiful mouth flattened. "Jannon has some history with being enslaved by a woman's spell. It may be why Tara's enchantment took him so easily."

"Would you care for more salt, my liege?" Jannon said. His mocking voice rang in the air as he approached them. "Not all my wounds have yet been scoured."

Kayla looked at the Fae warrior's god-like face, and glanced down at the bottle of blue wine he carried.

"Since you're already self-medicating," she said, "you probably wouldn't feel it."

"I am delighted you are back, Rowe." His copper-red hair wafted over his scowl as he bowed to her. "You may boot my arse all over the camp if you like. I would welcome it." He straightened and took a long swallow from the bottle. "My brothers, you see, have been treating me like a sick babe, when all I have been is a fool for a woman." He toasted Tara's cottage. "Again."

Kayla snatched the bottle away as he lifted it to his lips. Though it sloshed, she'd been quick enough. She handed it off to Ryan.

"That makes two of us, pal, but you don't see me getting plastered." She told him about Tara shoving her into the shadow portal. "There's a lot more to this than I think we know, so don't make any assumptions."

"But what she did to you, Rowe." He shook his head. "'Tis unspeakable."

"So was what Dirk has been doing to her." She glanced around. "Are you sober enough to steer me toward the stables? I'd like to check on the horses, and make sure they haven't stomped the dragon to death."

Jannon's mouth twitched. "Aye, if my liege entrusts me that far."

"Work will clear your head," Ryan said, and gave him a narrow look. "And you know what I will do to you if any harm comes to my lady, brother."

The other warrior sketched a deep, respectful bow. "On my head be it. This way, Rowe."

As Kayla walked with the big man toward an open-sided barn, his pain rolled off him in waves.

"We're pretty messed up, you and I," she said. "That doesn't mean we have to give up. Now that we know what she's been doing to us, we can move on."

"I have the unhappy benefit of experience," Jannon told her, his tone bleak. "Such betrayal lingers and preys on you. Just as you think you are healing, it rips you open anew." He picked up a bale of hay and carried it on his shoulder into the barn.

Kayla walked down the rows of stalls, greeting each horse with a touch on the nose and a smile. Sampson and Grania both greeted her with happy thoughts, but Titan took one look at her and nudged his stall door.

You are miserable. Let me out, and I will take you for a ride.

"Not tonight, Handsome. Too much work to do." She reached up to stroke the big white stallion's strong neck. "I need your help, though, if you're okay with being my bodyguard."

He turned his head to glare at the very last stall, in which the dragon motorcycle had been locked.

That monster is dangerous. If he turns on you, I may not be fast enough to ride you away.

"He's chained," she said, as she unlatched Titan's door. "But if anything goes wrong, you and Jannon need to get Ryan."

As she led the stallion down to the last stall, Jannon joined them.

"It is too dark to go for a…oh, bloody hell, no." He lunged between her and the dragon's door. "You cannot mean to release it."

"It's staying right where it is," she promised him. "I need to know why the Blackstones want me, and all I know is that I'm not a changeling."

She stepped around him and carefully unlatched the stall door. Jannon glanced at the bike, and drew a long dagger from his belt.

"Sheridan will tear my head off if you come to grief, lady. Very slowly, too. Remember that."

Kayla nodded and stepped just inside the stall. The motorcycle, which had been wrapped with heavy iron chains, blinked on its headlight.

"Sorry to wake you, Fallon, but we need to talk."

The dragon inside the motorcycle began sending his thoughts the moment hers touched him.

I will tell you what I can, my lady.

The dull gleam of the iron chains matched the tone of the dragon's thoughts, and Kayla touched one of the heavy links. "Are these hurting you?"

They prevent me from shifting, and block my power. But my bondage does not pain me. It is being separated from my brothers and sisters. Without them I am bereft.

"I can understand that," Kayla said. "I'm also sorry I have to question you like this, but we have to learn what the Blackstones have planned. I know they switched Tara with my real sister when they were infants. Where is my real sister now?"

I was left outside the night the changeling was put in her place. The dragon gave her his memory of being parked outside the house she'd shared with her father and Tara. *When the clan left your home, they did not have your sister with them.*

"Was she already gone?" As the dragon affirmed this, Kayla felt even more confused. "Then why did they leave Tara with us?"

For you, my lady. You were to be watched until it was time to take you. The clan believes you are the key to finding the spellsinger.

Kayla cocked her head back, but repeated everything to Jannon, who looked bewildered.

"The last Fae spellsinger was murdered by Dark Fae," he told her. "There have been no others since her death. Their gift is the rarest among our kind. It may be another ten thousand years before the next will be born."

"Well, even if this person exists," Kayla said. "I don't know who it is. Why do the Blackstones think I know where this spellsinger is?" Kayla asked the dragon.

You may not know, my lady, but they believe you are key to finding her.

Fallon showed her memories of conversations he had overheard between Dirk Blackstone and his father, Jarek. In every one of them they argued about taking the mortal girl Tara was watching. Dirk always pressed to take Kayla at once, but his father never agreed.

"They were waiting for something," Kayla told Jannon. "Or someone, maybe, to come to me. But the only person I haven't seen since..." She stopped herself and cleared her thoughts. "Thank you, Fallon. I'll talk to Ryan about what we can do to help you and your herd."

She gestured for Jannon to follow her outside, and once they left the barn she led him down to the lake.

"I think I know why the Dark Fae want me," Kayla told him. "They want to use me somehow to lure the spellsinger to them."

"You said you did not know the spellsinger," Jannon pointed out.

"I don't." She looked out at the shimmering water. "But Ryan and I proved that I have some Fae blood. My father was human, so it had to come from my mother. I haven't seen her in almost twenty years. She abandoned us that night, when the Blackstones left Tara in my sister's place. After what Fallon told me, I think it's possible she had another reason for leaving. Maybe to get my sister away before the Blackstones could take her."

Jannon's brows drew together. "You mean they came to switch Tara–"

"For the sister they really wanted," Kayla finished for him. "Maybe she's the spellsinger."

CHAPTER 4

JANNON WATCHED KAYLA head off with Ryan and Wallace to discuss the dragon's revelations, and considered looking for another bottle of wine. The men had transported most of their stores through the portal, and he wouldn't sleep tonight unless he drank himself unconscious. It was that or brawl, but no one would throw a punch his way now. His brothers all watched him, but their eyes held only pity. Tara had turned him into the camp's wounded pup. He shouldered another hay bale.

"Playing the stablehand, Ferguson?" a cool voice asked.

Jannon dropped the bale before he faced Gavan Waterson. "What are you doing here? You were left to guard the changeling."

"Aye, and I would, except she bleeds now, from her scalp." The other man touched the back of his head. "I cannot tell if the wound is genuine. She will not let me near her. But there is too much blood for it to be a scratch."

"She's in chains," Jannon said flatly. "She can't stop you."

Gavan grimaced. "She weeps, and says no one but you may touch her. Since I am not wont to force any female…"

"You and your soft heart," he said, pointing to the cottage. Jannon fell into step with him. But when Gavan led him to the cottage that Colm had assigned to him, Jannon jerked him to a stop. "You put her in my quarters? Are you daft?"

"She is in chains," the other man reminded him. "What difference does it make?"

He looked into Gavan's dazzling eyes, and saw they were slightly unfocused. "Go and fetch Wallace, brother. Bring him to me."

He waited until Gavan strolled away before he entered the cottage. Tara lay across his armchair, her eyes closed and her head resting on a blood-stained towel. Iron chains crisscrossed her thin body from neck to ankles.

Jannon didn't want to go near her, but the blood looked as real as the snowy paleness of her still features.

"You sent for me, changeling?"

She opened one eye. "Is that going to be my name now? Why not 'bitch'? I like that better. It's shorter than 'evil little bitch', too, so everyone will remember it."

The thready whisper of her voice drifted around him like the soft leather of a snare.

"You stole your name from Rowe's sister."

"Guilty as charged, but I didn't have one of my own." She pushed herself up into a sitting position, her movements slow and shaky. "Other than Blackstone, I mean. They never gave me a first name."

Jannon couldn't stand to look at her another moment, and went to the bathroom to find the first-aid kit. He then realized how ridiculous that was. As Dark Fae, she could heal only through pain or blood. He returned to the front room.

"I will not wound myself again to help you," he told her.

Tara smiled wanly at him. "Pain and blood, right. But there's another way. Come and take these chains off me, and we can do that."

Even clad in spellbound iron, the pull of her magick tugged at him. "You made yourself bleed. Heal your own wounds."

"I didn't do this." She shifted to show him the bloody towel. "Being dragged through that portal did. For your information, it nearly killed me."

Unable to resist, Jannon took a step closer. "Yet somehow you still breathe. Forgive me if I choose not to believe yet another lie."

The defiance in her expression changed to hurt. "I'm not lying, Jan. It felt horrible. Like it was trying to rip me in half." With difficulty, she pushed up her left sleeve, and showed him the large bruises that nearly covered her forearm. "It's like this all down my left side."

He crouched down in front of the chair to examine the marks closely. "Did something strike you from this side?"

Tara shook her head. "I felt something come after me. It grabbed me and tried to pull me back out of the portal."

His eyes narrowed. "We would not do such a thing to you, girl."

"I know." Her lips twisted. "I think it was my brother."

Being reminded of her Dark Fae kin made Jannon stand. "I will summon Wallace. He may have a spell that can repair the damage." He looked down as she clutched at his fingers. "I am no longer your creature, changeling."

"I don't want you to be." She peered up at him, and all the guile left her expression. "I'm sorry for what I did to you. The clan cast this spell over me when I was a baby, after my father cut me out of my mother's belly. I didn't even know about it until yesterday."

Jannon wanted to believe her, which more than anything about her disgusted him. He pulled his hand away from hers. "I am done with you and this game you play."

Before he reached the door Tara said, "They're going to kill me. They just have to convince Kayla it's the only solution. They're right, too. As long as I'm alive Dirk Blackstone will never stop trying to find me." She paused before she added, "When it's time, I want you to do it."

He turned around. "What did you say?"

"If I'm to be put down, I want you as my executioner. It's the only way…I can make up for…for…"

She closed her eyes, and slid onto her side.

Jannon swore as he hurried over to her, pulling her upright and resting her forehead on his shoulder as he examined the wound. Claw marks scored her scalp down to the bone.

"Fuck me," he muttered.

He took out his dagger and sliced his forearm. He held her head as he fed his blood to her, watching the deep wounds as they stopped bleeding and began to close.

The door to the cottage opened, and Wallace and Ryan stopped just inside the threshold as they saw him.

"She is badly injured," he told them, keeping his gash pressed against her mouth. "Bruises down one side of her body, and claw marks on her head. It happened in the portal."

Wallace approached cautiously. But after examining Tara he nodded his agreement to Ryan. The master of Forever Faire joined them, and lifted the blood-soaked towel from the chair.

"Gavan came to us," he said. "He showed signs of being under her sway until Wallace scoured her blood from his flesh. Even in chains, she is still able to enslave Fae to her through blood bond."

Ryan looked pointedly at the bright red smears on Jannon's fingers, where she had touched him.

"I know," Jannon said. As her wounds closed over and disappeared, Jannon took his arm from her. "You will have to do the same to me."

Wallace eyed him. "I believe not, brother. There is no spell trace on you. What you did here, you chose by free will."

"Aye," Jannon said, and looked down at the unconscious teenager's thin face. "But do not trust me, brothers. The grip she has on me has naught to do with magick."

CHAPTER 5

IN THE MANAGER'S office at the strip club, Dirk Blackstone watched his cousin examining the last of the wounded men.

"You mean to tell me two mortal whores did this? And escaped on my dragon?"

"They were not mortal whores," Beck said as he yanked a hair pin from the Dark Fae's pierced eye. He dragged a shivering stripper over to the man. "Take her from behind, and her pain will aid to speed the healing." He wiped his hands on a rag before he regarded Dirk. "The halfling did this. Kayla Rowe was with her. Your sister must have sent them through to us."

Blood pounded in Dirk's head. "Tara told you this?"

"I thought she told you." His cousin scowled. "Must we school this bitch again?" He ducked Dirk's fist. "Why do you wish to strike me? It is she who fucks us blind." He retreated a safe distance. "You think her your dog, but this stinks of trickery. She may now claim she kept your bargain, and yet we still do not have the spellsinger."

"Get out," Dirk yelled.

When Beck tried to speak again Dirk grabbed him by the back of the neck, hauled him to the door, and threw him out of the office.

It took destroying every stick of furniture in the dismal room to dispel enough of Dirk's fury for him to work a seeking spell. He never had to search long for his half-sister's mind, for a dreamshare spell had connected them since her birth. When he found her, however, a dull gray barrier prevented him from entering her thoughts. Only one thing could create such an obstacle—Tara had been imprisoned in spellbound iron—and the thought of her exposed and at the mercy of the Fae made him howl.

You came to visit. Tara appeared on the other side of the barrier, and smiled at him. *How sweet. Did you bake a file in a cake for me?*

Dirk glared at her, and then saw the blood painting her long neck.

They have harmed you? I will have their bowels wrapping my fingers.

We just got here. There hasn't been time. Besides, I thought you did this. Tara uttered a soundless laugh. *It must have been the portal.*

Dirk's chest filled with unseen stone. *They took you from me? Where? Where are you?*

Her smile widened. *Now why would I tell you that, big brother? I kept my word. I delivered the Fae to you. I'm free now.* She started to fade into a transparency of herself. *Free of you, and soon, this miserable life.*

I will never let you go. Dirk drove his fists into the barrier between them, feeling his knuckles split as the iron boundary repelled him. *Do you hear me, Tara? I am coming for you and the Fae.*

If only you had been kind, she whispered, her expression turning wistful. *I've been yours since we were children. All you had to do was love me, and I would have given myself to you. But there is no love in you, Dirk. Not even for me.*

The desperate, mewling part of him wanted her. *I will try to love you. Only come back to me...and bring the Fae.*

The last thing she gave him was a wistful smile, and a one-fingered salute.

A blast of amber and silver power hurled him out of the dreamshare, and Dirk returned to his body to see his fists oozing blood. He scrambled to his feet and strode out into the club. There wasn't a moment to spare.

"The Fae seek to escape us," he shouted at them, and seized the largest of the strippers. "We attack now."

The mortal female trembled as Dirk hauled her out of the club and shoved her on the back of a motorcycle. As he mounted in front of her and started the bike, his men's machines roared to life. He led them from the club to the faire grounds, which appeared empty. He passed easily through the gates formerly protected by a spell boundary. Dirk stopped his bike and climbed off, dragging the stripper with him.

"Search the property," he called to his men. "Find me the entrance to their wretched tunnels." To his cousin he said, "Bring me rope."

As Beck and the men dispersed, the terrified stripper fell to her knees in front of Dirk.

"Please, let me go. I won't tell anyone about you. I just want this to stop."

"So it shall."

Dirk grabbed her hair and jerked back her head. His blade soundlessly sliced through her soft neck before the whore knew what was happening. He tipped her forward until she bled out on the ground. His blade made quick but messy work of her, leaving only the thick sack of her skin, fat, and what muscles remained. As he'd done with the psychic, he stripped out of his clothes and donned the flesh like a garment. But this was no disguise. The misshapen and distended head and body would fool no one.

Beck returned with a coil of rope.

"The entrance is beneath the lodge," he said, and eyed the borrowed flesh with a smirk. "You mean to enter the tunnels in your pretty new girl suit? It will only repel the effects of the Fae crystals for a few minutes before it begins to peel away."

"That is all I need." Dirk yanked his trousers and jacket back on and shoved the stripper's hair out of his eyes. "Rope," he said, raising his arms.

His cousin tied one end around his waist. "Pull it taut if you need to be dragged out."

"Make sure you drag me out if I do," Dirk told him, "or you will never have your revenge on my father."

He entered the lodge, where the lingering spell trace of the Fae crawled against his borrowed flesh and read him as mortal. Beck followed him down to the basement, and stopped at the entrance to the tunnels.

"I can feel the bloody thing from here," his cousin said, scowling. "'Tis still open. Do not go through it."

"Do you think me an idiot?" Dirk checked the knot on the rope. "Be ready, Cousin."

Walking into the tunnel sent waves of nausea through Dirk as the crystals paving the passage activated. He could feel them pelting him with their light magick, seeking what lay beneath the dead stripper's skin. But he ignored the enchantment and made his way into the caves.

If Dirk had not despised the Fae with all his black soul he might have envied them the beauty and power of their hidden lair. All around him the crystals protecting their cave system glowed as he passed. They sparkled as they funneled power from the earth and transformed it into light. Their glittering facets focused on him, the source of the disturbance, but the stripper's skin reflected back only the presence of a mortal. He could feel the flesh beginning to thin, and increased his pace until he found the arch of journey stone and beheld its shimmering doorway. His gut clenched as he peered into it, trying to see what lay on the other side.

The mists began to clear, and two tall, powerful warriors appeared in the center, each holding a power crystal. Dirk ducked down behind a broad rock, and from there watched Ryan Sheridan and another man step up to the threshold of the portal from the other side.

Dirk's hands bunched into fists as he fought the urge to lunge through the portal at them. He knew the skin he wore would never last through such a jaunt. Once exposed to the portal as Dark Fae, he would be wrenched apart before he made it to the other side.

"I can feel someone on the other side, my liege," the man said to Sheridan. "We must close it now."

"Aye."

Sheridan lifted his crystal, touching it to the one held by the smith.

Dirk watched as the mists were swept away by the closing spell. For a few moments he glimpsed the place the Fae had chosen to flee. Oaks and pines hemmed a moonlit lake, and shaded dozens of old cottages there. It looked to Dirk like any of their faire grounds. But beside a dirt road that skirted a dark lake, he spotted a small sign.

Totten Lake Nature Trail Closed for Repairs.

The stripper's face sagged over Dirk's as he grinned and stood. Sheridan turned his head and saw him in the instant before the portal closed, and frowned.

"I have you now, you fucking madman," Dirk muttered.

Pain stabbed into his side as the skin suit parted, and

his own flesh was exposed to the wrath of the Fae crystal. He staggered out of the cave and into the tunnel, falling several times as his guise peeled away. Halfway out he collapsed and jerked on the rope.

A long moment passed before Beck began dragging him out. Dirk gritted his teeth as magick pummeled him. When his cousin at last yanked him from the tunnel, he promptly puked all over Beck's boots.

"I just had these cleaned," his cousin complained as he helped him to his feet. "So? Did you find them?"

"They're in Florida," Dirk said, spitting the last of the vomit from his mouth before he grinned. "By a large, deep lake."

Beck began to laugh.

CHAPTER 6

KAYLA USED THE last of her apple cookie stash to give the horses a treat before she stopped by the stall where Fallon had been left chained for the night.

"I've never taken care of a dragon," she admitted as she held out the last cookie. "But our herd loves these."

Reptilian jaws grew out of the front wheel guard, and delicately plucked the treat from her fingers before vanishing.

We have always been expected to fend for ourselves. You are kind, my lady.

"So are you." She patted one of the handlebars. "I'll arrange to have something more substantial for you in the morning." She hesitated before she asked, "You don't eat people, do you?"

We would, but your kind are very stringy, the dragon thought back. *If you will permit me to shift for an hour to make use of the lake, I can hunt for myself.* He showed her an image of a dragon swallowing a gator whole. *These creatures are especially delicious.*

"Works for me." She concealed a shudder. "Good night, Fallon."

When she left the barn Kayla glanced over at the nearby cottage where Colm had put her things. It was after midnight, and she would have to be up at dawn to feed and exercise the horses. But as tired as she felt, she knew she wouldn't sleep. In the space of one day her life had been turned inside-out.

How could she do this to me?

Kayla walked along the dirt path to the cottage down by the lake that Ryan occupied, and stopped in front of the door. She wouldn't whine to him about Tara's betrayal. That was something she had to handle on her own. She'd report on the herd, find out what their next move was, and see what she could do to help.

The door opened, and Ryan loomed over her. "You think so loud I can hear you inside."

"There's a lot on my mind." She glanced past him at Wallace, who nodded to her. "You're busy. I'll talk to you tomorrow."

"Wallace?" Ryan said, never looking away from her face. "Get out."

"Yes, my liege." The blacksmith exited the cottage, winking at Kayla before he strolled away.

Ryan drew her inside, guiding her around crates and boxes to a pair of chairs out on the small screened-in back porch. Beyond a short stretch of grass the lake shimmered under the moon's silvery glow. Artful silhouettes of the palmetto fronds formed a hedge of dark fans beneath the fuzzy drapery of Spanish moss on gnarled oak branches.

"I never thought I'd mind the heat." Kayla shrugged off her jacket and sat down with him. "I think Tennessee's winter turned me into a snow bird. Did everything go okay with the move?"

"Everyone and everything is present and accounted for." He paused for a moment, scowling a little. "I saw a mortal female in the cave, but I closed the portal before she could wander into it. She must have been one of the crew, come back for something left behind." Ryan breathed in deeply. "I do like how it smells here. 'Tis like walking through a garden."

"I used to plant watermelon seeds behind our house," Kayla recalled. "I had no idea they would take over the whole yard. I set up a little stand by the road to sell them. Tara would always try to steal some of the sample slices I set out for people to taste…" She stopped and shook her head. "I'm sorry. I promised myself I wouldn't talk about her tonight. I'm still processing, I guess."

Ryan reached for her, and before she could blink she was sitting on his lap. He tucked her head against his shoulder, and his big hand stroked gently up and down her spine.

"We never expect to be deceived or injured by those we love. We assume that our devotion is returned, and they would protect us against any pain, as we would shield them. Instead it tears wounds so deep that it seems impossible that they should heal."

Kayla could feel that tearing sensation now, in her chest. "I just can't believe it. She told me herself, everything. I kept thinking that she was lying. That it was some kind of awful story she'd made up to get out of trouble. When she looked at me, Ryan, her eyes were so empty, as if the sister I knew had been erased."

"That sister," he said gently, "was stolen from you."

"I know." That was another side of this horror—that her real sister had been taken from her. "What I don't understand is that I've known Tara my entire life. I've loved her since she was a baby, but I never knew her. The girl who shoved me in that shadow abyss was a complete stranger. How could I have lived with her all those years, and never once suspected who she really was?"

He tipped up her chin to look into her eyes. "You are not entirely mortal, and Tara was bespelled to enslave Fae to her. You saw only what she wished you to see: a beloved sister, for whom you would do anything."

"The worst thing is that you were absolutely right about her, and I wouldn't believe it. I forced you to keep her at Forever Faire. God." She pressed her hands over her face. "I've been such an idiot."

"You are safe now, and I will never permit that changeling to harm you again," Ryan said.

He slowly stood and carried her into the cottage. He murmured something in Fae language, and the crates and boxes disappeared as the interior transformed itself into a replica of his mountain cabin, complete with flames crackling in the old fireplace.

As he set her on her feet, Kayla saw frost scrolling over the windowpanes. "How did you do this? Are we back in Tennessee?"

"I brought winter here to us." He cradled her face between his hands. "What more can I do, love?"

She placed a hand on his chest, her fingers trailing over the weave of his tunic.

"I don't know if this is even possible, but could you help me find my real sister? If she's still out there somewhere, I need to know."

Ryan nodded. "I will speak to Wallace in the morning. He knows best how to track halflings."

"Thank you." Her shoulders sagged. "I owe you so much, Ryan."

"Then perhaps you can do something for me," he told her. "Will you stay and keep me warm tonight, love?"

$\mathcal{A}$S KAYLA LOOKED up into Ryan's brilliant blue eyes, she realized for the first time she didn't feel any guilt. Before tonight it had always seemed selfish to leave Tara alone to go to her lover, and steal a few hours together with him. Had that been part of the spell Tara had used to enslave her? How much of her life had been dictated by a changeling who had secretly hated her and her poor father?

Ryan pressed his mouth to her brow. "If you would rather be alone tonight, I understand."

"No." She gripped the front of his tunic as she stood on tiptoe to kiss him. The moment her lips touched his she felt her skin heat with the tingling warmth of his magick. "I'm staying right here."

"You are generous." A slow smile curved his lips. "I am glad I have a gift for you as well." He produced a small ball of wood carved to resemble a walnut, except it was hinged and had a tiny golden clasp. "'Twas why I asked Wallace to come."

Kayla felt charmed as she opened it, and saw the two

thin circles of amber crystal inside. Though different sizes, they were carved with the same intricate patterns.

"How beautiful," she said, but her eyebrows knit together. "You're giving me two rings?"

"They are binding rings. One is for you." Ryan took the smaller ring and slid it over her right index finger, which it fit perfectly. "The other I will wear." He put the larger ring on his left index finger. "Now close your eyes, and think of me."

As she did, Kayla saw a very clear image of Ryan standing with her in the cottage. She glanced up at him.

"Are the rings doing this?"

"Aye. I had Wallace enchant them so that they are connected through us." He lifted her hand so that their two rings touched, and a tiny cascade of stars showered over their fingers. "As long as we wear them, we will always know where the other is."

He'd done this because of Tara, Kayla suspected, and some of her pleasure deflated.

"I'll try not to get pushed into any other shadow portals." She traced a fingertip over the intricate whorls on her ring, and felt the tug of an old memory. "These patterns look so familiar."

"They are our names, and the words of the binding spell," he told her. "They are written in Fae language."

"'Kayla of Starling Park,'" she murmured, turning the ring on her finger to see the other side. "'Beloved of Ryan of the Forever Faire.'" She realized she was reading the inscription and caught her breath. "I've seen this before, Ryan. The words were different, but the writing was the same."

"Your mother may have worn one," he said gently. "Binding rings are common gifts among kin who are to be parted."

All the emotions she had been keeping in check welled up inside her. "My mother, Dad, and now Tara. In the end everyone leaves me." She blinked hard before she looked at him. "You're all I have left now."

"Come here, love." Ryan folded her in his arms. "We found each other, just as you said that first night by the campfire. I will never let you go anywhere without me." He kissed the top of her head. "For there is no place I would be, but at your side."

"Then we wouldn't need the rings, and I'm not giving mine back." She took his hands in hers, and drew him over to the thick rug by the fire. Kneeling down before him, she closed her eyes and thought of herself clad only by the firelight. Her clothes dissolved in a shower of light, leaving her bare to his gaze. "Now stand still, and let me practice my thought magick again."

Kayla stroked her hands along the outside of his strong thighs, grazing one palm over the thick bulge of his erection, before she slipped her fingers under the edge of his tunic. His flat, hard abdomen contracted under her curious touch, and the fabric covering her hand began to unweave itself. The threads of cloth came alive and snaked away from Ryan, collecting in a pile by Kayla's side. She glared at them, and they began reweaving themselves into his tunic.

Ryan smiled down at her. "That is an interesting alternative." He took in a quick breath as her fingers lured his belt from his waist, and made the leather strap bind his wrists behind his back. "You mean to make me your prisoner, love?"

"You have no idea what I want to do with you." Kayla drew her fingertip along the inseam of his trousers, which unstitched itself in her wake. "But you're about to."

His trousers and smalls dropped away from his hips, restitching and folding themselves in a neat stack by his tunic. Kayla dispensed with the magick as she unlaced his boots and tugged them away from his big, shapely feet. She placed a kiss on his instep and felt his calf tighten.

"You should not tempt me," he muttered, his voice hoarse as he watched her.

"I'm going to kiss you, that's all."

Kayla started at his ankles, and worked her way up to his knees. Every part of him fascinated her, from the smooth paleness of his skin to the bulge of tough muscle beneath it. She could sense the big, heavy bones that supported his massive frame.

"Kayla," Ryan whispered hoarsely. As she ran her hands up the back of his thighs, he groaned. "Release me so I may touch you."

"Not yet."

She smiled as she kissed the top of his thigh, and rose to her feet. Brushing her body against his, she moved around him, trailing her fingers across his flat belly. She could feel the heat of him now, and his skin grew damp as she nuzzled his bicep and shoulder.

"You're too tall, Sheridan," she said, and put her hands on his shoulders, pressing him down on his knees so that he sat on his ankles. "That's better."

Ryan's long, white-blonde hair tried to twine around her fingers as she stroked the top of his arms, and planted soft kisses against the sides of his taut neck.

"I like this belt," he muttered. "Do not make me destroy it."

"Patience is a virtue."

Delighted that she could drive him to the brink of losing control, she moved in front of him, and caught his handsome face between her palms. Looking at him awed her now as much as the first time she'd seen his mortal guise disappear. So much unearthly beauty, and it was all hers to love. She breathed in his scent, which had gone dark and heady, and brushed her thumb across his lips.

"I could just kiss you for the rest of the night."

His jewel-blue eyes closed. "I don't like the belt that much."

"You asked me to keep you warm." Kayla brought his head against her breasts, and rubbed one puckered peak against the seam of his lips. "How's this working for you?"

"You make me hot." He used his tongue to caress her tight nipple, but when he tried to latch on she shifted and teased his mouth with the other. "And hungry. Very hungry."

"That's good," Kayla said, as she straddled his thighs. She let him feel the soft brush of her damp sex on the tip of his straining shaft. "Because you make me wet. Maybe I can do something about all that heat."

"You can."

His arms bunched, and leather ripped. His big hands seized her waist, as his mouth covered hers, kissing her wildly as he lowered her onto her back.

Feeling the weight of him on top of her made Kayla arch up against him, her own self-control disintegrating. "Ryan."

"I should bind you and kiss you until you beg for me," he said, his voice strained. His expression turned fierce as he moved between her thighs, and guided his throbbing cockhead to her slick opening. "Only I must have you now. Do you want me, Kayla love? Do you need me inside you?"

She lifted her hips, lodging him just inside her clenching opening.

"What do you think?" She writhed against him as he sank into her, his swollen shaft stretching and filling her. "Ryan," she moaned.

"Let me see your eyes," he said. When she looked up at

him, his jaw tightened. "So much love. I do not deserve you, my lady. But this…" He drew out, and pressed back into her. "This I can give you, every night, every morning. Every time you permit me to touch your body, and taste your lips, and smell your skin."

"That's good." She linked her hands around his neck. "How open are your afternoons?"

He laughed, and kissed her, and went to work. The loving thrusts of his thick cock into the aching softness between her thighs was slow and thorough. Each stroke glided as smoothly as the silky, liquid heat that spread through her belly.

But Kayla sensed he was holding back, trying to make it good for her, and nipped his lower lip. "Stop being polite," she murmured, and put her mouth by his ear. "I want all of you, Sheridan."

"So you shall have me." He dragged her legs over his shoulders, shifting over her to drive deep and hard. "You tease me and kiss me until you drive me mad with longing. When all I can think is how I must fuck you until you explode around me with your pleasure. I want it, love. All your heat and delight. You will give it to me again and again."

Kayla felt his fingers circle around her wrists, binding her as he pumped deep and hard into her pussy. She heard the sexy sounds spilling between them, her soft whimpers and his deep grunts. Tension coiled in her belly as he sank himself home, moving faster, using his entire body. Heat flooded between her legs, moving higher, until her sex clenched in a spasm of pure pleasure. She gripped him tightly as the first explosion of her climax rocked her.

"Yes, yes," he crooned. "I feel you, love, I feel your heart embracing me. And here is mine."

Bliss shimmered through Kayla's body as she felt him

plow into her, his big frame tensing and shuddering as he began to come. The thick, heavy jetting of his seed wrenched her from her descent into another, impossibly hot climax that made her cry out his name.

Ryan rolled with her, holding her against his heaving chest as their sweat-slick skins glistened in the flickering glow of the fireplace.

"You owe me a belt," he whispered as he stroked the back of her head.

Kayla kissed his shoulder and sighed. "You're going to need more than one."

OLM MADE HIS final rounds of the new camp before returning to his cottage, where he found Christine inside, standing at the window. She had changed into a loose T-shirt and dark leggings, and let her new mane of sun-kissed brown curls loose on her shoulders. The bareness of her pale arms reminded him of all she had suffered before their resurrection, when one of the Blackstones' dragons had burned her alive. Although she had come back, all the colorful tattoos had vanished.

Both he and Christine had been brought back as blank slates, and Colm intended to fill hers with as much love as she would accept from him.

"What do you watch, my lady?" he asked. But as he joined her he saw the cottage she stared at. He tucked his arm around her waist. "Tara."

"I should have ended her for what she did," she said quietly. "I don't get her. I mean, anyone would kill to have someone who cared for them half as much as Kayla loves her. How could she be so hateful to her?"

"I cannot say," he admitted, "but she is here by her sister's request. Despite all, Kayla still cares for her."

"So do I. I think that's why I still want to strangle the little bitch so bad." She drew herself up and turned to him. "How's Gavan doing?"

"I sent him into town to get supplies." He hesitated before he added, "If you also stay away from Tara, in time your regard for her will fade."

"Yeah, I heard all about how she's been all magicked-up to make everyone love her. It didn't work that well on me." She glanced back at the cottage. "They don't do shame, do they? Her kind."

"That would require her to have a conscience, and feel remorse." His mouth flattened. "She has used Kayla all her life, and to my knowing has never once shown regret."

"Maybe she just didn't show it." As she heard herself Christine rolled her eyes. "Yeah, I'm definitely staying away from her." She forced a smile. "You hungry? One of the guys delivered some groceries, and I make the world's best bacon and cheese omelet."

Before Colm could agree a knock sounded on the door, and he grimaced at her before he went to answer it. Ryan and Wallace stood outside, and both looked grim.

"Forgive the intrusion," Ryan said, and smiled past him at Christine. "May we have a word with you both?"

Christine suggested they sit in the little kitchen, where she brought out a pitcher of iced tea she'd made and a tin of cookies.

Colm smiled at her as she sat down at the table with them. "You make an excellent housewife."

"Then you should make an honest woman of me," she countered with a wink. Before he could react, she said to Ryan, "How's Kayla holding up?"

"I left her to sleep. She is exhausted, and Tara's betrayal

has wounded her deeply." He sat back and eyed Colm. "My lady wishes to find her true sister. The dragon claims that the sister went missing with their mother before the Blackstones arrived to make the switch. Both may yet live."

"Let's say she's alive," Christine said. "How could you possibly find her?"

"'Twill not be easy," Wallace put in. "I could return to Tennessee and sweep their childhood home, but I doubt any life-energy she left behind yet lingers. As a halfling she will be also difficult to locate by the usual spells. Her mortal blood interferes. Or it could be…other matters."

Colm caught the sadness that flickered through the blacksmith's eyes. "You think her dead."

"The clan leader of the Blackstones is known for his particular lusts," Wallace said slowly. "There are whispers of how Jarek has raped and tortured every Fae woman captured by his clan before he kills them. If he took Kayla's mother and sister, 'tis likely he did the same to them. I would not be surprised to know that he also directed the dragon to surrender to us, so that he might give Kayla false hope."

"You can't tell Kayla that," Christine said. "God, her sister was just a baby when she disappeared."

"I would never, lady. And I may yet be wrong about them falling into Jarek's hands. Halflings are also very hard to track. 'Tis why my liege asked me to create binding rings for them." He gave Christine a wry look. "When I tried to locate you and Kayla through the shadow portal, I found no trace of either of you."

"Next time I'll drop some breadcrumbs." She nudged Colm. "Or someone could give *me* one of these nifty rings."

Colm placed a small golden box on the table in front of her. "Done."

"What?"

Colm knew he was grinning like a loon, but he couldn't stop himself.

Looking awed now, the dancer opened the box, and gently touched the glittering carved crystals inside.

"Guys, there's nothing more we can do tonight, right?" When Ryan and Wallace nodded their agreement, she gave them a brilliant smile. "Then, with all due respect, will you please get lost?"

Wallace chuckled, and Ryan clapped Colm on the shoulder before they rose and departed. Christine waved to them from the door before she bolted it and jumped on Colm.

He caught her by the bottom and found himself being thoroughly kissed. "What is all this now?" he said when she finally allowed him to draw a breath.

"You ringed me, my man." Christine covered his face with fervent kisses. "No one's ever given me one of those. You're going to wear the other one, right? Because Ryan already has one, and the blacksmith would only know to smash it with his hammer or something."

Her babbling amused him until he saw the tears glinting on her lashes.

"I will wear it proudly for the rest of our days," he said. "Sweetness, why do you cry now?"

"You picked me." She sniffed. "No one's ever done that, either. I mean I had boyfriends, but none of them were right. Not like you. I'm going to have to give you a very special lap dance." She drew back to look into his eyes. "You didn't give the queen a ring, did you?"

"She already wore her husband's." He kissed the tip of her nose. "And while I loved her, I always knew where her majesty was: in front of a mirror, sitting on her throne, or sneaking away to my bed."

Christine's expression grew solemn. "Did you have to call her 'Your Majesty' when you were doing it?"

"She preferred me to remain silent when she graced me with her affections, and she was never a female to talk much when seeking her pleasures." Colm hadn't thought of the queen since being restored to life, and now his memories of her seemed foxed and yellowed as a page from an ancient book. "Have I told you how much I love you this day, my lady?"

She pretended to count on her fingers. "Only nine times."

"I love you. Ten." He carried her back to their bedroom. "I adore you. Eleven. You have my heart. Twelve."

"And I have you." Christine finished unfastening his trousers and curled her fingers around his iron-hard girth. "Keep talking, my man. You're not allowed to be quiet around me."

"Yes, my love." He lowered her onto the bed. "Now, about this lap dance—can you be naked for it?"

AT DAWN KAYLA left Ryan sleeping in the cottage to go to the barn, where she fed the horses and removed the chains wrapped around Fallon.

"There's enough room by the lake for you to shift down there," Kayla told the motorcycle as she walked him out of the barn. "You can hunt for an hour, but you've got to stay out of sight."

Will you ride with me to the water, my lady?

The dragon's wistful thoughts came with the same surge of loneliness any horse felt when separated from their herd.

"Sure," she said, and climbed on. "Let's go."

Fallon kept his engine quiet as he took her to the lake's edge, and when she climbed off and backed away he shifted into his true form. This close to him Kayla could see he'd shed some damaged scales, which revealed the jagged scars in his hide. She gently touched one so deep her hand could fit inside it.

"That blast at the faire really did a number on you."

That is not from the battle, my lady. The dragon stretched out his wings, and made a purring sound of pleasure before he folded them again. *It feels good to be released.*

Kayla walked around him, inspecting the rest of him and finding a dozen more spots where he'd been scarred.

"Can't you repair your hide when you shift form?"

That is not permitted. Fallon yawned, and exhaled a small cloud of smoke. *Our masters enjoy seeing their marks on us.*

"The *Blackstones* did all this to you?" She felt sick. "Why don't you just eat them?"

Fallon's black lips curved up as if he were amused.

Would you have devoured your parent?

"My dad never physically abused me, but okay, I see the point." A thought occurred to her, and she said, "Is that why you're being so nice to us? Because you think we'll hurt you the way they did?"

No, my lady. I merely return your kindness to me. You could never do such things to me or any living thing. Our masters are very different from you.

As the dragon showed her memories of the abuse he and the other dragons had suffered, Kayla staggered back a step. The Dark Fae kept their mounts in filthy underground dungeons, where they were beaten for the slightest show of disobedience. Fallon had taken the most abuse, for he often tried to protect his siblings with his own body. As Kayla watched Dirk whipping him for some mistake, she spotted a small, pale face watching from a cage. Barely old enough to stand, the baby was naked, filthy, and obviously terrified by Dirk's sadistic punishment. Yet she didn't make a sound as she watched with haunted gray eyes.

"Tara," Kayla whispered, horrified.

They left the changeling child in our care, Fallon told her, and showed her another memory of the baby curled up with a sleeping dragon. *But we could not protect her from them.*

Kayla clamped a hand over her mouth to muffle a cry as she saw a big, craggy-faced man grab baby Tara by the neck and fling her out of his way. Dirk came and scooped her up, examining her almost indifferently as she squalled and squirmed. When she tried to bite him, he dropped her and kicked her back into her cell.

As the image faded from her mind Kayla felt numb. "How often did they abuse her?"

Dark Fae beat their young until they are absolutely obedient. The dragon showed her a bruised, battered Tara cowering in a corner as Dirk came for her. *The changeling remembers none of this. When she was bespelled, they scoured away her memories of them.*

Kayla spotted Christine coming down the path to the lake, and said to Fallon, "Go and hunt now. I'll meet you back here in an hour."

My thanks, my lady.

The dragon trudged down and slid into the water, displacing enough to make a sizable wave as he submerged. Christine joined her and watched Fallon's large shadow speed away under the surface.

"Going swimming with the monster?" the dancer asked. "'Cause if you dip so much as a toe in that water, I'm conking you on the head and dragging you back to camp."

"He's getting breakfast," Kayla said, turning to her friend. "I need to go and talk to Tara. Would you come with me?"

Christine's eyes narrowed. "Don't you remember what happened the *last* time you had a chat with that girl?"

"She can't do anything." She put her hand on the dancer's arm. "Please. It's important."

"All right." Christine squinted at her. "But the minute you start aw-honeying her, I'm conking everybody."

When they got to the cottage where Tara had been

secluded, the big Fae warrior standing guard refused to let them inside.

"I have my orders, my ladies," Donal told them flatly, his long, blue-black hair brushing his bulging biceps as he shook his head. "No visitors."

Christine smiled up at him. "We're not visiting her, sugar. We're questioning her." She patted his broad chest. "Don't make me go get Colm. He'll have you shoveling horse manure for a month."

"Please, Donal," Kayla said. She looked into his flinty dark eyes, and felt something knot in her chest. "We really do have to speak with her."

His stern expression softened. Then he checked left and right. He looked at each of them in turn, then tilted his head at the door.

"Five minutes, no more," he said, and opened the door for them. "Should I hear anything untoward, stay away from the door lest it hit you."

They went through, and he closed the door behind them. The cottage appeared empty except for a pile of blankets on the floor, and a tray of untouched, congealing food. Kayla heard the rattle of heavy chains from under the pile as a head of snarled ash blonde hair appeared.

Tara shrugged off the blankets and sat up, watching them without blinking.

"We're not going to hurt you," Kayla said. "We just want to talk."

"I don't," Christine muttered, and folded her arms as she watched the changeling.

The teenager smirked at her before shifting her gaze to Kayla's face.

Feeling this might go better if she showed some trust, Kayla walked over to Tara and crouched down at her eye level.

"You said a lot of awful things to me the last time we talked. You did a terrible thing, too." She saw the dried bloodstains on the neck of Tara's blouse and frowned. "Did someone hurt you?"

The changeling's thin shoulders hunched, and she looked away.

"Colm said she got hurt going through the portal," Christine said. "Jannon healed her."

"I didn't know," Kayla said, but Tara only glared at her. "If I had, I would have come sooner. I'm sorry. Is there anything you need?"

The chains clinked as Tara crawled around to turn her back on Kayla. She hugged her knees and stared at the wall.

Seeing the teenager's hunched spine should have felt like a rejection to Kayla. Instead it made her think of all the nights she had woken to find Tara sitting by the window in their room, rocking herself as she stared out at the moon. At the time Kayla had simply assumed she was depressed again. Now she knew better.

"Dirk's dragon came back with me," she told Tara. "I can read his mind, just like horses. He showed me how the Blackstones treated you when you were a baby. How they beat you–"

"You don't know anything," Tara growled, as the teenager lunged at her. But she abruptly came up short as Christine stepped on her chains. Tara seemed not to notice. "I'm nothing to you. Get out of here. Get out."

As Kayla rose and backed away, Christine stood her ground, keeping the chains tight.

"If that's how you treat the only person on this earth who ever loved you," the dancer said, "then you deserve to be chained like a rabid dog."

Tara turned her head to look up at Christine. "You

think being burned to death was bad? Wait until my brother comes for me, you slut. He'll take his time with you."

"Yeah, I think we're done here," Christine said, stepping around Tara and taking Kayla by the arm. "Let's go, sweetie. I need a bath. In Lysol."

Kayla almost made it to the door before she looked back at the teenager.

"I'll promise you this much," Kayla said. "He'll never touch you again."

Tara began to laugh, but when they closed the door behind them, Kayla thought she heard her sobbing.

Christine heard it, too, but steered her past Donal and away from the cottage. "She's faking it."

"She's scared and alone." Kayla took in a deep breath. "She thinks I hate her."

The dancer made an incredulous sound. "And you *don't?*"

"Remember when Colm told you that he didn't love you? That his heart still belonged to the Fae Queen?" Kayla stopped to face her friend. "You knew he meant every word he said. Did you give up on him after that?"

"Yes." Christine's mouth twisted. "No. But I wanted to, really bad."

Kayla pointed back at the cottage. "That girl has been doing whatever it takes to survive since she was a baby. She's been beaten, tormented, threatened and mentally abused. She was taken from her mother, and dumped with strangers. Her brother has been using her dreams to molest her for six years. We were her family, and we never had a clue. I can't even imagine how hard it's been for her just to get out of bed every day."

"But somehow she managed," the dancer countered.

"What was the alternative? Kill herself?" Kayla shook

her head. "She could have dropped me in her brother's lap, and her nightmare would have finally ended. But that's not what she did. I think when she opened the portal without telling Dirk first, she was obeying him—but giving me a chance to escape, too."

"She didn't try to defend herself when I clobbered her before I jumped in after you." Christine agreed, although she grimaced. "So what do you want to do? Make friends with her? I don't think that's going to happen."

"It doesn't matter," Kayla said. "Since she was born, Tara has been a slave to the Blackstones, just like the dragons. So I'm going to do what I would have if I'd known what was going on. I'm going to fight for her. I'm going to free her."

THAT AFTERNOON JANNON carried the last of the jousting gear into the barn's storage room, and held it as Kayla sorted it on the shelves. Though he was glad to be busy, there seemed little point.

"You needn't bother," he said. "'Tis unlikely we'll perform here. Lawrence cannot hire mortals if they cannot enter the camp."

"I have a feeling you guys are going to need to blow off some steam anyway." She hung the last hind guard on a hook and surveyed her tidy arrangements. "Christine told me you healed Tara again. Thank you."

He glanced down at his bandaged arm. "'Twas naught but a scratch." He saw how she was looking at him. "Wallace has declared me free of her magick. She controls me no longer, Rowe."

"But you still want to go see her," she guessed. "I feel the same pull. You want to love her, even when you don't. You want my advice?"

He heaved a sigh. "Not especially, but you are a woman. You cannot help dispensing it."

"Then here it is: stop hating yourself for being a nice guy." She patted his shoulder. "I'm heading into town with Christine to pick up some fresh groceries and stuff. Do you need anything for your arm?"

"'Tis not so bad as that."

As she headed out of the barn, Jannon tugged back the bandage around the wound to have a look, and went still when he saw the gash had vanished. He untied the cloth to press the unbroken skin, yet felt no pain. Something that Tara had told him before he'd healed her roared in his ears.

The clan cast this spell over me when I was a baby, after my father cut me out of my mother's belly.

At the time Jannon had thought the claim just another lie. Even if the mother had been mortal, the Blackstones would never kill a female proven capable of bearing children for them. She would be impregnated over and over …unless…

"Bloody hell." He trotted after Kayla. "Rowe, do you–" Though she stopped, he thought better of it. "Never mind."

Despite her puzzled expression, he continued past her and headed for the blacksmith's cottage.

Through the window Jannon saw Wallace sorting his tools on a table, and hesitated. If he went in and blurted out his suspicions the spelltracker would think him crazed. Quickly he wound the bandage around his arm before he knocked.

"Come in," the smith called, and hefted a sledge when Jannon stepped inside. "Care to pound some steel with me, brother? I've three swords wanting new edges."

"Another time." Jannon paused to choose his words carefully. "There is something that puzzles me, Wallace. Colm had so many wounds he should have died at once beneath the Blackstones' blades, but he lingered a time before he did. Why was that?"

"Longacre is strong as ten oxen, and he meant to shield Christine until she could be brought to safety." Wallace put down the big hammer. "Why do you ask?"

"She had been beaten bloody before he went to save her," Jannon reminded him. "Could her half-mortal blood somehow have kept him breathing a little longer?"

Wallace scowled. "Blood heals only Dark Fae, which Colm is not."

"As you say." Jannon began to pace as he tried to sort it out. "Mortals heal Fae and Dark Fae. Halflings may, too. We know Rowe has Fae blood, but she was able to heal Ryan."

"That was with sex," the smith pointed out, and then looked thoughtful. "Still, as a halfling she should not have been able to heal him so completely, or so quickly. 'Tis an interesting point. Perhaps it was their bond. Love is certainly more powerful than lust."

Jannon folded his hands behind his back to hide the bandage. "What if Kayla or Christine had been half Dark Fae?"

Wallace shook his head. "'Twould not have worked. Evil taints Dark Fae life energy. Our bodies will not absorb it. Longacre lives, and 'tis all that matters." Wallace came around the table and retrieved two bottles of ale from his cooler. "You cannot suspect either lady of being Dark Fae, brother. Christine has proven her Fae blood, and Kayla, too. Both fair shine with goodness."

Jannon had spent weeks watching Tara while she had worked as Forever Faire's seamstress. When she had not been sewing or repairing costumes for their performances, she had been fashioning garlands and wands to hand out to children. For all those times he had never once seen her use a straight edge, pattern or measure.

"Here." The smith handed an ale to Jannon. "It will

settle your prancing brain."

"Not tonight." He returned the bottle and headed for the door.

"Jan." When he looked back, Wallace seemed startled. "I have never known you to refuse a drink. What are you about?"

"Using my wits for once." He went out before the smith could reply.

He knew Donal stood guard over Tara, and he had no doubt Ryan had left orders not to admit Jannon, Gavan, or any lone Fae in to see the changeling. Even chained as she was, Sheridan did not trust her.

Jannon had felt nothing but anger with the girl since being released from her magick. Now he would know the full truth, even if it meant risking enslavement to her a second time.

Although they'd left Tara in the cottage originally assigned to him—and he'd moved elsewhere—Jannon had surveyed the little building when he'd first arrived. Like any warrior, he had determined its strengths and vulnerabilities, one of which he now exploited.

From the back he approached a window that could not be seen. From the exterior it was hidden by a high hedge with trumpet shaped flowers. On the other side of the window was a small, unused back room whose door had been locked. Jannon wasted no time wading into the thick foliage. Though the window was closed, he took a dagger from his boot. He easily worked the blade into the bottom of the window and lifted. The wood frame split and, with some twisting and scraping all around, the entire sash cracked. Jannon pried the window out and set it on the ground. He climbed through into the dark back room, unlocked the door, and slipped into the front room.

Blankets had been draped over the windows to block

out the light, and only a single camp lantern cast a feeble glow over the changeling. She sat cross-legged, with a long, looped string woven around her fingers. When she shook off the string she frowned, and turned her head to stare at him.

He held up his hands in a calming gesture. "I came to show you something."

"Then you'd better come closer, so I can see you."

Though Tara sounded indifferent, she kept her voice low enough that the guard would not hear her. That gave Jannon hope. He moved until he stood within the lamp-light, and peeled off the bandage. He held his arm out.

"This is where I cut myself for you this morning."

Her brows rose. "And?"

"Now there is not a mark on me." When she said nothing he tossed the bandage into her lap. "You healed me."

"That's funny," she said, her tone musing. "I don't remember having sex with you. Did you erase my memory of it, the way I think my brother does sometimes when he's extra rough?"

She had deliberately mentioned Dirk to anger him, but why?

"Your mouth on my skin did it." He tapped the inside of his arm. "But we cannot be healed by Dark Fae."

"Then it wasn't– Oh, I get it." Her lips curled into an unpleasant smile. "You think I'm using magick to heal you? While I'm chained? You really aren't very smart, are you?"

"I have watched you for a long time," he said. "You can measure anything with a glance. That is a Fae gift."

She made a rude sound. "Dream on, dude."

"Jarek Blackstone is known for his zeal in capturing our women." Jannon watched her eyes, and saw a flicker of fear pass through them. "He forces himself on them over and over until they die, or become mindless and are slain. Doubtless he enjoys their pain and degradation, but with your mother I think he had another aim. He wished to create a halfling who was not mortal at all."

Tara peered up at him. "So what if he did? I'm still a Blackstone."

"You are also Fae. One of us." He saw her eyes shimmer, and her lower lip tremble. "And you are in love with me. That is how you were able to heal me. You are not evil."

"I don't love you. I can't, I'm not—" Tara crumpled, and sobbed into her thin hands.

Jannon knelt down beside her, and pulled her against him, making soothing sounds as he smoothed her rumpled hair back from her brow.

"They have made you think you can be nothing more than Dark Fae. That was to control you, sweetheart. If you were, you could not use your Fae gift. You could never love anyone but yourself. You would have followed your sister into the shadows." He pressed his mouth to her temple. "Your magick is gone from me. What calls me to you is your Fae blood."

She swiped at her face before she looked up at him with her solemn gray eyes. "You still care about me, after everything I've done?"

He nodded. "You have my heart, my girl. Whether you wish it or not." He thumbed away a tear from her cheek. "We can be together, Tara. Once I explain it to Ryan, he will see the truth of you, as I do."

"Can we go together to talk to him?" She looked down at her chains and wrinkled her nose. "Oh, yeah, I'm still grounded. It's all right. There are just some things that you need to tell him for me, about the clan."

"I will bring him here to you."

Jannon curled his hand around the links, feeling the

burn of the iron on his skin. He saw the dark red marks it had left on her pale flesh and swore softly.

"It's okay. I move them around a lot." She looked down as he rearranged the chains so he could put the lock on the floor. "What are you doing?"

"Trusting you."

He took the blade from his boot again, set the tip in the keyhole, and forced it down with his considerable weight. Metal snapped and cracked and, when he gave the dagger a savage twist, the lock popped open. Jannon unwound the chains binding her, tossing them aside before standing and offering her his hand.

"Come, we will go together to Ryan."

Tara wobbled as she stood, and then stumbled into his arms. "I'm sorry."

The feel of her fragile form against him made Jannon wonder if he dared hope to someday make her his. He would have to wait until she was stronger. She would have to want him enough to offer herself. After what that sodding brother of hers had done, it might be a long time. Still, he could wait until she was ready. He wanted her no other way but willing.

"Let me grab my shoes," Tara said, slipping away to bend down to the pile of blankets, but she lost her footing.

Jannon reached to steady her, and didn't see the chain she flung at him until it wrapped around his neck. She used her shoulder to knock him off balance, and then straightened as he toppled onto his back.

"I'm sorry," she whispered as she wrapped another chain around her hand.

He had time to call out for the guard before she clouted him, but Jannon could only watch as she knelt beside him.

"I love you," he told her, hoping that would stop her.

It didn't.

$\mathscr{H}$ABIT KEPT KAYLA glancing in the rear view mirror. Or maybe it was the familiar surroundings.

"Everything is so green down here," Christine said, gazing out the passenger window. "Look at those orange trees." She gave Kayla a conspiratorial look. "Can we stop and grab some?"

"Sure. We can get shot for trespassing and thieving, too." Kayla turned to enter the parking lot of a supermarket and found an empty space. "I used to steal fruit when I was a kid, until a grove owner caught me in the act." She pinched the air. "Came this close to getting a rump full of rock salt."

"Ouch. Your farmers are mean." Christine climbed out and pulled off her jacket, tossing it on the seat. "Whew, it's hot. Is there a mall nearby? I could use a few more tank tops and some shorts."

"No mall, but there's a Target down the road." As they walked in and grabbed a buggy, Kayla noticed a dark blotch on Christine's left shoulder. "How did you get that bruise?"

The dancer tucked in her chin to look at the spot. "Oh, that? It's just an ugly old birthmark."

As they shopped, Kayla kept glancing at the blemish, with the growing feeling that it looked familiar. She put a hand on Christine's arm.

"Sorry, it's just…" Kayla took a closer look. "Did you show this to me before?"

"I doubt it, since I hate the damn thing. I got my first tattoo just to cover it up. The guy did a tribal turtle doodad." They'd stopped in the produce section, and Christine picked up a bunch of organic bananas. "The things we think are cool when we're sixteen. I kinda owe that dragon for scorching off all my ink."

Suddenly Kayla dimly recalled seeing it on a much smaller shoulder.

"Okay, this is really weird. Tara had a birthmark just like that, in the exact same place."

"Great, another reason to hate it," Christine said, then her brows drew together. "You said she *had* one. Did she get a tattoo over it?"

Kayla shook her head. "It disappeared. My dad said sometimes birthmarks faded, but I'm pretty sure one night it was there, and the next it wasn't." She thought hard for a moment. "The only reason I remember is because it was the day after my mother left us. When the Blackstones left Tara at our house in Ashdale."

"You mean– " Christine laughed. "Oh, no, honey. Lots of babies have birthmarks."

"That drunk at the strip club thought we were twins." As she studied the dancer's face, hope fluttered in Kayla's chest. "You weren't wearing any makeup that night." Kayla paused and deflated a little. "The only problem is that you're a little too old to be my sister."

"I don't know how old I am," Christine said and made a face. "No birth certificate, so no birthday. They guessed I was about two and a half. But I was always smaller than the other kids, and I didn't have boobs until I was in the tenth grade."

"We need to compare notes," Kayla said, grabbing her arm. She glanced around and saw the market had a small café area by the bakery. "Let's go get a cupcake or something."

Christine pushed the buggy in that direction. "Do they make them with rum?"

Once they sat down with coffees and a pair of jumbo muffins, Kayla felt almost afraid to start asking her friend more questions.

"All right," Christine said. "We've got a birthmark, we look like sisters, and I might be the right age." The dancer wiped some sugar from the top of her muffin and licked it from her finger. "What else would be proof? I don't know where I was born, but I was left at a hospital outside Gatlinburg. That's twenty miles or so from Ashdale."

Kayla stirred her coffee. "Do you remember anything about your parents?"

"My mom had light hair. Blonde, I think," Christine said. "It was so soft, and it smelled like flowers. Yours?"

Kayla nodded. "She came in every night to sing a song to us. I always fell asleep–"

"Before she stopped singing," Christine finished, as she visibly paled. "Her voice was like her touch. Warm and gentle."

Kayla leaned forward. "What were the words to the song?"

Christine shook her head slowly. "I don't remember any words. She sang, I don't know, like a–"

"Bird. She sang like a bird." Kayla eyes stung.

Christine jumped up from the table and went to the bakery counter. As Kayla used a napkin to wipe her nose, she watched Christine talk to the cashier. When she returned she had a mobile phone and a pen.

"Yes," she said into the phone as she sat down. "The number for social services, please." As Christine pinned the phone to her ear with her shoulder, she wrote a number on the palm of her hand. "Thanks." She dropped the phone into her other hand and dialed with her thumb. "This'll just take a minute."

Kayla sat on the edge of her seat, as Christine made her way through the social services bureaucracy.

"It's an emergency," she finally declared. "I need Janice Lynette's extension. Just put me through to her voicemail." She tapped the pen on the table as she waited. "My old social worker," she whispered to Kayla. "She'll remember me. We went to the same tattoo guy."

"Even so, it's been–"

Christine held up her index finger and forced a smile. "Ms. Lynette?" she said in a much stronger drawl. "It's Christine Marszalek. I don't know if you remember–" She paused to listen. "Well, I'm just fine, how are you?" Again she paused. "I know, I've been meaning to get in touch."

To give her some privacy Kayla got up and went to the restroom. Truth be told, though, it was Kayla who needed the privacy. She ran warm water over her trembling hands, then splashed it on her cold face. All the wretched feelings from her childhood had come rushing back, but she couldn't hate her mother anymore. If everything they'd pieced together was true, then she must have been trying to protect her real sister.

But why hadn't she taken both daughters? Was it because Kayla had been somewhere else with her father, and her mother couldn't wait? Or hadn't she been as important as her baby sister?

Kayla dabbed her face with a paper towel, not sure she wanted to know the answers. But she took a shaky breath and returned to the café. Christine was gaping at the phone on the table. Kayla half sat, half fell into the seat opposite her.

"What is it?" she asked.

Christine finally focused on her. "I told her I might have found some family, and asked if she had any more details from the night I was dumped at the hospital. She did."

Kayla tried to swallow in a dry throat. "And?"

"There were witnesses," Christine whispered. "She never told me that before. In the E.R., there were witnesses." Kayla reached across the table and grasped her hand. "My mother was blonde," Christine continued, with something like awe in her voice. She stared down at their hands. "She drove off in an old woody station wagon. The cops found it the next day, wrecked in a ditch. The woman was all messed up, so they took her back to the hospital. They were never able to identify her before she disappeared again." She met Kayla's gaze. "All she left behind was a huge stain on her hospital bed."

The world around them faded, and all Kayla could see was Christine's face.

"My dad had an old station wagon," Kayla said, barely able to get the words out past the constriction in her throat. "One of the woody kind." They squeezed each other's hands. "My mother took it the night she left us."

In the next moment, they were up and in each other's

arms. Kayla hugged Christine fiercely, and Christine held on so tight she almost couldn't breathe.

"Why would she take me and not you?" Christine sobbed.

Kayla felt as if her heart might burst. "I was in the city with my… with our Dad." She choked back a strangled cry. "Maybe getting you to a safe place was more important to her."

"Or maybe she was coming for you," Christine insisted. Her sister drew back and sniffed. "That road, where she wrecked her car? It runs straight through to Chattanooga."

The last knot in Kayla's heart slowly unraveled. She took Christine's face in her hands, staring at her through tear-filled eyes.

"You're nineteen years old," Kayla said in a trembling voice. "Your birthday is the thirtieth of December. When you were a baby you loved apple slices, and strawberry milk, and listening to Mom sing."

Christine's eyes went wide. "I remember a little girl," she said, as the tears streamed down her face. "She had a bunch of those toy horses with long manes and tails. They were in all the colors of the rainbow." Christine stared at her hair. "You always wore your hair in braids."

Kayla laughed a little. "Which you kept trying to gnaw on." She took Christine's hands in hers. "I want to know everything about you. Everything you haven't told me. Everything I've missed."

"I've been waiting nineteen years to tell you," Christine said with a laugh. "It'll take some time."

Kayla grinned, absorbing every detail of Christine's face. For a few moments, they could only look at each other.

"Sister," Kayla whispered, which made Christine grin.

"If it's all right with you," her sister said. "I'd rather not change my name. I'm kind of attached to Christine."

Kayla's smile faded. "Let her keep the name. That's the last thing she's ever going to steal from you."

CHAPTER 12

TARA WAITED UNTIL sunset before she covered the Fae warrior with her blankets and left the cottage. Refusing to eat had left her as weak as if she were still chained. She could smell the food the men were preparing for the evening meal. They'd find Jannon later, when they remembered to bring a tray for her.

If they remember, the snide side of her heart whispered. *Maybe they'll keep forgetting.*

Ryan and his men hadn't been cruel to her, but they hadn't bothered to be kind, either. The only reason they'd kept her alive was because of Kayla, and her idiotic ideas about her being damaged or something. Tara should have laughed in her face when she'd talked about the clan abusing her—or used it to coax Kayla into setting her free. Dirk would have.

The sound of heavy footsteps crushing the carpet of brown leaves made Tara duck down in some brush.

"I know naught about the Cloudstar," Gavan said, sounding miffed. "Our liege may hold a life-debt over them, but I doubt it will have much sway. Devalan has no love of outcasts."

"Aye, but his honor will outweigh his disgust," Colm replied. "We should take Jannon with us when we call on the clan. Devalan married a Ferguson, as I recollect."

"Doubtless to combat the seething heat here," Gavan said, his voice growing distant. "'Tis like one giant sweathouse, even in winter."

Once the men had gone, Tara crawled out of the brush and stood up to head for the spell boundary. Dirk had assured her that the changeling curse cloaking her would shield her from any spell the Fae cast against Dark Fae. It had worked in Tennessee. When she reached the protective barrier, however, the bruised side of her body began throbbing unpleasantly.

Going through the Fae portal had almost killed her. Pushing through this might just finish her off.

Tara smirked.

She stepped to the barrier's edge, spread out her arms, and walked into the boundary. Magic burned against the left side of her body, and purred against the right. By the time she stepped through she could feel every bruise down to the bone. She gasped, barely able to stay upright. But the lopsided pain brought forth her nightmare, and its meaning.

The beautiful Fae woman in the cell had been her mother. The thug with the blade, a bigger version of Dirk, was Jarek, her father. She had been the squalling infant.

Jannon had been right about everything.

I love you, he'd said.

"So what? Everybody has to love me."

Tara limped on, making her way to the opposite side of the lake.

She knew she didn't have to open a shadow portal

there. She could keep going until she reached town. It would be easy to find some tourists who lived far from Florida. Canadians were supposed to be nice people, and she could hitch a ride north with an older couple. By the time they reached the U.S. border they'd want her to move in with them, so they could take care of her and love her and never let her suffer again.

Only Dirk would find her, and kill them, and the nightmare would start all over again. No, she had to stick to her original plan.

Tara walked into the woods until she felt sure none of the Fae would spot her from the other side of the lake. Then she leaned against a nubby pine tree trunk and drew on the last dregs of her power. The moonlight shifted away from the pine's shadow, which darkened and expanded until it formed a large oval with glowing yellow edges.

Dirk Blackstone stepped through the shadow, his big body tense, and long daggers held ready. When he saw her, he sheathed one blade but kept the other in his fist.

"You took your time," he muttered, his gaze crawling over her with greedy thoroughness. "Where is she?"

Lying to her brother wasn't any more difficult than it had been with Kayla. "I killed her."

Dirk made a vicious sound. "You did what?"

"They were planning to use her when you came after them. It's why they let me go." She gestured at the portal. "So I'd bring you here."

Her brother inspected their surroundings. "Yet I see no Fae lying in wait for me."

"She's dead. Plan ruined." She gestured toward the portal. "Go back to Tennessee, Dirk. There's nothing left for you here."

He advanced on her. "I have you."

"No." Tara knew better than to run, so she pulled out

the blade she'd taken from Jannon. "You don't, and you never will again."

Dirk grabbed her wrist before she could plunge the dagger into his chest, and pried the hilt from her fingers.

"I think not, little sister." He bent his head closer to her, breathing in. "You smell like that Fae buffoon."

"That's because I fucked him." She let her expression go dreamy. "You never told me how good they are in bed."

Dirk gripped her by the throat and shook her. "You dare let another man touch you," he roared.

All she needed to do was push him a little harder. "He did more than touch. His hands were so warm on my skin. So much better than your cold, clammy touch. And when he put his cock inside me, it felt so good. He made me come over and over–"

Her brother flung her to the ground, driving his boot into her belly. Tara didn't resist that kick or the others that slammed into her breasts and back and face. She felt like she was back in the Fae portal again, only she wasn't going to make it out. Dirk was going to beat her to death this time, and that would be her penance for all the horrible, hateful things she'd done.

Tara retreated into a very small corner of her mind, where she kept the image of Jannon's handsome face, the spicy heat of his scent, and the wonderful rumble of his laughter. Finally she could answer him, even if he would never hear it.

I love you, too.

As Tara's mouth filled with blood, and her vision grayed, her brother dragged her up on her feet and shoved her into another man's arms.

"Hello, little cousin," Beck Blackstone said. "You've been naughty again, haven't you? Warms my heart to know you're keeping true to your blood."

"Keep her chained in my tent," Dirk told him. "Once we have the spellsinger, I will deal with her."

Tara forced her swollen eyelids open. When she saw what was slithering through the expanding shadow portal, she dragged in an agonized breath to scream.

"Never fear, Cousin," Beck said as he clamped his hand over her mouth. "We did not bring these beauties here to feast on you." He eyed Dirk. "Then again, you may serve as the last course."

KAYLA WALKED INTO the barn to find Ryan had done all her chores, and was saddling Titan and Grania.

"Hey, are you trying to steal my job?"

Although she had been looking for him to tell him the good news about Christine, something was up.

"I wanted to free you for the evening," he said. He adjusted one stirrup before swinging up to mount the big white stallion. He reached down to scoop her up and settle her on the cream-colored mare. "Unless you do not care to ride with me," he said, an impish grin stealing over his face.

Whatever he was up to, he was at ease. Kayla relaxed. Her good news could wait. She smoothed Grania's bronze mane under the lay of the reins.

"Is there a secret, underground, crystal city on our route?"

Ryan laughed. "Not unless we ride back to Ashdale."

I am willing, Titan thought to her.

So am I, Grania chimed in. *I have been idle so long there are cobwebs on my hooves.*

"That's a bit ambitious, even for Fae horses." Kayla rubbed the mare's neck. "So where are we going?"

"I must post a notice of sorts," Ryan said as he came alongside her to guide their mounts out of the barn. "Whenever we enter a new territory I make our presence known to any local clans or passing Fae."

That sounded pretty polite to her. "Why, so they don't accidentally walk into a faire run by outlaws?"

"I think of it as a courtesy, particularly when I am wont to call on a clan leader for a favor."

He trotted Titan to match Grania's shorter gait as they rode out of the camp. Then he gave Kayla a roguish grin before he let the big horse break into a rolling lope.

"Okay, sweetie," Kayla said, and touched her heels to the mare's side. "Let's show the boys how it's done."

Titan had a powerful, ground-eating gallop, but Grania had the advantage of a lighter rider and more stamina. Kayla also knew how to hold herself in the saddle to cut down on drag and best distribute her weight. After a minute they caught up with Ryan, and then moved to pass him. Titan lengthened his stride, but the mare was having none of that, and poured on the speed. Kayla let Grania run until they were a quarter-mile ahead, and then slowed her to a cooling walk.

"Oh, there you are," she said as Ryan and Titan finally caught up to them. "We were getting worried."

Grania whinnied as if she were laughing, and Titan gave the mare an evil look.

"You've raced before," Ryan accused.

"I placed first in my academy's annual four-forty sprint for charity." She offered him a prim smile. "Three years in a row."

From there they rode across the property to the north of the camp, which opened up into broad acres densely carpeted by feed grasses and clover. Kayla spotted white stacks of commercial bee hives tucked along the edges of the field. There were enough rolled bales of hay scattered along a dirt access road to keep their herd stuffed until next summer.

"This is all your land?" she asked as Ryan finally slowed the stallion at the start of a wide trail canopied by enormous weeping willows.

"It was, once." Ryan dismounted and lifted her off Grania. "I traded it to the Cloudstar clan in return for perpetual performance rights."

"So you can visit, but you can't live here." She watched him remove a large, dark sack from Titan's saddlebag. "You can't live anywhere but the lodge at Ashdale, can you? And I ruined that."

"The blame for that is on the Blackstone clan." He tucked her arm through his. "The traveling life is not so bad. We have grown accustomed to it."

Because they had no alternative, Kayla thought, and forced a smile. "Okay, so where are you putting up the notice that you're here?"

"Watch and see." Ryan emptied what looked like hundreds of tiny diamonds into his palm. Just as Kayla realized they were crystals from the caves in Ashdale, her lover swung his arm back, and hurled the tiny gems at the center of the trail.

Silent explosions of light burst in the dark air. They showered the grassy path and spread over the ground as stalks made of tiny stars erupted from the soil. The enchanted plants grew into emerald vines. The climbing plants spun around the drooping greenery of the willows and began to spiral up through them. Leaves sprouted and opened along the vines, and then thousands of tiny white and amber flowers bloomed. More little stars sparkled from their centers.

Kayla smiled with delight as she smelled honeysuckle and jasmine spilling into the warm night air.

"Amazing."

She went to one vine and touched the soft spikes of its honeysuckle blooms. The vine extended another shoot that wound gently around her fingers, making her chuckle.

"I was thinking you'd put up a flyer or something."

"Some clans use flowers to speak in their absence." He joined her, and touched the white blooms. "This means we have come for refuge." His fingers shifted to the jasmine. "And this, that we ask to parlay." He shook the vine, showering her with the little blooms.

Kayla brushed a few off her nose, but seeing the honeysuckle in her hair made her insides melt a little. Ryan always found a way to make her feel beautiful.

"This is actually pretty smart," she said. "If the locals see it, they'll just think they're flowers. Can you say something simple, like hello or goodbye?"

"A sunflower left by the hidden entrance to a clan's stronghold is a passing Fae's greeting," Ryan told her. "When we leave a territory, we bid farewell with lillies."

The scent of the vines made her feel a little drowsy and, oddly, aroused. "Do you use flowers for more personal messages? Something like 'Give me a kiss?'"

Ryan took a crystal from the sack and closed his hand over it. When he opened his fingers a delicate pink rosebud lay on his palm. He took it and stroked it across her lips.

"This means I want to kiss you." He moved it over her chin and down to the hollow of her throat. "This, I wish to embrace you."

Kayla glanced down to watch him circle the peak of one hard nipple poking under her shirt. Aching heat spread from her breast up her neck and flooded her cheeks.

"And that?"

"You tempt me." He released a few buttons of her blouse and traced the inner curve of her breast with the delicate petals. "I desire you."

She glanced over at the horses, and saw both had turned away and were happily grazing their way through a dense patch of bahia grass.

"No snuggery around here, I guess."

"We can make our own."

Ryan scattered the remaining crystals from the sack on the ground, making the soil glow before tiny ferns appeared. The soft, feathery leaves curled and interwove as they grew longer and thicker, until they formed a knee-high, fluffy carpet.

"Oh, I want one of these in my cottage." Kayla moved to the center of the enchanted plants, sinking down to caress the living bed. She looked up at Ryan, who stood watching her intently. "Just when I think I've seen all the magick, you show me more."

"Then you know how I feel." He knelt down before her, and took her hands in his. "Each time I look at you, I am enchanted anew."

"Keep watching."

She thought away their clothes and boots, and then pressed her naked body against his. Her hair twined with his as their body heat melded with the green scent of the ferns. She leaned back against his palms, offering her breasts to him as he came over her. He brushed his lips over her peaks, as gently as the touch of the rosebud, making her nipples pucker even tighter.

Ryan kissed every inch of her from her collarbones

down to her navel. She squirmed under the heated path, shuddering in anticipation. When he sat back to look at her, Kayla could hardly control herself.

"Open your thighs for me," he murmured, and produced the rosebud again, this time trailing it through the dark triangle curling over her sex. "I want to taste you."

"I was thinking the same thing." Kayla reversed herself on the luxurious bed, until the top of her head pressed against the hard muscles of his thighs. She cradled his heavy erection between her palms. "And I don't want to wait until you're through playing with me."

Ryan's breath caught as she tugged his hard shaft to her mouth. "You are an impatient woman."

"Mmmm."

She kissed a pearl of cream from the eye of his cockhead, and then enveloped him with her lips. As she lightly sucked him, Ryan lay on his side. She felt his breath on her thighs, and the sweet stroke of his tongue parting her.

Ryan laved her clit with slow, soft attention. His big hands gripped her bottom and brought her more firmly against his mouth. He shuddered when he felt her tongue caressing his girth, and groaned into her sex as she drew him deeper. His tongue rubbed her needy clit, making it pulse with delight. He stroked it to a throbbing fullness and then he went deeper, penetrating her slick opening to explore the softness within.

Kayla returned the torment by releasing him to kiss his tight, velvety balls, and sucked one gently between her lips until she felt him shake.

"Wait," Ryan muttered as he felt her nuzzle the base of his cock. He drew her leg over his shoulder as he buried his mouth between her thighs.

She took his cockhead in her mouth, slid him in, and took him deep. She held him and sucked in time with the sweeping caresses of his tongue. As his hot mouth covered her pounding clit, her fingers stroked the tightening bulge of his balls.

Ryan lifted his head to give her a pleading look. "You will make me spill."

She took her mouth away and smiled. "And how is this a bad thing?"

His big body tensed before he fisted his cock and brought it to her lips, feeding it to her until she curled her tongue against his shaft. His hips moved slowly as he glided in and out of her. He watched her intently, his eyes glittering with hunger.

"Ah," Kayla moaned around his thrusting length as she felt his thumb on her clit and two of his fingers push inside her pussy.

Ryan bent his head to kiss the inside of her thigh as he worked her with his fingers. His eyes narrowed as she tugged on him with each bob of her head.

The rasp of his thumb was almost too much for Kayla, as warmth flooded up into her belly. But she could also feel the swelling of his penis as it prepared to jet. Just as the first burst shot up through his shaft, Ryan caught her aching clit with his mouth. He tenderly sucked it until she arched and writhed against him. As she nudged her clenching mound closer, and his hips gently thrust, the climax overtook them.

Nothing felt as delicious as swallowing his spurting seed, even as her body was swamped with a thick, sweet bliss. Their muffled moans hung in the air, and stoked their pleasure. Kayla's belly clenched and unwound, only to clench again, as Ryan's massive shudder rocked the bed. The ferns clung to their skins, caressing them as they rode the waves of pleasure and the aftershocks that followed. When they finally stilled, Ryan slid from her mouth and drew his face back from between her thighs. As they both lay limp, Kayla breathed in the lush scent of his skin, mixed with the fresh green ferns.

"I want one of these in your cottage, too," Kayla murmured.

Ryan raised his head and looked at her with masculine satisfaction glowing in his sapphire eyes. "I will pave the world with fern beds."

Before she could reply Kayla felt a slight rumble under her. She sat up to peer out at the horses, who were still cropping grass. Beyond them a rapidly-moving silhouette of a big man on a bigger horse rode straight for them.

"Is that a clan guy, and should he really find us here naked and sweaty?"

Ryan instantly dressed them with a thought-spell and helped her to her feet as he watched the rider.

"It is Wallace, on Sampson."

The blacksmith wheeled his horse around to herd Titan and Grania to the trail, and didn't bother to dismount as he looked down at Ryan.

"Forgive the intrusion, but I dared not wait. Jannon has been hurt, and Tara has escaped."

CHAPTER 14

WHEN THEY ARRIVED back in camp, Ryan ordered Gavan and Lawrence to take the horses while Donal led them to the cottage where Tara had been kept.

"He must have gone in through the back, my liege," the grim-faced guard said as he opened the door. "I should have checked, but I thought Jannon free of her magick."

"He was," Wallace said flatly. "She found the means to bespell him again."

"While clad in spellbound iron chains?" Ryan shook his head and turned to Colm, who was kneeling on the floor beside Jannon. "That is unlikely."

As soon as Kayla saw the unconscious Fae she paled. "Oh, no. Please tell me he's still alive."

The sight of the brawler's bruised, blood-streaked face gave Ryan pause as well. "Will he live, Colm?"

"She hit him in the head, probably with the chains, but there are no other wounds." He glanced up at Kayla. "That dragon you brought with us has been circling the camp since you left. I know not what bedevils it, but it seemed to be looking for you." After soaking a cloth with a splash of firewine, Colm dabbed it on the side of Jannon's head. "Come back to us, brother."

"I'd better go see what's up with Fallon," Kayla said, her voice tight.

"Until we know where Tara is," Ryan told her, "you will stay away from that creature."

They all quieted as Jannon's eyes fluttered open.

"Oh thank god," Kayla said.

But when Jannon saw them, he frowned.

"Must you shout? 'Tis not as if you've never seen me–" His eyes widened and he shoved himself upright. "Tara."

"She's gone from the camp," Wallace told him.

Ryan saw the guilt steal across his warrior's features and glanced at Wallace. "Take Kayla to Christine, and stand guard over them until Colm and I join you."

The blacksmith nodded and left with Kayla.

Ryan crouched down to look into Jannon's shamed gaze. "You released Tara from the chains."

"I thought she had…after I told her about…oh, bloody fucking hell." Jannon pounded a fist into the floor boards, cracking two of them. "Aye." He told them about the encounter in a dull voice. "The moment she was free she clouted me. I wish she'd used a blade."

Ryan heard Kayla shout his name from outside the cottage, and dashed out to see her with Fallon.

"Get away from that thing!" he yelled waving her off.

"He's not trying to attack," she told him, and put a hand on the dragon's neck. "He was trying to warn the men about the Blackstones. They're here, with the rest of his herd, on the other side of the lake."

Ryan skid to a halt. He gestured for his men to follow him, and ran down to the edge of the water. Across the lake stood only more trees, but the shadows they cast writhed unnaturally over the surface of the water.

"My liege, they cannot cross the spell boundary," Wallace said. "It will protect us, and give us time to prepare." He looked down at the ground, and shook his leg. "'Tis odd, but I swear I felt something–"

Ryan grabbed at the blacksmith but only caught air. He watched in disbelief as he was jerked to the ground and dragged into the lake, disappearing with a splash. An ominous shape rose up a short distance away, water streaming from its mottled flesh as it swelled larger. The smell of rotting slime wafted over them as the giant creature lifted long, prehensile tentacles. It lashed out at the embankment.

"Retreat to arms," Ryan shouted as he dodged the limb the monster whipped at him.

As he ran toward the camp, he glanced back for any sign of Wallace. But instead he saw three other nightmares emerge to flank the tentacled creature. They moved from the water to solid ground.

Gavan appeared and tossed a sword to him. "How many?"

"Four." Ryan looked over at the lake behind him and saw how much that number had multiplied. "Twenty." He quickly took stock of the warriors streaming from the camp. "Sever the limbs," he called to his men. "Cripple them first. Pierce their brains or arteries after."

He jumped over a writhing tentacle. As he came down, he sliced it clean through with his sword. He drew on all his strength not to descend into his berserker madness.

"Colm," Ryan said, his fury building. "I will go for Wallace. Take the women out of here."

His second pointed to the sky. "Kayla just rode off on Fallon."

As more Dark Fae creatures crept out of the lake, a huge shadow passed over. Ryan looked up to see Fallon, his wings beating furiously, as he flew over the monsters toward the other side of the lake. Clinging to the space between Fallon's wings were two slight figures.

"No," Colm bellowed, looking as if he might go mad as well.

The dragon flew back to his masters, taking Kayla and Christine with him.

· · · · ·

The End of *Denied*

· · · · ·

Kayla's story continues in *Destined (Forever Faire Book Five)*.

For a sneak peek, turn the page.

DESTINED (BOOK 5)

CHAPTER 1

WARM, DAMP NIGHT air sifted over Kayla Rowe as she gripped the dragon's neck ridge and peered down at the lake below them. Dozens of enormous, slime-covered Dark Fae monsters slithered from the water as they attacked the men of Forever Faire. Although Kayla knew the Fae warriors all to be battle-hardened, superb fighters, they would soon be over-whelmed by the creatures.

You must free my brothers and sisters, lady, Fallon thought to her through their telepathic link. He began to drop down toward the trees. *Remove the keys from them, and tell them this.*

Kayla listened to the guttural string of sounds the dragon thought to her. "I don't think I can say that."

Fallon circled over the camp until he hovered above a cluster of large, powerful motorcycles.

Only remember it, and they will hear it in their minds.

"All right." She glanced back over her shoulder at her sister, Christine Marszalek. "I'm going to get the rest of the dragons. You and Fallon keep the Blackstones busy—but don't get too close, and stay away from the shadows."

"We've got your back." Christine said, handing her a dagger. Then she gave her a quick hug. "Be careful."

Fallon's long wings flapped rapidly as he dropped low enough for Kayla to jump to the ground. The air he displaced as he soared back into the sky blasted her for a moment. Then she ran to the motorcycles, yanking the keys from their ignitions as their engines roared to life.

Fallon sent me to free you. Kayla blasted the thought at the bikes as she waded through them. *He gave me a message, too. Listen to me.*

By the time she had run through her memory of Fallon's message, all of the bikes had gone silent. She wrenched out the last key and threw all of them into the woods.

A cacophony of dragon voices filled her mind. They roared and screeched, their rage almost tangible.

"Stop," she said through clenched teeth. She staggered back a pace. "*Stop.*"

It was like an ice pick being driven from temple to temple. Groaning, she dropped to her knees. Acid climbed in the back of her throat, and their voices crescendoed even higher. Tunnel vision took over, narrowing her sight. She was starting to black out. Despite the pain, she focused on the strongest thoughts.

Fallon is dead, one said, *killed by you and the Fae.*

"No," she said, gasping as she braced a hand on the nearest bike. She flooded it with memories of Fallon helping her and Christine escape the Blackstones. "He asked for sanctuary. I promised him we would try to free the rest of you. That's why I'm here. He brought me to you."

Kayla could sense some of the dragon herd listening.

She projected memories of her conversations with Fallon since giving him sanctuary. Scene after scene flowed through her mind, until finally the voices in her head gradually quieted. She took a shaky breath, and got unsteadily to her feet.

The biggest of the bikes approached and came to a stop in front of her.

You vow your men will not slay us?

"They don't want to hurt anyone," she said. "But they will defend themselves against any attack."

Why should we risk our lives to help you and Fallon? one of the other dragons demanded. *You offer nothing in return.*

Kayla nodded. "I have nothing to give you except your freedom—from cruel masters who don't care if you live or die."

The dragons thought to each other in their own language for several minutes, before the biggest backed away from Kayla.

We will transform and follow Fallon.

She concealed a huge wave of relief. "Have you seen Tara Blackstone?"

Master Dirk had her taken to his tent, the dragon replied, and showed Kayla how to get to it. *He beat her badly for trying to deceive him.*

Although she knew Tara wasn't her sister, the thought of the frail teenager being abused by Dirk made Kayla swallow against a new surge of bile.

"I'm going to free her. Please try to keep the guards away so I can."

The dragon's surly distrust seemed to melt away.

The little one is not like her kin. She is special to us. Be gentle with her.

"I will."

Kayla hurried off toward Dirk's tent. It looked like only

a few shelters had been pitched. Although the camp looked deserted, Kayla kept her head low. Dirk and his men were probably at the lake, but it didn't hurt to be careful. When she reached the tent, she peered through the flap first, then she slipped inside.

As her eyes adjusted to the dimly lit gloom, Kayla put a hand to her mouth.

Tara.

Her battered, drooping form had been tied to the center support pole. Her swollen eyes were shut and her thin arms loosely circled her abdomen. She appeared to be unconscious and barely breathing.

Fury, pity, and guilt warred in Kayla's chest. If Dirk loved Tara, then why did he treat her like his worst enemy? This wasn't love. It was twisted. Once more Kayla gave silent thanks that she had found Ryan before Dirk had gotten his hands on her.

As Kayla took a step forward, Tara lifted her head and gave her a ghastly, bloody smile.

"If you try to use my mouth again," she said, her voice ragged. "I'll bite it off."

"It's me, honey," Kayla said, rushing over to her. She knelt down to slice at the knotted cords binding the teenager's wrists. "I'm going to get you out of here."

Tara grunted and spat out blood.

"Why?" she wheezed. "I'm with my clan now. I belong to–" As she moved to avoid Kayla, Tara bit back a cry. "Don't touch me."

Kayla understood now why her breathing was so shallow. "Your beloved clan broke your ribs." She drew her razor-sharp blade across her palm. "Here." She held the gash closer. "It's okay. I want to heal you."

Tara turned her head away. "I don't want your blood or your help. Leave me alone."

"I forgot, you prefer to be beaten and abused."

Kayla touched her cheek, and a blue glow appeared under her fingertips that flooded over Tara's skin. Slowly the swelling and bruises faded from her face, and she stopped clutching her sides. But her eyes went wide.

"How did you do that?"

Kayla shook her head. "I don't know."

She had seen the same kind of light appear when she'd saved Ryan's life. But she'd thought it had been something between them. She stared at her hand. Did she have some kind of Fae healing power?

"We'll figure it out later," she said, and helped Tara to her feet. "Come on. We've got to move."

"You're being an idiot," Tara said and picked up an ugly-looking, spiked club. Though Kayla tensed, Tara went to the flap of the tent and looked outside. "My clan is circling around the lake to attack the Fae, so you'll have to go back through the woods. I'll hold them off as long as I can."

"If you're such a loyal Blackstone, then why did Dirk beat you and tie you up?" When Tara didn't answer, Kayla wrenched the club from her grasp, and threw it across the tent. "Did he rape you this time? Or is that for later, during the Dark Fae victory party?"

Her thin face paled. "It doesn't matter what happens to me now."

"Really? Okay. Why didn't you kill Jannon before you escaped?" As Tara looked away, Kayla came around to face her. "I'll tell you why. You couldn't do it. The same way you couldn't drop me in Dirk's lap when you pushed me through that portal. You're not like them—and I'll tell you why. Because they didn't raise you. I did."

The teenager pushed her away. "I'm not your sister."

"I don't care who or what you are. You may not want to be my sister, but I'm yours." She grabbed Tara's rigid shoulders and gave her a shake. "And for your information, that isn't because of your magick or your curse or whatever the hell the clan did to you. I love you. That's never going to change."

A profound weariness filled Tara's gray eyes. "But you know what I am—what I was born to be."

"That's their shit, not yours. You're old enough to decide who you are, and choose the family you want." Kayla pulled her close, wrapping her arms around the thin body. "Pick me, Tara. Screw the Blackstones. Be a Rowe."

Christine ducked inside the tent, making them both jump. Her pretty face was smudged with soot.

"Uh, ladies, I hate to interrupt the sister reunion, but it's time to go kick some slime monster ass and save our boys."

"The only way to destroy them is with dragonfire," Tara said, "or by keeping them out of the water. They can't survive long on land." Tara slipped free of Kayla's embrace and faced the woman she had so long ago replaced. "Or you could toss me to them."

"I vote for dragon bad breath," Christine said, and inclined her head toward the outside of the tent. "I've got Fallon and fourteen of his pals waiting to give us a ride back. I say we talk to them, girlfriends, and see if they'll switch sides."

Tara and Kayla nodded together. They left the tent, but as soon as the dragon herd saw Tara, they tried to crowd around her. She lifted her hands to stroke as many muzzles as she could before stopping in front of Fallon. Kayla gaped as the two eyed each other. Though she couldn't hear them, she was sure they were conversing. Evidently the teenager spoke fluent dragon.

The huge black dragon lowered his head to nudge Tara onto his back before he regarded Kayla.

Thank you for saving our little one, my lady. She is most precious to us.

Kayla knew the dragon had cared for Tara when she was a baby. Feeling the strong emotions pouring out of the entire herd, however, made her realize all the dragons considered the teenager as one of them.

"The clan is on the other side of the lake now," Tara said, holding her hand down to Christine and hoisting her up. "While they're attacking the Fae, the creatures will be vulnerable. I'll lead the herd against them."

"You do that," Christine said, "and Dirk will kill you the next time he grabs you."

Tara turned to face her. "He'll have to get through the dragons." She glanced at Kayla before she added, "and my Fae clan."

The dancer planted her hands on her hips. "About time you figured that out, kid."

As Kayla climbed up with the two other women, she opened her mouth to tell Tara to stay behind—that she and Christine could handle the dragons. But she stopped. Her days of being the overprotective older sister were over.

"Fallon," Kayla said, "drop me and Christine near our men." She glanced at her sister. "Ryan may be in berserker mode, so steer clear of him."

CHAPTER 2

*S*LIME AND BLOOD dripped from Ryan Sheridan's gore-spattered tunic as he hacked his way through a wall of inhuman, writhing limbs. When he reached his second-in-command, Colm Longacre, he used his long dagger to cut away the thick tentacle that was dragging him toward the lake.

"My thanks, my liege."

The other man's copper-colored eyes took on a wary gleam as he shook off the creature's remains and slowly backed away.

Ryan didn't blame him for his caution. He could feel the seething power of his ability growing inside him, which would transform him from a rational being into a mindless berserker. Once he descended into the madness, he would be virtually unstoppable in battle—and would kill anything that moved.

"The Blackstones are coming for us," Ryan said. He nodded toward the large, dark figures trotting around the lake toward their camp. "I will keep them occupied." He swung his blade at a one-eyed blob oozing from the water's edge, cleaving it in two. "Go and get the women."

"Wait," Colm said, looking over Ryan's head. "I think they come to us." Colm reached out and neatly caught Christine Marszalek as she fell from the sky. The curvy brunette gave him a brief kiss before he set her on her feet. "I should spank you until you can't sit for a week," he growled. He pulled a blade and threw it at another reaching tentacle, pinning it to the ground. "Or kiss you until you cannot think."

"Decisions, decisions," she said. The crystal ring on her finger glittered as she touched his cheek. "Hold that thought until after the battle, lover." She looked up at the enormous dragon hovering over them, giving the creature the thumbs-up.

But if Christine was safe, then where was–

He spotted Kayla a moment before she jumped and landed precisely in his outstretched arms. The heart-rending fear that she had been taken from him vanished. Instead it was replaced with the light, beloved weight of her petite body. She wasn't injured. She was grinning.

"I thought the dragon took you and Christine." He held her against him, breathing in her scent and feeling the strong rhythm of her heart thudding against his chest. "Kayla love. What were you thinking, going into the Black-stone's camp?"

"I thought I'd get my little sister back," she said, and looked up. "So I did."

Ryan followed her gaze to see Tara Blackstone peering down at them. The changeling gave them a grim smile as she gripped Fallon's neck ridge. The dragons turned and flew away. Though he didn't understand what had happened between the two women, the Dark Fae creatures were still rising out of the lake.

"You and Christine must go now," he told Kayla, and kissed her mouth before he put her on her feet. "Take refuge in town for the night, and leave at dawn."

"We're not going anywhere," she told him, and turned her head as a blast of fire lit up the night sky. "We've got help now."

Gavan Waterson joined them, his unearthly handsome features marred by a swath of deep gashes. "My liege, the changeling is using the dragons to attack the water creatures."

Colm looked confused. "She fights her own clan?"

"*We're* her clan now," Kayla told him. "Tara and Fallon and the herd will take out the monsters. But we have to handle the Blackstones."

Gavan wiped the blood out of his eyes. "How did you persuade the dragons to defend us?"

"Tara did that," Kayla said, then she gave the dancer a strange look. "I should also mention that we figured out who my real sister is: Christine."

As Ryan and his warriors stared at both women, the dancer bent and tugged Colm's dagger from the flopping tentacle. Without looking, she threw it at a Dark Fae running toward them. Thanks to her Fae gift of absolute precision, the blade buried itself in his chest and dropped him like a toppled statue.

"We can tell that story when we don't have Blackstone assholes about to overrun us," Christine said. "Kayla, come on. We need the horses."

"Wait a sec," Kayla said. She dashed over to Gavan, and reached for his face. "I think I can help. Close your eyes."

Ryan frowned as he watched her cradle his jousting partner's bloody face between her palms. "Kayla love, his wounds are not so grave, and you cannot heal him by... Blind me."

Blue light illuminated her hands and Gavan's face. As it sank into the warrior's flesh, the wounds marring it began to shrink and vanish. Ryan heard a low, soft sound humming in the air, and realized it was coming from her. He exchanged a look with Colm, who also watched the healing with narrowed eyes.

"There," Kayla said. She stepped back and smiled up at Gavan's uninjured features. "You look much better not shredded. Come on, Christine."

Ryan watched the women trot off toward the barn. His men came to flank him, but neither spoke until Kayla was out of earshot.

"When did your lady become a touch-healer?" Colm asked.

"I daresay she has always been." Ryan studied Gavan's face. "What did her power feel like to you?"

"Sunlight and rain," the warrior murmured back as he stroked his jaw. "She did not seem to know she was singing, but I felt it in my bones."

"'Twas said that spellsingers are deaf to their own magick." His gaze shifted. "The Blackstones come, Ryan."

"I know." He turned to Gavan. "Not a word of this to anyone." He glanced at Colm, who also nodded.

Jannon came out of the trees. "The bloody dragons are attacking the Dark Fae's creatures. They're burning them." He peered up at the fire-lit sky and gaped. "Is that Tara astride that monster?"

"Aye, she leads the attack against the monsters," Colm declared. He drew his sword as the first wave of Blackstones ran toward them. "Now let us dispatch their little brothers."

The rest of the Forever Faire warriors converged around them as they faced the Dark Fae. Ryan clamped down on his temper as he waded into the Blackstone attackers, who quailed as soon as they recognized him. It made them easy to disable and disarm. He had divested a dozen of their weapons when the women arrived with the horses. Mounting Titan, Ryan rode through the Blackstones, clubbing heads with the hilt of his blade as he searched for their leader.

"You must not have all the pleasure, my liege," Colm said as he rode up beside him, and reined in Grania. She tossed her head with impatience. "Save some for the rest of us."

Ryan scanned the fray around them. "Do you see that bastard who leads them?"

Dirk's men began turning and running to jump into the shadows, but Ryan heard Dirk shout furiously at his men to remain and fight. Ryan spotted him at the water's edge, kicking one of the dead water creatures. Ryan dismounted and strode to him.

"Sheridan," Dirk sneered.

The Dark Fae raised his sword and advanced a step before the smaller, rodent-faced man at his side hissed something to him.

"Your groom's sister suffers greatly in my care," Dirk said. "Give Kayla Rowe to me, and I will put an end to it."

"Indeed," Ryan said, and pointed up at Fallon. "From my view she seems to be having a wonderful time."

When Dirk looked up, Ryan punched him in the jaw. As the Dark Fae reeled backward, the smaller man lunged between them, and lifted his hand to the sky. A bolt of lightning blazed down, nearly striking Ryan. When his eyes cleared, both Dark Fae had vanished.

Jannon sheathed his sword as he and Colm joined Ryan.

"The dragons have charred the last of the water creatures," Jannon said.

That was all Ryan needed to hear. He tossed his sword

to Jannon and dove into the lake—directly where Wallace had disappeared. He swam furiously into the murky depths, past the burned bodies of the tentacled monsters. Though darkness gathered the deeper he went, Ryan pressed on. A mortal would have drowned, but perhaps not a—

There was a flash of gold in his peripheral vision. With his lungs beginning to ache, Ryan quickly changed direction. He darted around the swirling debris and saw it again, just ahead. It was the blacksmith's belt buckle. Ryan grabbed it, untangled him from a limp tentacle, and kicked frantically for the surface. When he and Wallace bobbed clear of the water, Ryan gulped air. He swam for the shore, dragging Wallace in his wake. Colm and Jannon waded in to help him carry the big man to the embankment.

"He is drowned," Jannon said, looking sick.

"The nine hells he is," Ryan said, and drove his fist into the smith's broad chest.

Wallace convulsed and choked out lake water. Ryan rolled him onto his side as he puked, and held him steady until he emptied his belly.

"That will teach you to go swimming before a battle," Ryan said, with a grin.

"My apologies, my liege," Wallace said, sitting up. He coughed a few times, and then scowled as Fallon landed a short distance away. The blacksmith pointed as his eyes widened. "The changeling rides that beast like a horse."

"She can also have him burn you to a cinder," Colm said as he helped him to his feet. "So I would stay on her good side now."

CHRISTINE WATCHED KAYLA send the last of the dragons to the edge of the dark lake to watch for the Blackstones. Jannon and Tara patrolled from Fallon's back as the dragon flew back and forth over the camp. Ryan had assigned his warriors to take night shifts patrolling the perimeter of the property. She was glad the men of Forever Faire weren't taking any chances, but unlike Kayla she didn't entirely trust Tara or the dragons. She'd follow her older sister's lead with the changeling, but she'd never turn her back on the teenager again.

Christine paused. *My older sister, Kayla.*

Christine had thought it would be tough to wrap her head around that new reality, but she already felt it in her heart.

"I'd offer you a pence for your thoughts," a low voice murmured next to Christine's ear, "but I suspect you'd use it to put out my eye."

Colm's strong arms came around her, tugging her back against him.

She turned in his hold to stand on tip-toe and kiss the hard line of his mouth.

"I like you with both eyes, mister. It's the dragons. After being burned to death, I'm not really a fan. Just stick close to me." She saw his expression and scowled. "Oh, you are so not leaving me here with the waffling changeling chick and her fifteen gigantic fire-breathing puppies."

"Ryan believes Dirk will summon more Dark Fae for the next attack, so he is sending me to seek assistance from the local Fae clan." Colm grimaced. "We are shunned by our kind, but the Cloudstar's clan leader owes Ryan his life, so he may agree."

She tucked her arm through his. "Then I'm going with you. I'm a halfling, and I've never been cast out or anything. They'll have to talk to me, right? We can say we were wondering if my mom was one of Cloudsparkles or whatever. That should get us in the door."

"You, my lady, are very sneaky." Her lover's mouth lost its stern lines. "Come, and we'll tell Ryan your scheme."

The master of Forever Faire approved Christine's plan, but he didn't look happy. "If Kayla is a Cloudstar, then as her sister by birth you might also be. But their clan leader has little love for halflings."

"Tough. He owes you." If Christine had learned anything while growing up in foster care, it was how to collect on a promised favor. "Plus I think Kayla and I have the right to know what happened with our mother."

Ryan gave Colm an odd look before he said, "So you both shall, I promise."

To avoid unwanted attention from a nighttime horse ride, Colm used one of the rental trucks to drive to Cloud-star territory. Christine used the dome light to fix her hair and put on some makeup, although there wasn't much she could do about her girl-next-door look now. She didn't mind the hair—she'd forgotten how bright her natural gold highlights were—but with all her tattoos and piercings gone she'd lost the illusion of toughness. That in-your-face edginess had also made her feel strong and safe when she'd started stripping. She twisted the crystal ring around the base of her index finger before she looked over at Colm.

"If I want to get inked or pierced again, will you give me shit about it?"

"If you say I cannot watch, I may." He reached over to take her hand in his. "Or perhaps I will have it done to me as well. I rather liked those little stars you had sprinkled on your arms."

That made her laugh out loud. "Can I pick where you get them?"

"I think not." He came to a stop at a red traffic light, leaned over and kissed her until she gasped. "I love you, woman. Ink, piercings or none." The sound of a beeping horn made him scowl. He peered at the headlights in the mirror. "Mortals. They have the patience of fleas."

For the rest of the trip Colm told her what to expect when they approached the clan, and some of the bizarre things Fae people did when meeting outsiders. Christine had no problem with being patted down, or giving a drop of blood to confirm her lineage. When her lover mentioned how she might have to be dunked in a cistern before entering the clan's hidden enclave, however, she protested.

"I'm already clean." She turned her head and sniffed her T-shirt. "Mostly. What, are they afraid of my half-human cooties?""

"The Cloudstar have a curious kinship with rain water," Colm said, and braked to make a turn onto a narrow dirt road. "They use it in many ways. It also powers the magick known only to their clan."

Christine huffed out some air. "Maybe they should have called themselves the Raindance people."

Colm drove several miles down the dark, bumpy road until he reached a broad swath of towering, full-branched trees. He parked on the side of the road, but left the headlights on. Then he came around to help Christine out of the truck.

"Have mercy," she said, tipping her head back to see the tops of the trees. Even against the starlight, they looked to be nearly a hundred feet tall. "I'm guessing these aren't native."

"They may have been, centuries ago."

He grasped her hand and walked to the tallest of the magnificent trees. He took out his crystal and touched it to the smooth gray bark. As he stepped back, a shimmering silver light outlined a long oval space that became a recess. Water formed a curtain of droplets across the space, slowing and then stopping as a Fae male emerged.

Christine gave the man the once-over. He was fair like Ryan and Wallace, but his coloring seemed much cooler. He was also lean and compact, a few inches shorter than Colm. He wore a thin white shirt and jeans that were so worn they almost matched. He confined his very long, white-gold hair in a loose braid that fell over his shoulder to his waist. His sea green eyes met Christine's.

"Clan Leader Devalan of the Cloudstar," Colm said, performing a respectful bow. "I am sent with an entreaty from Ryan Sheridan of Forever Faire regarding a lost Fae halfling."

"You speak a selective truth, Longacre." Devalan's voice had a liquid quality that tickled Christine's ears. When she cleared her throat to keep from giggling, he glanced at her. "I wager the halfling is but an excuse. Your master means to leverage the life-debt I owe him, and adds insult by sending his errand boy to collect."

"Whoa. Nice manners, Clan King." Christine turned to her lover. "I don't want to meet these people. If he's any indication, they're not worth my time. Let's go back to camp and find some hay to roll in, Handsome."

Devalan peered closely at her face. "*You* refuse to meet *us*?"

Colm stepped between them. "This is Christine Marszalek, whom my liege believes may share your bloodline. She is one of the lost Fae we met while wintering in the mountains."

Christine muffled a groan, while the clan leader jumped right on Colm's slip.

"You met more than one lost to us? Where are the others?"

"There's only one more, and she's my sister, Kayla," Christine said before Colm could reply. "She and our guys are holding off the Blackstone clan. More of them are coming, so we need your clan to help us kick some Dark Fae ass. That's where the debt you owe Ryan comes into play." She saw his face darken. "Thanks to Mom, I'm half-Fae, maybe even half-Cloudstar. You know I can't lie to you, so what do you say, Clan King? Want to grab your guys and give us a hand?"

Devalan produced a small dagger and slashed it across his palm before offering the hilt to Christine.

"Cross your blood with mine, and then I will answer." When Colm muttered something in the Fae language, the clan leader smirked a little. "He must love you. He just threatened to part me from my balls, should I harm you."

"Hurt him, and I'll make you wish he did."

Christine used the tip of the dagger on the end of her

finger, and squeezed a drop of blood from the tiny wound onto Devalan's palm.

The clan leader closed his eyes and fisted his cut hand. A silvery light briefly glowed from under his clenched fingers. When he looked at Christine again his eyes took on the same glow.

She couldn't decide if he looked pissed or afraid. "So are we kin, or not kin?"

"That is something we will discuss when I meet your sister." Devalan's eyes lost the unearthly glow as he regarded Colm. "I will send my warriors to provide aid to you and the outcasts. Tell your liege our debt is settled."

Devalan stepped back into the tree recess, over which spilled a curtain of water. When the cascade stopped a moment later the space had vanished.

"So I guess I'm not meeting the folks," Christine said, grinning up at Colm. "More time to find us some hay."

CHAPTER 4

"THIS IS SO weird," Kayla said as she inspected Wallace's unmarked ankle.

As with Gavan and Tara, all she'd had to do was touch him to repair the raw wound he'd acquired while being dragged into the lake.

"Maybe my mother could do it, too. I mean, you guys have your own doctors and nurses, right? You don't just use sex with mortals for healing, or there'd be a lot more halflings around."

The blacksmith looked as if he smelled a skunk.

"Right," Kayla muttered. As she stood, she looked at Ryan. "I think that's your cue to explain the stuff you've been keeping from me." Ryan's mouth flattened into a line. Kayla put her hands on her hips. "Why is Wallace dodging my questions? And why does Gavan keep staring at me like I meant to rip off his face instead of heal it? Any time now, Ryan."

"I will tell you, love," he said, his voice tight. "'Tis the matter of where to do so."

"The old grove," Wallace suggested. "'Tis the only place

where you may be protected while you, ah, remove any doubt."

"Okay, now you're starting to scare me," Kayla said and studied her hands. "Does this healing stuff have a dark side? Could I hurt someone without meaning to? Is that why you're so jumpy?"

Ryan put his arm around her shoulders. "We cannot speak of it here. Come, love. We will take a ride out to the grove. It is quiet and, as Wallace says, protected."

Kayla suspected she wouldn't get another word out of him about her power unless she agreed. "Let's go."

Instead of heading to the barn for horses, however, Ryan took her to one of the rental trucks.

"We could have Titan shift into bike form," she said as he opened the door for her. "He'd be quicker, and if you change your mind about riding horseback…which I'm guessing you won't."

Ryan shook his head as he helped her in. "'Tis not a time for Titan or any of the herd to be with us." When she started to ask why he touched a finger to her lips. "Please, my lady, no more questions until we reach the grove."

She slid onto the passenger seat, and he closed the door.

They took a dirt road from the camp to a nearby gated property. The headlights splashed across a faded sign for a tree farm, but she didn't recognize the company name. Ryan climbed out and used his crystal to open the gate, which closed silently behind them once they'd passed through it.

The road narrowed to a grassed-over trail flanked by dense, overgrown trees. Though she couldn't make them out in the darkness, the smell of citrus hung in the air. From the look of the moonlit land it hadn't been worked in ages. They passed an out building, its heavily rusted tin roof barely supported by three rotted timbers—and ivy growing from a neighboring tree.

The trail ended at a spread of huge oaks. They had grown together, their long, twisted branches entwined with each other. Something like Spanish moss hung like drapery from the canopy to the ground, but it glowed golden instead of gray, and grew in geometric shapes, like crystals.

"It's beautiful," Kayla said, as she climbed out and started to walk toward the trees. But she was brought up short by a big hand on her arm. "What's wrong?"

Ryan picked up a stone and tossed it in between two of the oaks. The golden moss seemed to come alive. It blasted thousands of tiny, glittering thorns at the rock while it was still in mid-air. It dissolved into dust.

She blinked. "I thought this was supposed to be a safe place."

"It is one of our old, sacred places," he told her. "It was created so long ago that the enchantment and the Fae who cast it are unknown to us. It is believed that the magick of this place will remain unchanged until the end of time."

Kayla felt even more confused. "Why bring me here?"

"The grove will not assault either of us, and I will tell you why once we have passed through the boundary protecting it." He touched her cheek. "You have only to trust me, Kayla love."

Kayla rubbed her face against his palm. "That was never in question."

Despite his reassurance, passing under the glittering attack moss made Kayla cringe a little. Happily not one thorn came flying at them. When they emerged on the other side of the trees, she stopped in her tracks. She gaped at what the ancient Fae had been protecting.

Immense oak trees had been magically shaped into an

enormous living pavilion. Rootlets wove together to make an intricately-patterned floor, from which a circle of chairs grew. She peered at the golden cushions on the seats of the living furnishings, and saw they had been woven out of the attack moss. A natural spring-fed rock pool occupied the center of the pavilion, shaded by dwarf tangerine trees full of ripe fruit. It was not nearly as large as the underground crystal city of Tarman, but it felt much older.

"Do you think someone lived here?" she murmured to Ryan as they walked toward the steaming pool.

"We believe ancient Fae used it to parlay with their enemies. The grove nulls any spell brought within its boundaries." He released her hand and walked to the other side of the pool. "The moss also attacks and repels every living thing except those of pure Fae blood."

"What?" Kayla said, backing up a step. "But I'm not." She glanced quickly at the grove around them. "Why doesn't it react to me?" She stared at Ryan. "And why are you standing over there?"

"I brought you here because I knew it would not, and for the next few moments 'tis better I keep my distance." He gestured at the pool. "Look at your reflection."

Kayla cautiously approached and glanced down. She yelped when she saw her hair. She reached for her pony-tail, dragging it over her shoulder to stare at the bronze and copper streaks that had appeared. As she flipped it back she felt the edge of her ear, which was no longer curved but subtly pointed. She then saw her fair skin had gone snow-white, and had acquired a faint glow.

"You said magick doesn't work here." She held up her hand, saw the difference in the smoothness and texture of her flesh, and still couldn't believe it. "So what did this to me?"

"Naught but the end of the curse cast over you, likely at

your birth." Ryan gestured around them. "Had I known you carried it, I would have brought you here at once. All of us assumed Tara had been cursed to appear as mortal, but it was done to you, Kayla." Her eyes went wide. "You are not half-mortal. You were cursed by your Fae parents in order to protect you. No one would suspect a mortal child to possess such power."

"Power?" Kayla said, as she felt something rising inside. It was so pure and light she half-expected to start floating in the air. "You mean the healing ability, and the telepathy with Fae animals."

Ryan shook his head. "*You* are the spellsinger, love."

CHAPTER 5

KAYLA LAUGHED. "NICE one. Okay, I might be part Fae, or even all Fae. But I'm definitely not a singer of any kind. I'm tone deaf." When he didn't react to that she frowned. "Oh, come on. You don't believe me? I've never sung a single note."

"You have, but you cannot hear it. Spellsingers are deaf to their own songs." He touched his neck. "When you healed me in the crystal cave I heard you singing under your breath. I didn't make anything of it at the time because I thought you were humming, and believed you to be mortal."

"I didn't hum," she said, scowling and shaking her head. "I never hum. I just have a healing ability. Super cool to be sure, but not spellsinger level."

"When you healed Gavan, and later Wallace, we all heard it. You sing so fast and so low 'tis like listening to a hummingbird's wings." He hesitated before he added, "You have one ability to share the minds of horses and dragons. Now we know you also possess this healing ability."

She threw up her hands. "I didn't ask for them."

"What I mean to say is that they are proof that you are Fae. Halflings never have two abilities. They do not have enough Fae blood to acquire more than one." He nodded at the water. "All you must do is try. Sing to the pool. Something brief."

She felt her stomach clench. "But I told you. I can't. I can never sing."

"Everyone can sing, love." He sounded patient, but his expression had grown slightly worried. "Resisting your birthright will only cause calamity. Please, try for me. Believe you can do it, and you will."

"I'm not allowed," she blurted out. An old memory came rising out of the dark mists of her childhood. "My mother told me that." Her skin went cold as she stared at him. "I remember now. She said I could never sing because I might hurt Tara."

Ryan nodded. "She would have added such a compulsion to the curse in order to protect your true form. Coming to the grove has removed it from you. You can sing now, and you must, if we are to be sure."

She dragged in a deep breath, and then tried to repeat a few words from one of her dad's favorite holiday songs. Her throat closed up so quickly she felt as if she were strangling.

"Breathe," Ryan told her. "Listen to what you feel inside."

Inside Kayla was terrified. Her lungs seemed to be shriveling, and Ryan's voice sounded very far away. She had felt this before, but she couldn't recall when or why. One by one the sounds of the night faded, leaving her in a pool of silence. She thought of Christine's saucy smile, and the sunlight gleaming on Tara's unbound hair, and took another breath. A frail, gossamer sensation fluttered in her veins. She felt rather than heard her voice leave her throat.

Hark how the bells, sweet silver bells.

Kayla stopped after the last word, and the air filled with the sound of ringing.

"Oh my god," she whispered.

She hadn't realized she'd sung the words until she felt steam rising over her. The water in the pool had also begun boiling. She gave Ryan a panicked look.

"You said magick doesn't work in here."

"Spells, and most abilities, do not," he assured her as he came around the pool. "Your power is much older than the grove, and far more formidable. I think your mother must have given you some training, however, for you did not lose control of it."

Horror raked her insides with rusty claws. "That's why you went over there. You thought I'd hurt you."

"I have never been in the presence of a spellsinger." Ryan drew her into his arms, and he didn't look at all afraid of her. "I was not certain what would occur once you deliberately tried to sing."

"And still you brought me here." Although she tried to smile, her lips had gone on strike. "You can't even go berserker on me to defend yourself, can you?"

He shook his head. "Here you have all the power, my lady."

"If you know anyone who wants it—besides the Black-stones—I'd be happy to give it up." She looked around them. "I'd better try to cool down this pool before it turns these tangerines into marmalade. Is that okay to try?"

When he nodded, the silence gathered around her again. But this time Kayla didn't resist the strange feelings. She allowed them to burble up and sang a line from a carol about a snowman. As before she couldn't hear herself, but the water stopped bubbling. Her pleasure in her minor accomplishment vanished as snowflakes began to fall over the grove.

"I can change the weather, too?"

"'Tis said there are no limits to a spellsinger's power." He touched his mouth to her brow. "Never worry, love. You will manage your ability."

She brushed some snow from his hair. "I don't seem to know how to turn it off without turning on something else. How do I stop the blizzard? Central Florida isn't ready for a white Christmas."

Ryan thought for a moment. "Try singing the snow song words in reverse."

She went over it in her mind until she felt she had it. Though it was awkward, once Kayla sang the line backward, the snow disappeared.

"It worked," she exclaimed. "And me with no Fae training whatsoever." She also felt a little light-headed, maybe from all the shocks she'd had over the last half hour. "Can we sit for a minute? I think I'm all sung out for now."

Ryan drew her over to the largest chair, where he sat down and pulled her onto his lap.

"I should tell you that no one can teach you how to manage your ability. There are no other spellsingers except you. I fear you must learn through practice."

"Maybe we could do that somewhere that isn't quite so sacred." She leaned her cheek against his shoulder, and then jolted up right. "Wait a minute. If I'm the spellsinger, then I was the one who blasted the Blackstones out of the faire grounds when they attacked us in Tennessee. How could I do that and not realize it?"

One of his big hands stroked her back. "The same way you healed me and the men: by instinct."

"No, I can't..." her voice trailed off as she saw how he

was looking at her. "All right. So I heal wounds by singing things I can't hear and that I don't know I'm singing."

"You'll know now, love." Ryan looked all over her new face. "There are other mysteries we must solve. One of your parents was not Cloudstar, I think. They have the fairest coloring among the Fae. We will have to trace your bloodlines."

"Christine and I are pretty sure that my mother died." She told him what her sister had learned from her social worker. "If my Fae father is still alive, why would he leave me to be raised by my human dad? Especially considering what I can do."

"I cannot say, but if you were my daughter, nothing in this realm or any other could keep me from you." He lifted her hand to his mouth, and kissed her palm. "All I may tell you is that I am not your father."

Kayla winced. "Boy, wouldn't that be the worst." Her jeans and shirt felt odd against her skin now, and she glanced down at herself. "Do you think anything else on my body has changed?"

Ryan circled one of her buttons with a fingertip. "We could have a look." When she nodded he set her on her feet and began undressing her. "Your hair is beautiful, and your ears are delightful. Your skin has the luster of pearls. You must stop wearing clothing with buttons." He undid the rest with a jerk of his hand.

"It's a shame we can't use thought-spell here," Kayla said. "Still, I don't mind the old-fashioned way. Think of it as unwrapping a gift."

"When I see you I cannot think." He stripped away her blouse and kissed her shoulder. "I should have realized you were Fae from your effect on me."

Once he removed her bra Kayla saw that her breasts had not grown any larger, but her nipples had lightened to the palest of blush pinks. Her navel had acquired a small dimple beneath its lower curve, too. Once she stepped out of her boots and jeans she saw all her body hair had vanished except for the neat thatch over her sex, which looked silkier and had lighter colors streaking the curls.

"No surprise tentacles," she said, and chuckled as she held out her arms and turned around for him. "What do you think? Am I good-looking for a Fae gal?" When he didn't answer her she glanced over her shoulder and saw him staring at her shoulders. "Don't tell me there's a tail back there."

"You have a mark." He reached out and traced his fingers over her spine. "It is blue, and shaped like a crescent moon." His hand fell away as she turned around to face him. "Fae are born unmarked, so your parents must have bestowed it on you for some reason."

"My own ink. Christine is going to be so jealous." She slipped into his arms, and where their skins touched they glowed. She also felt a new, tingling warmth spreading through her from every spot where her body pressed against his. "You have on too many clothes now, and we haven't done anything to celebrate our victory."

Ryan's arms tightened for a moment, and when he spoke his tone sounded strained.

"You are full-blooded Fae, Kayla. You belong with your kin, not me."

She tilted her head. "And yet here I am. You forgot, I picked you."

"I have not forgotten, and your choice was made when we thought you might be a halfling." His broad shoulders lifted and fell with his sigh. "Now that we know you are Fae, and a spellsinger, I am obliged to take you to your mother's clan. They will know what happened to your father, and why your mother cursed you to seem mortal."

"We can't do that tonight, not with the Blackstones regrouping out there." She attacked his clothes, undressing him until they were both bare. Where their skins touched more bright heat kindled. "You know, I'd really like to have *you* as my clan leader." She stroked the satiny bulge of his bicep before giving him a mischievous look. "Then I can say things like, 'What is your will, my lord?' and 'How may I serve you, my liege?'"

"You cannot serve me. You were never cast out by your clan." He watched her press a line of soft kisses across his chest. "You have broken no laws. You were hidden, not shunned, and if you do not stop that I will forget to be noble and show you my every desire."

"I like you better naked and not so noble." Kayla licked her tongue over one of his hard, flat nipples and swept her thumb back and forth over the other. "Will they kick me out of the Fae for serving you in ye olde sacred grove?"

"The Cloudstar might, if they find us here." His sapphire eyes shifted down to her tight-peaked breasts, and watched how she was rubbing them against the lower vault of his chest. "But Devalan knows naught of you, so we may stay a few hours."

While she kept her gaze locked with his, she lowered herself to her knees. She put her mouth to his thigh, which tightened under her lips, and bit him gently before tipping her head back.

"Showtime, my man."

Instead of taking advantage of her position, Ryan knelt with her so they were face-to-face.

"No fern to be had tonight, my lady." He took her by the arms and bent back, lifting her above him as he stretched out on the smooth trunks that formed the living floor. "I will be your bed now."

Kayla stretched out on top of him, savoring the feel of her petite form atop his big, tough body.

"You're a little lumpy, pal."

She wriggled down until her breasts cradled his thick shaft, and pressed her mounds against it so that he lay trapped between her curves.

"That feels nice," she murmured.

She massaged him with her breasts, moving over him so that his heavy cock thrust in and out of the soft, tight space. When his bulbous tip grazed her chin she bent her head to kiss the hot, straining dome. On the next stroke she gave him a slow, wet lick, making him groan out loud.

"I can taste how much you want me," she said. She loved seeing how his eyes narrowed when she gave him another leisurely lick. She recalled how Colm and the other Fae warriors spoke to him. "Tell me what you would have me do, my liege."

His big hands snatched her up from his thighs, and moved her over his groin.

"Spread your thighs, wench. I can feel the heat of you, now I will have your sweetness on me. Just so."

He lowered her just enough for his cockhead to rest against the drenched opening of her pussy. He jerked his hips, working the broad dome against her until her fluids made him gleam.

"That is not enough," he ordered. "Give me more."

The commanding tone of his voice gave Kayla a shivery thrill, and she braced her knees on either side of him. When he lowered her another inch she shimmied down his shaft until she engulfed him. The moment he began to lift her she tightened around him, trapping him inside her.

"You want me to make you wet?" she whispered. "Then I will." She thrust down with her hips, impaling herself on him. He stretched and filled her so completely she felt it from her heels to her head. One long, luxurious shudder snaked down her body. "I never want to move again. Oh, Ryan." She almost collapsed on his chest.

"Come here." He drew her down, keeping his swollen length inside her as he pressed her cheek to his shoulder. "I am your bed now, Kayla. Every night you will come to me for your rest, and we will sleep like this. Naked, and joined together. Your lips on my skin. My hands holding you close." He cupped the tight curves of her bottom as he thrust a little deeper into her softness.

"I can do that." She caught her breath as his fingers went exploring.

"I will do so much more," he assured her. "I will wake you with my tongue between your thighs, and my fingers plucking these sweet, blushing nipples. I will lick you as much as I wish. It will take a very long time to get enough of you for one morning—and then I will see you wrap your lips around me."

His murmured words had as much effect on her as the gentle thrusts of his shaft, and Kayla began to shake all over, her hands gripping his upper arms and then his shoulders as she felt her hair writhing around her face.

"Now you understand my every desire," Ryan told her, the pale golden tendrils of his long mane undulating as they threaded through her dark tresses. "All I want is you, naked and alone with me. I want to take you from dusk until dawn until noon. I would be your lover and sweetheart and mount. Like this, I am not your liege, my beautiful one, nor you my servant. We are made one and the same."

Ryan gripped her bottom as he worked her harder over his cock. His thumbs pressed into the soft notch between her tight curves, and nudged against her rosebud. She remembered how he had pleasured her in the crystal city's hidden snuggery, taking her virginal pucker and showing her all the delirious, dark delights she had never known. Now as he pressed one of his thumbs into the clenching ring of nerves Kayla cried out, pushing back against his hand and down on his shaft until their body hair meshed. As he worked his thumb deeper, she gripped his heavy girth from within and bowed against him as her belly tightened.

"I am going to pump you so full of my seed it will spill from you like rain," Ryan crooned, and gave her mouth a hard kiss as he plowed deeper into both of her openings. "And the next time we are alone, with time and privacy and a real, sturdy bed, I will have your lovely little ass again."

That sensual threat sent Kayla into a wild whirlwind of bliss as she came, crying his name and straining against him as an avalanche of sensation crashed over her. Another huge surge rolled over the first as Ryan thrust deep and held himself there, his cock jerking and pulsing as he jetted over and over into her pussy.

As they both went limp Kayla heard the harsh sounds of their mingled breaths, and felt his chest rising and falling beneath her face. She didn't know how long they lay like that, but realized she was content for the first time in her life. Finally though, she found the energy to push herself up and disengage their bodies. She rolled away to lay on her back and stare up at the stars. There were so many that the sky looked alien. She turned her head to ask Ryan why, but saw he had already fallen asleep.

"Such a man." She smiled a little as he grumbled and turned on his side.

She rose and gathered their clothes. They couldn't stay the night here, not with the threat of another Blackstone attack, but she could let her lover sleep for an hour or two. Ryan might not get another chance for a while.

She dressed as quietly as she could, and after placing Ryan's clothes beside him went over to pick one of the tangerines. While they'd been in Tennessee she'd missed the simple joy of being able to pick fruit from the citrus trees in her yard. As she broke open the tangerine she breathed in its sweet scent and smiled. Instead of dividing it into sections, she bit into it. The tangy juice spilled into her mouth and down her hand. It was like tasting sunshine itself. But before the heady nectar could run off her elbows, she hurried to the pool and dipped in her arm.

Two long, pale hands shot out of the water, and dragged Kayla down.

MOLD BLACKENED THE peeling paint on the walls of the bedroom. Broken windows allowed gnats, moths and lizards to come in and inspect the decaying furnishings and putrid piles of discarded clothes. The stink of sweat, urine and vomit came from a mattress so stained it resembled a sacrificial altar used carelessly and too often. The harsher, uglier stench drifted from the closet, where jugs of antifreeze, ammonia and drain cleaner were stored until the occupants ran out of their home-cooked drug.

Braced against the cleanest wall, Dirk Blackstone shoved the mortal addict away from him as soon as his minor burns had healed.

"Take her to the rest of the wounded," he told his cousin. "The worst may share her—and get rid of these damned chemicals."

"They're part of the potion which she and her friends inject daily," Beck Blackstone said, as he hefted the junkie under his arm. "If you wish to retain the female mortals to service us, you must permit them to make more of it."

Dirk's outrage had grown so much he thought his skull might burst. "Do you imagine I will stay in this privy one moment longer than I must, Cousin?"

"We have no other place here—unless you wish to return to the lake, and permit Sheridan, that changeling bitch, and our own dragons to finish us off."

His cousin bowed and trudged off with the limp female still tucked under his arm.

Beck's prediction burned hotter than dragonfire, but Dirk could not deny what he said. Nor could he turn a crushing defeat into what it should have been: a guaranteed victory. All of it came courtesy of Dirk's traitorous half-sister. Somehow Tara had been released and rescued, and persuaded to turn the dragons against their masters. She hadn't done it for Kayla Rowe, either. No doubt Tara imagined herself striking back at Dirk for beating her. He had the cold comfort of knowing that her Dark Fae nature had finally conquered the last remnant of her Fae mother's influence. For that he would rejoice, but not until after he punished Tara for daring to move against him.

He calmed himself enough to open a shadow portal, and through it sent the mindshare spell that allowed him to communicate with her. Offering her freedom in trade for the spellsinger had already failed. Nor would she have turned against him if she desired his forgiveness. He would have to offer something more tantalizing now: perhaps her own territory and a new clan of her own to rule. He knew how much his half-sister desired control over her own destiny. The prospect of becoming a Dark Fae clan leader would ensure such at outcome, along with formidable power and great wealth.

Please don't leave me here, she'd said. As a young girl Tara had often begged him in her dreams to take her back with him to the clan. *I want to be with you.*

Dirk had told no one of his intention to make his changeling half-sister his bride. No one but Jarek would have dared to object. But when the time came to bind Tara to him Dirk would make sure his father was already dead. Now that she had given her heart to that Fae scum who had taken her maidenhead, Dirk no longer wanted her as a wife. For that betrayal he would chain the little whore and make her watch as he cut the bastard she had fucked into ten thousand pieces.

You shouldn't do that, a very young Tara had told Dirk the first time he'd touched her. *You're a grown-up, and I'm only thirteen.*

Dirk's hands bunched into fists as Tara's image appeared briefly in the center of the glowing-edged shadow. Remembering how it had been with her made his cock hard, and it took all his self-control not to hurl himself into the portal.

"Sister."

Tara looked back at him for a long moment. "Not anymore." A moment later the portal collapsed in on itself and vanished.

Dirk felt even more stunned than he had when the dragons had attacked his father's monstrous creations at the lake. Tara had been taught how to open and close her own shadow portals, but Dirk had never shown her how to do the same with his. She must have discovered the secret on her own. Blocking him from her mind had not only closed the portal, it ended the mindshare spell that had allowed him to enter her thoughts and dreams since she was an infant.

Tara had never resisted him. She'd been his toy for so long he'd never imagined being kept from her thoughts. When he took her back from the Fae, he would have to prevent it from ever happening again. Perhaps he'd use one of his father's spells to render her as mindlessly devoted to him as Jarek made his own nightmarish creations. Mindless devotion could…

Dirk's hair stood on end. He knew exactly how to defeat Sheridan, and take Kayla Rowe away from the Fae.

The air in the room turned suddenly brackish as a portal opened in the far corner. It could only mean one thing: Dirk's time had just run out.

The Blackstone clan leader stepped through. His fine garments sparkled with dark jewels beneath the swirling dark cloak fashioned of spiny hide. Dirk knew his father enjoyed the bristling effect of the cloak, but its true value was in the lethal venom contained in each spine. Many had attempted to assassinate Jarek Blackstone, only to die writhing at his feet.

As his personal guard came through the portal, Jarek took in the filthy room. His thick, craggy features remained impassive as he regarded Dirk.

"You choose a pretty spot to shelter. Do you have her?"

"No, Father. The dragons made short work of your creatures before aiding the Fae against my men. I lost another seven to fire and blade before we could escape."

Since using Tara as a changeling had been Jarek's idea, Dirk took some pleasure in relating how she had betrayed the clan.

Jarek's heavy jaw worked as he listened, and when Dirk finished he ordered his guards out of the room.

"You cannot mean to hold me to account for Tara's treachery," Dirk declared. His head snapped to one side and his faced exploded with pain, as his father dealt him a back-handed blow. "I…I knew naught of it."

"It is just as well," Jarek said. "I have long suspected you and that half-Fae bitch of mine to be conspiring against me. Now it seems she alone did all the scheming. A pity you did not ferret out her intentions while you were mind-fucking the little whore."

It took all Dirk's will to go down on one knee and bow his head. Though pain fed his temper, it was stayed by the knowledge that to do otherwise would result in banishment.

"I but live to serve you, Clan Leader." He glanced up. "My mistake was in trying to use the changeling as bait. If you will allow me to set one final trap, I know how to lure the spellsinger to it."

Once Dirk related his plan, Jarek seemed almost amused. "I must have rattled your brains with that clout. What you speak of is suicide."

"Then you will be rid of me at last." He spat out some blood. "Give me leave, Father, and I vow I will deliver her and Tara to you."

"Very well." His father smiled a little. "Only know that if you fail again, Dirk, you need not return to report it. Bring me the spellsinger, or you will be banished from the clan forever."

CHAPTER 7

*T*HE SOUND OF running water roused Kayla from the dark, dull place where she had been floating. She could feel her sodden clothes clinging to her body, and smelled rain. Her wrists felt heavy, and when she twitched one she found it to be manacled to something even heavier.

"She's very dark, Father," a little girl's voice said somewhere near Kayla. "Lorcan said she's been living with outcasts. Are you sure she's one of us?"

"Completely, my sunshine," a mellow male voice said. "Now she's waking, so you must go to your lady mother. Quickly now."

Kayla opened her eyes to small slits, which allowed her to glimpse a child with curly white hair and a white dress hurrying out through a crystal-studded wooden doorway.

"Pretending to be asleep will not work, Kayla." The man came close enough for her to feel his body heat against her cheek. "Feigning death might, but I doubt you've developed your gift that much."

She lifted her eyelids to see a man with clear green eyes.

He had long, loose white-blonde hair, a remotely hand-some face, and what looked like a ball of foam in his long-fingered hand. She remembered that hand. He'd been the one to pull her into the grove pool.

"Who are you?" she said, struggling against the restraints. "Where am I? Why did you abduct me?"

"I will release you and answer your questions as soon as you promise not to sing while you are here." He waited for her to respond, but when she didn't he held up the foam ball. "Or I can stuff this in your mouth and tape it shut, and leave you here to stew."

"I won't sing while I'm here," she said, knowing full well she could do a lot more than sing, especially if this jerk had any horses.

He set the ball aside and began releasing her shackles. The water rose from her clothes in a mist, and wafted away.

"I am Devalan, Clan Leader of the Cloudstar. I have brought you to our stronghold so that you might be reunited with your kin." He helped her to her feet. "Wel-come to Nefele."

Devalan held onto Kayla's arm as he led her from the small crystal cave out into a city-sized chamber. The settle-ment that filled it in some ways resembled Tarman, the abandoned Fae city in Tennessee. This Fae stronghold, however, remained occupied by hundreds of the immor-tals. She could see them walking through the streets, moving in and out of their dwellings, and working in huge, open-sided hot houses. All the Fae wore various shades of white or light blue, and had the same white-blonde hair.

And then there was the water.

Pools shimmered across the length and breadth of Nefele, fed by innumerable columns of spring water. The downpour came from strategic openings in the rock ceiling over the city, which also fed smaller columns into funnel-shaped structures on every roof.

"Long ago the Cloudstar were called the children of the rain," Devalan said as he looked over his city. "Our legends say our first ancestors were born from a great storm of creation, and fell from the sky to walk the twin realms. It was through the pool that I sensed your presence in the grove."

"Really," Kayla said. She watched a towering, bare-chested warrior divert one of the columns into a series of water troughs. "Did your ancestors kidnap women, too?"

"You've as sharp a tongue as your halfling sister." His mouth flattened. "Your parents did not sacrifice them-selves so that you could join the outcast."

A pang of sadness jabbed at her heart. "My father is dead?"

He nodded. "Kelvan. You have his eyes." He offered her his arm. "Come. I will show you what they left behind for you."

Kayla didn't touch him. "You don't get to play the gentleman with me now, Clan Leader. Just tell me what you want so I can get out of here."

"He wants you to see the home where his sister lived with her first husband."

A copper-haired Fae woman with brilliant, pale blue eyes joined them. Instead of all-white she wore a vivid green tunic and close-fitted dark leather trousers. Across her back was strapped a long bow. The accompanying quiver of arrows hung from her waist.

"I am Jem Ferguson, wife of this addled-brained male." She gave her husband a hard look before she said, "Does my cousin Jannon yet dwell with the Forever Faire?"

"Yeah, he does." Kayla folded her arms. "Aren't you supposed to be shunning him?"

"Yes, but I was never very good at upholding the law. 'Tis why I married a clan leader. He seldom punishes me for defying it." Jem gave her a wink before she turned to Devalan. "Our daughter is with your mother, who is checking my baking again and finding it wanting. I am off to check my traps. Be kind to your niece, Dev. A delight meeting you, Kayla."

The clan leader growled something in Fae before he kissed her and watched her stride off. "As my wife proves, we are not unfeeling monsters. You and she would become good friends in time, I think." He eyed her. "And now you know I am your uncle. Your mother was my youngest sister. Her name was Valarya. I would show you where she lived before she was cast out. It is where you were born."

Valarya, Kayla's mind echoed. It was beautiful and somehow fitting. But the news of her father—of Kelvan—tempered any delight she might have found. Two fathers had died.

As Devalan gestured down the walkway, Kayla put the thoughts aside. Together they entered the city. As they passed other Fae she saw how they stared at her before bowing to Devalan. Some looked curious, but most of the Cloudstar seemed a little afraid, as if they expected her to attack them.

Devalan stopped in front of a house made of rough-hewn rock and polished wood, and used a crystal to open the entry. As Kayla followed him inside, sunlight illuminated the interior from columns of water pouring down each corner of the front room.

But it wasn't the light that stung Kayla's eyes. It was as though her parents had just stepped away. Everything was in place, from the tapestries on the walls to the table set for three. Instead of fruit, fresh white gardenia flowers had been left in a crystal bowl on the table. The scent made her remember the touch of her mother's hand on her cheek.

Her mother—Valarya—had always smelled of gardenias.

"We knew my sister was a spellsinger from the day of her birth," Devalan said as he moved slowly around the room. "Her wails nearly leveled my parents' home. They tried to protect her as best they could, but spellsingers are so rare they knew they could not hide her here forever. They arranged to foster her with another clan to the west, where she fell in love with your father. He was a gifted healer, so my parents raised no objections. They married and returned to us when Valarya became pregnant with you. When you were born, and we realized you had inherited your mother's ability..." He stopped and shook his head.

"That wasn't supposed to happen," Kayla guessed.

"No." He looked past her at the bowl of flowers. "Giving birth to another spellsinger placed my sister in even more danger, for such a thing had never happened in all our long history. Rumors began to spread that all the children she bore would share in her power."

Kayla sighed. "And then the Blackstones heard about it."

Devalan nodded. "By then the Dark Fae had learned of her existence, and yours. We were preparing to move you, but we were betrayed, and the Blackstones attacked. Your father died protecting you from Jarek Blackstone. He loved you and my sister more than his own life."

Kayla sat down at the table and picked up one of the flowers, cradling it between her palms.

"And for that you cast out my mother?"

"No." Devalan faced her. "Losing your father to the Dark Fae made Valarya even more determined to protect you. She had you marked so you could not be replaced by a changeling. One night she took you and vanished without a word. No one knew where she went, or how she lived. Then she returned to us without warning, some five years later."

The disdain in his voice made her anger simmer. "She came to you for help?"

He nodded. "The Dark Fae were hunting her again. They'd been in our territory for months. Others in our clan had already disappeared. When she brought your half-sister and the child's father, the clan was outraged. Our parents had no choice but to cast out Valarya for taking a mortal as a husband, and having a child with him."

Kayla got to her feet, grabbed the bowl of blooms, and hurled it across the room. Devalan jumped out of the way.

"My mother died trying to protect my sister, who grew up alone in foster care. The Blackstones replaced her with a changeling. Now they're coming after me." She watched his shocked expression for a moment. "I'd like to leave now."

"You do not have to. That is why I brought you here, Kayla. I knew of my sister's death when her blood joined the earth and its water." Kayla's mind flashed back on all the times she'd seen the Fae use blood. "But you had no part in your mother's transgressions," Devalan continued. "We can protect you from the Dark Fae." He came to put his hands on her stiff shoulders. "We are your blood kin, and you will be safe with us."

"Safe?" Kayla took a step back to break the contact between them. "What you did sentenced my mother to death, and took Christine away from me. My stepfather nearly drank himself to death while I raised a Blackstone changeling. All of it could have been avoided if you'd just helped her."

Devalan's expression darkened. "She chose her fate when she took a mortal husband."

"If there's a Fae Hell, I sure hope someday you and your entire clan burn in it." She went to the door. "I'm going back to Forever Faire. Now how do I get out of this gigantic toilet?"

CHAPTER 8

JUST BEFORE SUNRISE Tara Blackstone jumped down from Fallon's back and surveyed the still waters of the lake. During the long night she'd seen no sign of her half-brother or his men, but that only meant they were still gathering forces for the next attack. She had the feeling Dirk would be running on pure rage, especially after she'd blocked him from her mind.

You should go and rest, Fallon thought to her. *We will remain vigilant.*

Tara wanted to argue with him, but he was right. "Just watch the shadows," she muttered, and leaned against the dragon's neck. Kayla probably would have freaked out to see her cuddling with such a huge creature, but it comforted her exactly as it had when she was very small. "Did I do the right thing by coming back with her?"

You have lived so long in the dark, child, but you have never wanted it. We know your heart. He bent his head down to look into her eyes. *You have stepped into the light, of your own volition. Your lady mother would be so proud of you.*

"But my father will want me dead," Tara said, and touched his muzzle. "Be careful."

As the dragon flew off to continue his patrol alone, a tall, broad form came out of the trees. The sunlight blazed over his burnished copper hair, and sparkled in his cool eyes. Jannon Ferguson stopped a yard away from her.

"We've managed some breakfast, if you're hungry."

Tara had expected him to yell at her, and call her a bitch, and tell her to stay away from him—not invite her for a meal.

"No, thanks. I'm good."

"I know you are," he said and rubbed the side of his head. "When you are not clouting me with iron, of course. Then you are not so good."

"That's right. I lied to you, and tricked you. I hurt you. I left you chained up." She waited for him to react. "Well?"

"I think you are not very skilled at such treachery," Jannon said. "A Dark Fae would never have left me alive. Indeed, you should have lingered to torture me or have your way with me before you cut off my head or tore out my heart. You truly must stop allowing sentiment to hinder your evil ways. It is confusing everyone."

She pressed her lips together until she was sure she wouldn't laugh. "I think I hit you too hard, Ferguson. Your brains are scrambled."

"They were that, long before I met you, my lady." He held out his hand. "If you will not eat, then walk with me."

Tara told herself she was only humoring him as they walked hand-in-hand from the lake to a wide pasture dotted with round hay bales. The twilight mist was rising. It felt good to stretch her legs, and listen to Jannon's deep voice as he told her about some of the performances they'd given here.

"'Twas so hot during the shows we could not wear our

helms for the jousts. The sweat would blind us. Ah, there is the field."

He stopped by a fence and pointed to a clearing where the old arena had been set up.

Tara leaned against the fence beside him, and looked out at the spot. Grass covered the dirt where Jannon and the Fae had once rode with their lances and armor. It even sprouted through the mulched-over trail that the spectators had walked to the stands. In a few years the field would revert to what it had been before the performers came.

Is that what would happen to her? Now that she didn't have to pretend, what would she become?

"I do not like seeing you riding that dragon," Jannon said. "I think of you falling, and then my belly knots, and I want to find a very big net. Do you think they sell them in town?"

He was trying so hard to chat her up that Tara had to take pity on him.

"I can never be with you," she said simply, and rested her chin on the top rail of the fence. "I am a changeling, and Dark Fae. I've been taught things that would turn your hair white. The Blackstones created me to do bad things. That's who I am. You have to accept it."

"No, I do not. Neither will Kayla. She did not raise you to be evil. Her love made that impossible." Jannon turned to her. "Do not wrinkle your nose at me. I have seen the goodness in you. I have felt the love you hide in your heart. I think some of it is for me, or you would have chopped off my head when you had the chance."

"You just won't give it up, will you?" Something must have gotten in her eye. She had to blink hard. "When I rejoined my clan I was going to take you with me, Jannon.

Have you chained in our dungeons, and make you my slave." She swiped at her eyes. "My love slave."

"A waste of time," he said, "for I am already that." He tipped up her trembling chin. "Say what you will. You know I am yours, my lady."

"I love you, but–" Inside her chest something pounded, but it couldn't be her heart. She didn't have one. "I've also betrayed everyone, including you. I've done terrible things to my sister. My brother has been coming into my dreams and using me for sex for years, and I let him. And sometimes? I liked it."

Jannon's jaw tightened. "You were but a girl, and he never said he was your brother."

"Yeah, well, I never asked. All I cared about was my own pleasure." She ducked her head. "After what he and I did, I don't know if I can…be with anyone else. He ruined me."

He tugged her close, and kissed the top of her head. "All you have to do now is heal, my lady. However long it takes, I will wait for you. We are immortal, after all."

Tara wanted to believe that, more than anything in the world. But if there was one thing she'd learned in her short life it was the futility of hope.

"Dirk's been controlling me since I was born. He's taught me a lot about the ways of the Dark Fae." She swallowed hard. "I don't want anything to do with him, but there's still a connection between us. He can get to me whenever he wants. I'm fighting it, Jannon, but I don't know if I can break it."

"You can, and you will."

She shook her head. "You can't know that."

He drew back and looked into her eyes. "I can and I do," he said. "Because I will help you."

It was all there in his face. He believed every word he

said. She swallowed past a constriction in her throat, and looked away.

He put his arm around her shoulders. "Now come. If you still do not wish to eat, then you may watch me. I am so hungry that grass begins to look appetizing."

THE SOFT LIGHT of dawn roused Ryan from his sleep, and he rolled over to put his arm around Kayla. When he felt wet wood he opened his eyes to find only splash marks where she had been.

"Kayla?"

He got up and jerked on his clothes, cursing at the fastenings as he scanned the empty grove. Sunlight made the golden moss sparkle as it shifted in the light breeze, but there was no sign of his beloved. A splash made him spin around to see Kayla surfacing in the pool. She wiped the wet hair out of her face and spat out some water.

"Morning."

"A fine time for a swim, my lady." He knelt down to hoist her out of the pool. "You should have woken me."

"I wasn't swimming." She shook herself and tugged at her drenched shirt. "Devalan Cloudstar grabbed me while you were sleeping. He took me for a visit to Nefele, where he introduced me to his wife and showed me the sites. He offered me sanctuary, too."

Ryan went still. "He did what?"

"Wasn't my idea." She twisted the long tail of her hair to wring it out. "P.S., Devalan is my uncle. My mom was his youngest sister."

Ryan heard fury in Kayla's brisk tone. "Do I need to end him?"

She pretended to think. "No, but only because I liked his wife, and they have a kid." Her mouth flattened. "Auntie Jem asked about Jannon. Should I say hi to him for her, or is that not a good idea?"

Silently he cursed Devalan for putting her through this. "You owe naught to the Cloudstar, love."

"Oh I wouldn't say that."

Clearly she was troubled. "What else happened in Nefele?"

Her hands fisted. "I saw the place where I was born, and found out why my mom died. They use water instead of crystal to power things. Oh, and they have a thing for wearing white. I'd hate to be the Fae in charge of laundry."

Whatever the Cloudstar had revealed to her, it had shaken her to her core. "What more then, love?"

"My dear old uncle wanted me to stay. He said he and the clan would protect me. This after they sent my mother to her death because she married the wrong guy."

Her knuckles turned white. The air around them began to vibrate.

"Kayla," Ryan urged. "Focus." She glared at him, her topaz eyes burning into his. He quickly scanned around them and pointed. "Focus on that tree."

"The tree?"

"It is not a tree," Ryan said softly. "It is Devalan."

Kayla took in a quick breath, and then began to sing. The voice that poured out of her was hard and angry, and filled with pain. It lashed out as a wave of enormous, glittering power. It blinded Ryan for a moment as it scythed through the pines. When his vision cleared he saw every tree in front of Kayla had been flattened into the ground. The trunks and branches of the largest lay half-buried. The rest had been reduced to heaps of needles and splintered wood.

Kayla swayed for a moment, and then abruptly sat down on the stump.

"I think I need to join your next anger management class. If Devalan had been standing there…"

"He would be toothpicks." Ryan sat beside her. "You sang only for a few seconds, and your voice destroyed a forest. You drove off a herd of dragons and the Blackstones. Jarek knows the power you possess. It is why he will never stop hunting you."

"Okay." She leaned against his shoulder, and in a dull voice asked, "What if we cut my vocal cords? If I can't make a sound, I can't hurt anyone. I can live without a voice."

Ryan would have felt sickened by her suggestion, but he remembered how his clan had reacted when they discovered his brutal gift.

"My kin wanted to place me under an enchantment that would remove my emotions. The logic was that if I couldn't feel anything, I would not shift into a berserker."

She shuddered. "That's disgusting."

"They thought I could live without emotions," he said. "After my wife and son died I went into the madness for so long I almost did not come back from it. When I did, and I was cast out, I decided to retreat to a place where no one could find me. It was much the same as what my clan had wished to do."

Kayla gave him an uncertain look. "What made you nix that idea?"

"I didn't. When I arrived in the remote mountain spot I

had chosen for my hermitage, I found Colm already there, building his own. He convinced me that we could be brothers in exile, and help each other— and so we did."

Ryan smiled as he remembered those far-gone days. All that had mattered was hunting, staying warm, and speaking of anything but the past.

"Wallace came to us a year later, after he had been cast out, and offered to serve as our smith and spell tracker. Then Gavan wandered into our camp, and challenged me to a joust. We built our first arena, borrowed some horses from the local mortals, and went at it. I knew from the moment he lowered his lance that he wished me to kill him."

She smiled wanly. "But you didn't."

Ryan shook his head. "I did unhorse him three times before he dragged me from my saddle and tussled with me in the dirt for an hour or so. Then we decided to go into town and get very drunk." Not mentioning the twin sisters he and Gavan had met at the tavern seemed politic. "'Twas an interesting night."

"I bet." Kayla looked out at the devastation, and the humor faded from her expression. "Ryan, I can't use my power against the Blackstones. If they attack again, and you and the guys get in the way... I won't risk hurting any of you."

"When I saw you and Christine fly away on that dragon, I thought I would lose control. I am certain my men entertained the same notion. Still they remained at my side and fought. They had faith in me, as have I in you." He took her hand in his. "That and my eyes turn black first, so doubtless they were watching them."

"Oh, no doubt." She stood up from the stump and tugged him to his feet. "Come on. Everyone will be wondering where we are."

CHAPTER 10

WHEN THEY RETURNED to camp Ryan took Colm to patrol the perimeter, and check the dragons standing guard at the lake. As Kayla watched them go, Christine joined her.

"So, I'd say you two went skinny-dipping," Christine said, eyeing her. "Only your clothes are all wet. Then there was that great big boom we heard from where you were. I'm pretty sure it wasn't an orgasm, but if I'm wrong, honey, I want all the details."

"I know Colm told you I'm the spellsinger," Kayla said. "So don't annoy me." She glanced at her sister. "It's not weirding you out, is it?"

"Not really. I mean, you can talk to horses in your mind. *That* was weird." She bumped her shoulder against Kayla's. "By the way, I saw Tara and Jannon eating together at breakfast. Think she's going to be all right now?"

"If Dirk doesn't get at her again, yeah, I hope so." Kayla glanced up at the clear sky, and watched Fallon fly across it. "What are they waiting for, anyway?"

"More of their skunk kin to poot at us, I imagine." Christine gestured at some archery targets one of the men had set up. "Let's go do some shooting. It always makes me feel better to put an arrow in something."

"I need to work on my control." Kayla told her sister about what she'd done in the pine thicket. Then a thought occurred to her. "How do you get everything so perfect when you use your ability? Is there something you see in your mind when you're thinking about it?"

Christine shook her head. "I never think about it. If I do, it just messes me up. Come on, I'll show you."

After retrieving some bows and arrows from Wallace's cottage, Christine took Kayla to the makeshift range and moved two targets into place.

"Taking any shot is always about two things: seeing and feeling." She notched an arrow and raised the bow. "I look at what I want to hit. *Really* look at it, and see everything about it: how big it is, the distance between me and it, anything in the way, and the spot where I think I can do the most damage. Then I go into myself, in that place where my little trick comes from, and soak it up. I don't know what to call it—power, energy, talent, whatever—but it's like water. I jump in." She raised the bow. "And I shoot."

Kayla watched the arrow fly and bury itself in the center of the target.

"And you really don't think about it at all?"

"I don't have to. I trust myself. Always have." She handed the bow to Kayla. "Now your turn. Show me some magick, girlfriend."

Christine had to show her how to hold and draw the bow before she stepped away. Kayla looked at the target. Not thinking about shooting seemed bizarre to her, but she focused on the target and saw the spot she wanted. Reaching into herself for the power that she had only just discovered was strange, but it was there. Kayla only knew one song about arrows, and as she released the bowstring she sang four words from it. Her arrow whizzed through the air and landed in the exact spot she'd chosen: dead center.

Just as Christine began clapping her hands the target exploded, showering them both with bits of straw, paper and shattered arrow.

"Yeah, I think we need to work on that power part." Her sister shook out her hair. "And can you heal half-mortals by touch? 'Cause I'm thinking that might come in handy, too."

The sunlight dimmed, and Kayla felt something cold splash on her head. She glanced up to see dark clouds billowing over the camp—too quickly to be natural.

"Christine?"

Fallon flew beneath the clouds, and a shaft of lightning struck him, sending him hurtling to the ground.

"Oh, shit, it's them," Christine said. As a hard, cold rain suddenly pounded down on them, Christine grabbed her hand. "Run."

As they fled toward the cottages Kayla squinted through the rain at the sky. It was black with shadow portals. Sickly yellow light glimmered as more of the Blackstones' nightmarish water creatures fell onto the dragons standing guard. As fire blasted from their roaring mouths, it hit the rain and turned to steam. The tentacled monsters dragged them into the lake, extinguishing their flames.

"Kayla," Ryan shouted.

She looked over to see Ryan and Colm running toward them, only to be buried beneath a huge creature falling from the sky.

"Colm!" Christine screamed, as she and Kayla ran toward them.

She grabbed some branches from the trees they passed and flung them at the monster.

Colm struggled out from under it as it retreated from Christine's attack. But it oozed into the lake before Kayla could reach it. She caught a glimpse of Ryan's bright hair before the monster submerged, taking her lover with it. Jannon, Wallace and the other Fae warriors rushed past Kayla, their swords drawn as they dove into the lake. A moment later all of them came flying out of the water to land on the ground and in the trees.

Kayla's throat tightened as a shadow spread over the lake, covering the seething watcr until it became a bottomless abyss.

Titan, she thought, reaching for the mind of the giant stallion. *Please, come and help us.*

We are trapped.

The herd leader sent back an image of shadow portals enveloping the barn.

Should we try to break through them?

No, Kayla thought back to him. *Stay away from the shadows.*

Christine helped Colm to his feet. "Is that one of their portals?"

Kayla looked across the lake at the Dark Fae walking out of the forest. Dirk Blackstone carried two huge blades, and wore a full suit of black armor. He paused long enough to smirk and salute her with one blade before he stepped into the shadow covering the lake, and slowly sank under it.

"He'll kill Ryan," Kayla whispered. She turned her head to meet Colm's gaze. "I'm going to sing. You and the men take cover. Now."

Ryan's second nodded, and shouted to the men to retreat before he snatched up a struggling Christine and ran.

Kayla ignored her sister's furious shrieks as she blocked out the sounds around her and gathered her voice. She knew if she used too much power she would vaporize the shadow barrier, as well as Dirk, Ryan, and the entire lake. If she didn't use enough, Dirk would kill him.

She sang words that seemed to come from a deep, unknown place in her memory. The words came to her in her mother's sweet voice. The power rolled out of her, but when it touched the shadow masking the lake, it blasted backward, knocking her off her feet.

Kayla struggled to a sitting position. "What the–"

A thin hand grabbed her and helped her up.

"The shadows reflect your power," Tara told her. "You can't dispel Dark Fae magick."

Kayla looked into the changeling's calm gray eyes. "But you can."

"Yes." Tara turned toward the lake. "When I lift the shadow, remove the water. The creatures can't live long without it. It will let the men get to Ryan."

Kayla nodded, and stepped up beside Tara as she began murmuring under her breath. When she extended her hands they began to darken and glow with gray light, which shot out and encircled the lake. The shadow lifted inch by inch into the air, until Kayla could see the water. Her mother's song poured into her mind, and she sang it to the lake.

The water rose along with the shadows, curling into a huge funnel. It whirled up into the storm clouds, churning like an inverted sea. Rain pelted Kayla's face as she sang the last of the words. Her heart clenched as the funnel exploded, blasting the sky clear.

In the empty lake bed, the sagging creatures that had been left behind crawled aimlessly. But at their edge, not far from her, she saw Ryan and Dirk fighting. Her lover only had a short dagger against the long swords Dirk used to hack at him.

"No," Tara said, gripping her shoulder, when Kayla lurched forward to help him. "That's exactly what he wants. Dirk will use you as a body shield."

"But—"

Tara gripped her with both hands. "Don't you see? It's so predictable." Kayla watched Ryan leap clear of the whirling blades before Tara cut off her view. "It's a trap."

More Blackstones appeared on the other side of the lake, but one of them stared across at Kayla. He looked older than the others, and had a smirk on his face that made her stomach turn. Tara looked over her shoulder.

"That's my father," she said flatly. "Jarek Blackstone."

Kayla looked at the girl's tormented expression. "Don't ever call a rapist your dad. You know who your real father was. His name was Rowe, like yours."

Jarek shouted to the Dark Fae as he led them onto the lake bed. Colm and the men of Forever Faire did the same. Christine dashed for Kayla.

"You stay right here," Christine told her as she handed Tara a dagger. "Come on, little sister."

Tara grinned back at her before they followed the men.

Kayla felt worse than useless. Just as she'd warned Ryan, it was too dangerous to use her voice. Should she grab a blade? Her sisters had.

Above the growing din, a ringing clang of steel grabbed her attention. Someone had gotten a sword to Ryan! He parried Dirk's blades with such force that sparks shot off the clashing weapons. Dirk feigned a thrust at Ryan's midsection, and swung his other sword for his neck. Kayla pressed her hand over her mouth. But an instant before the blade reached him, Ryan dropped low. With a blinding speed that belied his size, he ducked under the sword and stepped in—and drove his dagger into Dirk's thigh.

"Yes!" Kayla screamed.

The wound immediately spurted blood. As Dirk rose, Ryan knocked the Dark Fae back onto his ass. He kicked him in the chest, laying him out flat.

As though summoned, Tara emerged from the mass of battling warriors and hurried to Dirk's side.

Kayla held her breath, but Tara looked away from the fallen Dark Fae, and stepped back to stand beside Ryan.

"Yes," Kayla muttered, pumping her fist as she strode onto the muddy lakebed. "That's my sister."

"Come here," Dirk demanded, lifting a hand to Tara. "Heal me, or I will bleed to death." When she didn't move he tried to grab her leg, and she stepped back. "Tara, come to me, now. Don't let me die like this."

"You won't," an ugly voice said.

Jarek Blackstone appeared over his son with a battle-axe. He brought it down before Ryan or Tara could react. He decapitated Dirk with one single, horrific stroke.

"For you, berserker," Jarek said, as he kicked the head toward him.

But then he pivoted, flinging the blade hidden in his other hand directly at Ryan—as Tara stepped in the way. Though Ryan grabbed for her, it was too late. The dagger thudded into her chest, all the way up to its quivering hilt. She staggered backward into Ryan's arms.

"No!" Kayla screamed.

"Tara!" Jannon yelled.

His horrified shout cut through the din of the fighting, as he rushed to her. Kayla's legs gave out, as she sprawled in the mud. But she crawled the remaining distance, as Jannon and Ryan lowered Tara to the ground.

Tara glanced down at the enormous hilt, but then looked at Jannon.

"Be brave," she said to the Fae warrior, his face a stricken mask. Then she smiled at the Blackstone clan leader. "You lose."

Jarek snarled, but when Ryan jumped to his feet the Dark Fae darted away.

"Kayla," Jannon said.

"I know," she said.

Without thinking, she snatched the blade out of Tara's chest. As the wound gushed, she pressed her hand down over it.

"Come on," she muttered. "Come on."

The blue light appeared, and the flow of blood stopped, but Kayla could feel the slowing beats of the badly damaged heart.

"No, no, no," Kayla gasped. "God, please, no. *Tara.*"

"Can't heal me," her sister whispered from dry and pallid lips. "Too much Dark Fae blood." Tara looked up at her with an expression so peaceful it made Kayla sob. "Don't…cry." Her thin hand came up to wipe a tear from Kayla's cheek. "Gives you clown…nose."

The hand fell, and Tara went still.

As Jannon uttered a torn sound, Kayla furiously shook her head.

"No," she ground out through clenched teeth. "I won't have it."

She closed her eyes and, unbidden, the words of the resurrection song flooded into her mind.

No blood stains love's blade.

No valiant heart shall be ended.

That which was made is unmade.

That which was broken is mended.

Nothing happened. Even though Kayla waited, there was no explosion. She opened her tear-blurred eyes to see Jannon staring at her.

"Can you not–"

"I tried," Kayla cried. "It didn't work. I tried!" The tears streamed down her face. "I don't understand."

Jannon's mouth twisted as he tenderly cradled Tara's limp form to his chest. He gently stroked her hair, and choked back a sob.

"The Dark Fae was the death of her," he whispered.

"Sheridan," said a familiar voice, as the sound of the battle intruded.

Though Kayla didn't look up, Ryan answered. "Devalan."

"The blood of my kin called through the earth's water," the leader of the Cloudstar said.

As though she were seeing it from a distance, Kayla realized Tara's blood had mixed with the watery mud. Tara was a Cloudstar? A white cloak appeared in front of her face, and she looked up into Devalan's grim face. Only as he draped the fabric over Tara's body, did Kayla see the resemblance in their pale blonde hair.

"You must leave," he said, as water began to stream around them. He looked at Jannon. "Now."

Jannon got to his feet, hugging the precious bundle to his chest. Ryan helped Kayla to stand.

Devalan drew his sword and addressed Ryan. "May we be of service to the Forever Faire?"

"Aye," Ryan said. He briefly touched the white cape. "Aye, that you can."

Kayla followed Jannon to the shore, and Devalan raised his sword. From all sides of the lake warriors dressed in white came out of the forest, riding on streams of water as if they were surfing over the ground. The Cloudstar wove in and out as they effectively cut off the Blackstones from retreat, and closed in around them.

"Keep her safe," Jannon said, and kissed the top of Tara's head before he went after Ryan.

With shaking hands, Kayla used Devalan's cloak to cover her sister's peaceful face. As she knelt, her heart collapsed inside her. She saw that face, from the time Tara was a cooing infant to her first day at school. So many birthdays streamed by, so many walks from the bus. Then there was the day she began her job at the fabric store. Kayla had almost begun to smile when she remembered the first time the Blackstones had found her sister. She had failed Tara so many times. Kayla took in a shuddering breath. But this one hurt the most. She would never have a chance to make it right.

Almost dispassionately Kayla watched the Cloudstar easily overwhelm the Dark Fae. The white-clad warriors drove the Dark Fae back to the men of Forever Faire, who quickly dispatched them. She thought she would feel nothing until she saw Jannon corner Jarek Blackstone between him and Dirk's cousin, who turned and drove his sword into the clan leader's back. Jannon finished him with a quick thrust, and then frowned at Beck, who grinned before he threw himself on Jannon's blade.

The last of the Dark Fae fell beneath Ryan's blade, and he lifted it over his head to the shouts and cheers of all the warriors. His eyes found Kayla's, and the love in them touched her like a physical caress.

Once the men left the lakebed, Kayla carefully used her spell-song to draw the water the Cloudstar had brought with them to cover the bodies of the slain. Sunlight sparkled on the shimmering blue ripples as they closed over the dead, and then it was as if nothing had happened —almost.

Ryan came to her, and took her in his arms. "She saved my life," he said lowly.

Kayla nodded against his chest. "She saved us all."

CHAPTER 11

THAT NIGHT THE men built a bonfire, and gathered around it with the Cloudstar warriors. They shared the bottles of Fae wine that Lawrence brought out from their stores. Fallon and most of the other dragons survived the battle. They shifted into bike form before they joined the horses in an open field. The Fae herd grazed peacefully, but kept a watchful eye on the visiting Fae.

Kayla stood outside Jannon's cottage, where they had placed Tara's body. She gazed at the circle of men around the fire. The pale, handsome faces of her uncle's warriors stood out. She didn't know a single one of their names, and yet all of them were related to her. It seemed outlandish to have such a large family, not that she would ever think of them that way. Now that Tara was dead, Christine was the only family that mattered.

"You should join us," Devalan said, appearing at her side. He offered her a bottle of firewine. When she shook her head he took a drink from it. "My men are very curious about you."

"You only fought because you owed Ryan," she said. She

started to move away, and came up short as her uncle caught her by the arm. She yanked it away from him. "Don't be a jerk. I can sing as much as I like here."

"We fought because you are still Cloudstar," Devalan told her. "You may be a spellsinger, but you do not see what is before you. We are a powerful clan, Kayla. Join us, and you will be cherished and protected."

Cherished and protected? Like her mother? Like Tara, who'd shared Cloudstar blood?

"No, thanks. Oh, here, I forgot." As she handed him the blood-stained cloak she had brought from the cottage, she spotted Ryan coming toward them. "Excuse me."

"If he pesters you," Ryan said, embracing her, "I will send them on their way. 'Tis tradition to mark a battle with hospitality." He kissed her forehead. "I care little enough for tradition."

"It's not that," she said. "It's Jannon." She looked at the cottage. "He won't leave her, and I want to…" She could hardly believe she was saying this. "I need to get her ready for the funeral."

Ryan nodded, his face grim. They made their way back to the little place, and Ryan went inside. He emerged a few minutes later with Jannon, who looked exactly as bad as Kayla felt. Once they walked away, she took a deep breath, slipped inside, and went to the back room.

Jannon had lain Tara's body so carefully on his bed. Fresh tears stung Kayla's eyes when she saw that he had already cleaned the blood and dirt from her face. He'd wrapped his finest tunic over her blood-stained clothes. Kayla hugged herself. He'd also brushed out Tara's hair so that it framed her face like soft moonbeams. She looked like an angel. Kayla gingerly sat down and took Tara's cold, stiff hand between hers.

"I'm going to miss you so much," she said quietly. "I'll

sleep under one of your quilts every night, I promise. And every time I order pizza, I'll get half anchovies and hot peppers. I don't know if I can eat them, but they'll always be there for you."

As the tears began to fall, Kayla leaned over and kissed Tara's pale cheek. The drops glistened on her sister's face, and Kayla closed her eyes. This is not how she wanted to remember Tara. But try as she might to call up a happier image, all she could see was that damned lake—and her blood seeping into the ground. She bowed her head and grimaced. Her Cloudstar blood had saved them, as much as her Blackstone blood had doomed her. Kayla sniffed and wiped at her nose. Tara had said it herself.

Too much Dark Fae blood.

Well that wasn't a worry any more.

Dark Fae blood?

Kayla went still for a moment before her eyes snapped open. She furiously swiped away the tears and stared at Tara's white face. Could what she be thinking possibly be true? There was only one way to find out.

Kayla put her hand on Tara's chest.

As expected, the blue glow appeared, but Kayla wasn't going to give up so easily this time. As with the arrow, she didn't try to control the healing. Instead she pictured the outcome. In her mind's eye, Tara's heart was whole. The damaged muscle knitted together. It became whole and strong, ready and willing to pump blood.

Kayla half-grinned to herself. What blood would it pump?

"Fae blood," she said out loud.

When Tara had died, she'd nearly bled out, her Fae and Dark Fae blood mingled. Kayla pressed her hand down harder, and saw the blue glow flare. But now it was up to Kayla to heal her, and she knew one thing for certain: her sister would have Fae blood. She saw it so clearly, she had to smile.

The healing light ran like wildfire over Tara's entire body.

"Yes," Kayla breathed, putting both hands on her chest. "We are Fae."

As Kayla squeezed her eyes shut, she concentrated. A sweet memory of Tara filled her vision. She was sewing, and humming that wordless tune their father whistled. Kayla smiled. Now she knew the words. The sweet sound filled her soul. Her mother had sung it to her and Christine. How she wished Tara could have been there to hear it! Kayla nodded to herself. She would hear it now.

No blood stains love's blade.
No valiant heart shall be ended.
That which was made is unmade.
That which was broken is mended.

Light teased the edges of Kayla's eyelids. She stopped singing and opened her eyes. Millions of white stars swirled around the room, weaving in and out. They circled and grew denser as they shrank into a glittering ball of blinding brightness. As she squinted the light fell onto Tara, disappearing into her chest—but then her body convulsed.

"Oh, no," Kayla gasped, as she backed away from the bed in horror. "I didn't mean–"

She clamped both hands over her own scream.

Blue light raced through the delicate veins under Tara's ashen skin. Her entire body vibrated with a hum that filled the room. White stars formed on her lashes, and then her blue lips. Streaks of blazing light threaded through her hair, and raced beneath Jannon's tunic. Her body floated, growing brighter and whiter until Kayla could barely see her.

Ryan, Jannon and Devalan burst into the room just as the light disappeared. Tara fell back to the bed.

For a moment, there was stunned silence, and it seemed no one could move. But Jannon stepped to the bed, only to stumble back—as Tara sat up.

"Blind me," Devalan muttered.

Tara cocked her head at him, then swung her legs over the side of the bed. She tugged away Jannon's tunic and stood up, looking down at herself before she met Kayla's astonished gaze. Gold now glittered in her white-blonde hair, and her eyes had acquired an emerald color.

"I'm alive," Tara said, touching her own cheek. "How?"

"My niece brought you back to life with a resurrection song," Devalan said.

"Kayla?" Tara said, reaching out to her.

Kayla wrapped her up in a bear hug, lifting her off the floor. "Tara," she whispered into her hair.

"All spellsingers can do so," Devalan continued. "Though it seems that my niece can also purge Dark Fae blood. Very powerful, I must say. I have never heard the like."

"Then it was Kayla who brought back Colm and Christine," Ryan said.

Tara kissed Kayla on both cheeks, and slipped out of her arms. She stepped in front of Jannon, who still stared at her in disbelief.

"Were you brave?" the teenager asked with a shy smile.

He nodded, and touched a piece of her hair. "I cannot believe you are come back to me."

Ryan exchanged a look with Kayla, and by silent agreement, they herded her uncle out of the room. Colm and Christine waited outside. Although questions filled their faces, Ryan caught Colm's eye and nodded at Devalan.

"Come, Clan Leader," Colm said. "I have a fine bottle of

rainwine from the old country. I can think of no one I'd rather drink it with than you."

Although Christine trailed after them, she kept glancing over her shoulder at Kayla, who could only manage a smile.

That left her with Ryan, who held out his hand. Kayla took it, and went with him to his cottage, where he sat down with her in the big armchair by the fire. They sat like that for a long time, neither of them speaking.

"This was the reason Jarek Blackstone wanted my mother, and then me," she said quietly, and looked up at his handsome face. "Because we could bring the dead back to life. There is no greater power than that among the Fae, is there?"

Ryan shook his head. "He would have attained true immortality. With you as his slave, he would never again fear death of any kind. He might have also planned to force you to have children, in hopes of building an army of spellsingers."

"I'm so glad that man is dead," she said, and slumped. She felt completely drained and wondered if resurrecting Tara had cost a great deal of her power. "Come to bed with me?"

Without another word he carried her into his bedroom, and undressed them with a thought before curling up with her under the covers.

"Sleep now, love," he said, kissing the top of her head. "I will be here when you awake."

AS RYAN SAW off Devalan Cloudstar in the morning, the clan leader insisted Ryan and the rest of his men accompany Kayla to his stronghold the following night. He promised a proper victory celebration with a feast and revelry and performances by the Cloudstar's finest dancers and musicians.

"The Blackstones were a blight upon our kind for too long," Devalan said. "And your protection of my niece has earned you a place at our table."

Ryan thought of Kayla, who still slept in his bed, and how much she had disliked her first encounter with the clan.

"My lady may not wish to attend, Clan Leader."

Devalan's eyes narrowed. "If you wish her to be your lady wife, I suggest you overcome her reticence."

Ryan took the time to personally thank and clasp hands with each of the Cloudstar warriors who had come to their aid. He knew full well the victory might not have happened without their numbers. None of the Fae responded with anything but the proper form, but still he saw the reservation in their expressions. Devalan's men might boast of defeating the Dark Fae clan, but they would not mention they had done it fighting alongside a band of outcasts.

Tara and Jannon emerged from his cottage to take breakfast with the rest of the Forever Faire warriors. They treated the resurrected changeling with a mixture of awe and delight. As Ryan walked back to his cottage, he was happy to see Tara smiling, and Jannon laughing. They had both done so much to earn the happiness that glowed in their faces.

Inside the cottage he removed his boots so he would not wake Kayla, and walked softly back to the bedroom to look in on her. She lay sprawled on his side of the bed, her pale body gilded by sunlight. He could still see the faint bruises under her eyes that had been so dark last night after bringing Tara back. But her breathing sounded easy, and a light flush of pink tinted her cheeks.

Ryan wanted to stop time so that he never had to let her go. Yet if she chose to join her clan, he would lose her forever. They had made promises to each other, but that was before he knew she was a spellsinger. The Cloudstar also knew it, and they would want her in their keeping.

Kayla opened one eye. "You lied to me."

Ryan came over to sit on the side of the bed. "I cannot do that now that the curse has been lifted." He frowned. "Why do you think I have?"

"You said you'd be here when I woke up," she said and yawned. "That was an hour ago. I think you owe me now."

He loved how she looked when she was drowsy. It made him wish he could bolt the door for a week.

"How may I repay my debt, love?"

Kayla glanced down at his tunic. "Do you have to be anywhere for the next couple hours?"

When he shook his head she pressed her hand to the

center of his chest, and closed her eyes. His clothing unfastened, and he stood to allow the garments to remove themselves from his body. The empty clothing then walked over to the dresser, folded themselves neatly and formed a tidy stack.

Kayla lay back before she beckoned for him to join her. But as Ryan stretched out his big body over hers, she turned under him. She got on her hands and knees to rub her bottom against his belly.

"Put your arms around my waist. I want to show you something."

Ryan sent a quelling thought to his stiff cock and did as she commanded, rocking a little as their bodies lifted off the mattress to float above it.

"You have been practicing your thought-spells."

"I think about that night you did this to me and made me think I was dreaming." Slowly she rubbed her damp sex against his rigid shaft. "You still do, every time we're together."

He shifted, bringing the full bulb of his tip to nudge her slick opening. Suddenly he couldn't wait another moment to have her.

"I'm coming into you now, love."

Kayla cried out her delight as he thrust into her. Her softness was wet, heated, and welcoming to his hard invasion. Ryan lifted her hips against him to forge deeper with every stroke, plunging into her again and again until she whimpered and writhed beneath him.

They fell to the mattress, and he dragged her over to the side, crouching and bracing his feet so he could work himself for her pleasure. Fucking her like this felt primal and savage and darkly arousing. It made his shaft swell until their fit grew so tight they both groaned.

Ryan reached under her to cup her pretty breasts, and

murmured how it pleased him to tease her beaded nipples while he plowed in and out of her. He watched Kayla's fingers curl into the coverlet, and jerked out of her to turn her over to face him. Watching her eyes as he slowly pushed back inside her made his balls tighten, but he was not ready to empty his seed into her. He bent his head to suckle her, lashing her tight peaks over and over as he gave her slow, heavy thrusts of his cock.

Her hands gripped his hair, becoming trapped by the twining strands as she brought his face to hers.

"Kiss me."

As he did, her sweet tongue glided against his, mimicking his stroking. She took her lips from him, and looked into his eyes. Something was amiss.

"What is it, love?"

"Now that the curse is lifted, I think I can get pregnant. Somehow, I just feel it. I'll have to talk to Wallace about it, but...I want to." She looked all over his face. "I want your child in me. Will you give me your baby?"

Her request made Ryan's self-control snap. He pumped into her, eager to fill her with his love and the dream of a child. She wrapped her legs around him, her eyelashes fluttering. Her skin took on a golden glow as her climax burst around him. The strong, rhythmic contractions dragged him with her, and he jetted into the center of her delight.

He kept his shaft nestled in her as he held her through the last tremors of bliss. Kayla cuddled against him, her lips parting on a low sigh before she fell asleep.

Ryan held her and allowed himself to imagine the child she wanted, and that he knew could never be.

KAYLA SUSPECTED THAT all of Nefele had turned out for their clan leader's cele-bration. She and Ryan led the warriors of Forever Faire through the streets of the water city to Devalan's dwelling. Hundreds of Fae dressed in fantastic outfits of white lace, silk and satin smiled at them as they passed huge tables filled with beautifully-prepared platters and bowls of food. Wine replaced water in the five fountains outside the clan leader's huge mansion. Enchanted crystal goblets floated around each fount, waiting to be plucked out of the air and filled.

Colm left them to accompany Christine on a tour of her clan's city, and the rest of the men spread out to enjoy the food and drink.

"He really knows how to throw a party," Kayla said to Ryan. "I'm sorry we couldn't talk Tara or Jannon into coming. Both of them have family here."

"I believe they had their own private party planned," he told her.

They paused to watch a group of graceful dancers

performing on a platform made of a geyser and whirling crystal disks. Beneath the watery stage a large orchestra performed gorgeous music on the Fae's strangely-shaped instruments. The most impressive was a wide pyramid of glass tubes filled with different levels of water, which a single giant Cloudstar played with silver sticks.

"Our guests of honor," Devalan declared. "Welcome back, Niece."

He climbed down the steps of the pavilion to bow before Kayla.

"Thanks for inviting me this time," she said. A little girl was hiding behind him, and Kayla smiled at the shy child. "You've got a funny tail, Clan Leader."

"I'm not a tail," the girl protested. She popped out, her white curls bobbing as she planted her hands on her hips. "I'm Larya."

"I'm your cousin, Kayla," she said, bowing to the child, who giggled with delight. "This is Ryan Sheridan, the master of Forever Faire."

Larya's pale green eyes took him in. "He's very large. Are all his clan so big?"

"Do you mean to subject our guests to interrogation?" Devalan asked her as he rumpled her tiny curls. "Will you ask your mother to come to me, my sunshine?"

"Yes, Father." With one last look at Kayla Larya hurried off.

Something about the child's name finally clicked. "You named her after my mom, didn't you?"

"I was very fond of Valarya, and never agreed with what my parents did to her." Devalan cleared his throat. "I will not press you tonight, Niece, but I would know soon if you wish to return to the clan." He eyed Ryan. "You are aware that if you and Sheridan marry, he will also be welcomed into the clan."

"But not the rest of the guys," Kayla guessed.

Devalan gave her a pained smile. "Marriage to you nullifies his exile, not that of his men." Jem came to join him, and he kissed her cheek. "I must attend to some duties they expect of clan leaders. I hope you enjoy the festivities."

"Just when I think I can like the Fae," Kayla said, "they say something that makes my blood boil." She sighed. "Can we find a place where we can talk?"

Ryan took her down by of the springs that supplied the clan with their water power, and sat with her on a bench to watch the glinting, darting dance of the tiny fish that occupied the pool.

"Your uncle did not have to offer to end my exile. He is within his rights to cast you out for becoming involved with me."

"Yeah, I'm surprised, too, seeing that his parents did that to my mother. Maybe that's the reason he isn't." She laced her fingers through his. "Would you want to join the clan?"

"It is tempting," he admitted. "Few things are more joyous than living among our own kind in our true realm. But I cannot leave my men, or Forever Faire."

She looked away. The last thing she wanted to do was make him choose, but she had to ask the hardest question.

"What if I became pregnant? Would you join the clan to be a father to our child?"

"Did you consider that the child might be another spellsinger, or a berserker?"

She had. "It wouldn't matter to you or me. Either way, our kid would have the best possible parents in the world to deal with it."

He smiled sadly and shook his head.

"I will return in a year to visit you." He rubbed his thumb

over her knuckles. "Even with your uncle's indulgence, we cannot stay long in this territory. You might visit me in Ashdale. Now that the Blackstones are gone, we can rebuild the lodge and winter there each year. It will seem long at first, but I promise you it will be worth it when I return"

"Don't bother," Kayla said as she stood up. Ryan gaped up at her. "I'm not going to be here next year. I also don't need a Fae family."

She tugged him off the bench to a spot they'd passed, with a splendid view of the city.

"You cannot live alone," he said, "or pretend to be a mortal. You will have no protection. 'Tis too dangerous."

"I'll have plenty of protection," she said, and gave him a deliberately bewildered look. "You're not firing me, are you? Because you have to know, Sheridan, I'm the best groom you've ever had. Will ever have, for that matter."

"You mean to stay with Forever Faire? With me?" he tacked on. He gestured to Nefele, but never took his eyes off hers. "When you could have all this?"

"What, Drippyville? Look, I like water as much as the next gal, but in way smaller amounts. Ice cube trays. Teapots. The occasional secret trysting pool. Besides, I look terrible in white." She grinned at him. "I told you, Ryan. I pick you. I'll always pick you. Forever Faire is my clan, and you are the love of my life." She touched her belly. "And, if Wallace is right about my fertility, my baby daddy, too. So think marriage, but no Drippyville."

"I want to marry you," he said, his earnest face beaming and his eyes alight. "Right now."

He scooped her off her feet, as she gave a surprised yelp. At breakneck speed, he carried her down to where his men and the Cloudstar had gathered around a long table. Gavan and Wallace were there, as well as Colm and Christine. When Ryan set her down, curious eyes turned their way.

Ryan solemnly took her hands in his. "You have only to say how you feel for me, Kayla Rowe, before all your kin."

Kayla caught Christine's eye, smiled, and turned back to Ryan.

"I love you, Ryan Sheridan, and I will be your wife. Forever."

• • • • •

THE END

• • • • •

More sizzling paranormal romance awaits in *Rescued* (*Silver Wood Coven Book One*).
For a sneak peek, turn the page.

LACHLAN
Immortal Highlander Book 1

Chapter 1

KINLEY CHANDLER HAD expected a perfect day. So of course, she got one. Gray-green sagebrush and bright bush sunflowers carpeted the bluffs above the golden sands where she walked. As dawn peeked over the horizon, the Pacific spread its endless indigo skirts to tease the shore with lacy white flounces. Manic, black-tailed gnat catchers flitted about in pursuit of their insect breakfasts. They uttered scratchy, catlike calls whenever Kinley strayed too near. The rising sun felt good on her face as it heated the briny breeze of the San Diego coast.

This is where I should be.

As she skirted a tidal pool, Kinley wondered why she hadn't come here more often when she'd been stateside. She'd never hiked the entire half-mile trail through the reserve. Atop the cliff in the distance, above a private beach, was the millionaire's sprawling, fake Italian mansion. Once it had annoyed her, but now it didn't bother her at all.

She could stay right here, happily.

Forever.

"Captain," a soft voice said, accompanied by a tentative touch on Kinley's left forearm. "Time to wake up."

The beach from Kinley's memory winked out of existence as her nose filled with the bleak cologne of old wounds, bleached linen and hand sanitizer. She breathed through the frantic fear bubbling up inside her as she reminded herself that this was America, not Afghanistan, and she no longer occupied a combat zone, but a room in San Diego's finest VA hospital.

She didn't have to fight anymore. She'd lost her last battle, and she was going to be a good loser.

Opening her eyes meant seeing the pitted ceiling tiles that had been her only sky for the last two months. The machines connected to her body beeped like robotic wrens. Their smudged screens displayed dismal numbers. She focused on them, as evaluating her condition always drove off the pathetic panic caused by her PTSD. She could see that her pulse was too low, and her body temp too high. Her blood oxygen level hovered a digit above borderline. The fever meant she probably had a budding infection in her mangled right leg. If her shredded gut had gone septic she'd already be comatose or dead.

Kinley focused on the ward nurse's round face. Brisk smile, forced cheer, dark circles under her eyes—a burnout or a treasure in the making.

"Heya," Kinley said.

"Good morning," the tired woman said as she began

detaching lines and rearranging bags of fluids. "Feeling up to your appointment with the new therapist?"

"Can't wait," Kinley said. An orderly pushed a wheelchair into her room, and only when he parked it next to her bedside did she comprehend that it was for her. "I thought she was coming to me this time."

"She wants you up and about, Captain." The nurse drew back the bed linens. "Here we go." She nodded to the orderly, who helped shift Kinley into a sitting position. "One, two, three."

Being moved woke up her broken body, which protested with a dozen different spikes of pain. The wheelchair rocked as they settled her emaciated ass into it, and her IV line tangled with the stethoscope around the nurse's neck. Kinley felt her patchwork abdomen throb in protest, but kept silent. If she complained they'd pump her full of opiates, and no way did she want to be high with the new shrink. No one knew about her PTSD except a medic who had been with her during one of her worst episodes on her second tour. He'd knocked her out, and then later told her how to deal with it so she could remain on active duty.

"Hang on," the nurse muttered, and extricated herself from the tangle. "There." She shooed away the orderly and peered at Kinley's battered face. "You okay?"

Sweat beads popped along the edges of her lank hair as the pain swelled, and for a moment she thought she might puke or pass out. She shoved it back and bared some teeth.

"Never better."

"We'll take it slow," the nurse promised as she wheeled Kinley out into the corridor of Medical Palliative Care Ward Four, which most of the staff referred to privately as Morgue Prep. "Have you met Dr. Stevens yet?"

"Maybe. All these shrinks look alike to me."

Kinley couldn't get comfortable in any position, so she

opted for the least painful, which meant on the only uninjured part of her body: her left forearm. Though she didn't feel much in her right arm, the cast was too heavy to lift.

"She seems pretty nice. Very experienced." The deliberate heartiness in the nurse's voice took on an edge. "You're going to give her a chance, aren't you?"

"I won't make this one cry, like that kid who wandered into my room," Kinley said. "Unless she's a wimp around the really disfigured terminals, like the last one."

"You're going to live, Captain," the nurse chided, making the lie sound almost believable. "You'll turn around any day now, and start healing, and get back on your feet."

"Sure," Kinley said and glanced at the dressings covering her mangled right leg. Her surgeon would be amputating it mid-thigh, assuming she ever got strong enough to go under his blade again. "Any day now."

Dr. Geraldine Stevens occupied a smallish office just outside the psych ward, and came out with a ready smile. "Good morning, Captain Chandler." Thankfully she didn't try to shake Kinley's hand. Her gaze shifted to the nurse. "I'll call when she's ready to return to her room."

Kinley had already seen the inside of the office too many times, so she eyed the new shrink. Dr. Stevens sported a gray blazer with a turquoise-blue linen dress that looked new. But her charcoal pumps looked old enough to be comfortable. She was somewhere between forty and fifty, a head shorter than Kinley, and about twenty pounds overweight. Her careworn look suggested that she was actually concerned for her patients. Or she might be married to a jerk who made her life hell at home. The doc hadn't opted to wear perfume or makeup, but she had some product in her curly brown hair that smelled of cherries and almonds.

Behind her the Veteran Administration's ICARE program poster hung like subliminal propaganda.

I care, she cares, everybody cares. We're all such good liars.

"Do I pass inspection?" Dr. Stevens asked as she sat down behind the desk.

Let the mind games begin, Kinley thought. "Do you want to?"

"Everyone wants approval, Captain. If we didn't, we'd live like tigers or polar bears, and eat each other." The shrink fussed with some drawers until she found a pen. "Before Dr. Patterson left for Chicago, he briefed me on your case."

"Did he say nice things about me?"

Probably not. Patterson had been a humorless ass who hadn't been able to look at Kinley for more than three seconds at a time.

"Did you want him to?" Dr. Stevens said, smiling at her witty turn around as she opened a thick patient file. "You were injured during the rescue of a downed air crew. According to your commendation, you ran into crossfire to pull them out of the wreckage, which insurgents subsequently blew up with an improvised incendiary device." She frowned. "You didn't suffer any burns at all?"

Kinley had never been burned in her life. Not once. In the explosion it was as if the fire went *around* her. But she couldn't explain that without sounding like she needed to be transferred to the psych ward.

"I was thrown clear," Kinley said and shrugged. "Luckily, right into the Hawk."

The explosion had blasted her head-first into the side of her team's Pave Hawk rescue helicopter. She hadn't even dented the reinforced steel hull, but the impact had smashed her nose, cracked her cheekbones, and dislocated her jaw. A secondary blast had dropped the wing of the downed plane on her leg, crushing it. At some point during that party she'd also taken six bullets in the back and gut. They'd patched her together as best they could at Bagram. Eight weeks later her body and face resembled something a very drunk Picasso might have drawn.

But hey, at least she hadn't been burned.

"You're very fortunate, given the circumstances," Dr. Stevens said and flipped through more pages. "During your sessions with my predecessor you've insisted that, aside from your physical condition, you feel fine."

Shifting in the wheelchair made Kinley's lower spine burn like a lit fuse. "I do. I got out alive, my brains aren't scrambled, and everything can be fixed or cut off or whatever. Life is good."

"Dr. Patterson mentioned you feel so fine, in fact, that you've been refusing pain medication." Dr. Stevens arched brows that had been plucked too thin. "According to your chart you're also not eating much, and several nurses have noted that you sleep most of the day."

"That's from the TV." She put a little more weight on her forearm to keep the pain bomb in her back from detonating. "Game shows and soap operas are better than tranqs."

"Are you pretending to be asleep so you don't have to eat or speak to anyone? Is that why you haven't had any visitors since you were admitted? Have you even told your family that you're here?" When Kinley didn't answer Stevens closed the chart and gave her a direct look. "Captain Chandler, you should know that I've been working with disabled veterans for twenty years now."

Why did they always offer that as reassurance? Maybe it was in the VA shrink handbook: *Assure patient of your proficiency in dealing with ruined soldiers. Gain their trust. Then screw with their minds a little more.*

"Good for you, Doc."

It was a shame Stevens hadn't read her entire file, or she'd know exactly why Kinley had never had any visitors.

"I know military culture," the shrink insisted, "and the highly unrealistic expectations soldiers have of themselves and others. You're constantly pressured to 'accept the suck', as they say."

"It's actually 'embrace the suck'," Kinley said, her mouth hitching into a smirk. "Although my personal favorite has always been 'If you can still twitch, don't bitch.'"

Dr. Stevens didn't return the smile. "I think you're hiding your condition from your friends and family. You also seem to have no interest in recovery. Unless you start fighting for your life, Captain, you won't be twitching much longer." She paused to look into Kinley's eyes. "You'll be dead."

"Well, then, I guess I'll have to work on my attitude," Kinley said. She knew doctors always liked to hear that kind of suck-up bullshit. It might also stop the nurse from putting her on a gastric feeding tube. "I am pretty tired now, though. Could I go back to my room, please?"

"I have a better idea." The shrink stood and took a giant purse from the bottom drawer. "Your primary has cleared you for a short day trip. Let's go for a drive."

* * *

The chance to leave the VA hospital silenced Kinley, who had never expected to see the outside world again. Even the discomfort caused by being loaded by the electric lift into the handicapped van didn't seem so bad, not while sunlight poured over her like warm, liquid gold. But as the shrink drove north from downtown and took the I-15 out of the city, Kinley began to feel uneasy.

"Are you sure this is a *short* day trip?" she asked. "Because it looks like we're heading for Seattle. Not that I'd mind, but I think the charge nurse might freak out."

Dr. Stevens shook her head. "We'll arrive at our destination in twenty minutes, and spend an hour there before we return to the hospital. You'll be back in time for lunch."

Kinley guessed the vagueness was calculated, an attempt to coax her into asking questions about where they were going, or chatting about how wonderful it was to be out in the real world again. She also knew the surest way to confound a shrink was to use their tactics against them.

"That's good. I have things to do."

Like asking about a transfer to hospice, where she could die in fucking peace.

Once they left the city behind, hills and valleys rose and fell on either side of the interstate, and Kinley could see mountains ahead. They passed Lake Elsinore, and then left the freeway to head west toward the rugged chaparral-covered mountains. The road bisected acres of sparsely-strewn sage and scrub oak, punctuated by huge boulders that gleamed gray and orange in the morning light. Once they had passed a small fire station, Kinley saw a sign indicating where Dr. Stevens was headed, and almost laughed out loud.

"You're taking me to Horsethief Canyon?" Kinley said. She hadn't been there in years but, as the signs on the freeway said, it was part of the Pine Creek Wilderness. "Are you serious?"

"It's a lovely spot for a hike," the other woman said as they slowed and turned. She parked the van in an empty lot with bike stands and a water trough. "There's a paved riding trail here we can use for you."

Kinley could have made a fuss about not being well

enough to hike anywhere, even in her wheelchair, but going along with the crazy shrink's idea was easier. This might be her last trip outside, too.

"Okay."

Dr. Stevens unloaded Kinley and her chair, grabbed her purse, and almost set it in Kinley's scrawny lap. But she must have seen Kinley tense or maybe she'd just thought better of it. She left it behind the driver's seat, locked the van, and pushed Kinley across the lot to the promised trail. The weeds that crisscrossed it jostled her wheels, but Kinley ignored the discomforts as she looked ahead toward the slopes. California's long drought had left much of the area barren, and she could see an old watering hole that had dried up, but the raw, rough rock formations were stunning. More water-polished stones marched up to the edge of a cliff, and made her imagine the waterfall that had once cascaded down them. Before the drought it must have been a magical spot to go swimming.

"I don't think we'll go that way," Dr. Stevens said when they came to the fork in the trail, and turned to push her up toward a large oak grove. "We should have a better view past the trees."

When they reached the oak grove Kinley looked up at the canopy of the gnarled tree limbs. Here the trees looked much more mature, with thick, curving trunks and densely-leafed branches. Dandelion seeds floated like so many unused wishes through the dappled shade between the oaks. Beyond them Kinley could see a gap in the brush, and part of a dried-up riverbed. What lay on the other side of the grove must be the old waterfall overlook.

As Kinley caught the scent of the oaks—a slightly smoky and heavy fragrance—she thought of someone she hadn't in years, and smiled. Her grandmother Bridget would have loved the spot. She'd always taken her tea out in the afternoon to sit under the giant black oak. As a little girl Kinley would sit there and listen to stories about brownies, kelpies and selkies that her grandmother had told her.

Even as a child Kinley had been a skeptic. "Do you really believe in such things, Gran?"

"I do, for we've magic in our family," Bridget said firmly. "That's why I'm able to find your toys when you forget them. Lost things call to me. My own mam could charm wild birds with her singing. They'd come and eat seeds, right from her hand. She always said it comes from our Scottish blood."

"Then what's my magic?" Kinley asked.

Her grandmother tapped her cheek. "I can't tell you yet, sweetheart, but whatever it is, it's strong. I've felt it in you since the day you were born."

Bridget had been babysitting her when Kinley's parents had left for a weekend getaway, and had helped her through the horror and grief after their plane crashed in the sea. She had even gone before a judge to argue that although she was seventy and a widow, she could raise her granddaughter better than the foster care system.

Bridget Chandler might have looked like a sweet old lady, but she had a will of iron. The judge had granted her full custody of eight-year-old Kinley.

"Still awake?" Dr. Stevens asked.

Kinley nodded as the old guilt dragged at her. Bridget had taken care of her for the first few years, but as the old lady aged and grew frailer the situation reversed. A month before graduating high school Kinley had come home to find her grandmother under her oak tree, looking as if she had fallen asleep. The stroke she'd suffered had been so massive that it had killed her instantly.

At the funeral at Bridget's church, Kinley had sat alone

in the family pew. Both of her parents had been only children born to older parents. They hadn't had her until they were in their mid-forties. Her grandmother had been her last living relative.

There hadn't been much money left after the funeral expenses, so enlisting in the Air Force had allowed Kinley to go to college and get her degree, and make a new life for herself.

The military had become her family after that, and now they were gone too. Kinley had no friends outside the service, and no hope for the future. Reconstructive surgery could restore some of her face, but the nerve damage would always make her resemble a post-party piñata. Once they took her leg she'd be crippled for life. No man would fall in love with a disfigured amputee. She'd be alone, again, and this time it would be forever.

There really is no coming back from this.

Kinley had always thought as much, but when she saw the oak grove, and what lay beyond it, she understood.

"I think this is a good place to take a break," Dr. Stevens said, breathing a little hard. She set the hand brake and looked around before she eyed Kinley. "How are you feeling?"

"Okay." Her back screamed, her leg throbbed, and her eyes stung with unshed tears, but she also felt oddly, utterly calm. Letting her expression go soft and wistful, she asked, "Can I borrow your phone? I'd like to call home."

"Of course," Dr. Stevens said and reached to her jacket pocket, but then she glanced back to the lot. "I left it in the van." For a moment, she studied Kinley's face. "I'll go and get it, if you promise to stay right here."

One last lie, and she would never have to tell another. "I'm not going anywhere, Doc."

The shrink hurried off, no doubt elated by what she thought was a break-through. Kinley felt a little guilty as she watched her go, but that melted away as soon as she looked through the oak grove. Once the other woman was out of sight, she released the hand brake, gripped the left wheel and rolled herself forward into the trees.

The incline of the trail sloped down, helping her propel the chair toward the edge of the cliff. The overlook was a drop of at least seventy feet onto the rocks. Death would be instantaneous, and the whole thing would look like a tragic accident.

Kinley didn't feel afraid.

Gran, I'm coming. Please, please be waiting for me with Mom and Dad.

Bits of dandelion fluff caught on her eyelashes, somehow spangling her vision. The roar of her heart in her ears turned to the sound of wind through the trees, whispering all around her. This was good. She was going to have a good death. Since her life had sucked, that was a nice surprise.

Suddenly, halfway to the edge, her wheelchair stopped, hurling her to the ground—but Kinley never landed. Inexplicably she kept falling, her broken body plummeting through endless shadows, with the old oak trees stretching and curving until they formed a tunnel around her.

I must be dead.

But if she was, how could she still think?

Memories began pouring through her, from the blurry images of her parents waving goodbye to the years with her grandmother to the morning she had set out from base on her last search and rescue mission. Her sucky life had been too short, but Kinley had only one true regret: she'd never shared it with someone.

She'd been too busy taking care of her grandmother to

get involved with anyone in her teens. At college she'd had a brief fling with a jock, who had turned out to be a selfish ass. The service had supplied an endless amount of men, and as much sex as she wanted. But the stress of being in a war zone had made real relationships impossible.

If only I'd met someone to love!

The tunnel of trees closed over her as she headed into darkness. But as she plunged downward a strange warmth spread through her body. As her pain vanished, relief flooded through her. Tears sprang to her eyes at the sudden and sweet release. But in moments, a new, powerful energy replaced it. It surged down her body and into her limbs until sparks flew from her fingertips. Kinley screamed as she emerged from the tunnel and landed in darkness on her hands and knees.

As she struggled to catch her breath, Kinley stared at the ground. It wasn't rocks at all, but...mud? Stinging, icy rain poured over Kinley as she scrambled up from the slush. But as she looked down at herself, she froze. All the surgical pins holding together her shattered leg had disappeared. She was putting her full weight on it and all she felt was strong, sturdy support. Her back felt brand-new. She pressed her now-unbroken right hand against her abdomen, which felt flat, firm and unmarked. The last time she had touched her belly it had been spongy and latticed with long, stapled incisions.

Kinley's hands shook as she brought them to her face. She felt her straight nose and high, curved cheekbones. Smooth skin covered everything, and she could feel her fingers against it.

"Oh, my god. How...?"

Drenched and shivering, she wrapped her arms around her miraculously healed waist and turned around, squinting against the downpour. She stood in a clearing of wild grass surrounded by oak trees, but nothing looked like Horsethief Canyon. Thick stone posts poked up from the grass in a rough circle around her. They resembled oversize gray bullets and on each were primitive carvings of swirls, animals and huge, sideways letter Z's. The symbols glowed a fiery orange-red that quickly faded.

From beyond the dark oaks came the sound of metal clashing and deep, male voices shouting, and then dozens of men fighting with swords burst into the clearing.

· · · · ·

BUY LACHLAN
Immortal Highlander Book 1

DO ME A FAVOR?

You can make a big difference.

Reviews are the most powerful tools I have when it comes to getting attention for my books. Much as I'd like it, I don't have the financial muscle of a New York publisher. I can't take out full page ads in the newspaper—not yet, anyway.

But I do have something much more powerful. It's something that those publishers would kill for: **a committed and loyal group of readers.**

Honest reviews of my books help bring them to the attention of other readers. If you've enjoyed this book I would so appreciate it if you could spend a few minutes leaving a review—any length you like.

Thank you so much!

For a complete, up-to-date book list, visit
HazelHunter.com/books.

Get notifications of new releases and special promotions
by joining my newsletter!

DEDICATION

For Mr. H.